I0606650

Ace My Heart

LAYLA PINE

CONTENT WARNING

This book is an adult romance, containing multiple, explicit intimacy scenes. It is intended for 18+ audience.
This book contains scenes / references to the following, which may be distressing for some readers:
Murder
Physical abuse
Verbal abuse
Non-consensual elements during consensual sex
Cyber bullying

Ace My Heart
First Published by Layla Pine Author 2022
This Edition Published 2024
Copyright © 2022 by Layla Pine

All rights reserved. No part of this publication may be reproduced, stored or transmitted in any form or by any means, electronic, mechanical, photocopying, recording, scanning or otherwise without written permission from the publisher. It is illegal to copy this book, post it to a website, or distribute it by any other means without permission.

This novel is entirely a work of fiction. The names, characters and incidents portrayed in it are the work of the author's imagination. Any resemblance to actual persons, living or dead, events or localities are entirely coincidental.

Layla Pine asserts the moral rights to be identified as the author of this work.

Designations used by companies to distinguish their products are often claimed as trademarks. All brand names and product names used in this book and on its cover are trade names, service marks, trademarks and registered trademarks of their respective owners. The publisher and the book are not associated with any product or vendor mentioned in this book. None of the companies referenced within the book have endorsed the book.

Cover Art by Vas Design

Second Edition
ISBN 978-0-6455770-0-6

For the little girl I used to be, who dreamed of being a writer. And for all the little girls and boys out there who are still dreaming.
And for Connie. We don't know how long you'll be with us, my little furry baby, but now you're immortalised in words…

Contents

CHAPTER ONE
Quarter Final Curse

*D*ear God, *pardon my French, but please don't let me fuck this up!* I prayed fervently, rocking back and forth, my hands between my knees so I didn't have to watch them shake.

My mother would kill me if she knew I routinely swore at God. Then again, she'd probably just be happy that I was speaking to him at all.

She'd be full of smug, pious words if she were here: *I told you, Melanie, didn't I tell you? It's the curse! You haven't been going to Church enough. When was the last time you went to confession? Probably not since school! God will forgive your sins if you confess, and he'll lift the curse. But you've turned your back on the Lord, so of course he's going to punish you.*

I'd always imagined that if God wanted to curse me, he would do something truly biblical, like give me syphilis, or send a plague of locusts to munch on the pot of basil I was slowly murdering on my windowsill.

But why would he curse me at all? I hadn't turned my back on him. I still had faith. I just didn't think that worshipping God meant listening to some 'celibate' dude in a black dress tell me how to behave.

I continued pleading with Our Heavenly Father. I had a drought I needed to break.

God, if you're listening to me, I'll do anything! I'll come and light candles this Sunday. Hell, I'll even go to the nearest church after the match and light them straight away. I'll try my best to stop swearing. I'll go and visit Mum more often. Please don't let me lose another quarter-final!

I stopped short of offering to swear off sex; it was a hollow promise anyway. How can you swear off something that you haven't indulged in for months?

My sex life was another drought that I was waiting to break, but I couldn't exactly pray to God about it. I mean, what would I say? *Dear God, please send a big throbbing man with a big throbbing penis in my direction?*

"Are you ready?" a stern voice wafted above me. I was in full-fledged panic attack by then, and for a second, I thought it was God talking back to me. Well, close enough, at least in his opinion.

It was my coach, Steve Herbert. He wasn't exceptionally tall, but he was all lean muscle. His grey hair was cropped as close to his skull as possible without using a razor, and his blue eyes stared down at me, filled with expectations. He looked more like an Army drill sergeant than an ex-pro tennis player turned coach.

He could see the freak-out happening behind my eyes. He slapped me.

"Ow!" I shouted, putting a hand up to my face where I could feel the stinging outline of his palm. "That wasn't very nice, Steve!"

He chuckled at me without a scrap of humour, "I'll be nice to you when we're *not* at the Australian Open. Right now, you're paying me to help you win. If that means slapping you out of hyperventilating, I'll do it."

I stood up and walked shakily over to the mirror in my change room, inspecting my cheek for damage. There was a bit of a red mark, but nothing serious, and in a few minutes I would be red all over anyway. Melbourne in January was always scorching.

And just like that the tremors in my hands returned. Melbourne in January meant Australian Open. Australian Open meant me competing. Competing meant the curse.

Steve strode up behind me and gripped me by my arms, shaking me enough that my teeth clanked together. He was just slightly shorter than me, but Christ he was strong.

"Listen to me Melanie Black, you're going to go out there and you're going to smash the crap out of Gordana Slavonisovich. You're a better player than her, and you deserve to beat her!"

"But the curse!" I wailed without thinking. I knew the second the words left my mouth that it was the worst thing to say to Steve.

"This is why I forbade your mother from coming down here to watch! All this shit about curses and turning your back on Jesus. You're the only one who has the power to determine whether you win or lose! Now go and warm up. You're going to beat Slavonisovich. You did last time you played her!"

"That wasn't a quarter," I muttered under my breath. Thankfully Steve didn't hear me. I moved over to the treadmill and set it to a jog.

All warmed up, I checked the strings on my racquet: a Martel XIV Pro that I was trialling at this tournament as my previous endorsement deal had just expired. Martel was the bee's knees on the professional tennis circuit, and they didn't have any Aussies on their sponsorship books. I planned on being the first one.

Now all I had to do was go out there and smash Gordana and I would be one step closer to a lucrative sponsorship deal with Martel. I was decked out in all their gear at no small expense to myself. But if it all worked out it would be so worth it. If I could just win my quarter-final. And that was a *big* if.

I hadn't won a quarter in the last five tournaments. I'd made it to the quarters every time, and every time something happened that would fuck it up: a twisted ankle; coming up against my hoodoo player, Katinka Norieva; getting stuck in my own head; losing my confidence completely; etcetera, etcetera, etcetera.

I was about to drown under a tidal wave of 'I just don't have it anymore'. If I didn't win this, I may as well just pack it all in and move home with Mum, marry some good Catholic boy she stalked for me at church and start popping out the rugrats.

That thought shuddered me out of my depression better than

anything else could have, and it came at just the right time, as the bell went off inside the change room to let me know it was time to head out onto the court.

I gritted my teeth, adjusted my purple skort and strode past Steve. He nodded approvingly at the steel in my gaze and followed me into the tunnel that would lead me out onto Rod Laver Arena; my first ever match on the famous court.

The screams of the crowd echoed down the tunnel as I made my way closer to the harsh sunlight reflecting off the blue Plexicushion playing surface. The adrenaline kicked in then, and the blood in my veins pumped faster. I stepped out of the tunnel, blinded temporarily by the Melbourne summer sunlight and deafened by the roaring spectators.

Why had I been worried? This was *my* home crowd! As my eyes adjusted to the sunlight, I gazed around the court, waving at the fans.

"Marry me, Mel!" someone screamed. I laughed, blowing a kiss in that direction.

'Black'll Smack Ya!' signs were held aloft all over the place. But one banner caught my eye, and I had to chuckle to myself when I saw it. *'Smash 'em Smellie!'*

There were only two people in this world who called me Smellie, and while I'd known they were going to be in this crowd, seeing the banner gave me a boost of confidence that I hadn't known I needed. I blew a kiss in that direction too, hoping that Brad and Amanda would know it was for them.

Smellie was my high school nickname. Not because I reeked or anything; some dickhead kid back when we were thirteen called me Smellanie once as a joke, and it just kind of stuck. I figured owning it was better than acting all hurt by it, and even though I'd been out of school for four years now, Brad and Amanda still used it as a sort of badge of honour, for being the friends who'd stuck with me the longest.

And now they were about to watch me in my first ever Australian Open quarter-final. I *had* to win this one.

Slavonisovich was serving first. I got into position as the crowd quieted to watch the match.

I knew I was a better player than Gordana. I just had to pretend that this wasn't a quarter, or convince my brain that there was no such thing as a curse. Not easy when you've been raised by a highly superstitious Catholic.

I took a few deep breaths and I was in the zone. Nothing existed for me at that moment except for the court and Gordana Slavonisovich.

The sun was murderously hot as Gordana served to me, and I smashed it back over the net into the far corner of the court. She didn't make it in time and the ball bounced away. The crowd applauded as the umpire called, "Love fifteen!"

Well, that was a good start. But it was far too soon to discount the curse. I had to keep my head in the game.

It wasn't long before the sweat was dripping into my eyes, and I wiped it hurriedly away with the sweatband on my wrist. I was up three games to one, and I was settling into my groove.

Gordana was up to serve. She tightened her white-blonde ponytail and bounced the ball in front of her a few times. Just before she served, I heard a voice in the crowd, "You can do it Smell!"

Thanks Brad, I thought as I rallied Gordana. His shout had stoked the fire inside me. I just hoped they didn't kick him out for it.

The sun continued to pound down on us as Gordana and I fought with each other across the court. She began to flag a little as the first set was called: I won six-four. A lot of the northern European players had difficulty handling the Australian heat.

But I wasn't about to start relaxing any time soon. I still had to win another set. And I was feeling the heat too, although as an Aussie I was better acclimatised. I towelled off and adjusted the strings on my racquet. The Martel XIV Pro had been working really well for me so far.

"Just keep working," I told it under my breath as I swapped ends with Gordana. She shot me a look of hatred as we passed each other. I flinched. Sure, we were competitors, but that was a look you'd give your mortal enemy. I glanced up to the coach's box to see

Steve shaking his head minutely out of the corner of my eye. *Don't get riled by the Russian*, that look said. I smiled grimly at him to let him know that I wasn't biting. Well, not *literally* biting, anyway.

If she wanted an enemy, I would give her one. I would pound her right into the Plexicushion.

I rallied and volleyed and served like my life depended on it, concentrating only on smashing the ball at Gordana with enough force to break her bones if it hit her.

It took me a couple of seconds to register when the umpire called the match – I'd won in straight sets!

As my surroundings slowly came back into focus, the roar of the crowd increased in volume. I walked towards the net in a daze and clasped Gordana's hand over the net.

"Congratulations," she said in her matter-of-fact Russian accent. There was no trace of the hatred I had seen earlier as I thanked her with a tired smile.

And then it sunk in. I'd broken the drought! I'd beaten the curse! I'd won my first Australian Open quarter-final!

I leapt into the air, punching at the sky. I probably looked like a massive tosser, but I didn't really care. The crowd was screaming; they loved seeing an Aussie get up in Melbourne.

A bunch of dude-bros in the front row were wolf-whistling at me. "We'll help you celebrate, Hot Stuff!" one of them shouted drunkenly as they all thrust their hips in my direction. I rolled my eyes but couldn't help my grin. I'd won a quarter-final, even drunk jerks couldn't ruin my high.

I did on-court interviews with Wolf Sports and Channel Four. I spouted something about working on my focus and keeping my cool, before escaping to the change rooms for an ice bath.

Steve was waiting for me, grabbing me and swinging me around before returning me to the ground. "I told you there's no such thing as a curse!" he laughed at me.

I smiled back wickedly. "Maybe it's just that God finally answered my prayers," I teased, not truly believing it.

Steve rolled his eyes and then got serious.

"Okay Mel, you're into the semis, there's no time for you to be complacent now. You're up against Norieva. We need to talk strategy later over dinner."

I grinned fiercely at him. "Of course. Now get out so I can freeze my tits off in peace."

I sank into the ice water, trying not to wince. I thought about how Brad had clutched at his balls when I described to him the sensation of first getting into an ice bath.

"Oh jeez, Mel, why would you do that to yourself? I think my testicles have gone into hiding just thinking about it!"

I chuckled, glad that Brad and Amanda had been able to use my family passes. I wondered idly as my body started to go pleasantly numb if their presence had made a difference to my game today. Maybe.

This could be the tournament you win, Mel, I reminded myself. Katinka Norieva next, and then who? Probably Saturn Phillips – she hadn't missed a final for ages. It would take some sort of miracle for me to beat her. But hey, if I could believe in curses, I could believe in miracles, right?

I climbed out of the ice bath and hopped straight into a hot shower, rinsing the sweat out of my hair and enjoying the warmth.

Julie the physio was oiling up my back when Steve walked in. I was naked except for the towel over my arse, but it didn't really matter because Steve had been my coach for six years now; he'd seen it all, and it really didn't interest him.

"So, Norieva," he began. I grunted – not much else I could do when I was face down on a massage table.

"Her volley is her biggest weakness, so you need to focus on your short return. She'll be getting you moving around a lot. How's your ankle?"

"It's fine," I mumbled into the vinyl as Julie's fingers moved lightly over my right ankle, the one that I had rolled in the first of my cursed quarter-finals, to check for any swelling.

"Mel, I'm so proud of you; that was a convincing win. You keep up that sort of form and you'll have no problems with Norieva."

"Thanks Steve."

I relaxed and let Julie work her magic on me, riding the high of my win. I wasn't about to let myself start worrying about the next match. Yet.

I wasn't cursed. Now that I'd won I felt very blasé about the existence of the curse in the first place.

It had just been a drought, a drought that was broken now. I wondered when I'd get time to work on breaking my other drought.

CHAPTER TWO

Snuffleupagus Pubes

I scoffed down another mouthful of salmon pasta, stretched out on a comfortable sofa in front of the big screen TV in the players' retreat. I couldn't believe how lucky I was to have this little bit of downtime. The press conference had been shorter than I had anticipated.

Clayton Banks, another Aussie playing his quarter, aced Ric Fontaine and I gurgle-cheered through a mouthful of carbs.

"Well, hey there gorgeous!" a warm American accented voice said behind me. I recognised it immediately. Holy shit! I bolted upright, swallowing my mouthful without chewing it properly.

"Oh, don't get up, Mel. You just played a hard match. Congratulations by the way." I turned my head, relaxing my stiff posture with some effort. He rested his elbows on the back of the lounge, leaning closer flirtatiously.

"Hi Pete," I replied breathlessly. Oh shit, was that a piece of salmon caught between my front teeth? I sucked at it with my tongue, trying to look inconspicuous. "When's your quarter?"

"Tomorrow night. I wish Donatello Herrera was in worse form. It's gonna be close, that's for sure!"

I rolled my eyes. Pete Levine was the number one men's singles player. He was the odds on favourite to take out the Australian Open. He was also really bad at feigning modesty.

"Come on Pete, you know you're going to smash him!" I said. Pete laughed, the sound sending a shiver down my spine. He turned all the power of his deep brown eyes on me, ruffling one big hand through his dark curls. I had to wipe my mouth – was I drooling? I'd always thought Pete was hot, but we hadn't really had much to do with each other in the two years I'd been playing on the pro circuit.

"So, I guess it's been a while, hasn't it?" he asked, a twinkle in his eyes. My mouth popped open. How could he possibly know that? I mean, I'd been wondering if hymens could grow back, but I was hardly advertising the fact. I shifted uncomfortably, tucking one leg under myself.

Pete chuckled. "I mean, it's been a while since you've won a quarter-final." He didn't really need an answer for that, but I shrugged.

"Hey, everyone goes through a dry spell now and then." I was flattered that he paid enough attention to my career to even know that.

He put his hands on my shoulders, his fingers caressing the sides of my neck. Reminding me again about my *other* dry spell. Well, I certainly wasn't feeling too dry now, not with his big warm hands on me, and his breath in my ear as he leaned down to whisper.

"You're very tense, Mel," he said, his hands still moving against my neck. I *was* tense; every inch of me was zinging with sexual energy. I think Pete could sense it.

"You're staying at Savoy Tower, aren't you?" Pete asked quietly. I nodded mutely. If I opened my mouth I was worried I would screech out, *"Take me now, you big handsome beast!"*

Pete exhaled a deep breath. It tickled at the nape of my neck. I shivered involuntarily.

"Well, maybe you might like to pay me a visit tomorrow night, after my quarter? I'm in room 1537," he suggested breathily.

Saliva flooded my mouth, but before I could compose myself to respond, Pete's hands were off me and he was gone, leaving me gasping and aching in very naughty ways.

I'd lost my appetite, but I forced myself to finish the bowl of pasta. It sounded like I was going to be burning extra calories a bit earlier than my semi-final. At least, I hoped so, with every single fibre of my being.

I couldn't have been more grateful that I *didn't* offer to swear off sex in my little promise to God before the match. I'd just have to figure out how to sneak out past Steve; he wouldn't approve of this late-night rendezvous.

Was it wrong of me to even be considering sneaking out to meet up with Pete Levine? I mean, I had to play the most important game of my career in two days. But … I needed this. Besides, relieving that particular form of tension would probably help my game. That was my line, and I was sticking to it.

Pete was rumoured to be a bit of a Playboy, but I didn't buy into labels like that. What two consenting adults did together in private was their own business and no one else's. It wasn't up to anyone but God to judge them. I didn't think God would judge me too harshly for this. After all, he made me, and he'd given me a very active libido. One that, self-care notwithstanding, hadn't had a proper workout in quite some time.

I wondered how the infamous Pete Levine would stack up compared to my one and only sexual partner.

Grant Johnson and I had had a long, sordid relationship. We'd popped each other's cherries at fifteen, he asked me to move in with him at eighteen (thank God I said no to that one), and last year he met me at the airport when I arrived home from a tournament, with a blonde ditz by the name of Susie Keens hanging smugly off his arm.

"Sorry Mel, it's been over for ages. I just couldn't find the right way to tell you."

What a nice way he found of doing it, arsehole!

Since Grant, I'd promised myself I would stay celibate, and throw myself into my career. Which was why I was now ranked twenty-third in the world and hoping to climb a few rungs.

Grant had left me a year ago. And a year without sex for someone who spent the previous six years having a *lot* of sex had been torture.

I was so ready for a hook-up. Pete was gorgeous and I'd heard some wildly hot rumours about the size of his dick. I wouldn't get emotionally attached. He got my motor running and he apparently felt the same way about me. All in all, it seemed pretty perfect.

By the time I had decided one hundred percent to knock on Pete Levine's door the following night, I was in the elevator on my way up to the seventeenth floor of Savoy Tower, where Steve and I had rented a three-bedroom apartment for the duration of the Open.

The third bedroom had been reserved for my mother, but Steve had banned Mum because of the whole curse thing. I'd assumed that by then it was too late to re-book a smaller apartment.

You know what they say about assume: Ass. You. Me.

I unlocked the door, hearing the TV blaring inside. I narrowed my eyes suspiciously.

"Hey Stinky, you broke the dreaded curse!" a deep male voice dripping with ego greeted me. I couldn't see him because he was lying down on the lounge, but I knew who it was, and I groaned.

"It's not Stinky, it's Smellie, and I only let my *friends* call me that." I retorted. Steve's son Joel just brought out the worst in me.

"Whatever, Stink." He unfolded his six-foot-four frame off the lounge and slouched into the kitchen, pulling *my* organic kombucha out of the fridge and sculling it straight from the bottle.

I clenched my fists. "Well, now I know why your dad kept the three bedrooms, don't I? Why are you down here anyway? Oh wait, let me guess, you quit *another* job, right?" I used my most cutting tone. Joel grinned at me, totally unfazed.

"Actually, Stink, I'm taking a little holiday before I start seeing clients next week." He took another massive gulp of the kombucha before pulling a glass out of the cupboard.

"You want some?" he asked, tilting the bottle towards the glass. I shuddered.

"Uh, no thanks," I muttered crossly, thinking about all the back-wash that had just gone into the bottle. Joel shrugged, took another slug and put it away, launching himself back onto the lounge. I growled at his retreating back and rummaged through the stocked pantry before emerging with my favourite post-game treat: a humble Caramello Koala.

I followed Joel back towards the lounge and sat down on the floor, reaching out to stretch my hamstrings and focused my gaze on the TV. A dreadful sitcom was on.

"What clients? Wait, let me guess, you've got a job as a male escort?" I asked as I peeled the wrapper from the object of my chocolatey desire.

"Yes, well I absolutely missed my calling there," he replied with a wink and a leer that made me cringe. "I'm starting my own personal training business, didn't Dad tell you? I figured he would've mentioned it, since he wants you to train with me a couple of times a week."

I bit into the feet of the koala as I turned and watched him, eyes narrowed. Joel had been a personal trainer for a while now, but he'd had a string of jobs with gyms all around Sydney, which he never seemed to want to hold onto. He had a problem with authority. I had a private theory that it was because he hated being told he wasn't allowed to do things like wink at female patrons or challenge other guys to wrestling bouts. He said that people just didn't get his sense of humour. I was one of them.

I'd always wondered why he hadn't followed his father's footsteps into tennis – I'd played a few friendly matches with him and there was no doubt that he could have been great if he'd put his mind to it.

I would never tell him to his face, but I had a feeling that running his own business was probably going to be a success. He wouldn't have to kowtow to anyone else's ideals, for starters. And he certainly looked the part. His tall, broad physique was toned, tanned and totally cut. I was sure that he waxed his chest and back just so it was impossible to ignore how defined his muscles were.

I didn't want to think about where else he might wax. Not that I would *ever* go there, but in my sex-starved state, dick was never far from my mind.

So yeah, he was a specimen. Men would employ him because they wanted to look like him, and women would employ him because it would mean they got to perve on him for the duration of their training session. Not to mention the motivation factor: *if I just lose that extra ten kilos, I might have a chance with a man like him.*

Vomit!

"You trying to burn a hole through me, Mel?" he asked me, sprawling out further on the lounge. He was so tall there was no room for me to sit, not without having some part of him touching me.

I sneered around my chocolate.

"Just trying to figure out what kind of ape you are," I retorted, turning back to the TV.

"Let me make it easy for you, I'm the sexy ape you secretly want to bone."

I scoffed. "More like the ape who constantly grunts and beats his chest. You're so full of yourself. Want to know the worst kept-secret in the world? Not every woman wants you!"

"No, but you do." He thought he was so funny.

I groaned in frustration. "Dream on, pal!"

"Hey, you just let me know when you're ready to take a ride on a *real* man, Stink. I'll happily break you in."

I leapt to my feet, a growl rumbling in the back of my throat. I was just opening my mouth to inform him that I had an appointment tomorrow night with a real man, one with chest hair and everything, but at the last minute I caught myself and snapped my mouth shut so fast that I gagged on my own saliva.

"Don't choke on your last bite of Caramello, Stink," he warned, smirking up at me from the lounge.

I found my breath and lost my temper. "*Don't* call me Stink, you oversized doofus! You're the biggest knob I've ever met! If I could —"

The door opened with a bang and Steve strode in.

"Mel, calm down, don't let him get to you. Joel, stop teasing her and move over so she can sit down. Have you eaten, Mel?"

I took several deep breaths while Joel sat upright and patted the cushion beside him. I plonked myself down, folding my arms over my chest. Joel rested his arm along the back of the sofa behind me, his fingers draped so they tickled my shoulder. When I wriggled, he snickered at me under his breath so his father wouldn't be able to hear.

"Yes. I had salmon pasta."

"And she just inhaled a chocolate marsupial," Joel added unhelpfully.

Steve sighed. "Joel, I told you to be on your best behaviour! Mel's got a very important game ahead of her. I don't want her stressed out."

Joel rolled his eyes. Steve didn't see it, but I did, and I scowled at him. He winked back at me.

"I was just trying to help her lighten up a bit, Dad – she's way too tense. Seriously Mel, you need to chill out." Oh, so *now* he was all concerned about my welfare!

"Well, why don't you go do some Yoga with her? That'll help her relax."

"Mel?" Joel turned to me, sounding so sincere that I knew that I would look like the immature one if I didn't comply.

I followed Joel out onto the balcony. It was large enough for both of us to use, and it was nice to be in the fresh air. It was getting to be late afternoon too, so the sun was low enough that the worst of the heat was gone.

Stripping off the long pants that I had been wearing in the air-conditioned players' retreat, I stood waiting in my tiny training shorts. Joel eyeballed me. I ignored it. I could rise above his childish behaviour. You really wouldn't have guessed that he was five years older than me by the way he acted.

"Nice arse, Stink," he whispered as he moved into the Warrior. I followed.

"I don't know why I used to want an older brother. If I'd had one as annoying as you, I'd have killed him by the time I was twelve!" I hissed.

"Don't forget your breathing. In through the nose, out through the nose." He moved flawlessly into the Sun Salutation, his muscular frame in frustratingly perfect balance.

I worked on breathing evenly, and it wasn't long before the familiar postures, and the sound of Joel's breathing matching my own *did* calm me down. I knew I shouldn't let him get under my skin, but he had a knack that he'd perfected over the five years we'd known one another.

I gave Joel a small smile of thanks as I stepped back into my sweatpants and slid the balcony door closed behind us. I was feeling much more limber and much less tense.

My mobile rang as Steve served up dinner. Joel was in the shower, so I was having a moment of peace. When I saw who it was, I grinned.

"Brad!" I answered.

"Smellie! Congratulations!" he shouted over the din of a packed pub. I almost wished that I didn't have to be good tonight because it would be great to be out with him and Amanda. But then I remembered that I was about to play in an Australian Open semi-final. I wouldn't give that up for a few beers, even with my besties.

"Thanks. You'll be there for my semi-final, right?"

"Wouldn't miss it! You were incredible – I've never seen you play that well before!"

I laughed. "Well, thanks, I think. Let's just hope the next match is even better."

"I'm sure you'll be fine. Amanda has something to tell you, hang on."

"Oh my God, Mel! Thank you for inviting us down here!" Amanda yelled.

"You're welcome! I didn't realise you were that big a tennis fan."

Amanda laughed. "I'm not. Oh, I mean, I really enjoy watching *you* play. But, Mel, I met this guy today in line for snacks. He's here at the bar tonight. He's super cute, and you wouldn't believe it, he lives in Sydney!"

"Oh, wow. Well, you were obviously meant to be here, to meet him!"

"I hope you don't mind, I kind of name dropped that you're my friend. He's a big tennis fan, he's super impressed."

I snickered. "See, having a semi-famous friend is working out for you tonight!"

Amanda's giggle was suddenly muffled, and I heard a male voice in the background.

"And … she's flirting again," Brad said. "It's kind of sickening to watch to be honest."

I chuckled. "Let her have her fun – you never know, it might turn into something more."

"And in the meantime, I can have another beer and watch the tennis highlights," he said cheerfully.

"A worthy evening. See you tomorrow, Brad."

I hung up the mobile and slid into a chair at the dining table. Joel was already seated, still topless after his shower. His smooth chest gleamed, and he raised an eyebrow at me as he flexed his taut pecs. He was waiting for me to ogle him. I didn't give him the satisfaction.

He decided to torment me another way. "Ooh, Bwaddles, I wuv you so much, mwah, mwah!" Joel puckered up his lips at me. I gave him a sugar-coated smile.

"Oh, don't be jealous, Joel. Brad's just a friend. I know you have a thing for him, but I'm sure if you just keep pining … well anything's possible."

"That's enough, both of you!" Steve snapped as he plonked the food down on the table. I picked up my cutlery and ate in silence, eyeing Joel crankily. He looked smug, and I hated that. How did he annoy me so much, but nothing I said ever seemed to break through his smarmy exterior?

My nerves started to peak just before dinner the night Pete was playing his quarter-final. All day I'd felt them jangling in the background, in the gym, and out on a practice court with Steve. Luckily, Steve didn't like to work me too hard on my days off, or he would have noticed just how out of the game my head was.

After dinner, we all turned to the TV to catch Pete's match against Donatello Herrera. Steve and I sat on the lounge, and Joel sprawled on the floor, leaning back so his head was touching my thigh. His hair was soft and it tickled. I should have pushed him away but I didn't.

I was too busy getting hot under the collar watching the sweat dripping off Pete, thinking about what he'd offered for tonight.

Joel tilted his head, his hair caressing my knee, and I looked down. His legs, stretched out in front of him, almost reached the TV. He was so tall! I sneaked a look at Steve out of the corner of my eye. Steve was a good head shorter than his son. I wondered how he had spawned such a monster. It wasn't like Joel's mum Sandra was a giant.

Joel didn't really look like either of his parents, with his deep-set eyes and strong jaw. Even his short, dark brown hair was nothing like the pictures I had seen of his parents when they were younger. Sandra Herbert was blonde and Steve had blue eyes like his son, but his hair had been sandy brown before he went grey.

As I had expected, Pete beat Donatello in straight sets. He hardly even looked puffed at the end of it. I found my cheeks warming as I thought gratefully that he'd have plenty of puff left for me.

Steve got up and stretched. "Well, I'm turning in for the night. Don't stay up too late please, Mel. You need your rest."

I sighed shakily. Could I be experiencing a little pre-coital stage fright? It was a new sensation for me. Joel cocked an eyebrow at me. I stuck my tongue out at him.

As Steve clumped off down the hallway, I stood and paced the kitchen. My hands were sweating. I wiped them on my pants.

I needed something else to focus on, otherwise I was going to wind myself up so tight I'd be the worst lay Pete Levine ever had.

Normally I treated myself to Caramellos only on match days, but desperate times… I snatched another from the cupboard and tore the wrapper off with gusto, sinking my teeth into the feet, savouring the chocolatey goodness as I chomped my way up the tiny koala. I moaned when the caramel hit my palate.

"Christ Stink, are you eating that thing, or fellating it?" Joel said. I narrowed my eyes. He was leaning on the kitchen bench, staring with avid amusement.

I popped the head into my mouth, sucking it slowly, throwing my head back and making a sex sound. Joel watched, eyes glinting.

I swallowed the last bit of deliciousness and smiled at him.

"Bet you enjoyed watching my foodgasm!" I spun on my heel and headed down the hallway. Joel's chuckle followed me, leaving my skin tingling in irritation. Why couldn't I get under his skin the way he did mine?

I turned into the bathroom I would now have to share with Joel for the rest of our stay. I ran the shower cold – I needed to calm down. I soaped myself up, washed my long, chestnut brown hair and blow-dried it straight.

I studied myself in the mirror. My skin was nicely tanned from the summer, my brown eyes warm. Ever since I'd gone through puberty, I'd had boys … and men … telling me that I was gorgeous, but I'd never really paid my looks much mind. As long as my body did what I wanted it to – win me matches – I was happy. But I couldn't help wondering what Pete would think of it. Would he like the sleek line of muscle in my thighs? Would he appreciate my breasts, a decent handful, but nothing to really write home about?

Shaking my head, I wrapped the towel around myself and sneaked across the hallway to my bedroom. I wasn't sure what I should wear down to Pete's room. I settled on a pair of cropped denim shorts and a singlet; cute and comfortable. It was also not too hard to get out of. My face heated up again at that thought.

Dressed, I sat on the edge of my bed and tapped my feet on the floor, glancing every few moments at the clock. I didn't know how long it would be before Pete would be back in his room.

It was close to eleven when I decided I'd given him enough time. I opened my bedroom door quietly and crept down the hallway. The TV was on, volume low. Joel was still up. Oh great. Well, I wasn't going to let that scare me back to bed.

Taking a deep, fortifying breath, I walked out like it was perfectly okay for me to be sneaking off in the middle of the night on the eve of my Australian Open semi-final.

"Where're you going, Mel?" Joel asked quietly from the lounge. I turned to look at him from the door.

"None of your business," I hissed. I put my hand on the door handle, ready to open it and make my escape.

Jesus, he moved fast! He was standing next to me in less than a second, leaning against the door so I couldn't open it.

"Well, you've made an effort for someone, haven't you?" He looked me up and down, reaching out to run long fingers through my shiny, straight hair. I smacked his hand away.

"Like I said, it's none of your business. Now let me out!"

"Not until you tell me who you're meeting."

I rolled my eyes. "Why do you care? I can go meet whoever I want!"

Joel stared at me expectantly. But I wasn't giving in. I wasn't telling him anything.

"Well, I thought it might have been Lover Boy Brad, but you're not wearing any shoes, so it's someone in this building."

I snorted at him. "Brad is *not* my Lover Boy, he's my friend. I know you've never been able to have a platonic relationship with a member of the opposite sex, but *surprise*, it's possible."

Joel gazed down at me, that familiar sardonic grin on his face. "I have a platonic relationship with you, Stinky. Although I guess I'd be willing to change that." He very obviously looked down at my cleavage. "But you still haven't told me who you're meeting."

I was very close to blowing my stack. "Okay, let's just get one thing straight. Whatever you consider a platonic friendship, this" – I gestured wildly from him to me – "isn't it." I tried to push past him, but he wasn't budging.

"It's Pete Levine, isn't it? You were practically panting earlier when we were watching him play. Honestly, I didn't realise you were into the Snuffy look."

"The ... what?" I asked.

Joel snorted. "You know – from *Sesame Street?* Come on Stink, you must know Pete is renowned for his stellar chest rug."

I tried not to show any emotion in my expression. How had he figured it out? I decided to be blunt with him, then maybe he'd leave me alone.

"Okay, you got it, do you want a medal? I'm going downstairs to have lots of wild woolly mammoth sex with Pete, because it's been a long time between drinks, and I really need a root, and I've heard that he's got a *big* trunk. Are you happy now?"

The smug look on his face slipped away as I spoke. His eyes were stern, lips down turned.

"Mel, I'm going to be serious for a moment here."

I choked back a sarcastic laugh, waiting for him to explain himself.

"D'you really think this is a good idea? I mean, you've got the biggest game of your career tomorrow. Is a bang with the grizzly man worth ruining that?"

I knew deep down he was right. But hearing it from Joel made me more determined than ever to continue with my plan.

"I'm going downstairs and I'm having sex with Pete Levine. And I don't have to justify that to you or anyone else. It won't affect my game. If anything, it'll help me relax." I hoped so – every tendon, every muscle in me was crackling with tension.

Joel shrugged and moved aside. As I opened the door and walked out, he stuck his head out after me.

"Well, have fun. Don't get too many Snuffleupagus pubes caught in your teeth."

I kept my shoulders stiff until I was in the lift. Then I let the laugh out. Joel was truly sick, and I shouldn't find him funny. But sometimes, I just did.

CHAPTER THREE

Find A Mojo, Lose A Mojo

Pete was shirtless when he answered the door. My breath caught in my throat as I eyed him up and down, taking in his broad shoulders, the forest of black curls on his chest and stomach.

"Well, you're a sight for sore eyes, Melanie Black."

With that, he dragged me in and slammed the door shut. He pulled me to him, his hands suddenly all over me, his mouth pressing urgently against my own. His dick was hard and jabbing up against my hip bone, almost painfully. His lips parted and his warm tongue sought mine.

My nerves were consumed by a flare of heat, and I responded with a fierceness that surprised me. I arched my body against his, tangling fingers into his dark curly hair, dragging his face even closer to mine.

The bed was only metres away, but it suddenly seemed like that was too far. He tugged at my singlet, and I raised my arms up helpfully, allowing him to drag it off. The appreciative moan that escaped his lips when his hands met my bare skin reverberated all the way through me. I ran my fingers down his torso, enjoying his shuddering response.

I unbuttoned my shorts and let them drop to the ground, stepping out of them hastily while fumbling with the drawstring of his pants. He reached down and undid them in one fluid movement.

Slipping them over his hips (and his big throbbing dick), they fell to the floor.

His mouth was on my neck, his teeth gently grazing the skin of my throat. I gasped hoarsely, running my hands down the warm expanse of his back, sliding them under the waistband of his boxer briefs. He moaned again, like an animal. Wet heat gushed from my pussy at the sound.

His fingers were on my back, holding my hair away as he unhooked my bra. The clasp popped open and he tore it off me, one hand already cupping a breast, pinching and twisting at my nipple enough to make me gasp in pleasurable pain. His breath was hot on my throat as his other hand slipped between my legs, his fingers exploring my wetness.

I reached down and gripped the thick, pulsing shaft that had been pressing insistently against me, stroking him frantically.

"Fuck, Mel, you keep that up and this'll be over before it even begins," he muttered hoarsely into my ear, nibbling on my earlobe as he plunged a finger into me.

"Well then, you'd better get this," I gave him a dirty squeeze, "inside me." I was panting, rolling my hips to ride his finger, giving him a taste of what he could look forward to.

With a grunt, Pete lowered me to the floor, fumbling for a condom in the pocket of his discarded pants. The next few minutes were a delicious, throbbing blur of tangled arms and legs, of his warm body pressed against mine, inside mine.

Afterwards, we both lay panting on the floor beside the lounge. His legs were still entwined with mine, and his fingertips trailed up and down my torso, in between my breasts, all the way down and then back up again. I shivered with the sensation, with the pleasant aching between my thighs. The rumours were absolutely true – he was *very* generously proportioned.

I sighed with sleepy, post-sex satisfaction. Pete nudged at my shoulder once. I ignored it. He shoved me a bit harder.

"Mel! Gorgeous, you're gonna have to get up. You don't want to fall asleep on the floor – think about how much you'd hurt in the morning."

That roused me. I had a match to play tomorrow. I'd forgotten about that in my horny haze. I pulled myself up with a groan and ran a hand through my messy hair.

"Fuck, Mel, you are so damned sexy!" Pete groaned, pressing his hands against my hips. I was suddenly wide awake again.

"Well, you're not so bad yourself," I replied coyly, peeking at him through my lashes. He pulled me closer. I gasped, he was loaded and ready for round two.

"Do you think we can make it to the bed this time?" he asked, and I giggled, letting him pull me in that direction.

In the early hours I very quietly let myself out of Pete's apartment and tiptoed towards the lift. I'd left Pete sprawled on his bed, snoring.

Swiping my card in the door, I eased it open as quietly as I could. The TV was off, but Joel had left the kitchen light on. I wondered if that was his way of apologising for being a douche earlier.

I sneaked up the hallway and into my bedroom. I really wanted a shower, but I was afraid to have another one in case I woke Steve. I pulled off my clothes and slid naked into the sheets.

It was two-thirty. I really needed to sleep.

I couldn't.

God, did I just do something really stupid? I asked as I stared into the darkness. I didn't get an answer.

I sat up, reaching for my phone to turn on the music quietly. But even the husky, romantic tones of Jace McKenzie, my favourite singer, couldn't relax me. If anything, I felt more tense now than before being pounded twice by Pete.

The sex had been decent. Pete had moves, said the right things – he told me how sexy I was, how much I turned him on, how hard he was about to come.

But it just hadn't felt right. How was it possible to feel like I'd used Pete, and like Pete had used me, at the exact same time?

"Did the trunk live up to its reputation, Stink?" Joel whispered as he opened the door. I slipped further down under the covers – if he found out I slept naked, I'd never live it down.

"Who invited you in?" I whispered through clenched teeth. He sat down on the edge of the bed.

"I invited myself. Was the Wookie sex as hot as you'd been hoping?"

I grimaced, overwhelmed by the need to unpack it with someone.

"I'm not sure … I mean the sex was fine … more than fine, but I don't know. Something was missing," I muttered.

"A foreskin maybe?" Joel asked cheekily.

I fought my twitching lips. "Are you telling me you have one of those?" I asked before thinking about how inappropriate that was.

Joel raised an eyebrow, his hands slipping to the tie of his shorts. A weird little sound gurgled out from the back of my throat.

Joel's lips curled upwards, and he folded his arms. "I'll leave you to ponder that one on your own, Stinky."

"I really need to get some sleep now, Joel," I grunted. He stood up. My stupid, traitorous eyes snapped straight to his crotch. He noticed and his grin widened as he moved to the door.

"Good luck with that."

He left silently, and I squeezed my eyes shut to try and clear the vision of the more-than-friendly bulge in Joel's pants.

Oh God, how was I going to be able to sleep at all with that vision stuck in my head?

Apparently I could.

***

I woke up what felt like minutes later to Steve thumping on the door.

"Get up, Mel!" I could tell from the tone in his voice that he had some idea about what had happened last night, and he wasn't happy.

I felt hungover even though I hadn't had even a sip of alcohol, and sore, not just between my legs. Not a good sign. Struggling out of bed, I padded my way across the hallway to the bathroom. The door was locked. I banged loudly, rubbing at the sleep in my eyes with my other hand.

"Joel, hurry up! I need to shower!" I shouted. The lock clicked and the door swung open.

"Trying to save a bit of time by undressing on the way to the bathroom?" Joel leered down at me.

In my groggy state I'd forgotten that I'd slept naked. I couldn't even bring myself to care.

"Please get out of my way," I sighed. Joel stood to one side of the doorway, naked himself except for the towel wrapped around his waist. I had to squeeze past him to get into the room.

"You know, Mel, you look very nice naked. Maybe I could join you in the shower? Help you wash off the stink of Eau de Bigfoot?" he murmured.

"You could try," I retorted. "Depends on how attached to your testicles you are. And keep it down will you – your dad does *not* need to know about last night."

As I closed the bathroom door, I heard him reply in an undertone, "I think he's already figured it out."

I tried not to think about that as I tied my hair back and showered hurriedly. Rubbing sunscreen into my face, I winced at the dark circles under my eyes. Oh well, nothing I could do about it now. Hopefully some coffee and breakfast would perk me up.

I tucked one foot under me as I sat down in front of a bowl of Weetbix and fruit.

"Sit straight Mel! You don't want to twist your back like that!" Steve snapped. I complied obediently, chewing on a fingernail. Joel gave me a sharp look. I stopped chewing and focussed on eating my breakfast.

I was overtired, disgusted with myself, and now Steve was mad at me. Could this day have started any worse?

After breakfast, I tied the laces on my tennis shoes and adjusted my boobs in my training singlet. If I thought I'd been shaking in my shoes before the quarter-final, I was having my own personal earthquake today.

"Deep breaths, Stink," Joel reminded me from the table. He

peered at me over the top of Buff magazine, reaching out to squeeze me on the arm. "You'll be fine, don't work yourself up into a lather."

"Careful Joel, if you keep it up like that, I'll start thinking that you actually care." I was proud that my voice didn't tremble.

"Hey, I'm your personal trainer now. I'm all about ensuring not just your physical fitness, but your emotional wellbeing too." He grinned lopsidedly at me before burying his nose back in his magazine.

To distract myself from the nerves, I walked over behind him and read over his shoulder.

"Wow, *'Butt Clenches for Every Situation'* sounds really … deep." I commented wryly.

Joel turned to me and winked. "Good to see you can still read, Mel – I've heard that one-night stands with overly hairy men can cause blindness, you know."

Steve walked back down the hallway, scowling. Sweat broke out all over me, trickling between my shoulder blades. I reached down and pinched Joel hard on the arm, feeling a sick satisfaction when he flinched. He'd snitched. I was sure of it.

"Ready?" Steve asked in a clipped tone. I nodded and walked to the door, picking up my racquet bag. Steve shouldered the rest of the gear.

"I'll see you over there. Good luck, Stink!" Joel called out.

I nodded and headed out to the lift. Steve followed in silence.

Neither of us spoke until we were almost at the Park.

"Mel, you know I've never tried to tell you how to live your life outside of tennis, and I know it isn't really any of my business, but couldn't you have waited until the Open was over before leaping into bed with Pete Levine?" Steve finally asked.

Fuck you, Joel, I thought. He must have gone straight to his father and dobbed me in last night.

"You're right, Steve, it's *not* any of your business," I growled. Steve's teeth clacked together. He always did that when he was furious about something.

"If you fuck this up today because you were too busy spreading your legs last night …" His angry tone became pleading, "Mel, you've worked so hard to get to where you are. Don't let yourself down because of a man."

I knew that everything he was saying was true, and that just made me even angrier. And since I didn't want to be angry with the person I really should be – myself – I settled for being angry with Steve.

"Get fucked, Steve. I *have* worked hard, and I really don't think that a little bit of sex is going to spoil things."

Steve grunted. "Well, all I can say is I hope it was worth it."

The car pulled up at the player's entrance. I leapt out. A small crowd of people were milling, looking equal parts embarrassed and starstruck as they held out phones for selfies. I posed stiffly for a few photos as Steve unpacked the gear from the hire car. My mood was foul, which wasn't going to help my game, but I just couldn't drag myself out of it.

"Mel, you're acting like a spoilt, slutty little brat," he grated at me, not bothering to keep his voice down. People were staring.

I gaped at him. What did he expect me to say to that? I closed my mouth with an effort and stormed off in the direction of the change room.

I rounded on him as he appeared behind me in the room.

"Stop treating me like I've already lost the game!" I shouted. He looked at me sadly.

"Well, it's a foregone conclusion if you can't get rid of this attitude and calm yourself down."

Steve turned away from me, mumbling into his mobile.

"Are we going to go and hit some balls?" I asked when he hung up.

"You are. I'm not. I don't think I'm the right person for you to be around right now. Joel will meet you at court nineteen in ten minutes. Be back here at two."

I silently grabbed my racquet bag and left.

God, what's wrong with me? I beseeched as I strode towards the practice courts. I could have gotten into one of the little buggies that trawled the length of the Park, but the nervous, angry energy zinging through me demanded that I walk. *Why am I feeling like this?*

No answer.

Last night I'd scratched an itch. But it was like a mozzie bite: instead of feeling relief, it had become more inflamed and irritated.

By the time I entered court nineteen, Joel was already there, wearing cotton exercise shorts, a singlet, joggers, and a cap covering his dark hair.

"You dobbed me in!" I accused. Joel nodded curtly.

"I freely admit it. I was hoping I'd be able to talk you out of it, but failing that … he deserves to know. This is his career too, and if you fuck up, it means he's fucked up."

That stopped me in my tracks. I'd never thought of it in those terms before. Joel was right; Steve only ever had my best interests at heart.

"Jeez, could you make me feel any worse about it?" I muttered. Joel shrugged, a wry expression on his face.

"Let's hit some balls." Joel hit one in my direction. I returned it – not hard, just enough to feel the muscles in my shoulders and back working.

Within minutes I could feel the angst leaving my body as I concentrated on returning the ball to Joel. He didn't push me hard, but he didn't slack off either. He warmed me up and he calmed me down. It was just what I needed.

Eventually he deflected one of my balls, signalling that I was warm enough now. I walked towards the net.

"Feeling a bit better now, Stinky?" he asked. I glared at him until he dropped his eyes from mine.

"Sorry. Mel."

My lips twitched into a faint smile. "Yes thanks, Joel."

"Listen, don't let fighting with Dad get to you, okay? Just focus on playing the game to the best of your ability. And don't let what happened last night affect your mojo either."

We walked off court, Joel stopping me at the gate. "I'm heading back to the apartment to shower and change now. Go eat, stretch, practise some mindfulness if you can. I'll be in the crowd. Good luck."

I squeezed his arm. "Thanks again, Joel. You know, you're not such a dickhead when you're really trying."

"I know, but it's just too much effort to try that hard *all* the time," he replied with a grin as he walked off. I headed back, making a quick detour via the player's lounge for some takeaway meals. I returned to the main arena and my change-room feeling much more serene.

Steve was sitting with his head in his hands. I walked in and sat down beside him, handing him one of the containers and opening the other.

"It's okay, Steve. I'm feeling fine now. I'm calm."

He looked up at me and his eyes seemed empty. "Just try your best, Mel. That's all I've ever asked of you."

I nodded. I'd let him down, that much was obvious.

I didn't even think that begging God for one more chance was going to help me today. That didn't stop me from trying though.

Please God, just one more little win. I know that I was supposed to come and light a candle for the last one, but ... I knew I had no excuse. God owed me no favours.

I spent the afternoon stretching and trying to meditate. I wished there was time for a nap; I was starting to feel my late and sleepless night.

The bell for my match went off, but it felt too early. I walked down the tunnel in a daze, and I didn't register the noise of the crowd like I had before.

Norieva eyed me calculatingly across the net. My heart started up an unnerving rhythm that didn't bode well. Norieva was ranked above me and was seeded far higher than me in this tournament. But I shouldn't let that sort of attitude get in the way.

I took my place, ready to serve. My mind wasn't in this game and that was a worry. There were too many non-tennis related thoughts zinging around in my brain.

I served to Norieva. She returned the ball with a high-pitched grunt. I wasn't a fan of the grunt. It didn't make the ball go any faster or any more in the direction you wanted it to. And silence often put off my opponents better anyway.

We rallied for a little while until she sent a ball right into my opposite corner. I couldn't make it there in time. Love-fifteen. I shook my head, and up in the stands I could feel Steve's disapproval like a laser beam in the back of my skull.

The first set was at five-love in Norieva's favour when it happened. She smashed the ball across the net into the far corner. I spun on my right leg to try my hardest to get over there in time. That was when I felt a sensation in my ankle that was both excruciatingly painful and dreadfully familiar.

As I fell towards the Plexicushion, it was all I could do not to scream out a whole bunch of swear words. In fact, I think I probably did.

It was more than just twisted this time.

Shit!

A medical officer was with me within seconds. I dreaded imagining what Steve was thinking up in the stands. The medical officer's mouth was a grim line in his otherwise business-like expression, as he helped me to hobble to the side of the court and assessed my ankle.

"I can't treat this in a time-out, Mel," he told me. "It's a sprain. You're going to have to forfeit – there's no way you'll be playing on with an injury like this."

I sighed but nodded. The medical officer called the umpire over so I could officially ruin my Australian Open chances.

"Your mind wasn't on the game, Mel. That's why this happened," Steve snarled darkly as he stormed into the change room.

"Not what I need to hear right now Steve!" I hissed back, wincing as Julie turned my ankle this way and that. I tried not to yelp with the pain – instead I almost bit through my lip. I'm a bit of a sook when it comes to pain.

Fuck, fuck, fuck!

Oh God, I'm sorry! I should've come and lit a candle instead of screwing Pete Levine last night!

"We could have strapped it, given her some pain meds and she would've been fine!" Steve shouted suddenly, making me jump. My ankle burned.

"If you'd sent her back out there you may as well have just kissed goodbye to her career!" Julie snapped. "Go have your temper tantrum somewhere else!" She pulled a whole bunch of stuff out of her bag.

"Okay, this is called a Cryo-cuff. It's going to compress the injury, and pump —"

"I know what a Cryo-cuff is, Julie. Just put it on and then please, will someone get me an anti-inflammatory?"

Steve returned, standing over me and glaring down.

"What the fuck were you doing out there, Mel? You shouldn't have been in a situation where you could have missed that ball!"

I breathed deeply through my nose. It took more than ten seconds for me to be calm enough to open my mouth.

"Steve, it's done now. There's nothing either of us can do to change that."

"I don't fucking believe this!" he grated through his teeth as he stormed off again.

Julie packed my swollen ankle into the cuff and set it to the correct compression. "Just let him stew for a bit. He'll calm down eventually." She started hooking up the water. I watched in vague interest, hoping that she'd give me some painkillers as soon as she was done.

"Did I hear someone calling for drugs?" a deep voice asked from behind me.

"Oh my God, thank you! How did you get in here, Joel?" I asked as he held out a pill and a bottle of water to me. I downed them gratefully.

"I'm your trainer now, remember? Steve got me an All Access pass." Joel looked way too pleased with himself. Julie looked up at him and smiled. She hadn't finished setting up the Cryo-cuff. Joel only ever called his dad 'Steve' when he was trying to impress someone.

Sure enough, he turned the full force of his smile on Julie. She blushed, strands of her red hair falling about her face. I rolled my eyes. Joel turned to me and winked. God, he just couldn't help himself!

"You should eat something with that medication, Mel." He put down the bag that was slung over his shoulder and unzipped it, dragging out a Tupperware container and a fork. He handed both to me. I opened it and immediately felt my jaw ache as saliva flooded my mouth.

"Uh, yum!" I exclaimed at Sandra Herbert's signature chicken and rice salad. It was one of my favourites; packed with nuts, herbs and cranberries. "How did you get this? Your mum didn't send it down with you, did she?" I asked Joel, who stared at me like I was some sort of stupid person.

"I made it," Joel replied, slowly like he was talking to a half-wit. I shrugged and tucked in. It was delicious – even better than his mum's, although I'd never tell him that. A little moan of enjoyment slipped out. Joel grinned.

"Yes, the man can cook," he boasted. Julie goo-goo eyed him. I eyeballed her in frustration.

"Is that cuff on properly?" I asked sharply. Julie came to her senses and went back to work, but I noticed her sending longing glances in Joel's direction. I had a feeling I knew whose bed he'd be sharing that night. The thought sent an odd, sick feeling through my stomach. I screwed up my face; did I really hate having a mental image of Joel shagging Julie so much that it was nausea-inducing?

"All done!" Julie said in satisfaction. She manoeuvred my leg so that it was elevated, patting me on the knee, but she was looking over my head at Joel.

"How long do I have to keep this on?" I asked. Julie flicked her gaze down at me, lips pursed in annoyance.

"Oh, gee, *sorry* for having the hide to injure myself and force you to do your job!" I snapped. Joel's hand fell on my shoulder.

"Settle down, Stinky," he murmured. I growled under my breath. Julie blushed.

"Two hours would be good. You can do a second session if you think it's needed, but you will have to give the ankle a break for at least half an hour in between. You need to go and get some scans done tomorrow to check for any fractures. Just rest up in your hotel tonight. I'll come round later and strap it up for you." She was directing her words to Joel again. I gave up fighting it. Why not let him deal with it? He was my 'trainer' after all.

"Thanks Julie," Joel replied suavely. I almost choked on my last mouthful of rice salad. "Can I get your number to tee up a time we could get together?"

Julie recited her number to Joel, who programmed it into his phone. I couldn't wait for her to leave.

"She'll need a chair to be moved out to the car, and back up into the hotel. I'm sure there's one around here somewhere."

Julie beamed at Joel once more, gave me a cursory glance, and walked out. I lay back down against the bench. Joel took a seat by my head.

"You know she's way too old for you," I said.

Joel grinned. "Jealous, Stink?"

I gagged. "You wish! Now, can we please get out of here before the reporters start bashing the door down? I have no intention of giving interviews today."

Joel patted me on the cheek and walked off to find me a wheelchair. I wrinkled up my nose at the thought of him wheeling me out. I wondered where Steve had gone. He was probably so mad that he couldn't stand to be near me.

I'd been waiting for months to break the quarter-final drought, and I'd done it. I'd been waiting almost a year to break the sex drought, and I'd done it. Was it too much to ask that I just have a good match against Norieva? Not even a win, but just a good, solid match? One where I didn't injure myself badly enough to forfeit? Why was it that I couldn't just have everything in my life fall into place for once?

CHAPTER FOUR

Dutch Courage

"I'm pretty confident there's no fracture, so that's a good sign," Julie said as she finished strapping my ankle with a compression bandage. "But I still want you to get some scans tomorrow."

Julie had arrived, wearing a leather ultra-mini skirt. I wasn't sure it was appropriate attire for a woman who'd be pushing forty, but I had to admit she managed to rock it. She was tall and had long, slender legs, naturally curly red hair, and a smattering of reddish freckles across her nose which made her look younger than she was.

Joel smiled his signature smile at her, and I swear her knees almost gave way. Joel was damn handsome when he turned the charm on. And he knew it. That was the problem. I didn't think his impressive body was big enough to hold his enormous ego.

Julie excused herself to use the bathroom. I propped my ankle up on the armrest of the lounge and turned my sly gaze to Joel, who was leaning over the back of the lounge, watching me with a smirk.

"She probably needs to change her Depends," I commented lightly. "You shouldn't smile at old people like that – they're liable to wet themselves."

Joel chuckled. "Say what you want, Stink, but you know that later on tonight, when you're in bed all alone, I'm going to be making her wet herself in a sexy way. I like a woman with a bit of experience. Now, if you'd been with more than one guy, I might be interested, but I don't give lessons to beginners, sorry."

I propped myself up on my elbows and glared at him. "Oh, hand me a bucket, I think I'm going to puke! Besides, I *have* been with more than one guy."

Joel straightened. "Sorry, Mel, but the yeti you boned last night doesn't count."

If I'd had use of both my legs I would've gotten up to punch him, but I couldn't, so I settled for throwing the remote at him. I missed, and he picked it up with a grin and sat it gently down on the armrest beside me.

"You know what's funny, Joel?" I asked, forcing a breezy tone through clenched teeth. "That you actually believe that the only reason you haven't slept with me is because *you* don't want to."

He gazed right at me then, turning the full force of his very blue eyes onto me. I tried my hardest to meet them with defiance.

"Mel, one day you'll realise that you want me."

"Oh, God, I *really* hope so. I just can't *wait* to be another notch on your bedpost!" My voice dripped with sarcasm.

Julie cleared her throat behind us. Joel flinched and turned around. I could see her face over the back of the sofa. She looked a little put out. I guess she'd heard the last part of our conversation. *Well, take that, Joel. Maybe you won't be making her 'wet herself in a sexy way' tonight after all!*

"Ready to go?" Joel asked her. She smiled at him and I took back my last little thought. Julie was clearly all too eager to fall under the Joel Herbert spell.

"You both have a *really* nice time tonight!" I called insincerely as they headed for the door. "Don't worry about me; the invalid will just look after herself for the night."

Joel sighed and turned around. Julie had brought a pair of crutches with her, and they were propped against the wall just inside the door. He carried them over and put them on the floor beside me.

"No need to milk it, Mel," he said in an undertone. "You'll be fine. Steve will be back in no time. I'll see you tomorrow."

He stood up and walked back over to the door. "Don't wait up!" he called as he ushered Julie out.

The thought of Steve returning before Joel kind of terrified me. Joel might be annoying as all Hell, but he had a knack for defusing his dad's explosive moods.

And now I'd be left to cop the full brunt of it, while Joel romanced my physiotherapist.

I was sobbing before I even had a chance to work out what was making me feel so upset. I forcefully rubbed at my wet cheeks, wishing the tears away.

My phone rang. With a shaky sigh of relief that someone out there wanted to talk to me, I reached for it.

"Hey Brad," I mumbled. I made a pathetic effort to sound like I wasn't crying, but he wasn't stupid.

"Are you okay, Mel? Are you in pain?" he asked anxiously. I was touched by his worry.

"Nah, just down about the match. And feeling a little lonely."

"What, isn't Steve there?"

I shrugged. "Nope. And Joel just left to screw my physio."

Brad snorted. "Why does *that* not surprise me? I am surprised that Steve left you all alone with a sprained ankle though."

It was my turn to snort. "I'm not. We had a massive fight."

"Why?" Brad was curious.

"Oh, it's a long story, but the gist of it is that he's pissed at me because I lost."

"That's bullshit! I mean, it's not your fault that you fell over and sprained your ankle!"

"Well thanks, it's good to know that someone's on my side." Even if it was in part my own fault.

"I'm always on your side, Mel. Do you want to grab dinner? Amanda moved her flight up to get back to work, I just dropped her at the airport, but I'm still down here until tomorrow evening. Maybe we could get Uber Eats, watch some crappy TV?"

I smiled, feeling heaps better already just at the thought of having Brad with me.

"Sure, that sounds great. I'm in room … actually, I'll meet you in the foyer."

Brad inhaled through his teeth. "Are you sure that's such a good idea? You're not supposed to be moving on a sprained ankle." Brad would know, he was studying medicine at Uni.

"It's okay, I've got crutches. I want you to take me somewhere if that's alright?"

"Um, okay. I'll be there in about twenty."

I arrived in the foyer long before Brad was due, so I took a seat in one of the tub chairs and sighed. People looked at me with funny expressions, some of them even surreptitiously pointing their phone cameras in my direction. Great, I was infamous now: the tennis player who stuffed her Australian Open chances by falling over. *Fan-fucking-tastic*. Just what I'd always wanted to be remembered for. I'd been playing the pro circuit for two years now; I thought I'd gotten pretty good at ignoring the unwanted attention.

Didn't stop me wishing I could do a Russell Crowe and chuck my phone at them.

"Looking good, Mel!" Brad's mellow voice was like music to my ears. I looked up and beamed at him.

"You have no idea how great it is to see you!" I gushed.

Brad grinned, looking so boy-next-door it was almost criminal. His floppy dark blonde hair fell into his grey eyes, never looking quite tidy enough. His smile was bright and lopsided, and his teeth weren't perfectly straight, giving him an approachable air. He was tall and lean, dressed casually in a pair of shorts and a black t-shirt.

"So, where do you want me to take you?" Brad asked, helping me to my feet and tucking the crutches under my arms.

"I need to get to a church," I replied, hobbling out the front door. Brad helped me down the three steps, where his car was idling in the valet parking area.

"A church? Mel, you haven't been inside a church since high school." Brad sounded dubious.

"Exactly. Clearly I'm overdue. Besides, I broke a promise to God, and I need to make up for it before he sends worse shit my way."

Brad shrugged. "Your wish is my command."

The smell of frankincense inside Saint Eric's hit me, bringing back memories of sitting in the pew in high school, waiting for my turn at confession. Nervous, sweaty-palmed memories of not wanting to tell the preacher just what dirty sexcapades I had gotten up to over the weekend. Memories of taking my Hail Mary's without complaint, only to never actually recite them.

Shaking the cloak of memories off, I hopped over to the altar. After all, I hadn't come for confession; I was here to light a candle just like I'd promised I would. I reached for my handbag for a two-dollar donation, before realising that I hadn't brought it with me. Just my phone and the electronic room key in my back pocket.

I turned to Brad to beg for a loan, but he was already standing there with a wry grin on his face, a coin held out to me.

"My treat," he whispered. I smiled at him and took the money, slipping it into the donation box and taking a candle.

Brad helped me kneel down in front of the altar, and then politely moved away so I could pray in peace.

I lit my candle from one of the other little stumps that were still burning there and sat it in among them.

God, first up, I really need to thank you for watching out for me in my quarter. I felt you with me during the match, I felt your strength supporting me.

I'm also really sorry, I made a promise and I broke it. I needed your guidance today and I couldn't find it. I kind of feel like that's probably a bit my own fault, really. And it's made everything so much harder.

I'm going to need your help, to find the patience and the humility to mend this rift with Steve. I feel so awful that I let him down. I let me down too. And I let You down …

Now, I know that I don't really have a right to be asking you for anything else right now. But … after last night – and I know you know what I'm talking about – there's something that's been playing on my mind. It's not tennis related, promise …

I took a deep breath and squeezed my eyes tighter shut, hoping that if I concentrated hard enough God really would pay attention.

Please, God, help me to find a guy. Not one who just thinks I'm hot and wants to screw me, but one who will take the time to get to know me, with all my crazy fucked-upness, and who can love all of me. One who can help me to ... to trust him, because after ... well, everything, I just really need some help with that.

Oh, and if you have time, can you give Joel Herbert genital herpes? If he hasn't got them already that is. Thanks God.

Finished, I looked around, and Brad walked over and helped me up. "So, what do you want to do now you've got that off your chest?" he asked.

"Let's get pizza and booze and have a night in."

A few glasses of vodka and juice and several slices of pizza later, and I was feeling much better.

"Why don't we do this more often?" I asked as I turned to Brad who was sitting on the floor beside the lounge, his head resting against my knee. The TV was on quietly in the background. Not on the tennis – I'd had enough tennis for one day.

Brad smiled at me. "Because you're an athlete, Mel. You can't eat and drink like this every night." Oh Brad, always the voice of reason.

"Why aren't you drinking?" I asked him.

"Because I have to drive back to my hotel soon," he looked down at his watch, "Mel, it's almost midnight."

I shrugged. I didn't feel very drunk, but I wondered how much my head would spin when I stood up.

"You could stay here tonight."

Brad looked very deeply into my eyes and shook his head sadly. "I don't think that's such a good idea."

"Why not?" I insisted. "I doubt Joel's coming home tonight – you could sleep in his bed."

Brad paused for a moment, then shook his head again.

"I can't. It's too ..."

I raised my eyebrows at him.

"Too what?" I demanded.

Brad refused to look at me. "Nothing. Don't worry about it."

I shrugged, reaching for the box of pain meds Joel had left on the coffee table. Brad snatched it away and glared angrily at me.

"Are you insane? No pain killers for you while you're drinking!"

I grunted crossly. "If you say so, Dr Jacobs."

Brad watched in silence as I poured myself another vodka and juice.

"I don't think …" he began, his voice trailing uncertainly.

"That I should be drinking more? Well, I've got to numb the pain somehow." I took a slug of my drink and winced; too much vodka. Brad, ever the intelligent one, took my cup and diluted it with more orange juice as he changed the subject.

"Mel, why d'you keep Steve on as your coach if he's so horrible to you?" Brad took my hand and held on tight.

"He's a great coach, Brad. He cares and he really wants me to succeed. He does have some … unique motivation methods," I laughed blithely, "Like the other day he slapped me."

Brad's breath hissed through his teeth. "He hit you?" he asked, incredulous.

"Well, I was working up to a panic attack about the quarter-final at the time. He was just snapping me out of it."

"By physically abusing you!" Brad's face was thunderous. This conversation was totally souring my buzz.

"Brad, I'm really tired, I think it might be time to call it a night." I sat up and screwed the cap back on the vodka.

Brad stood up, then looked back down at me. "D'you need help getting to bed?" he asked.

I shook my head. "I'll be fine. You get going. Thanks for keeping me company tonight."

Brad leaned down to kiss me lightly on the cheek. "Any time, Mel. You know I'm always here for you." Brad pushed a piece of hair out of my face. "Take care, Smellie." His footsteps faded, then returned. I opened an eye, as he handed me a bottle of water.

"Time to hydrate now, I think," he murmured. Before I had a chance to thank him he walked to the door, and I heard it snick quietly closed behind him.

I lay down, wondering if Steve planned on coming back tonight.

I hated knowing he was mad at me, and he had every right to be. The apology was burning my throat. Or was that the vodka?

My phone beeped.

> Brad: Hey Mel, ran into your coach in the foyer. He was about to throw down with Pete Levine, but security broke it up. Pete got into the lift, but Steve headed into the bar. Don't expect him any time soon. Sleep well.

Well, there went my apologetic feelings. Steve had no right to be yelling at Pete – it wasn't Pete's fault that I'd played so badly! It was mine. He should have come up and screamed at me instead.

Clearly Steve had been drinking. He didn't drink often, but a couple of times I'd seen him get very messy. I should go down and confront him before he started a brawl.

I struggled into an upright position, suddenly realising that I was a bit drunk too. Well, good. Nothing like a bit of Dutch Courage.

I picked up my crutches and lurched to the door, heading down the hallway towards the lift. Inside, as my finger paused over the button that would take me down to the ground floor, the last slug of vodka hit me. Squinting at the blurred number panel, I moved my finger and pressed another button instead.

CHAPTER FIVE

"I am so sorry about Steve!" I exclaimed as soon as Pete opened the door. I didn't even give him a chance to let it sink in that it was me leaning drunkenly outside the door of the apartment.

Pete looked me up and down, his eyes lingering on my boobs before flitting down to my ankle, all strapped up in the compression bandage.

"Don't mention it," he murmured. "How's your ankle, gorgeous? That was a nasty fall."

Pete crouched down and rested my right foot in his hand. His fingers trailed up my calf, sending delightful little shivers all the way through me. He looked up, his brown eyes blazing.

"I just feel really bad that Steve yelled at you," I persisted. I vaguely registered the slurring in my voice. "Is there anything I can do to make it up to you?"

I tried my hardest to look sexy, despite the swollen ankle, the crutches, and the drunkenness.

Pete stood up and held the door wide open for me. "I can think of something you might be able to do."

I shambled through the doorway, taking the initiative and heading straight for the bedroom. I sat down on the edge of the bed, propping the crutches against the wall and tearing off my singlet and bra.

Pete leaned against the frame of the door, watching me with his arms folded across his chest, a hot smile on his face. I pouted at him, sitting in my shorts and beckoning to him with one finger.

He walked over to the TV cupboard at the foot of the bed, where I could see an iPad, Pete's phone and a whole bunch of the usual mess of a person who has been living out of a suitcase. I watched, vision blurry, as he fiddled with something on the cupboard, and when he turned around, music was playing quietly in the background.

"Nothing like some tunes to set the mood," he purred as he pushed me back on the bed, and I forgot about everything else.

There was light streaming in through the open blind when I woke up. My mouth tasted like bile, and my head and my ankle were throbbing like nobody's business. I had that dreadful moment where I was completely disoriented.

"Oh, God, where am I?" I grunted, sitting up, and then wishing I hadn't when the room spun.

"Well, good morning sleepy!" Pete greeted me from the door-way, wearing nothing but a pair of boxer-briefs, a glass of water in one hand. He held it out to me, and I took it gratefully, guzzling it down greedily.

"Easy there, tiger!" Pete chuckled, taking the glass from me and kneeling down beside the bed. I blushed, realising that I was naked. It was stupid – I'd been naked the whole night. I winced as some of the things we'd done last night came back to me in mortifying bursts. And then I winced some more as the throbbing in my ankle intensified.

I looked down. Pete was very gently unravelling the compression bandage from my ankle, returning my gaze with a soft smile.

"I know it hurts, gorgeous, but if you want to take a shower the bandage has to come off. You want a hand to get in there?"

My eyes started to water. I blinked furiously at the tears, but I couldn't suppress the surge of gratitude that flooded me. Pete was acting really sweet … *why* was Pete acting so sweet?

"I think I can make it, if you hand me the crutches," I choked out. He stood up and held a hand out to me. I took it and he helped me lever myself off the bed. He held me steady with one hand while he propped the crutches under my arms. He walked in ahead of me and ran the shower, the steam billowing out.

"There you go," he said. I handed him the crutches again and hopped into the cubicle. He draped a towel over the top and then left, closing the door behind him.

"Call me if you need me, okay?" I heard his muffled offer through the door.

I sighed, letting the hot water soothe my throbbing head. I opened my mouth and let some water trickle in.

Back in the bedroom Pete had picked up my clothes and had folded them neatly at the end of the bed. That brought on a fresh wave of prickling in my eyes. What had gotten into me? I was on the verge of blubbering for God's sake!

I sat down on the bed and struggled into my underwear and shorts, clipped my bra back on and dragged my singlet over my head. The compression bandage was rolled up beside me. I picked it up and looked at it. I had no idea how to wrap my ankle properly.

I was about to tuck it into my pocket, hoping that Steve was over his anger and would re-strap it for me when I got back upstairs, or that Joel would know how to do it, when Pete returned, juggling another glass of water and a plate of toast and Vegemite.

He passed it to me with a smile. "I know how much you Aussies like your Vegemite," he said softly as he knelt down in front of me again, plucking the bandage from my other hand.

"Eat," he said, and proceeded to strap my ankle up nice and tight. I managed to force down the toast. He'd been a bit heavy handed with the Vegemite, but I could forgive that. No one who wasn't a true Aussie knew how to spread the mightiest of 'mites.

Ankle all strapped, he stood up. He was dressed now in his tennis gear. Of course, he had his semi-final this evening. He would be heading over to prepare.

I finished off the last crust of toast, and Pete helped me to my feet, taking the plate into the kitchenette. I put the crutches under my arms and headed towards the door.

"Thanks for this morning," I murmured to him as he came up behind me. I felt his lips on the back of my neck.

"No, gorgeous, thank *you* for last night!" he sighed with feeling. His hands snaked around my middle, and he leaned closer to kiss me on the cheek. "I'll be remembering it until the next time I see you. Are you still in Melbourne tonight?" I heard the hope in his voice and I giggled.

"We're booked until the end of the Open, although Steve might change our plans now," I replied. "Why? Do you want me to come down again tonight?"

"Mmmm hmmm," he groaned against my skin, his lips on my shoulder. "If I win, I can't think of a better way than celebrating with you, and if I lose … well, you can help me forget about it."

"Okay," I agreed. "Good luck this evening."

"Thanks," he whispered. He opened the door and let me out into the deserted corridor, blowing me a kiss before closing the door behind me.

With a grin on my face, I made my way towards the elevator.

The doors slid silently open on the seventeenth floor and I staggered out on my crutches. The hallway turned sharply to the right, and our room was at the very end. I pulled my key out of my back pocket, limping down the hall.

The door wasn't fully closed. Swallowing back the sudden, inexplicable tightness in my throat, I leaned heavily on the crutches and pushed it open. The apartment was in darkness. All the blinds had been drawn the night before, and I'd switched off the lights as I'd left. Obviously, Joel wasn't back yet, or if he was, he'd had such a sleepless night that he'd just gone straight to bed. Steve was likely sleeping off a hangover.

I moved crutches-first into the gloom. There was a funny smell in the place. In my sensitive hungover state, it made me gag. I reached out to flick on the light switch.

What I saw when the light came on − what was all over the floor, all over the walls, sticking to the bottoms of my feet, took the strength out of my legs.

Then it was dark again. Blessed dark.

My eyes opened. My face was pressing wetly against something sticky and slimy. The smell was overpowering. I swallowed hard and groaned weakly. My body hurt from the fall. How long had I been unconscious?

"Mel? Oh shit, Mel! Thank God! You're alive!"

"Am I?" I asked, trying to push myself off the floor and sliding in the goo that covered me. "I kind of wish I wasn't."

"Don't move – the ambulance will be here soon," Joel hissed. I couldn't see him.

"What happened?" I asked groggily. The sticky, coppery fluid on the floor got into my mouth and I lost it. The toast I'd just eaten came straight back up.

Once it was all out, I managed to push myself up to sit against the wall just inside the doorway.

"I don't know," Joel muttered, his voice cracking. I tried to wipe the blood from my face, but I only managed to smear it around more. I focussed on the puddle of vomit near my knee – it was much easier to look at than the body on the floor … Steve's body.

Joel walked the long way around the prone form of his father, sprawled out in an awkward position, his eyes open and staring sightlessly. It was hard to tell what had happened to him – there was so much blood. I didn't want to look, but my eyes kept straying back to it.

Joel crouched down in front of me, a tea towel in his hand. He dabbed at the blood on my face, on my arm, on my chest.

"Are you hurt?" he asked, his voice shaking. I shook my head. I didn't feel like I'd ever be able to talk again.

"Shit, Mel, I thought … I thought you were … I thought they'd gotten both of you."

I kept shaking my head.

"Are you sure you're not hurt?" he asked again. His hands were trembling. His voice trembling. I reached out one bloody hand and gripped his tightly. He clung on like his life depended on it.

"Is he …?" I whispered. I couldn't finish the sentence.

Joel turned away from me, his eyes squeezed tightly shut. We both knew, but saying it aloud was just too much. Joel slumped against the wall beside me. I put my head on his shoulder and closed my eyes.

God, what have you done? Why would you let this happen? What did Steve ever do to you? He didn't deserve this!

Suddenly there were people everywhere. I was being lifted onto a gurney and EMTs were checking to make sure that none of the blood that was soaked through my clothes belonged to me. Joel was having similar treatment. They didn't even look at Steve. I wanted to scream at them to check him, to save him, but I couldn't find my voice.

I felt like I was watching the whole scene from a great distance. I was wheeled out of the room as more police arrived. Hotel staff were standing around, their faces white with a greenish tinge. I thought I probably looked the same way, under all the blood.

Joel walked like a zombie into the lift with me and the medical team. There was a streak of blood on his cheek and his shorts were smeared with it. He found my hand and I wound my fingers through his.

I was separated from Joel as soon as we arrived at the hospital. When they cleaned me up and satisfied themselves that I wasn't bleeding, they relaxed a bit. Someone took the bloody bandage off my ankle and checked out the damage there. They sent me for scans. Well, Julie had said I should get it checked out, I just hadn't imagined that it would pan out *this* way.

I lay there in the hospital gown – totally naked underneath because all my clothes had been soaked through with blood – and exhaustion claimed me.

I woke up to the sound of a throat being cleared.

"Miss Black, sorry to wake you, but we need to ask you some questions."

I cracked my eyes open and there were two men in suits standing by the bed. One had his phone out and he was muttering the date and time into it. My body went cold.

"Miss Black, can you please run through the events of yesterday evening for us?"

I swallowed dryly. I looked around for a glass of water, but of course there was none.

"Is Steve …?" I forced the words out through my parched lips.

The taller detective nodded gravely at me. "I'm sorry, yes." They knew what I meant. They were investigating a murder, and I was the first person on the scene after the crime. Of course they would need to talk to me.

They waited for me to answer their question. I racked my brain – yesterday evening seemed so long ago.

"Okay, um … well, when Joel left, Brad – my friend, Brad Jacobs – called me and I asked him to come and pick me up."

"What time was that?" the shorter man, the one holding the recorder, interrupted.

"Um, that would have been about seven thirty, I think. I met him down in the foyer and he took me to Saint Eric's church, so I could light a candle.

"Okay, so after that we stopped at a bottle shop, and then we picked up some pizza … and we went back to the apartment."

"Was Steven Herbert there when you returned?" the taller detective asked. I shook my head. The shorter one murmured into the phone.

"We had dinner and hung out for a while. Brad left just a little before midnight."

"Did you see Steve after that?" I shook my head again, and again shortie described it into the recorder.

"But Brad sent me a text message to tell me that he saw Steve going into the bar downstairs in the hotel as he was leaving." I realised that Brad was the last one of us to have seen Steve alive. I felt a pang of sadness that threatened to overwhelm me. I swallowed around the dry lump in my throat.

"And then, did you go to bed?" the taller one prompted, not unkindly.

"No," I replied, flushing. "I went downstairs and spent the night in someone else's room."

The detectives didn't bat an eyelid at that. "Whose room was it?"

"Pete Levine." I whispered.

"Can you speak up a little please, Miss Black?" the taller one prompted.

"Pete Levine," I answered, enunciating each syllable carefully.

"And what time did you head back up to your room?"

I shrugged. "I don't know exactly, but it was probably about nine."

"And can you describe for us what you found when you returned?"

I paused, gathering my thoughts. I tried to focus only on the facts. "I got out my key, but when I got to the door it was already open. It was really dark inside so I flicked the light switch, and then I saw the blood, and I fainted.

"The next thing I remember is waking up in a pool of it, and Joel was there."

"You didn't notice anything else out of the ordinary? Was Joel already in the apartment when you got back?" the shorter one asked gruffly.

"Well, I didn't really have time to take much in before I was unconscious on the floor, but I'm pretty sure I was the only one there."

"And did Joel Herbert tell you where he had been all night?" shortie persisted.

"He left at about seven last night with Julie Green, my physio. He was expecting to spend the night with her."

"Thank you, Miss Black. Will you be remaining in Melbourne for a while?"

I shrugged. "I don't know. I had planned to stay until the end of the Open, but now …" All I really wanted was to go home and curl up in a ball in my familiar little apartment, and cuddle my cat.

"Where's Joel?" I asked. The two men shared a meaningful look.

"He's being interviewed in another room. He might have to stay down here for a few days."

That wasn't a lot of information, but it told me a hell of a lot about what was happening.

I sat up sharply. "Listen, Joel wouldn't … do this, I don't care what you think!" I snarled at them.

A nurse poked her head around the curtain. Shortie glared at her, but she held her ground, pushing the curtain aside and bustling through to check on me.

"We're just making initial inquiries, Miss Black. Where will we find you if we need to follow up?"

I knew that as soon as they left, I was ringing Leopard Airlines and booking the next available flight home. I rattled off my address.

"Thank you for your time." The taller man smiled at me. Shortie scowled, and they breezed out through the curtain.

The nurse smiled sympathetically at me. I asked her if I could make a phone call. I had no idea where my mobile was – probably back at the apartment and now a piece of evidence in a murder investigation.

I phoned the airline and thankfully they had two seats available on the last flight back to Sydney. I booked them both, reciting my credit card number over the phone to them. I was pretty sure that Joel would be allowed to leave – I mean, we both had airtight alibis for last night. I knew he would want to get home to his mother.

Oh God! Had anyone called Sandra to tell her? I was halfway through dialling her mobile before I realised that I couldn't make that call. It wasn't my place. I hoped that she'd been told by a police officer knocking on her door, and not when she turned on the morning news. The lump in my throat throbbed.

Trembling, I dialled Brad's number.

"Hello?" He sounded panicked.

"Brad, it's Mel."

I heard his shaky exhalation over the phone. "Mel! Thank God! I've been freaking out all morning wondering where you were! I'm over at Savoy Tower – I came to bring you brunch. There are police everywhere, they have the whole seventeenth floor blocked off … I've had cops hounding me about who I am and what I did last night and who I was with. They wouldn't tell me if you were okay, or where you were or anything!" Brad's voice quavered.

"It's okay, Brad. I'm at the hospital – they brought me here because they thought I was hurt, but I'm not." I took a deep breath, preparing to break the news. "Steve was …"

"I know," he muttered over the phone. "I'm down in the foyer, and there's a TV with the news going – it's all they're talking about. There are cameras outside. The police asked me to stay until they can sit down and get a statement from me. Have they spoken to you yet?"

"Yeah, they wanted to know what happened since the last time I saw Steve. I told them that you'd been over and that you saw Steve when you left about midnight."

"They don't think you had anything to do with it, do they?"

"I don't think so … hey, when they come to get your statement, can you ask them if I can have my stuff back from the apartment? I'm catching the nine forty flight home tonight. D'you reckon you could ask them to bring it over to the hospital?"

"Sure thing, Mel. Is that the Leopard flight?"

"Yep."

"I'm on that one too. I guess I'll see you at the airport. D'you want me to come and pick you up from the hospital?"

"No, that's okay. I'll find my own way. Just tell the police that I really need my stuff – I don't even have my phone and wallet, so it'll be hard to get on the plane."

"Okay, Mel. I'm so glad you're alright. I'll talk to you again as soon as I can."

"Thanks, Brad. Bye."

I closed my eyes for a moment, exhaustion creeping over me.

Bulging eyes.

Gaping mouth.

Blood.

I sat bolt upright, swallowing back a scream.

The nurse popped her head in. "You've got a visitor."

Joel slumped in, pale under his tan. He collapsed into the chair beside the bed and looked down at his hands. I hid my own shaking ones under the blanket.

"Joel, I'm so sorry," I whispered.

He looked up and a ghost of his usual smile flitted across his face. My heart lurched, my throat constricting.

I coughed. "Are the police done with you? Did they say you could leave?"

He nodded. "Yeah, they're done."

"I booked us tickets home tonight," I said quietly.

"Thanks, Mel. I just got off the phone with Mum. I have to get home."

I watched him trace the bloodstain on his shorts with his index finger. I couldn't think of anything to say that would make him feel better. I don't think that there *was* anything I could say.

"The bastard butchered him," Joel blurted out, the words echoing in the little curtained room.

My breath caught in my throat. "What?" I managed to ask, then wished I hadn't. I didn't want to hear in any detail what Joel meant.

"His chest looked like it had been put through a meat grinder." Joel choked on the words.

I retched, but there was nothing in my stomach to vomit up. It felt like there was nothing left inside of me at all. I was just a big hollow shell. I was lost.

God, please look after Steve, and tell him I'm sorry, and I love him.

CHAPTER SIX

Coachless

We arrived in Sydney to a frenzy of photographers, TV crews and journalists outside the arrivals area.

Joel managed to think quickly, and we dodged the bloodthirsty pack by hiding in among a huge group of tourists who were milling around looking lost. There was no way either of us were in any shape to be interrogated by journalists – not that it would have stopped the hungry press from going for the throat.

Brad, who could pass by the cameras with no one the wiser, ducked off ahead of us to get his car and have it idling by the entrance so we could jump straight in. He had insisted on the plane that he would drive us both home. Between Joel, in Rose Bay, me to the east in Vaucluse, and Brad in Double Bay to the west, we were practically neighbours.

As we pulled into the drive of the Herbert family's palatial waterfront monstrosity, I turned around from the front seat and patted Joel on the knee.

"Are you sure you don't want me to come in?" I asked quietly.

Joel shook his head. "Thanks, Stink, but it's all good. Aunty Dianne's here with Mum."

I felt loneliness drop like a lead weight in the pit of my stomach. I hadn't known my dad, he died when I was little. Steve had been like a father to me. In that moment I realised with a cold jolt that I wasn't really a part of Steve's family.

The silence on the trip from Joel's house to my apartment was complete, but not uncomfortable. I felt like anything I might say would be too trivial for the situation we were living.

Brad eventually broke the silence.

"Poor Joel, I really feel for the guy."

"Hmm," I agreed. If there were words to express how I felt about it, I wasn't clever enough to come up with them.

We pulled up at my apartment building.

"Night, Brad. Thanks for the lift." I opened the door, but Brad hopped out quickly and helped me out of the car, putting my crutches under my arms and getting my luggage out of the boot.

"How're you going to make it up the stairs?" he asked me, looking dubiously at my strapped ankle.

I sighed, glancing up at the three flights of stairs ahead of me. Crutches and stairs simply don't mix. I took a deep breath and bit my lip to prevent the tremble that was about to turn me into a blubbering mess.

Brad saw right through it and with a wry expression on his face, he wordlessly took my bags, propped me up against the wall and removed the crutches, then sprinted up the three flights with the ease of someone who has full use of his legs. I managed a watery smile, rolling my eyes.

When he returned, panting slightly, he turned away from me and bent down.

"Hop on."

"Um …" I mumbled uncertainly. I was only maybe an inch shorter than him and probably more muscled. I didn't think he could cope with a piggyback ride over three floors.

"Just get on, Smell!" he growled. "I'm stronger than I look, you know."

I snorted but awkwardly clambered onto his back, warm through his t-shirt. His neck felt damp with sweat. Poor guy – carrying me up three floors probably wasn't the way he'd like to be spending his evening.

To his credit, Brad didn't complain about my weight once. But by the time he was outside my door, I could feel his body trembling with effort. He let me slide to the floor, where my crutches were waiting for me.

"Thanks," I murmured. Brad dropped his hands to his knees and took a few panting breaths, holding a finger up to me to wait.

"Thought you were stronger than you looked?" I teased.

Brad straightened up, chest rising and falling as he fought to catch his breath, his face red. "Are you going to be okay on your own?" Brad asked, a hint of doubt in his voice.

I shrugged as Connor wound his way around my good leg, pressing his grey and white head against my shin and purring like crazy.

"I'll be fine. I mean, I've got Connor after all." I didn't want to think too much about being alone. Physically I could cope. Mentally … I had no idea how that was going to pan out.

Brad bent down and picked Connor up, holding him so I could give him a pat. He yowled demandingly in my face, blowing fishy breath all over me.

"Okay, Connie, I'll get you some food. I bet Grandma hasn't been feeding you properly."

Normally when I travelled, I entrusted Connor's care to Amanda, but since she'd come down for the Open, I'd had to rely on my not-so-reliable mother. Mum … well let's just say the thought of her having unrestricted access to my apartment was horrifying.

I hobbled to the kitchen and scooped out some biscuits for him. He heard the noise and leapt out of Brad's arms, gallivanting into the kitchen with a yowl.

I watched Connor scarf down his kibble, knowing better than to try and touch him while he was eating. I still had scars to remind me why that was a bad idea.

"Well, I'll just get going then," Brad said from behind me. I jumped – I hadn't heard him follow me into the kitchen. I guessed I would probably be a bit jumpy for a while.

My stomach churned and my vision blurred. I closed my eyes to try and clear my head.

Gaping mouth.
Bulging eyes.
Blood.

I snapped my eyes open, biting the inside of my cheek.

"Okay," I mumbled.

Brad closed the space between us and enveloped me in his long arms.

"Do you want me to stay?" he asked, rubbing soothing hands up and down my back. I shook my head against his shoulder and he stepped back, peering into my eyes. "I'm serious, Smellie. If you need me, I'm here."

I shook my head again, gripping the kitchen bench behind me so he wouldn't see my hands shake. "You're the best, Brad. But I'll be fine."

"Well, I'm only a phone call away. I'll need to get used to late night calls anyway once I graduate."

I managed a weak smile and hugged him again. I stood at the open door and, gripping Connor like he was a snuggly toy, watched him walk down the stairs to his car.

I needed to be alone.

Alone felt terrifying.

"Well, Connie, you're going to sleep under the sheets with Mummy tonight, okay?" I crooned shakily. Connor eyed me with the disapproval that only a cat can muster. At least he didn't struggle out of my arms.

Blood.
Bulging eyes.
Gaping mouth.
I scream …

It was the scream that woke me. It didn't stop, even as I launched myself out of bed, catapulting Connor off my legs. My ankle throbbed painfully.

I realised as my throat burned that the noise wasn't stopping because *I* was screaming. I locked my jaw shut and hopped over to flick on the light, chasing the shadows and the remnants of my nightmare away.

It was just after five. I'd managed a solid four-and-a-half hours sleep. Great. Well, I doubted I'd be getting back to sleep now. I pulled an oversized t-shirt over my naked body.

Crutching my way out to the kitchen, I flicked the switch on my coffee maker and grabbed the milk from the fridge, sniffing it and screwing my nose up at the sour smell. Sighing, I pulled down a carton of long-life from the cupboard and cracked it open.

A nice, sweet latte was my best bet to chase away the clinging cobwebs of the nightmare.

I sat in a chair at my table and nursed that coffee as the sun rose through the kitchen window.

A knock at the door startled me out of an exhausted haze. I winced as I collected my crutches.

Brad was standing on the other side, two takeaway coffees in hand. He eyed my stretched-out t-shirt briefly as he entered.

"Uh, you might want to get dressed. The police just pulled up as I was getting out of my car and they look like they mean business."

I groaned and made my way back to the bedroom, fear swishing in my stomach.

I rummaged through my wardrobe and found some clean underwear and a cotton summer dress that I couldn't ever remember wearing. I wasn't normally a dress sort of girl, but it would be easier to put on than shorts. I yanked it on over my head and picked up my crutches as I heard another knock at the door, and Brad's footsteps as he answered it.

There were two police officers: a short woman with shoulder-length brown hair, dressed in a smart pant suit, and a chubby middle-aged man with a bald spot and old sweat stains in the armpits of his off-white shirt.

"Miss Black, I'm Detective Coughlin and this is Detective Taylor," the man began. I eyed them warily before sitting down in my armchair and gesturing towards the lounge. They sat, serious expressions pulling their mouths downwards.

"Have you remembered anything more about what happened the night before last, Miss Black?" the woman, Detective Taylor, asked.

I shook my head. "There's nothing else to remember – I already told the police in Melbourne everything."

"Well, we thought you might want to change your story. You see, our colleagues in Victoria had a chat with Pete Levine last night, and he says that you didn't spend the night with him."

I gaped at them in disbelief. Why would Pete lie about it? He'd never cared if people knew about his little affairs before!

"Why did you say you spent the night with him, Melanie?" Taylor asked, her eyes narrowed.

"Because I *did*!" I spluttered out. "I went to his room just after midnight, and I didn't leave until about nine the next morning!"

"And what were you doing in Pete Levine's room?" Taylor persisted.

"What weren't we doing? I think we tried just about every position known to man, and some that aren't!"

Brad's face was a carefully calm mask at the edge of my vision.

"Okay, so you're insisting that you spent the night in bed with Pete Levine, and he insists that you never set foot in his room," Taylor spoke very clearly, like she thought I didn't understand her properly.

If I had seen Pete Levine then, I would have thrown one of my crutches at him. Followed by the other one. And then whatever else I could get my hands on.

"Well, obviously one of you is lying," Taylor continued, "So why don't you just come clean now, Miss Black?"

"I'm as clean as they come, Detective," I replied, barely keeping my voice calm. "Why are you so sure that I'm the one who's lying? Don't they have CCTV in Savoy Tower? Couldn't you just look to see me going into Pete's room? Or for that matter, couldn't you just see who it was who …?"

Taylor cleared her throat, cutting me off. "The Savoy's CCTV currently only covers the lobby, restaurant and other public areas. They use dummy cameras in the guest-only areas."

"Dummy cameras?" I asked, confused.

"Devices that look like cameras as a deterrent, but they don't actually record or stream any footage."

"It's made our job a lot more difficult," Coughlin added and Taylor threw him an icy look.

"We aren't here to discuss issues of hotel security," Taylor said. "We're here to follow you up, Miss Black."

"Well, consider me followed up."

"So, you're sticking to your story?" Taylor asked.

I glared at her angrily. "I'm sticking to the truth! How about you go and question Pete Levine a bit further?" I suggested.

Taylor must have caught my mood because she stood. "Oh, rest assured, Miss Black, our colleagues down in Melbourne are with him as we speak. We'll get to the bottom of this. You're not by any means off the hook."

I swallowed, but I held her gaze. I knew I'd done nothing wrong, and it would only be a matter of time before they knew it too.

The pair walked back to the door. Coughlin stepped out into the hallway, but Taylor turned and eyed me with dislike from the doorway.

"Don't leave town, Miss Black," she muttered. I slammed the door in her face and turned to Brad, bursting into hysterical laughter.

"I wonder how long she's wanted to use *that* line!" I gasped. Brad smiled, but I could see the concern in his eyes. I sobered up a bit.

"Pete Levine?" he asked. I could hear a hint of some emotion in his voice, but I couldn't quite place it. I flushed.

"It was just a bit of harmless fun. He's a nice guy," I replied.

Brad rolled his eyes. "Oh, he sounds delightful – he won't even admit to spending the night with you!"

I flinched, Brad's words hitting me like a slap.

"Mel … you just …" Brad moved closer, the anger on his face softening. He reached up and stroked my cheek with his thumb, staring down at me. I met his gaze for a moment before looking away – his grey eyes were too intense for me.

My phone rang, thankfully distracting both of us. I hopped over to where I had dumped it on the table the night before and answered.

"Melanie! Why didn't you call to tell me you were home?" my mother's shrill voice demanded. I held the receiver away from my ear. Brad could hear the screeching too. I winced and he grimaced.

"I got home really late last night, Mum," I replied. "You know I was just about to call you." I crossed my fingers behind my back to excuse the little white lie.

"Mrs Rodriguez down at the newsagents said she saw a police car outside your building just a moment ago. You're caught up in this whole Steve Herbert thing, aren't you?"

I bit my lip, nostrils flaring as I got my emotions under control. "What Steve Herbert thing, Mum? Oh, you mean that my tennis coach was …" I cleared my throat. *"Murdered.* That is what you mean, isn't it?"

"Yes, that's what I mean. I'm worried about you! Are you in any trouble?"

I sighed. There was no use in trying to make my mother understand.

"No more than usual, Mum," I mumbled.

"I think you should go to confession, it'll make you feel better."

"I'll see if I can fit it in somewhere," I lied.

"I'll let Father Shannon know to expect you."

Yeah, right. Like he hadn't heard *that* one a thousand times before.

"Okay, Mum. Bye." I hung up before she had a chance to say anything else.

"Mel, I've got to get going," Brad said apologetically. "I've got a meeting at Uni at twelve, I just wanted to drop by and see how you were holding up. Oh, and to give you this. Sorry, it's probably cold now." He handed me the lukewarm coffee.

I smiled gratefully as I took a sip. "It's sweet and caffeinated. That's ninety-nine percent perfect, I'd say. Thanks Brad."

"Are you sure you're okay?" he asked tentatively. I pressed my lips together, nodding.

"It was a bit rough last night, but … coffee helps!" I attempted chipper. I think I almost pulled it off. "Do you have time to drop me off at Joel's house?" I asked, slipping my unbandaged foot into a flat sandal. I looked up at him to see him nodding.

"Time to stop by the florist on the way?"

Another nod. I chucked my wallet, keys and phone into my bag and shuffled my way to the door.

Armed with a bunch of David Austin roses, we approached the Herbert mansion. The number of cars parked out the front was insane. My shock rapidly turned to disgust when I realised they belonged to the photographers and camera crews milling on the pavement. Luckily, the house was completely private from the road, with an eight-foot fence and solid timber gate.

Brad pulled up by the gate and put his window down to punch in the code I muttered as quickly and discreetly as possible. Cameras went off and my name was shouted as the vultures noticed me in the car.

And then we were in, the gate closing behind us. Thankfully the media circus had the sense not to trespass.

Brad pulled the car up at the front door. I brushed my lips very briefly across his cheek as I opened the door.

He smiled sadly at me. "Tell Mrs Herbert I'm thinking of her," he said as I clambered out of the car.

"I will," I promised.

I made my awkward way up the front steps, juggling the flowers and my crutches.

The Herbert house still gobsmacked me. It was one of those places that always looked like it was straight out of an interior design magazine. The furniture was ultra-modern, the floors were always spotless, and the pool glistened in the sunlight – there was never a leaf or a spider in that pool.

The huge front door swung open as I lifted my hand to ring the doorbell. I looked down at Sandra Herbert, immaculate as usual, blonde hair perfectly styled, lipstick flawless.

I held the flowers out to her. "Hi Sandra," I murmured.

Suddenly the words of consolation I had planned got stuck on the rock in my throat.

She took the flowers from me, eyes glistening. "Thank you, Mel. It's good to see you." She reached out and wrapped her arms around my waist. I hugged her back around the crutches, desperately blinking back my own tears.

She broke away and beckoned me inside. I followed, the rubber feet of the crutches squeaking on the gleaming polished Blackbutt floorboards of the entryway.

The house was built clinging to a cliff. We entered a large foyer, with two sets of stairs. One set led up to four bedrooms up top. Sandra took the other set, heading down to the rest of the house. I hopped along gracelessly after her.

Down a level was the living and kitchen, a monster open plan space with gleaming white leather and glass furniture, splashes of blues and greens reflecting the colours of the harbour. A glass wall which slid away opened out onto a sunny deck.

Yet more stairs took us to the ground level, with a huge theatre room, gym, and a bar and rumpus space bigger than my entire apartment opening onto a manicured garden, which in turn gave way to a tennis court and a glistening pool with a waterfall edge that tricked the eye into thinking it spilt into Sydney Harbour itself.

Sandra glided through the garden towards the pool cabana. I heard children splashing in the pool, giggling and squealing. The sound seemed completely at odds with the fact that this was a house in mourning.

"Dianne's kids are here," Sandra explained. Dianne was Sandra's younger sister and she had four kids ranging in age from seven to twelve. Probably too young to really understand that Uncle Steve wasn't coming back. "Joel's entertaining them in the pool. He's been so strong. Make yourself at home, Mel. I'll go pop these beautiful flowers in some water."

I was surprised Sandra had another vase handy; the living room already looked like a florist.

Dianne glanced up at me from a table laden with food and

smiled wistfully. "Hello, Mel. Good to see you again. It's been a long time."

I smiled at Dianne and took a seat beside her, looking out to the pool and the harbour beyond. Three of the kids were sitting on the edge of the pool, staring intently into the water. Suddenly Joel burst to the surface, the fourth kid standing on his shoulders. The kids all giggled hysterically as the child did a somersault off Joel's shoulders.

Joel turned then and spotted me. He waved, his smile not quite reaching his blue eyes.

He turned to the kids and said something that I couldn't make out. They all protested, but he climbed out of the pool and grabbed his towel, walking towards the table. He stood and dried himself directly in front of me. I couldn't help but stare at the beads of water rolling off his skin. He'd stood there on purpose. He might be grieving, but some Joel Herbert traits just worked on autopilot.

Dry at last, he came through the gate and pulled a chair up opposite me. I thought he was going to sit down, but he lifted my right leg onto it.

"Remember the RICE principal, Mel: Rest, Ice, Compression, *Elevation*. We need to keep this up for another twenty-four hours, then you can start doing some light exercise. Swimming to begin with." He gestured towards the pool.

I couldn't believe that he was focusing on my rehab at a time like this. But to be honest, it was much easier for me to think about my ankle than to try and come to terms with Steve.

He piled a plate of fruit in front of me. "You need to make sure you eat right while you're recovering."

I glared at him. "I eat great, thanks," I snapped. It felt better to stay in this familiar territory with Joel. The territory of insults and sarcasm.

"Okay, Stink, just listen to me. I'm your trainer, remember? I know what's best for you. I spent a lot of hours the other night talking to Julie about how best to get you back on track as fast as possible."

I really wanted to retort with, *"Oh, when on earth did you have a chance to talk about me, in between the bouts of scorching sexy-time?"* But I couldn't say that with his mother and aunt and four small cousins in hearing distance.

Instead, I bit forcefully into a strawberry. The juice dribbled down my chin. Joel chuckled at me as I wiped it away with the back of my hand.

"You can put Stinky in a dress, but that won't make her act like a lady," he commented lightly. I scowled.

"Now, now, Joel. Just be nice to her. She's your only client so far. You know how to be charming, so be that," Sandra reprimanded him as she elegantly smeared some Brie onto a cracker.

I choked on a giggle.

"Mel prefers me to talk to her like this, Mum. If I turned the charm on her, she wouldn't be able to concentrate on anything else," Joel argued teasingly.

Sandra turned to her son with a perfect smile that matched his. "Okay, Joel. I'll let you learn these lessons your own way."

Joel leaned down to kiss his mother on the forehead. "Thanks, Mum. Hey Stink, let's go inside where you can elevate that ankle properly, and we can talk about your rehab."

I rolled my eyes but took his hand and he pulled me to my feet. I reached for my crutches and tucked them under my arms, striking out towards the house.

When I reached the stairs, I stopped. Going up stairs was difficult on my crutches. Seeing my expression Joel's lips twitched, and in a single smooth movement, he snatched the crutches from me and swept me off my feet – literally, not in the romance novel sense, of course – carrying me up to the living room.

"What was that for?" I asked as he put me down, wishing my face wasn't on fire. "Your *hero rescues the damsel* act isn't going to work on me."

He grinned at me, and again I noticed how it didn't reach his eyes. "Isn't it, Stink? I think it already has and you're just in denial."

I snatched my crutches back from him indignantly and hobbled my way over to the white leather sofa, plonking myself down and swinging my legs up onto the lounge. Joel tucked a couple of cushions under my foot before heading for the kitchen. The fridge opened and the blender whizzed. I watched an oddly phallic cloud formation steam across the sky, and by the time it disappeared Joel was at my elbow, handing me a green smoothie.

"Don't spill that on the lounge or Mum will have me flogged!" he warned before settling his towel-clad butt on the floor. I took a sip – it was surprisingly delicious.

"How are you holding up?" I asked.

His eyes flashed with the pain that he had been hiding so well earlier. "Barely, to be honest. I'm just so glad that Mum wasn't there to see … She's being so strong, but I know it's draining. It's good to have Aunty Dianne and the kids here to distract her."

I didn't miss how he talked about his mother rather than about himself. Typical male, avoiding talking about his own feelings.

Although I guessed I was just as guilty of that as he was.

"When's the funeral?" I asked.

"They're doing an autopsy today, so once they're satisfied with that, they'll release him. We're working around Friday."

We lapsed into silence again.

"The police came by my house this morning," I said quietly, breaking the silence. Joel looked at me sharply.

"Why?"

I fiddled with the hem of my dress. "Apparently my alibi didn't match up. Pete-The-Arsehole-Levine denied that I spent the night with him."

Joel's jaw dropped. "Why would he do that?"

I shrugged. "Embarrassed maybe? I don't know. I haven't spoken to him and I don't want to."

I felt the tears prickle at my eyes again, and I blinked them determinedly back. I had too many emotions about too many different things swirling in my head – Steve, Pete, my injury – that if I let those tears out, I was worried they would never stop.

"Why would anyone be embarrassed about …" Joel trailed off. I hazarded a glance at him, but he was looking in the other direction.

"Well, I have nothing further to tell the police. If they want to question anyone further, it better be Pete."

Joel grunted. "Well, good for you, Stink," he said, "So, once this is all over and done with – the funeral, and your injury and all – are you going to look for a new coach?"

I looked down at my hands, twisting in my lap. "I don't know, Joel. Obviously, I'll need someone. But I can't think about it yet."

"I was thinking … maybe … if you want to, that is … you could consider letting me coach you. I mean, Dad taught me everything he knows … knew … and I know your game back to front. I know your strengths and weaknesses, and … I just wanted to put my hat in the ring."

It did make sense, in a strange way.

"Let's just see how you go getting me back to match fitness, okay? Then we can discuss it." Great answer, Mel. Noncommittal but perfectly reasonable.

"Fair enough, Stinky. Now on that subject, I've put together a fitness and rehab plan …"

For the rest of the afternoon we put aside the fact that he was fatherless, and I was coachless, and we put aside the fact that ninety-nine percent of the time he drove me insane, and we worked out how to get me back on the court.

CHAPTER SEVEN

Viral Sex

"It hurts!" I complained to Joel. His eyes pierced me and I knew that I wasn't getting out of this so easily.

"Just five more laps and then you're done!" he called from the shallow end of the pool where he was waiting for me. "If you swim back to me, I'll do the last four with you."

I grunted and kicked off, gritting my teeth against the tenderness in my ankle.

The early morning sun glistened over Sydney Harbour, the temperature promising to zoom up into the forties before lunch. Joel waited for me at the shallow end leaning against the edge, his tanned pecs glowing.

I made it back to him and lifted my leg out of the water, sticking my ankle in Joel's face.

"Are you sure we're not making it worse?" I asked. I watched as his gaze slid along the length of my calf before settling on my ankle, his fingers probing gently around the joint.

"It's still a bit swollen, but it's not getting worse," he reassured me. "Nice pins by the way, Stink."

I grimaced. "I'm serious, Joel. Are you sure we're not jumping into this too soon?"

He rolled his eyes. "Believe me, it's not too soon, Mel. And if you think this is hard, you're going to hate me tomorrow!"

He sounded altogether too satisfied with himself about that.

"And I thought your father was a hard-arse," I muttered. Joel froze.

I swallowed. "Listen, Joel, I didn't … I'm sorry."

Joel shook his head, refusing to meet my eyes. "No, don't worry about it. It's all good."

It clearly wasn't. My stomach churned with guilt. It just still felt so surreal. A few days ago, I would have made the same comment and Joel would've laughed and agreed with me.

Joel swam away and I followed, my complaining silenced.

We finished the last four laps and Joel immediately got out of the pool and dried himself, not even trying to show his gorgeous body off. I knew then that I'd really upset him. I followed him out of the pool, careful not to put too much weight on my ankle. I wasn't allowed to use the crutches anymore, but I still needed to be tentative. I towelled off and slipped a singlet on over my swimmers.

"Joel, I'm sorry. I didn't think."

Joel glanced away as he collapsed into a chair on the deck. I followed. Sandra had laid out some cereal and fruit for us.

"I've been waking up screaming in the middle of the night," Joel muttered as he poured cereal. I turned to stare at him. He usually wouldn't open up to me about stuff like this.

"Me too," I replied. "The nightmares are … intense."

Joel nodded as he topped his cereal with banana. "It freaks Mum out. She has no idea just how bad it was, really. I mean, she knows what happened, but … the blood, Mel. And the look on his face." Joel's shudder matched my own. I remembered those parts all too clearly.

He cleared his throat, his expression calmer, although his eyes remained dark. "Maybe you should come and stay here, Stink, until your ankle's better. Then I won't have to come and pick you up for training at the crack of dawn every morning."

I paused, considering the offer. Living alone wasn't ideal at a time like this. Waking up after a nightmare to no one. No tangible reminder that I wasn't the last human left alive on Earth.

"What about Connor?" I asked.

"Your cat can come stay too, I guess. *If* he doesn't claw the furniture or take a shit on the carpet."

I sneered at him. "My cat is perfectly house trained!" I replied. "Are you sure Sandra won't mind us coming to stay?"

Joel shook his head immediately. "I think Mum would be as happy as I would be to know that …" His words trailed off. I found myself blushing, although I wasn't entirely sure why.

"Okay, Joel. Just until my ankle's better though." *Only until I can sleep through the night again*, I added silently to myself. I wondered if Joel hadn't been angling for me to stay for that same reason. No, his mum had probably put him up to it.

We ate in peaceful quiet, watching Sydney Harbour become bluer as the sun rose. My hair had dried into beachy waves by the time I finished my cereal.

"So boss, what's on the agenda for the rest of the day?" I asked. He put down his own bowl and stood, stretching. His skin rippled over his stomach muscles mesmerisingly. I bit my lip, but he heard my sharp inhale.

"It must be hard, having something you want so badly right in front of you and not being able to admit to yourself that you want it."

"I have no idea what you mean," I said, standing up and limping my way back inside.

"Okay, Stink, let's get you moved in with me." He said into my ear, walking beside me as I hobbled up the stairs towards the front door.

"Let's get one thing straight here – I'm not moving in with *you*. I'm staying in your mother's house for a while so that I can get myself back in shape," I snapped as I opened the front door and made my painstaking way towards Joel's car – a blue BMW M4. Joel thought it was hot. I told him it was super wanky. I secretly loved riding in it, but I'd never admit that to him.

I slid into the leather seat. Joel put a towel down on his seat and sat down.

"Lift your butt, Mel!" he commanded. I grimaced as I lifted my swimmers-clad behind off the seat so Joel could put a towel down to protect his precious vehicle. Somehow, he managed to trail a couple of fingertips over my butt as he straightened. I shivered, pursing my lips so I didn't squawk at him. He wanted my reaction – he *always* wanted my reaction, and I had to stop giving him the satisfaction.

We were slipping into our usual habits: him teasing me, me trying not to bite. It was easier than being serious. Being serious brought Steve to the forefront of my mind, and that made me feel sick and dizzy and on the verge of tears all at the same time. I wondered if it made Joel feel the same way, but I was too afraid to ask.

The road outside was thankfully clear of people – Sandra had engaged some private security who were very good at intimidating loiterers. Joel gave a salute to the two large men posted outside the gates as he pulled onto the road.

"Now I know how celebrities feel," I muttered. Joel chuckled humourlessly, turning down the music.

"So, how come Braddles hasn't been sleeping over? I thought he'd be all about the night-time comfort."

"I … need to be able to cope with this on my own," I mumbled.

The nightmares had plagued me again last night. *Blood. Gaping mouth. Bulging eyes. Screams.* I shuddered. Joel noticed.

"People want to help, you know, Stink," Joel replied. "None of us should have to do this on our own. You can always call me, I'll come and keep you warm." And we were right back to teasing.

"Connor keeps me plenty warm, thanks. Besides, you should be with your family, not with me."

Joel huffed out a breath. "You are family, Stink. Pretty sure Mum likes you better than me."

"It kind of didn't feel like it, when I asked if you wanted me to come in the other night. I …" I trailed off, reluctant to tell Joel about my pang of loneliness that night.

Joel didn't respond straight away.

"I assumed you were just being polite," he eventually said. "Besides, I figured you and Lover Boy needed some alone time. Sex is great for taking your mind off things. I almost invited a 'friend' over myself. I would have if Aunty Dianne and the kids weren't over."

I grunted. "For starters, Brad's *not* my lover boy – we're just friends. And secondly, too much information, Joel. I really have zero interest in your sex life."

Joel sniffed. "Brad's got it bad for you, Stink."

I gaped at him. "Brad so has *not* 'got it bad' for me! He's just a friend!"

"Uh-huh. A friend who wants to marry you and have babies with you."

"Ugh," I grumbled.

Joel pulled into my building's car park. I looked up and sighed when I saw who was waiting in one of the visitor parks.

Joel followed my gaze, and his lips pressed together into a thin line. He knew what my mother was like. He pulled into a parking space and slid out of the car. I reluctantly followed suit.

"Hi, Mum." I tried to sound happy to see her.

Mum approached me, her expensive dye-job brown hair swinging around her shoulders. She pressed her hands with their French-polished nails to my cheeks.

"Melanie! You're looking too thin! You're not eating right. Did you go to confession? Father Shannon said he was looking forward to chatting with you."

I shrugged out of her grasp, unlocking the building door and holding it open for her. Joel brought up the rear, his eyes hidden behind his sunglasses, his expression unreadable.

"I'm eating fine, I haven't had time to go to confession, and unless Father Shannon needs to tell me that Christ's second coming is upon us, he can wait."

Mum turned and gave Joel an unimpressed once-over before turning back to me. "What's *he* doing here?" she whispered sourly.

"Mum, his name is Joel, you've known him for years, and he can hear everything you're saying." I leaned closer to her. "Maybe you might want to express your sympathy?"

Mum threw a glance at Joel. "He's in the Lord's arms now," she said. Joel nodded once, lips still tight. Sometimes it was best not to speak to my mother. I wished I didn't have to.

"Mum, I have a lot to do today. I've got to get my stuff over to Sandra's. I'll see you later."

I thought she might argue, but she just sniffed and stormed back down the stairs, slamming the door behind her.

"Sorry about that," I muttered, turning to Joel.

A tear tracked its way from under his sunglasses, down his cheek until it came to a stop at the corner of his lip.

Oh shit. My eyes started prickling too. I reached a hand up, brushing that tear away with two fingers. Joel huffed out a big breath, turning away and taking the stairs two at a time. I followed more tentatively, blinking furiously so my own tears subsided.

"What do you need me to do?" Joel asked brusquely as I unlocked the apartment door. He was all business now.

"Um, I'll just grab some clothes and stuff, and then you can take that down to the car while I get Connor sorted."

Joel seemed happy with that. He flung himself onto my lounge and switched on the TV while I went into the bedroom and sorted through the clothes still sitting in my suitcase from Melbourne. I'd only unpacked the dirty stuff, so I shoved in a few fresh items.

In the bathroom I chucked my essentials into my toiletries bag and stuffed it into the front section of my suitcase, wheeling the whole lot back out to the living room.

"Okay, I'm all packed, bet you didn't think I could –"

My words were cut short as I saw what was playing on the TV.

"After spending the night of his Australian Open semi-final loss answering questions for police, tennis star Pete Levine has been given leave to return home to the United States."

Some footage flashed up of Pete leaving Melbourne Police Station, a lawyer between him and the camera.

"Levine, a person of interest in the murder of tennis legend Steve Herbert, was released from police custody late yesterday evening. Levine was staying at the Savoy Tower Apartments in Southbank, where Herbert was found stabbed to death on the morning of January 28th.

"Levine was the main lead in this case, so it looks like police are back to

square one, Karl," the reporter said, and the vision flickered back to Karl Franks, host of Early Mornings.

Joel flicked the TV off, dropping the remote onto the lounge beside him. I collapsed down on his other side, feeling like I would puke. Finally, the gravity of the situation hit me like a tonne of bricks. Joel turned to look at me, his face tight.

"Well, one good thing came out of that – if Pete came clean, the police won't harass you anymore."

I couldn't find the energy to even shrug. I couldn't care a scrap about whether the police thought I was a murderer or not. Steve was gone and he wasn't coming back. Hearing people who'd never known him talk about his death in such an emotionless way triggered something inside of me.

The sobs rattled out of me and my eyes quickly became so filled with tears that the room was just a watery blur. Once they started, they wouldn't stop. My stomach ached, my eyes ached. My heart ached.

An eternity later, as the last hiccups started to subside, I wiped my red, swollen eyes, and took a shuddery breath.

Joel's warm side was pressed against me, his strong arm around my shoulders, squeezing gently.

I looked up at him, my sight still bleary. His lips were pressed into a tight line, his jaw clenched. It must've been so hard for him to keep his cool. I wondered if he cried alone in his bedroom where no one could see how much he was hurting.

And here he was, comforting me as I fell apart over the death of his father.

I reached out a hand and gently massaged the tense muscles of his jaw. He opened his mouth, sucked in a little breath, and stood.

"Let's get this stuff back to my place, hey?" he murmured, dragging my suitcase out the door. I heard it clatter down the stairs.

"Connor!" I called shakily. His little grey and white head popped out around the hallway door, and he galloped over to the kitchen. I scooped him up and limped into my spare room, dragging down his cat box. His little body tensed, pinpricks of pain shooting through my arm from his claws.

"No, Connie, no vet; we're going on a holiday – someplace nice!" I promised, thrusting him into the cage before he could draw blood. He yowled in disapproval as I closed the little barred door.

I collected all his other paraphernalia and waited at the top of the stairs for Joel to come and help me. He didn't. I leaned on my left leg, tapping my fingers against the bannister. Still nothing.

With a sigh, I picked up Connor and struggled my way down the stairs with him. I was out the door before I realised what had kept Joel. I froze as he came and stood beside me, taking the cage with the yowling Connor in it.

"Miss Black. Would you mind coming down to the station with us to answer a few questions?" Detective Taylor asked. I gulped, glancing pleadingly at Joel, not that he could help me.

He met my eyes, a grim expression on his face, "Call me when you need me to pick you up," he offered, before loading Connor into the car, holding his hand out for my key. I passed it over, Joel squeezing my fingers briefly.

I sighed and clambered into the back seat of the police car. Detective Coughlin was waiting behind the wheel. I was surprised that Taylor let him drive – she didn't seem to let him do anything else.

I sulked in the back seat on the drive to the station. The detectives didn't seem to notice. That suited me just fine.

God, what is it this time? Why can't they just leave me alone?

Coughlin played the gentleman by opening the door for me when we got out in the underground car park at the station.

Inside I was ushered into a little room that looked exactly like the ones in the movies. There was a two-way mirror on the wall and a voice recorder on the table. I sat in a hard-backed chair, Taylor opposite me, Coughlin by the door.

Then Taylor spoke to the voice recorder, "Interview with Melanie Black, in relation to the murder of Steven Herbert …"

My skin went cold as she stated the date and time. This was no joke. This was really fucking serious.

"So, Pete Levine corroborated your alibi," Taylor began, tapping a pen against the table in the most annoying way and looking up at me from under her sharp fringe. Why did she need a pen when she was recording this interview?

"I heard," I replied. *Told you so!* I screamed inside my head.

"But there was something interesting about his story. Would you care to take a look?" Taylor's voice was smug. My palms broke into a sweat. What did she mean, *'take a look'*?

Taylor nodded at Coughlin, who switched off the lights and left the room. Taylor flicked on the TV screen. I had no idea what was going on until a too-familiar figure appeared on a bed on the screen, tinged with the green of a camera with night vision. I heard my slurring voice and I felt the blood rush to my face.

I thought I'd remembered everything about that night with Pete. Apparently, there was a lot that I hadn't. I couldn't take my eyes off the screen – it was like a car wreck. I wanted to block my ears, block out the animal moans that were coming out of my mouth.

Taylor picked up an identical remote to the one Coughlin had used and flicked the video into fast forward. I thought it was bad watching it in real-time, but seeing myself on a screen sucking Pete's dick and getting banged doggy-style in high speed was pretty horrific too. Pete had managed to position me so that, even in night mode, you could see *everything*.

Oh God.

Taylor didn't slow down until the little time bar showed four-thirteen AM. Pete obviously hadn't bothered to press stop when he'd caught on camera the part he wanted to.

Taylor turned to me as I continued to stare at the screen. You could see the sleeping forms of both of us in the bed. She was waiting for my reaction, but I was frozen, horrified. The video rolled on.

Then I saw it. I saw myself climb out of the bed and hobble drunkenly off-screen. My brow furrowed in confusion. Taylor continued to stare at me as she pressed fast-forward once more. The minutes ticked by. She pressed play. I watched myself clamber back into the bed and roll over.

"An hour and twelve minutes, Miss Black." Taylor picked up the pen again and tapped it against the table. I chewed on my lip. What was her point?

"You can come back in now, Coughlin!" she shouted. The older man returned and flicked the lights back on. I squinted from the glare.

"So?" I asked, confusion tainting my tone. I remembered all too well curling up in front of Pete's toilet bowl and hurling up half-digested pizza and too much vodka and juice.

Taylor looked at me like I was missing some really important point. I waited for her to get to it.

"Melanie, the coroner has declared that Steve was murdered between three and five AM."

Oh. Oooooh.

Fuck!

"This is serious, Melanie. This almost puts you in a worse position than you were in before Pete came clean. You and Steve fought earlier in the day, and you're seen leaving the bed of the man you insisted was your alibi around the time the murder took place, creeping back immediately after. It doesn't look good. Did you know Pete was filming this?"

The blood that had stained my cheeks while I watched myself fucking on camera swiftly drained away.

Honesty is always the best policy, Mel.

"I didn't know that he was filming. I wish I still didn't! But I didn't have anything to do with Steve's … with what happened to Steve." Tears were threatening. "You must be able to see that I was really drunk – I mean who does that sort of thing sober?"

Coughlin's mouth twitched at the corner. I couldn't hate him, not the way I hated Taylor, who gave me a stony stare.

"If you were as drunk as you claim, can you remember with any clarity what happened in that hour and twelve minutes?"

I closed my eyes. "Before morning. I remember getting up and spending a long time on the floor of Pete's bathroom, getting to know the inside of his toilet bowl and the contents of my stomach, very well." I opened them again, pointing to the screen. "Plus, you can see my crutches right there, propped up on the wall beside the bed. Unless you think I crawled out of the apartment, up two floors and, somehow managed to …" My throat closed around the words.

Steve … lying in his own blood.

I gripped the edge of the table until my knuckles were white.

"Is that all you have to say about this?" Taylor asked in disbelief.

I cleared my throat and Coughlin handed me a box of tissues. I took one and wiped at my leaking eyes. "Yes."

"So, at no time from midnight until nine the next morning did you leave Pete Levine's apartment?" she prompted.

"That's right. Can I go now?"

Taylor's eyes flashed and she turned to Coughlin for guidance. It was the first time I'd seen her take cues from him.

"We haven't got anything that we can hold her on."

Taylor scowled and stood, her chair clattering to the floor. I struggled to my feet, my ankle still very tender. As I turned to the door, Coughlin winked at me. I shuddered. He would absolutely have seen that video, even if he didn't stay for the replay.

I hobbled from the room and Coughlin led the way to the main entrance. I took a seat just inside the door, pulling my phone out. My hands were shaking and my chest felt too tight.

Gaping mouth.

Blood.

Bulging eyes.

I pressed my hands to my stomach. While Steve was being … I had been vomiting up too much alcohol. After being secretly filmed drunkenly fucking.

I couldn't call Joel. I just couldn't. I didn't want to have to explain to him, and I knew he'd bug me until I told him everything. What I really wanted to do was forget what I'd just seen.

Like that was ever going to happen.

I clicked onto the Uber app. Ride sorted, I lay my head back against the vinyl seat, stretching my injured ankle out in front of me.

"You look thirsty."

I squinted up to see Coughlin holding out a little plastic cup of water to me. I took it gratefully and downed it in one swallow. The older man smiled indulgently at me.

"Sorry about Detective Taylor. She gets so serious about things sometimes, but she doesn't always see the bigger picture."

It seemed unprofessional for him to be telling me this when I was apparently on their 'people of interest' list. I nodded, hoping to end the conversation.

"For the record, I've never thought you were a suspect, but you know how it is – we have to explore all avenues," he continued.

I nodded again. He didn't leave.

"You clearly have something else you want to get off your chest," I muttered.

He laughed nervously and reached into his pocket, pulling out a tennis ball. He thrust it under my nose, followed by a Sharpie marker.

"My son Randy's a big tennis fan. Would you sign this ball for him?" Coughlin asked shyly. I managed the remnants of a smile, plucking the ball from his hand and scrawling a signature onto it.

"Oh, thank you Mel! He'll be stoked!" Coughlin gushed, finally returning to his job.

My phone pinged. My Uber had arrived.

The driver was polite and silent, which suited me fine. I rested my head against the seat, staring vacantly at the city buildings as we crept through traffic.

Blood.

Gaping mouth.

"Stop!" I shouted. The driver smashed on the brake and looked worriedly at me in the rear-view mirror.

"Do you want to get out?" he asked in clipped English. I couldn't speak, my throat was locked. I shook my head and coughed.

"Keep going," I grated. He looked at me sternly for a moment longer, until the car behind him honked and he accelerated once more.

"I thought you'd call when they were through with you, Stink," Joel said as he opened the front door to let me through.

"I didn't want to bother you – I Ubered instead."

Joel's eyes narrowed and he pressed a knuckle under my chin, tilting my head up, "Everything okay?" he murmured.

I tried a smile. It felt too tight. "Just peachy," I replied. I wasn't going to explain what I'd just seen at the police station.

"I put your stuff up here in the biggest guestroom," he said after a pregnant pause. He led me up to the top level of the house, along a loft-style hallway and through a door on the left.

Connor was lounging on the bed, as if he already owned the place. I noticed with surprise that Joel had set up his kitty litter and put bowls of food and water down for him in the enormous en suite.

"Connor won't want to leave if you start treating him like a king," I said, narrowing my eyes at Joel.

His grin nearly knocked my feet out from under me. Damn it, why did he have to have such a gorgeous smile?

"So, Stink, what did the cops have to say?" he asked as he sat on the bed beside me. Trust Joel – his curiosity would always get the better of him.

"Well, Pete gave me an alibi, but it turned out to be more of a curse than a blessing."

"Why?"

I shook my head, lying back against the plush mattress and putting an arm over my eyes so he couldn't see me. "I really don't want to talk about it."

I waited for Joel to insist, but he was distracted by his phone buzzing. As I peeked at him, he pulled it out, staring down at the screen for what seemed like forever.

"What is it?" I asked, sitting up again.

"There's this sports gossip blogger: tennisfanboi. He always Tweets about you. I have Twitter set to notify me when he posts. I just got a …"

And then I heard a sound that I had hoped never to hear again in my life. At first, I thought I must have just been reliving the humiliation, but then I heard Joel make a choking noise. I sat bolt upright, looking at him. His eyes were wide, and there was a strange, shocked expression on his face.

"What is that?" I demanded. Joel didn't look away from the screen. Instead, he tilted his head to the side and stared intently at what I wished *wasn't* the video of me and Pete. But I knew it was.

"Looks like Levine's alibi has gone viral … Jesus … is that … even possible?"

Joel's voice had taken on an odd tone. I groaned and reached over to snatch the phone from him. He pulled away from me, eyes still fixated on my gyrating hips on his phone screen.

"This *is* the alibi, right?"

I was about to die of embarrassment. "Yes, that's the alibi! But if you can pry your eyes off your phone, you might like to know that Pete left his hidden camera running after we fell asleep, and it shows me getting out of bed for an hour or so right at the time that …"

That stopped Joel in his tracks. The animal sounds were still coming from the phone, but he wasn't watching them. He was looking at me in shock.

"What, they think *you* …" he rasped.

I sat on my trembling hands. "I don't know – one of them probably does, but they don't have any real evidence. I told them that I'd spent that hour embracing the toilet bowl. Why did Pete lie in the first place? And why did he decide he needed to give the police this footage? And how the fuck did it get onto Twitter?"

"Did you say, 'hidden camera'?" Joel asked. I nodded, wishing the video would just finish.

The sounds stopped. I turned to look, finding Joel's phone screen blank, his knuckles white as he gripped it.

"You didn't know he was filming."

"Nope," I replied.

"Fuck. Pete Levine, what a fucking piece of shit." Joel's voice was dark.

"Yep."

And then I had another horrible thought. If the video was

already on Twitter, then it wouldn't be long before the whole world knew about it. And when that happened my hopes of finding another sponsor would fly out the window.

"So long, Martel," I muttered.

CHAPTER EIGHT

Funeral Photography

Joel and Sandra were talking quietly to each other in my living room while I struggled into a black pencil skirt. I grimaced at the thought of how sweaty my thighs would be on a day that was threatening to top forty-five.

I teamed the skirt with a dressy, deep blue blouse, and a pair of black flats.

I'd deliberately worn no makeup so I wouldn't leave panda eyes and tear tracks all over my face. I brushed my hair and tugged it back into a low ponytail.

I really didn't want to leave the house today. I really didn't want to leave the house ever again.

If it wasn't for the security Sandra still had posted at their gate, I'd have been hounded every time I set foot outside their house. I'd turned off the voicemail feature on my phone, and only answered calls from friends and family. I'd made the mistake of answering unknown numbers a few times.

They all wanted the same thing: what did I have to say for myself in the wake of the Black-Levine sex-tape scandal?

My answer? *"No comment."*

What I really wanted to say? *"Leave me the fuck alone!"*

I dawdled out to the lounge room. Sandra and Joel both fell

silent and looked up at me. I got the distinct impression that they'd been talking about me.

"You look lovely, Mel," Sandra commented as they both stood up.

"Thanks," I replied shyly. Joel put a hand on the small of my back, leading me gently out the door and down the stairs to his car. Sandra refused to take the front seat when I offered it to her.

"You need to stretch your leg out, Mel. Steve would never forgive me if I made you squash up in the back with a sprained ankle."

I didn't speak much on the trip to the church. I wiped my clammy hands on my skirt, sneaking a glance at Joel. He was wearing black pinstripe pants and a dark blue shirt and tie, but no jacket – it was draped over the spare seat in the back.

There would be a swarm of media outside the church. My heart lurched and I scrubbed my palms on my skirt again.

"Stink," Joel murmured. "You okay?"

"I'm …" I began, chewing on a nail, then thought better of it and put my hand back into my lap. "I don't want to talk to press. I don't want today to be about … you know."

Sandra totally knew what I was referring to, but I still felt a hot flash of mortification discussing it while she was in earshot.

"Whatever happens, Mel, know that we are all here to support each other," Sandra said. "You're family. And we Herbert's stick together."

My eyes overflowed at Sandra's words, and I frantically swiped at the tears with the back of my hand. It was too early to start with the waterworks – I had the whole funeral to get through yet.

Sure enough, when we parked on the street not far from the church, we could already make out a wall of cameras outside. Joel and I shared a meaningful glance. We couldn't let them derail today with questions about me and Pete Levine. And we *definitely* couldn't let them get anywhere near Sandra.

I bit my top lip and together we got out of the car. It only took one of them shouting, "Mel! Melanie Black!" and they were all converging on us.

"Head down, don't react," Joel muttered in my ear as he gripped my elbow and, tucking his mother under his other arm, we stepped into the fray.

"Mel, are you and Pete Levine an item now?"

"How many times have you slept together?"

"Any plans for a sequel?"

Joel's fingers were almost bruising as he parted the sea of vultures like Moses. I watched the ground, face on fire. Wanting to scream at all of them that none of this should ever have been any of their business, but the lump in my throat wouldn't subside. My eyes burned.

Finally, we breached the doorway. No media was allowed inside.

"Breathe, Stinky," Joel reminded me as we walked towards the front of the church, Sandra stopping to greet and hug people. Joel kept hold of my arm.

Dianne and the kids were already there, sitting in the second row. A tall, handsome man with a strong jaw, dark hair, and eyes like Joel's was seated in the front row, and he stood to envelope Sandra in a hug.

"That's my Uncle Ben," Joel explained as he steered me to a seat in the same pew. "He just flew in from the Middle East."

The man hugging Sandra looked nothing like how I'd imagined Joel's uncle. He and Joel looked more like brothers – the family similarity was striking, more striking than it had been between Joel and Steve.

Joel clocked my bewildered expression and chuckled humourlessly. "He's a *lot* younger than Dad."

I fidgeted in my seat, listening to the low hum of voices behind us. I dreaded to think what they were saying.

"I don't …" I mumbled, starting to rise, to move further back, but Joel cut me off.

"You heard what Mum said in the car, Stinky. You're family. You sit here with us." He still had his sunglasses on. Without thinking I reached out and took them off his face, folding the arms and sticking them in my handbag. His mouth twitched, but neither of us had the energy for a proper smile.

The priest took his place at the pulpit and my heart rate kicked up a notch. I'd managed to keep my eyes off the dark wooden casket in the middle of the room, until now. It loomed bigger than ever into my vision.

Bulging eyes.

Blood.

Gaping mouth.

My fingernails bit into my palm and I turned away from the coffin, trying to get my blurry eyes to focus instead on the smiling photo of Steve set up among an array of yellow and pink flowers.

Joel's fingers gently untangled the fist I'd made, and placed my hand palm down on my leg, giving it a quick pat.

Ben was called up to deliver the eulogy. I tried to focus as he began to speak, but I felt Joel's warm shoulder shaking against mine.

He was crying. Oh fuck.

My eyes prickled, the lump in my throat, which felt like it had been there since the morning this all happened, thickened and hardened and became something truly painful.

I reached across and grabbed his hand, squeezing, leaning my head against his shoulder. He drove me crazy most of the time, but right now he needed a friend. Right now, I could be that friend.

"Steve and Sandra had one of the best marriages I have ever known," Ben continued, his voice quavering. "The love they have for each other will continue on even now that Steve is with God. Sandra, I know that Steve is up there, waiting patiently for the time when you'll join him again. One day I hope that I find someone who I can love the way Steve loved you."

Joel pulled his mother against his other side as she wept quietly. I reached across, grabbing her hand and wrapping my fingers through hers.

To everyone else in the church, we would look like a family. Sandra's two kids, comforting her. In some ways, Joel was like a brother to me. An annoying older brother. In other ways … well …

Joel could never be my brother.

When the service was over, Joel stood to join Ben and the funeral attendants to wheel the coffin out to the hearse.

"Follow along behind, but stop just inside the church door, okay? I'll come back in for you both," Joel muttered to Sandra and me as he took his place at the coffin. I grabbed onto Sandra's hand, heart thundering. How unfair, that she couldn't even be there to watch her husband be driven away to the crematorium.

As if to remind me why, the frantic clicking of cameras outside reached us. Hot, tight emotions bubbled in me as Joel and Ben walked out the door.

Sandra turned from me and greeted people as they filed from the church, hugging and kissing, and murmuring, "Thanks for coming," and, "Yes, back at the house, I'll see you there."

I stood idle at the door, suddenly feeling out of place, peering through the door as the coffin disappeared into the hearse.

"Smellie," a voice murmured behind me, and I turned into the waiting arms of Brad. Amanda stood beside him and rubbed my back as I gasped desperately for air. I buried my head in the spot where his neck met his shoulder.

Brad pulled me away from him and kissed me on the forehead, passing me over for Amanda to wrap her arms around me.

"It was good of you to come," Joel murmured to Brad as he joined us. I listened from my safe place with Amanda. Brad and Joel hadn't ever really gotten along all that well, so I could hear the stiffness in Joel's voice.

"It was important for me to be here for Mel," Brad replied. "She was very close to your father."

Joel nodded. "I know. It's like having a sister sometimes." I screwed up my nose at that.

"Are you coming back to the house for the wake?" Joel asked. Brad shook his head.

"Thanks for coming, guys. It really means a lot to me." I gave them a watery smile. Brad moved in and hugged me again.

"You're welcome, Smellie. See you again soon?"

"As soon as I know what's happening with my ankle, and whether I'm off to Dubai in a week." The tickets had been booked for months, and Joel had managed to change Steve's flight into his name. I thought he was being a bit optimistic, but I hadn't said anything.

I said goodbye to Brad and Amanda, who moved out of the pew and made their way out of the church.

Julie popped out from a pew about two-thirds of the way down the church and approached us. She hugged Joel quietly, tear tracks all the way down both cheeks. She turned to me then and put her arms around me. I stood stiffly in her embrace, patting her back awkwardly. It seemed weird that she was here. I didn't think she knew Steve all that well.

"You coming to the wake?" Joel asked her. She shook her head, swiping a fresh tear from her face.

"I don't think that's a good idea," she replied. Joel nodded, as if that made all the sense in the world. What had happened between them in Melbourne? Maybe more than just a night of fun? Maybe she was here for Joel?

I clenched my jaw as Joel promised to be in touch with Julie in the next few days. Why was he getting in touch with her? He pressed a kiss to her cheek and she walked away.

"I'll take you out to the car now, Stink, before everyone leaves the church and the media have you all to themselves. I'll come straight back for Mum."

I nodded, not wanting to think about him and Julie, or about why he had to escort me to the car under the cover of a crowd.

Joel gripped my elbow and together we marched through the church doors. Cameras clicked feverishly and TV crews converged.

"Mel Black!"

"Melanie!"

"Is your career over now?"

"Ignore it, Stink," Joel muttered, marching me out the church gate and down the street to his car. He unlocked it, handing me into the passenger seat.

"I'll be back as quickly as I can. Keep the doors locked," he commanded, turning back towards the church.

I slumped against the seat and put my face into my hands. God, I hoped that Joel and Sandra weren't too much longer.

"Mel!"

I instinctively glanced up, to find a camera pointing through the windscreen. Groaning, I turned away, keeping my head down and my hand shielding me from the photographer.

Hurry up, Joel! I pleaded silently.

"What, no smile for me, Mel? I thought you loved the camera! Can I get a moan like you gave Pete Levine? Did you know that Grant is marrying Susie Keens?"

My head snapped up at that, and the jerk got a bunch of shots of my shocked expression.

"Get the fuck away from her you piece of shit!"

Joel appeared with Sandra under his arm. He elbowed the photographer out of the way. I could hear frantic clicking outside the car as Joel got his mother in and slid hurriedly into the front seat.

"I don't believe that arsehole!" Joel fumed as he drove away. I shook my head, not having the energy to find words. I was utterly spent. All I wanted was to curl up into a little ball in my comfy king-sized bed in Sandra's house, cuddle Connor, and sleep.

"My ankle's really sore, Joel," I said quietly. I spun in my seat to look at Joel's mother. "Sandra, would you mind if I kept to my room this afternoon, rested up a bit?"

Sandra smiled sadly at me. "Of course not, Mel. Don't we all wish we could do the same?"

"Did you ever imagine that you would marry Grant?" Joel asked me quietly.

I shook my head. "Of course, my mother would have liked nothing more, but no. We were never going to work long-term – I can see that now. He's egotistical enough that he needs a woman who will make him feel important. He couldn't have that with me – he was too jealous of my career."

Joel surprised me by smirking in my direction. "Stink, every man wants a woman who'll make him feel important."

I rolled my eyes. "Joel, your ego's just as out of control as Grant's!"

He shook his head, still smiling. "You've got a hell of a lot to learn about men, Stinky. But just a bit of advice now: everyone wants their partner to make them feel important. It's just that everybody has a different idea of what important means."

"How would you know? The only lasting relationship you've ever had is with your hand!"

Joel chuckled but didn't respond. As usual, that frustrated me more than if he bit back. I'd thought he wouldn't be able to go a day without being a smart-arse. It turned out I couldn't either.

CHAPTER NINE

Uncle Ben

We had one more day until we flew out to Dubai. In that time, I hadn't gone a single day without that lump in my throat reappearing at odd times to choke me. Nightmares still woke me. I no longer screamed out loud, but the strangled gasps that shocked me awake were somehow more horrifying.

One more day of strengthening my ankle. Joel and I were on the tennis court. I balanced on my injured ankle and bounced a ball on my racquet. I'd had a proper ankle brace fitted to offer some extra support. It was still plenty sore, but the pain helped me focus.

Mostly. Today I was too distracted.

Every private thing Pete and I had done together had been analysed over and over by news outlets, sports gossip bloggers and Twitter. I doubted anyone on social media had missed it. This morning I'd finally snapped and gone into social media blackout, deactivating all my accounts until further notice. I had no emotional space to deal with the abusive DMs and comments on my previous posts, about what a whore I was, how I was a bad role model, how I was going to Hell. There were even a couple of death threats peppered throughout.

"Go to the police, Stink, for fuck's sake!" Joel had said. "That footage getting leaked, all this abuse – it's fucking illegal!" He seemed even more incensed than I was about the whole debacle. Like a protective older brother.

I was sure I already knew who leaked it – fucking Pete Levine. I bet *he* wasn't being called a whore. More likely receiving virtual high fives.

At least when I had contacted the police to make sure it was okay for me to leave the country – that they wouldn't try to stop me at customs – I'd been given the all-clear.

I lost my concentration for a second, and the ball hit the frame of the racquet, ricocheting away across the court. Joel grunted and retrieved it. I put down my left leg, taking some of the weight off my injured ankle.

"Focus, Mel! Your mind's wandering," he said in a clipped tone. He handed me the ball. "Your head's not a hundred percent in this. Physically you're fit enough to compete, but mentally you're struggling!"

I scowled. "Of course I'm not mentally prepared for this! How can you expect that with everything that's going on?"

Joel took a deep breath.

"Stink, Dad would have wanted you to keep going. All he wanted was for you to succeed and he knew that you could do it. Don't let him down now. He wouldn't want you to get distracted. He'd want you to go to Dubai and play your heart out. Do him proud."

I gritted my teeth, clearing my throat to dislodge the lump. What he was saying was totally true. I took a few deep breaths and set the ball on my racquet, lifting my left foot once more. Joel picked up a racquet too. I guess he thought that I'd feel better about it if I wasn't the only one looking ridiculous.

"Time for a break yet?" a deep voice asked. Joel gave me a sharp look and shook his head minutely as Ben sauntered onto the court. He leaned against the net pole and folded his arms across his chest, watching me intently. I put too much force into a bounce and lost control. Ben picked up the ball and grinned a white, toothy smile at me.

"Ben, we're trying to work here, and as you can see, Mel's easily distracted." Joel actually sounded grumpy. Ben continued to smile, his eyes on me.

"Well, maybe it's time for a break – you've been out here for two hours. It's hot, why don't you come inside and have a cold drink, something to eat?"

I waited for Joel to decide. He looked at me, and he must have seen in my face how over it I was. He sighed and put his racquet down. I followed suit, relieved.

"So, are you staying much longer, Ben?" I asked as we all made our way back inside and up the stairs to the main level, where Sandra had made sandwiches. He shook his head.

"No, I'm going back home tomorrow. I've got a big project going on at work, so I could only get a week off."

"And where's home?" I asked, taking a bite out of a salad roll.

"Dubai," Ben replied with a grin. "I run Meerkat Engineering."

"Holy shit!" I gasped. "You *own* the business that sponsors the Dubai Tennis Championships?" I asked. Ben chuckled.

"No. Well not entirely anyway. I'm an executive director." He smiled smugly at me. "I always loved tennis, but I was never good at it the way Steve was – I must have missed out on the sports gene. By sponsoring the Dubai Championship, I still feel involved."

I took another bite of my sandwich, mentally readjusting my picture of Ben. I'd assumed that he was living off Steve's wealth. But he'd built his own fortune. He went up a lot of notches in my estimation.

After lunch had settled, Joel suggested that I get in the pool and swim some laps. I ducked back inside the house to change, feeling Ben's eyes following me.

I had a couple of pairs of swimmers with me – a deep blue one piece that was very practical for exercise, and a little yellow string bikini, which wasn't practical at all, but was great for tanning. And if you wanted to impress someone.

I thought about Ben sitting out there, watching me swim. I put on the yellow bikini and strutted back out to the pool. I had the satisfaction of watching Ben's eyes bug out when he caught sight of me. I pretended I hadn't noticed and continued into the pool, slipping into the water.

Joel appeared out of the house, wearing a pair of Speedos which left very little to the imagination. I tried not to let my eyes follow the definition of the V shape of his lower abs, pointing directly down towards his … *stop, Mel!*

He raised his eyebrows when he saw my bikini, but he didn't comment, hopping into the pool and pushing off from the end, his long muscular body cutting an easy path through the water. I followed him, conscious of Ben's eyes on me as I moved.

I think I'd done about fifteen laps when Ben appeared at the pool side wearing board shorts. I stopped for a moment and looked up at him. He might not have inherited the sport gene, but he had definitely not missed out on the hot gene. I was struck again by the similarities between him and Joel.

"Mind if I join you?" he asked, not waiting for Joel to give him permission before he hopped into the water. Joel scowled as he stopped swimming to tread water, glaring at his uncle, who was beaming at me.

"So, what's an average day of training for you?" Ben asked, standing in the water, his hair wet and water beading off his smooth chest. Sporting gene or not, he worked out – no one had a body like that without working out.

I rolled over and floated on my back, my boobs sticking out of the water.

"Well, at the moment I'm not on my regular training schedule because of the ankle. But normally I would do drills on the court every day for an hour or so, morning and evening, then thirty minutes of weights once a day. I try to swim at least four times a week too – it's good for relaxing, and it helps condition my heart and lungs without the wear and tear on my joints. And of course, I play friendly matches a lot."

Ben's eyes lingered on my stomach, my breasts, before sliding up to my face. "Maybe we could have a friendly match tonight? That is, if your ankle is up to it." Ben looked to Joel, as if seeking permission. He nodded, a strange glint in his eyes.

"I was going to suggest that we play a game tonight, so if Ben wants to do the honours, that's fine." He seemed satisfied for some reason. I had no idea why. I'd given up trying to figure out what Joel got his jollies from a long time ago.

Sandra walked out onto the deck then. "Mel, you've got visitors!" she called. I swam to the stairs. Joel grunted.

"You're supposed to be preparing for a tennis tournament, not socialising," he muttered. I threw him a dark look.

"Oh, don't get out, Mel!" Sandra called. "I think they're hoping for a swim as well."

Brad appeared, grinning, followed by Amanda, holding the hand of a tall, lanky guy with a pretty face and dark blonde hair. I threw a questioning glance at Brad as they dropped their stuff.

"The guy from the tennis," Brad mouthed at me, before pulling off his t-shirt and leaping into the pool.

Amanda dragged off her sun dress, speaking quietly with the guy, who shifted uncomfortably.

"Hey," I called out to him, and he glanced up, a hint of pink on his cheeks. "I'm Mel, nice to meet you …"

"Thomas," he replied, a small smile pulling at his lips. Amanda nudged him with her elbow and leaned in, saying, "I told you she wouldn't mind."

And the pair of them joined us in the pool.

"We figured that if you weren't going to have a chance to see us before you left, we'd make an effort to come see you." Brad said, swimming towards me.

"I'm so glad you did!" I replied, splashing Brad and laughing when he shrieked. Amanda and Thomas introduced themselves to Ben as he dragged a couple of pool loungers into the water.

Joel brushed past me on his way out of the pool, his lips pressed together, shoulders tight. Amanda swam over to me.

"What's up with Joel?" she asked, watching his dripping body with wide eyes as he stalked towards the cabana.

"Don't stare at him like that when your new boyfriend is right over there!" I hissed, smacking her lightly on the arm. "He's probably annoyed; this is our last chance to train before we get on a plane for fourteen hours."

"Why does he care so badly? I mean you train so hard, what's wrong with an afternoon off?" she persisted.

I narrowed my eyes. "He's got a lot on his mind at the moment, with everything that happened with Steve, and putting his training business on the back burner to help me out, and leaving Sandra alone while he flies overseas to support me."

Oh God. My bad mood, my lack of focus, me snapping at him, and now distractions in the shape of Ben, Brad, Amanda and this Thomas guy. Joel was stressed and I was making it worse.

"Joel!" I called out. He turned, water still trickling down his washboard stomach. "Come back – we haven't finished training."

He sighed, but half smiled as he dove elegantly back in, swimming underwater until he surfaced right in front of me. I moved back – my boobs were touching his chest, which was just way too personal.

I turned to the others. "Sorry, guys, we'll only be another twenty minutes or so."

Amanda shrugged and hopped back out of the pool, Thomas in hot pursuit, but Brad looked from Joel to me, his brows furrowing ever so slightly.

Ben stepped in to save the day. "Hey mate, come on, let's leave the professionals to do their thing. I'll get you all a beer."

Brad gave me a tiny nod and swam to the steps. I threw Ben a grateful smile. He winked at me.

I turned back to Joel, who set the pace for another twenty minutes of solid swimming that left me shaking at the end. Joel, hardly even puffing, grinned wickedly at me. Damn he had some stamina.

Sandra invited my friends to stay for dinner. She'd put together a buffet of foods – salads, cold meats, sweet potato bake. Brad looked like he was in seventh heaven; his parents rarely ate at home, so I think most of the time he existed on pizza and two-minute noodles. He grinned at me around a mouthful of food.

I watched with a warm heart as Thomas took Amanda's hand and smiled at her. He seemed smitten; it was adorable.

We watched the sun set on the harbour, letting our food settle. When it was dark, Joel jumped up, rubbing his hands together.

"Okay, Ben, let's see how you fare against a pro." Joel sounded way too keen for this match. I wondered what he had up his sleeve. I went inside to change. Amanda followed me.

"So … this Thomas guy seems nice," I commented, climbing the stairs to my bedroom. A smile split Amanda's face.

"He's amazing!" she gushed. "He works in IT, he has a really cute apartment, he's –"

"You've seen his apartment?" I exclaimed. "Amanda, are you two …"

She flushed prettily, flicking a strand of blonde hair out of her face. "Of course not! You know I'm saving the V card for my husband."

I opened the bedroom door.

"Oh, Connor's here!" Amanda commented. The cat circled her ankles – he had a soft spot for Amanda, being his designated feeder whenever I was out of the country. She picked him up and held him to her as I stripped out of my now dry swimmers and pulled out a sports bra, singlet and some training shorts.

"You look like you've moved in here, Mel – your stuff's everywhere," she commented lightly, sitting down on the edge of the bed. I avoided her gaze.

"Yeah, I've been staying here lately. It's just easier, with training and all, to be close to Joel. And you have no idea how hard it was to be alone in my apartment after …"

"Smell, you don't have to justify it to me – I can't even imagine … But tell me, is there something going on between you and Joel?"

I glared at her. "Joel's my trainer, and I guess sometimes I would call him a friend. But no, just, *no*! I couldn't go there!"

"Couldn't, or wouldn't?" she asked quietly, not looking away from Connor.

I grabbed my socks, ankle brace and shoes. "Wouldn't. End of conversation."

She shrugged and put Connor back down on the bed. He yowled once and pranced up to my pillow, settling down for the night.

Back out on the deck I tugged the brace onto my ankle. Joel knelt, his big hands sweeping over my ankle to check the brace position.

"Don't overdo it, Stink," he muttered.

"I won't," I promised him as I tied my shoes.

"And go easy on Ben, okay? He's your warm-up tonight. You'll need it." He smirked. Yep, he had some agenda he wasn't telling me about. I scowled at him.

"You're so cute when you're annoyed, Stinky," he teased, tweaking my nose, which only frustrated me more.

"Hey, we might go," Brad said, as Amanda and Thomas gathered their things.

"No, it's okay, it's just a friendly match, you're welcome to stay and watch," I replied, standing up and stretching. Brad shook his head.

"That's okay – you'll want to get a good night's sleep before you leave tomorrow." Brad kissed me on the cheek. I flung my arms around his neck and hugged him tight.

"Good luck in Dubai, Smellie. Knock 'em dead!" he whispered into my ear, his arms circling my waist.

"Thanks Brad. I'll call you when I get there."

"Promise?" he asked, leaning back and holding his pinkie finger up to me. I clasped it with my own.

"Promise."

I hugged Amanda goodbye too and Thomas stepped forward, offering a timid hand for me to shake.

I grinned. "Hopefully I'll get to see you again when I'm back in the country," I said, gripping his hand.

"I … I'm around as long as Amanda will have me," he stammered. Aw, he really was adorable!

Ben, Joel and I made our way down to the court. Joel flicked a switch, flooding the court with bright white light. I picked up my practice racquet from where I had left it that morning, and Ben picked up the other one. Joel tossed a ball in my direction. I caught it on my racquet, and taking Joel's advice, I served the ball slowly to Ben.

He missed. Not only did he miss, he tripped over in the process of missing. Joel snorted quietly. I gave him a sharp glance, and he passed me another ball.

Ben missed every serve, so I offered him the ball to serve.

He served it into the net. Seven times in a row. The eighth time he actually got it over the net and into the service box. I returned it and he hit the ground with the racquet. It ricocheted up into his face, slicing him above the eye.

As he slumped off the court, pressing the heel of his hand to the cut on his forehead, I couldn't even really call it a game. I wasn't sure what to call it.

"Sorry, Mel. That wasn't a good practise for you. I told you I missed the sport gene." Ben shrugged, still managing a grin even with a bleeding head. He dropped the racquet and walked back into the house to seek out a first-aid kit.

Joel looked so self-satisfied I wanted to slap him.

"You knew he couldn't play, you let him make a fool of himself!" I accused. Joel laughed, reaching out and picking up the racquet that Ben had relinquished.

"He's making enough of a fool of himself all on his own. Maybe he would have played better if he wasn't so busy making goo-goo eyes at you."

My head snapped towards Joel, who was moving around to the other side of the net, picking up a couple of balls.

"Is that jealousy I hear in your voice?" I asked him sharply.

He pouted at me. "You'd like it to be, wouldn't you, Stink?"

I grumbled under my breath, but I took my position on the base line. Joel served hard, and all the frustrated thoughts left my mind – I had to concentrate to make sure I didn't miss the ball.

Joel didn't hold back on me. I realised that he always had in the past – he'd never played me this hard before. He'd never played me to beat me.

And that's exactly what he did.

I was puffing by the time he let up.

"How's your ankle?" he asked as he collected the balls and took my racquet from me.

"Tender," I admitted. "Apart from that I feel okay, except for my wounded pride."

He huffed out a laugh. "You did really well, Stink. I thought I'd own you, with your ankle and all. But you held your own."

I snorted in disbelief – if he called that holding my own, I would hate to see what he would call me having a bad game. I walked back into the house and sat down on the weights bench, pulling my shoes and socks off. Joel put away our stuff and came to inspect my ankle.

"Hmm, it's a little swollen. Maybe we'll ice it for ten minutes or so." He went to the freezer in the bar at the other end of the enormous rumpus room, and pulled out an ice pack, returning and strapping it to my ankle. He looked up at me from his position crouched on the floor.

"I wasn't going too hard, was I?" he asked worriedly.

I smiled. "No, Joel. It was actually good – I needed to test myself out before Dubai."

He grinned crookedly at me. "I know. That's why I had to give you a go; Ben wasn't any help at all."

I shook my head at him. "Why did you let him do it? Were you trying to make a fool out of him?"

Joel chuckled. "No. Well, maybe. He just really wanted to play you, who am I to discourage him?"

He stood up and hauled me off the seat. He gripped my elbow as we mounted the stairs, but I shrugged him off – I didn't need any help.

"I'm going to shower," Joel said, "When I'm done, we'll take that off and look at it again. Are you all packed?"

I nodded as he headed up towards his bedroom.

I went out to sit on the deck, propping my leg up on a chair, and staring out at the night lights of Sydney. I wouldn't see them now for a fortnight, and then I'd be back for only a week before I headed to Indian Wells.

Ben came and sat down beside me. As if he could read my thoughts, he murmured, "It's a beautiful city, isn't it?"

I nodded, feeling like no words could really describe just how beautiful it was to me.

"I've travelled a lot in the last ten years, Mel, and I've seen some pretty amazing places in that time. But nothing compares to Sydney. No matter how long I stay away, it's always home to me."

"I'm hearing you," I replied, taking a sip from the bottle of water that Joel had left on the table at dinner.

"I love Dubai – I love that every day I wake up and there's something new being built. It's a place of great opportunity for someone like me. But when I find the right woman, and I settle down and start a family, I can't think of anywhere but here that I would raise them."

"So, you're flying tomorrow?" I asked, changing the subject. Ben's conversation topic was becoming a little too strange for me.

He nodded. "Early flight. What time does yours leave?"

"Ten thirty."

"It's a pity we're not on the same flight. It would have been good to spend some more time together. But I'll see you both once you arrive anyway."

"You will?" I asked, confused. Ben nodded.

"You and Joel are staying with me in my home. I had organised it with Steve before … but Joel knows all about it now, anyway. It's far too big for one bachelor, it'll be nice to see your lovely face over the breakfast table for a bit."

I found myself blushing. This man I'd barely met was going a long way towards sweeping me off my feet – in the romance novel sense.

"Yeah, that sounds really nice, thanks, Ben," I said. He beamed at me.

"What sounds really nice?" Joel asked, sauntering out in his pyjamas.

When I say pyjamas, I really mean a teeny pair of boxer shorts. And nothing else. I kept my eyes fixed firmly on the city lights twinkling across the harbour.

"Ben just told me we'll be staying at his place while we're in Dubai."

Joel took a seat opposite me, effectively ensuring that I had to look at him.

"Oh, it will be lovely, Uncle Ben!" Joel remarked, putting one of his feet up on the table. I could see up the leg of his boxers. I was only able to establish that I couldn't see *everything* because I was staring so intently. I dragged my eyes away with an effort, turning back to Ben.

"I'm looking forward to it," I said.

Ben grinned back at me. "Me too," he replied, standing up and touching me once on the shoulder. "I'm turning in – damned early flight. I'll see you over there." I looked up at him, and he leaned forwards, eyes intent on my lips.

Joel cleared his throat and Ben straightened. He patted my shoulder again and walked into the house.

I glared at Joel. "What was *that* all about?" I demanded.

He shrugged, a silly grin on his face. "Come on, Mel, let a man have some fun."

I rolled my eyes. "You never seem to do *anything* but have fun. At other people's expense."

Joel laughed and unfolded himself from the chair, crouching down to take the ice pack off my ankle. His long fingers were gentle and warm on my skin as he inspected the swelling. I shouldn't enjoy it so much when he fussed over me like this. But without my permission, my skin heated, a flush creeping up from where he touched me until I felt it all over. I sucked in a little breath.

"It looks great, Stink. Now go have a shower. The car's picking us up at seven thirty."

I stood, stretching. Joel, still crouched on the floor, looked up at me with an odd expression on his face.

"What?" I asked. He straightened, his body suddenly very close to mine. Close enough that I could feel the heat emanating from his bare chest. Close enough that my nipples puckered and an ache throbbed between my legs. I pressed my thighs together, biting my lip to try and distract myself from my inexplicable arousal.

Oh God, why did you have to wrap Joel Herbert in such pretty paper?

"Goodnight, Stinky," Joel whispered against the skin of my cheekbone. He stepped back from me and walked inside. I let out a shaky breath.

As I hopped into the shower, it seemed that every nerve ending in my body was tingling. That tingling became a jangling as I ran the soap over my skin.

It's Ben who's making me feel this way, I told myself firmly. *He's as hot as Joel, he's successful, and seems really nice. He obviously likes me.*

And the jangling kicked up a notch when I thought about staying in his house with him for the ten days we would be in Dubai.

Yep. It was Ben. It *definitely* wasn't Joel.

CHAPTER TEN

Judging A Book By Its Cover

"I can't wait to get to Ben's house and have a nice long shower," I said as Joel helped the driver pile our suitcases and my tennis gear into the boot of his car.

"Don't get your knickers in a knot, Stink. We'll be there in no time."

We hopped into the back seat of the car, and I relaxed back against the leather as we left the airport, peering out of the tinted window at the city rising out of the desert. It was stark, but there was a sort of beauty to it – the way the ultra-modern skyscrapers jutted out of the barren landscape.

Joel pulled his phone out from his shorts pocket and studied it. I leaned closer to read it over his shoulder.

"Oh, great! How did I get Norieva first round?" I wailed. Joel gave me a sharp look and I snapped my mouth shut.

"It shouldn't matter who you play first round. You just focus on being the best *you* can be."

"But is the best I can be going to be better than Katinka Norieva?" I muttered. I was all kinds of nervous. This would be my first professional tournament without Steve. Every eye would be on me, waiting for me to fail. Waiting to leap on my mistakes. Waiting to harass me about Pete.

"Have some faith in yourself, Stink, it's all about thinking positive." Joel smiled at me in his most winning way. I tried not to smile back at him and failed miserably. I was beginning to realise that his upbeat mood had a way of rubbing off on me, even when I tried to fight it.

When we pulled up out the front of Ben's building, I craned my neck upwards – completely amazed at the sheer height of it.

"He lives *here?*" I asked incredulously. Joel chuckled as he handed me my suitcase.

"Yep – penthouse."

I gaped at him, his laughter intensifying. "Never picked you for a gold digger, Stinky."

I adjusted my expression and scowled at him. "Not everyone is as shallow as you, Joel. Sometimes people look for deeper connections in a relationship."

Joel snorted. "Mel, I know all about deep connections. Every woman who connects with me gets it deep."

I pretended to puke. "Seriously, why do you always have to make everything about sex?" I snapped over my shoulder as I dragged my suitcase awkwardly up the steps. Joel appeared beside me and took the suitcase from me, hefting it easily along with his own and my tennis bag, and carrying the whole lot the rest of the way. He put them down at the top and pulled out a card, which he scanned on a panel. The heavily tinted glass and steel doors swung inwards silently.

Joel turned to me with a grin. "Because, Stink, you can have the most profound connection with a person, but nothing will ever come of it if they can't satisfy you in bed. We're all just animals ruled by our hormones really."

I eyed Joel with irritation as the lift took us very quickly up to the top floor. The doors slid open with a quiet whooshing noise and my mouth fell open.

The lift opened directly into the apartment. I turned to Joel in disbelief. He grinned at me.

"How is that secure?" I demanded. He lifted the cases out of the elevator and the doors closed silently behind us.

He held the card up to me. "This has to be programmed to

bring you to this floor." I sneered at him and turned back to the apartment.

The floors were polished concrete. The large kitchen was industrial – the benches stainless steel, with black doors and drawers. The whole floor seemed open plan, with the long narrow dining table made from metal and concrete forming a barrier between the kitchen and the living area, where an ultra-modern leather sofa sprawled in front of the biggest flat screen television I had ever seen.

Hallways opened off from either end of the space – one to the side of the kitchen, and the other at the living room end. I guessed these led to the bedrooms.

Directly in front of me, behind the dining table and through the tinted glass wall, was an indoor swimming pool – it was roofed in glass to let the sunlight in but kept out the worst of the heat. There were exotic plants in a garden along the far side of the pool, and nestled among them was a spa.

"And you thought Mum and Dad were rich," Joel murmured in my ear as he led the way. He took my stuff through a doorway, along a wide hall and into a massive bedroom with a king-sized bed and en suite. He propped my suitcase up against the bed and sat my tennis gear on top of the covers.

"Shower," he commanded and then turned for the door. "Then we'll swim some laps before dinner."

I was tired and jet-lagged and cranky, but I did as I was told, and I surprisingly didn't feel too bad as I pulled my training swimmers on.

Joel was waiting for me in the pool already, wearing his Speedos. He more than filled them out – oh God, why did I have to have *those* thoughts about *Joel*?!

"Oh, I was looking forward to the itty-bitty yellow bikini again." Joel commented mockingly as I slipped into the pool beside him.

"Well, I wish *you'd* cover up more, but we don't always get what we want, do we, Joel?" I responded, pushing off and swimming a length of the pool and back.

Joel grinned lopsidedly at me. "You only wish that because you hate it that you crave a piece of this." He ran those big hands down his rippling abs.

I groaned. "I thought we were here to train, not so that I had to listen to you wax lyrical about how great you are."

Joel shrugged and pushed off from the edge of the pool. "Okay, Stink, let's see if you can keep up with me with your racing togs on."

I admit, I had trouble. I might be an athlete, but Joel was something else entirely. He was naturally good at everything physical that he tried his hand at. It drove me berserk.

Joel climbed straight out of the pool and dripped his way over to the spa, pressing a button to start the jets and sliding under the bubbling water.

"Come on, Stink, this is the relaxing part!" He beckoned me over with his head. I wasn't sure if it was a good idea to join him in there, but I walked reluctantly over and climbed in.

The spa was nestled among the tropical plants, so you almost felt like you were in a hot spring in the middle of the jungle. It would have been a really romantic setting if I hadn't been sharing it with Joel.

"So, let's talk strategy." Joel was all business now. "Norieva's weakness is her volley, so concentrate on your short returns. She's very fit though, and she'll be getting you moving a lot to try and take advantage of your weak ankle."

My breath caught, the lump that I'd been combatting with some success swelling in my throat. A garbled sob burst from me.

"What's up, Stink?" Joel asked, moving closer and leaning down to look up into my face. I looked away from his aqua eyes.

"You sounded … just like your dad …" I choked out. Joel sighed and he moved closer until his arm pressed against mine. My head tilted until it was resting against his shoulder.

"I miss him too," he murmured. "It's still so fresh. I'll think I'm okay, and then it's like a bolt of lightning to my chest."

I rubbed at my throat. "I … whenever I'm not keeping myself busy, I get a sudden flash of … of the things I saw – *we* saw," I admitted in a hoarse voice. "And for a moment my heart feels like it stops, and it won't start again."

"Do you still dream about it?" he asked. "Because I do. It's not shocking enough that I scream anymore, but I still wake in a jolt, and I'm sweating and icy cold."

"When will it stop?" I asked through my tears. I felt Joel's shoulder move in a shrug.

"No idea, Stink. But you know, I'm always here if you need to offload. I feel like I can't really talk to anyone else about this. You're the only one who ... gets it."

"Same, Joel," I managed.

"You know, he wouldn't have wanted us to dwell over it when you've got a tournament to play."

I nodded. I wouldn't think about Steve. I wouldn't.

I leaned my head back against the edge of the spa, closing my eyes. Minutes trickled by in comfortable silence. I focussed on Joel's body, warm next to mine.

Something brushed against my thigh. And again. Up and down, so gently it tickled. It was at once soothing and ... stirring.

"Joel?" I asked quietly.

"Hmm?" he responded.

"Is that your hand on my thigh?" I opened one eye to peer at him. He was peering back at me the exact same way. The tickling touch didn't stop.

We stared at each other for a long moment. His knuckles continued to feather tiny circles up and down my outer thigh.

I was holding my breath. Why was I holding my breath?

"It's definitely your hand ... on my thigh ..." I reached down and placed my hand on top of his. For a second Joel's fingers curled around mine, then his lips twitched and he slid his hand away.

"I thought it was *my* thigh I was touching. Jeez, Stinky, haven't you ever heard of a razor?" His voice was soft.

I gathered myself, throwing him what I hoped was a withering look. "That's the worst excuse for feeling a girl up I have ever heard. You must be getting really antsy – I mean it's been what, weeks since the last time you got any?"

"But hey, it felt good, didn't it?"

Damn him, he was right. I climbed out of the spa like lightning, willing myself to get it together.

"Where're you going?" he asked casually, leaning over the edge of the spa and watching me.

"I'm going to shave. Wouldn't want you mistaking my leg for yours again."

"Well, when you're done, come back out here and I'll check again to make sure they don't feel too similar."

I groaned and escaped inside, dripping water all over Ben's beautiful floor. Oh, what would he care anyway? He probably had a full-time maid.

It's never a good idea to shave when you're angry and preoccupied. I nicked myself twice when my silly brain wandered, picturing me going back out there, climbing into the spa and asking Joel to check how smooth my legs were.

What had gotten into me?

I busied myself with blow drying my hair until it hung in glossy waves down my back. The noise of the dryer helped to drown out my sudden, weird, intrusive thoughts.

I rummaged through my suitcase, pulling out a little sheer white top, a black bandeau bra, and a pair of denim cut-offs.

When I walked back out into the living room, Joel was lounging on the lounge, showered and dressed in shorts and a white t-shirt. He raised his eyebrows at my attire.

"You didn't need to make an effort for Ben, you know, Stink. He's not all that fussy when it comes to women."

"Well, that's one thing he has in common with you, isn't it?" I responded cuttingly.

Joel grinned. "Someone with talents like mine has a responsibility to society to share them around."

I plonked myself down on the lounge, not too close to him. "Oh, that's right, I forgot. You're a 'Sex God'." Sarcasm oozed out of me. Joel moved closer, leaning over until his muscular arms caged me, his face inches from mine.

"You want me to take you to Heaven, Melanie Black?" he

murmured.

I groaned, hoping I wasn't blushing. "Ew, Joel! You are a walking cliché, you know that don't you?"

He sat back with a snicker. "You love it."

I had nothing to say to that.

"Seriously though, Stink. Ben's very obviously holding a torch for you. He's going to want …"

"What, Joel? What's he going to want?" I interrupted.

"To sleep with you. At a bare minimum."

I gaped at him. "Are you serious?"

Joel's eyes blazed. "I've never been more –"

The elevator door hissed open, and Ben stepped out, beaming in my direction. Joel snapped his mouth shut, but he flashed me a pointed look.

"Hi! How was your flight?" Ben gushed. He turned around and lifted a heap of brown paper bags out of the elevator.

I stood up and walked over to him. "Long. What can I do to help?"

His eyes roved over me and for a second he didn't respond.

"No. Sit down, Mel, you're a guest," he chided me gently, carrying the bags over to the kitchen.

"What are you cooking, Ben?" Joel asked smugly. I gave him a cold stare before turning back to Ben, who was unpacking the bags onto the bench.

Ben grinned at Joel. "You know I can't cook, Joel. But I just picked up a feast fit for a queen." He winked at me. I heard Joel snort in the background, but I ignored him.

"Smells good – what is it?" I asked, leaning over the kitchen bench.

"Well, I figured since this is your first time in Dubai, we should have some authentic Middle Eastern cuisine." He started setting out platter after platter of food.

"Uh, how many people are you feeding tonight?" I asked. There was *so* much food.

"Well, I didn't know what you'd like, so I just got a bit of everything. There's Pide and Baba Ghanouj, and Loubia B'Zeit to start with, then there's some Shish Kabobs, Tabouleh and Fattoush Salad, and Kibbeh Nayeh, and Baklava for dessert."

I had only a vague idea what most of those things were, but I was so impressed by all the exotic names and his polished pronunciation that I couldn't wait to try it all.

"Sounds delicious!" I said, watching as Ben laid out the first course on the table. Joel unfolded himself from the lounge and came to sit. Ben sat himself down to Joel's right, and I sat to his left. He poured us all a glass of white wine.

"To new ... friendships," he said quietly as he raised his glass, watching me intently. I blushed as I raised mine to his and took a sip. Joel smirked into his glass, raising his eyebrow in my direction.

Ben watched me anxiously as I tried everything and seemed delighted when I proclaimed that I liked it. It was awkward, how hard he was trying to please me.

When he got up to make coffee, Joel stood and stretched, yawning.

"I think I'll turn in for the night. Mel, are you sure you want to try the ... Baklava?" he asked, voice dripping with innuendo.

"I'm sure it will be fantastic," I told him, not able to meet his eyes.

Joel shrugged, sauntering over to the hallway leading to our bedrooms. I scowled after him.

Ben brought the coffee to the table, along with a couple of slices of Baklava. I turned to him with a forced smile, suddenly nervous to be alone with him. He set the dessert down and sat in the seat Joel had vacated. I took a sip of my coffee.

"I wanted to tell you earlier, but it felt a little weird in front of Joel – you look stunning tonight."

"Thanks, Ben," I mumbled, scooping up a spoonful of Baklava so I didn't have to meet his intense stare.

"Mmm, this is amazing!" I said. Ben grinned as I polished it all off, gathering my empty bowl and taking it to the kitchen, before coming back and standing behind my chair.

"Well, I was sort of hoping that we might be able to work off the extra calories together," he murmured and his hands found my shoulders. I felt the goosebumps rise on my skin.

"Um … really?" I squeaked, suddenly nervous. How had Joel known? What had he been about to tell me before Ben arrived home?

"I'm looking forward to getting to know you, Mel," Ben whispered, and his hands moved up to my face, his lips to my hair. "I feel like we will be good together."

Something about his tone sent a warning alarm deep in the back of my mind, but it fled when he suddenly tilted my head back and kissed me. His lips tasted of the sweet Baklava and the bitter coffee.

I parted my lips, touching my tongue to his.

Ben broke the kiss, watching me. His eyes were bright, and blue, and so much like Joel's. Heat pooled low in my belly. *Why not?* I thought recklessly, standing and turning to him.

Ben took my hand and led me towards the other hallway that led off the kitchen towards the master suite. He pressed me down on the edge of his enormous bed and stood before me. He unbuttoned his shirt folding it neatly and setting it on top of a chest of drawers nearby, turning back, his broad, muscular chest glowing in the dim light.

"Your turn," he murmured, gesturing to my clothes. After a confused pause, I pulled my top off over my head, dropping it to the ground, followed by my bra.

Ben watched me with an inscrutable expression as he unbuckled his belt, stepped out of his trousers and folded them up too, putting them with the shirt. He slipped off his briefs and stood, arms folded, dick semi-hard, and gazed pointedly at my shorts.

"You're not naked yet," he said darkly. My stomach fluttered as I unbuttoned my shorts, lifted my hips, and pulled them and my underpants off in one go, kicking them away. Ben's eyes darkened, roving over me appreciatively, but not … hungrily. Not desperately.

He walked towards me and climbed onto the bed, kneeling over me, until his dick was bobbing in front of my face. I scooted back, putting a little space between us. He pressed me down with one hand, one of his legs nudging between mine.

"You look good on my bed," he muttered, eyes skating down my body. He reached a hand between my legs, and with a sharp jab, one finger was probing inside me.

I gasped. I wasn't as wet as I usually would be before a guy fingered me, and the friction wasn't exactly comfortable.

"So tight," he mumbled, taking hold of his cock and stroking himself in time to the thrust of his finger. "I hope I'll fit."

"You will," I reassured him, trying not to wince as he added a second finger. "If you just —"

But he removed his fingers and reached into his bedside drawer, pulling out a condom, tearing the packet and rolling it down his length.

"Are you ready?" he asked. I bit my lip.

"Do you have any lube?" I whispered. There was no way he'd gotten me wet enough for his girth.

He nodded, grabbing a tube from the drawer and spreading it on himself with methodical efficiency. He leaned closer, until his arms caged my shoulders, and his knees were between my thighs. He spent a moment manoeuvring himself into position, then slid inside me.

Although it wasn't painful, I did feel very stretched. I was so not into this. It felt more like I was conducting a business transaction than having sex.

Ben moved inside me rhythmically, like he was counting along with his thrusts. I closed my eyes because I couldn't handle looking up at him. I felt his lips touch my shoulder and I placed my palms on his back.

"Mel, this feels so good," he whispered in my ear. *In what universe is this good sex?* I wondered. I decided to take matters into my own hands.

I pressed him back from me, and when he looked down in surprise, I whispered, "Let me on top."

His eyes darkened further, and his lips twisted in what might have been disapproval, but he complied. I straddled him, slipping down onto him, rocking my hips back and forwards. I put my hands on the head of the bed, closing my eyes. Focusing only on the sensation, and not overthinking the rest. Things definitely felt better this way, with me in control.

Ben's hands met my hips, and he held me still, thrusting upwards into me.

Once.

Twice.

Three times.

He groaned, his body shuddering beneath me. Had he just *come?* Just as I was actually starting to enjoy it?

I clambered off and sat on the edge of the bed as he lay panting. Disappointment flooded me, along with some other, gut churning emotion.

The mattress moved as Ben stood, walking into the en suite to discard the used condom. He returned, leaning against the door jamb.

"Would you like to sleep in here with me tonight?" he asked. I turned around and forced a smile onto my face.

"I think I'd better go back to my room," I said as I stood, climbing back into my clothes. "Tomorrow's a busy day."

A brief flash of emotion lit Ben's eyes, but he smiled understandingly. "Of course. If you'd feel more comfortable in your own room, then I'll see you in the morning."

He took my hand and kissed the back of it, then sauntered back into the en suite. I watched his impressive body move. That body should have been made for sex, but it just … wasn't. I shook my head as I left the room, closing the door behind me. How was I supposed to face him in the morning?

The TV was on in the living room. Oh great! This was going to be one awkward conversation. I decided it wouldn't help to pretend I couldn't see him there, sitting on the lounge.

"I thought you were going to bed," I said lightly, continuing to walk past like nothing untoward had happened.

"I couldn't sleep – jet-lag," he replied, not taking his eyes off the TV. "How was the Baklava?" he asked quietly.

I flushed. "It was great."

"And … what about the sex?" He turned and fixed his azure gaze on me intently. I looked away, my stomach swirling. There was no point in denying it.

"It was …"

"He's a bit old for you, don't you think?" Joel interrupted.

"I like a man with experience," I retorted on autopilot. Arguing with Joel was easy. Easier than thinking about what had just happened in Ben's room.

He rolled his eyes. "I know I don't get to dictate what you choose to do in your spare time, Mel, but just don't do what you did in Melbourne. You've got a great opportunity here. Your ankle might not be exactly where I would like it to be, but your fitness is otherwise excellent. Don't throw this away."

I hated it when he talked sense.

"I think you care about what I just did with Ben more than you'd like to admit."

His composure didn't even falter, which instantly frustrated me. He climbed off the lounge and sauntered casually around it until he was standing in front of me, about a foot away. I looked up into his eyes.

"Like I said, Stinky, I have no problem with what you choose to do in your private life."

"Then you won't mind if I go back for round two of the best sex of my life," I lied. His mouth twitched.

"Mel, whatever happened in there, it wasn't even close to the best sex of your life."

I snorted, but it came out a little unsteady. "How would you know?" I asked. Joel moved closer to me, gazing down at me with those blue eyes that were a lot like Ben's only … hungrier.

"Well, for starters," he murmured, trailing one hand down my arm, "if you've had good sex, you breathe differently." My breathing became shallower and noisier without my permission.

"And your legs go weak," he continued, letting his hand trail down to my waist and slipping his fingers up under my top to caress my hip. I locked my knees so he wouldn't notice how my legs were turning to jelly.

He leaned closer, until his mouth was beside my ear. His breath fanned against my neck, and his free hand reached up to press against my sternum, right between my suddenly heaving breasts. He whispered, "and your heart goes crazy."

My heart hammered under his palm and hot, achy need rushed through my blood and between my legs. I clenched *everything* to stop myself from making the sound that was sitting at the base of my throat, clamouring to be moaned out.

Joel took his hands away and stepped back with a triumphant chuckle.

"See, Stinky? You just had better sex with me than you did with Ben, and I didn't even have to take a stitch of clothing off you."

I groaned. "I wasn't excited, you tool! The thought of getting naked with you is horrifying enough to make me breathe differently and lose my balance!"

"Ah, but your heart gave you away."

I scowled, disgusted at myself — mostly because what he'd just done to me was all kinds of hot. But he was *Joel* — it would totally be like having sex with my brother. Wouldn't it?

Hang on a second — why was I even letting my mind take me there?

I stormed back to my room, Joel's deep, amused laughter following me. Why had I decided to let him come with me on this trip again? Oh, that's right, because he knew my game, and he knew his stuff, and he was surprisingly really good at coaching me. Damn, I hated it — I just wanted to find a reason to be genuinely angry at him and I never could.

I flung myself face down on the bed. And the worst part was that everything he had said was right. I shouldn't be doing anything to compromise my game. And he was right about how I felt after really good sex. And he was right that he'd made me more excited barely even touching me than Ben had by actually sticking his dick in me. And all of this put together just made me more annoyed at him.

With 20/20 hindsight, sleeping with Ben had been a huge mistake. And I wasn't going to make that mistake twice. I wondered if Ben would be expecting a repeat performance. My brain could easily work itself into confused, worried knots over this, but I was suddenly exhausted, to the point of feeling like my eyelids were weighted down with concrete.

Thank you, jet-lag.

CHAPTER ELEVEN

Last Night In The Desert

"You did great, Mel. Your form was fantastic through second and third sets. Yu Yang is an absolute freak! I wouldn't be surprised if she takes out the whole tournament," Joel comforted me, passing me my water bottle.

I took a slug. "And hey, I beat Norieva first round!" I puffed, stripping out of my dress and heading for the ice bath and a rub down with a local physiotherapist Joel had contracted.

Yu, only sixteen and the youngest player at this tournament, had surprised me in the first set, beating me six three. I'd clawed my way back in the second set, ending it at six two, but it hadn't been enough. She'd taken the match in the third set.

Joel had convinced the WTA that I would immediately walk from any press conference the second any questions relating to Steve or Pete Levine were asked. As a result, the press conference had been my favourite kind: short and sweet.

We ducked into the players' lounge for a free meal and then we left the tournament. It was a weird feeling, but one that tennis players have to get used to. You come to a tournament and your aim is to go all the way. When you bow out after only a couple of rounds, it feels a little empty. The hardest part is taking it in your stride and moving on, preparing for the next one.

"Stink? You on another planet?" Joel asked me as we climbed into a hire car. I shook myself.

"Oh, no, just thinking about how strange it is to be so worked up to make something happen, and then it just … doesn't."

Joel chuckled. "You're not the only person in the world to have felt that way, Mel."

"Have you ever felt that way? Like, really, have you ever wanted something so badly, it aches, but no matter how hard you try, you can't have it?" I looked over at him. He glanced at me for a moment, before pulling his sunglasses out of the breast pocket of his polo shirt and putting them on.

"Of course not. I always get what I want," he replied. But I caught a hint of something odd in his tone, and after that he didn't look at me for the rest of the car ride. Sometimes I just couldn't figure him out.

"So, what are we going to do now?" I asked as we rode the lift up to Ben's apartment. Joel still had his sunglasses on.

"If you don't mind, I'll try and get us on an earlier flight home – I want to get back to Mum. Just as long as you don't mind your *hot sex* with Ben being cut short." He grinned cheekily.

I grimaced. I hadn't been back to Ben's room after that first night. I'd used the excuse that I needed to focus on the tournament. What excuse was I going to use now?

The doors snicked open into Ben's apartment. Afternoon sunlight was streaming through the glass roof into the pool. The water glimmered enticingly.

"I think I might take a dip," I said to Joel as I headed towards our bedrooms.

"Mind if I join you?" he asked.

I looked at him in surprise. "Since when have you ever asked permission before?"

He took his glasses off and grinned wickedly at me. "Right, don't know what got into me for a moment there, Stink." He disappeared into his bedroom.

Inside mine, I pulled on my yellow bikini – I wasn't planning on swimming any laps today. I grabbed a towel and returned to the pool area, sliding into the comfortably cool water and floating on my back.

Joel sauntered in, wearing board shorts for once.

"Oh, you covered up for me – thank you!" I called cheekily. He jumped into the water beside me, sending little waves over me.

"And you decided to uncover for *me*! How thoughtful of you." He ran a couple of fingers across my exposed belly. I gasped, inhaling a mouthful of water.

"Jesus, Mel, the pool is supposed to stay outside your lungs!" Joel cursed as he hauled me upright and patted my back as I coughed and spluttered.

"And your hands are supposed to stay away from my bare skin," I grunted, still catching my breath. I looked up to see his eyes glinting with … something I couldn't name.

He took a step towards me. "Why fight this, Mel? It's inevitable, you know."

"What exactly is inevitable, Joel?" I asked, stepping backwards.

He advanced on me again. "That one day you're going to snap, and you'll beg me to touch you *everywhere*." He stepped closer again, skating his fingers across my ribs. My skin burst into goosebumps under his touch. My breath caught in my throat. My nipples puckered as his fingers flitted up, stroking the undersides of my breasts through the thin bikini fabric.

Something in me *did* snap then. I lifted the string of my bikini top over my head, letting the triangles drop away from my breasts. I glanced down long enough to see how my nipples jutted towards him lewdly, before biting my lip and looking back to Joel. His mouth was a perfect 'O'. My heart pounded, even as I took another step backwards, out of the reach of his questing hands.

"Take a good look, Joel, because this is the closest you're ever going to get."

"Uh, aren't you two a little old to be playing 'you show me yours, I'll show you mine'?" Ben's deep voice asked from the side of the pool. He was stunning in his conservative work suit, but it didn't make me tingle one little bit. I hastily put my boobs away, avoiding Ben's gaze, cheeks flaming.

Joel cleared his throat, eyes still intent on me. "If we'd gotten to the part where I showed her mine, we would have been playing a *much* more adult game."

What the fuck was I *thinking*? I climbed out of the pool, wrapping my towel around me and rushing back into the house. I heard Ben's footsteps, but Joel's voice called him back.

"I wouldn't follow her if I were you."

My chest tightened and I wheezed as I ducked into my room. Had Joel been warning Ben about my bad mood or warning Ben about something else entirely?

Not my circus, not my clowns, I told myself as I closed my bedroom door on the humiliation.

Safe alone in my room, I flung the towel down and tore my bikini off, jumping into a shower hot enough that I wouldn't feel the heat of my embarrassment. I'd just offered my tits to Joel! Had I been trying to shock him? The way my nipples had strained towards him suggested otherwise …

I scrubbed shampoo into my hair, cringing. I almost hadn't moved away when those big hands were reaching towards my breasts; a little voice in the back of my mind whispered sordid things about what might have happened if Ben hadn't arrived when he did.

God! Why did I put myself in that situation? With Joel *no less?*

My phone rang. Jumping out of the shower, I half wrapped a towel around me and grabbed for it.

"Mel! Hey, I was live-streaming your game. That Chinese chick is a *freak*!"

"Hi, Brad. Yeah, she's something else alright."

"Are you upset?"

I shrugged. "A little bit. But I played hard, so it's just a lesson learned. Joel's going to try and get us an earlier flight so that he can spend some time with his mum before we leave for California."

"Great, Mel! I miss you. I would say Amanda does too, but she's been too busy with Thomas – it's almost sickening how cute they are together."

"Oh God, Brad, I forgot," I gasped, "I promised to call you as soon as I arrived, and I didn't and that was six days ago! I'm so sorry!"

Brad laughed lightly. "It's okay, Smell. I figured you were busy: you've got enough to think about when you're competing. Besides, I can live vicariously through Joel's Instagram updates."

"Joel's Insta … is he posting *me* on Instagram?"

"Honestly Mel, don't you check your notifications? He tags you in everything."

"I've banned myself from social media. I still have a sour taste from some of the shit people said about me."

"Well, Joel definitely takes a lot of great shots of you."

"I'm sorry I forgot to call. I'll make it up to you – let's catch up for dinner and drinks. You, me and Amanda, and Thomas too I guess, when I get home."

"Sounds great, Mel. I'd better go, it's late and I start clinical placement tomorrow."

"Good luck!"

I hung up the phone feeling much calmer – Brad had that effect on me. I lay back on my bed and closed my eyes, working up the motivation to get back in the shower to condition my hair.

"Hey Stink, I'm sorry about before, okay? Are you –" Joel stopped short as he eyed me naked except for my towel that had fallen open. I leapt up, tightening it around me.

"Christ, Joel, don't you know how to knock?!" I demanded. Then it sunk in. "Hold on, did you just *apologise* to me?"

Joel choked out a cough and met my eyes, a hint of a smile on his face. "Yes, I did apologise. I guess I owe you another one – sorry for walking in on you in the middle of … going to town on yourself?"

I glowered through my blush. "I wasn't 'going to town', thank you very much, and you should *always* knock no matter how you expect to find someone, before you enter their room."

He cocked a smile at me. "But then I'd never get to see you in all your beautiful nakedness!"

I nudged him back out the door. "I'm sure you'd cope."

He braced his foot in the door to stop it from closing, and he stared right into my eyes.

"I am sorry about before. Ben asked me to tell you to shower and get dressed, because he's taking us out for dinner tonight. And also, I've got us on a flight tomorrow."

"Oh. Okay. Um, what's the dress code for this dinner? Casual I hope …"

Joel's brow furrowed. "Stink, when it comes to Ben, there's no such thing as casual." He took his foot out of the door and walked away. I watched his retreating back, an ominous tingle shooting up my spine.

No such thing as casual.

God, I prayed fervently as I conditioned my hair, *please get me out of this mess without hurting Ben's feelings, or making him mad at me.*

I hurriedly dried my hair and threw clothes around the room in a desperate attempt to find something that would be suitable for a fancy restaurant. I hadn't really packed anything appropriate. I travelled to play tennis, not socialise, so I rarely packed anything fancy, especially for the Middle East; where covered shoulders and knees was a dress code requirement in most places.

In the end I only really had one choice – a pair of fitted black pants and a cream blouse.

"Ugh!" I snarled as I tossed the items onto the bed.

There was a knock on the door. Obviously, Joel was learning. And good timing too – he had good fashion sense, and wouldn't hold back if he thought I should start panicking about my attire. I opened the door.

"I wasn't sure if you would have brought any evening wear, so I got you these – it's only fair, considering I sneaked this whole dinner thing on you." Ben handed me a garment bag and a shoe box through the door with a grin. "I hope it all fits."

He closed the door behind himself, and I tried to swallow down the panic threatening to overwhelm me. I was in a worse conundrum than before – I could either wear what I had brought and risk offending Ben, or I could wear what he had bought me and risk him getting totally the wrong impression about us.

I unzipped the garment bag and staggered back in shock.

The gown was cream, with a delicate gold pattern through it. Floor length and mermaid cut, it was semi-modest at the neckline, with little capped sleeves.

It looked *very* expensive, and that shocked me. But the thing that scared me the most was that it looked like a *wedding* gown. What was Ben thinking? I couldn't wear this!

But then I looked down at my black pants and blouse splayed on the bed, and I realised that I had no idea where Ben was taking me, so I'd be stupid not to wear what he'd chosen.

I swallowed down the panic and started undressing.

When I was clothed again and my hair pinned up on top of my head, I slipped on the gold kitten heels that I'd found in the box. Everything fit perfectly, which only creeped me out more; had Ben gone through my luggage to check my size? I took a deep breath and opened the door.

Joel was walking past as I stepped out. He froze, took a step back, and I watched the look on his face with dread as he took in what I was wearing.

"Wow," he muttered under his breath. I felt my skin get hot all over. But then he cleared his throat and quirked his lips. "You scrub up okay, Stink!"

I tried to smile sarcastically back at him, but I was so nervous it mustn't have looked right, because his own face softened in response.

"I look alright?" I asked shakily.

He grinned at me, nodding. "Ben's not going to want to let you go home so easily after seeing you like that."

The smile fell from my face. That was exactly what I *didn't* want to hear.

Joel was wearing a sand-grey suit, with a light cream shirt, gold tie and a pair of cream snakeskin shoes. He gestured for me to walk out in front of him, and I did so nervously. I actually felt like a bride on her way to the church. Except this was an arranged marriage and I was being bought with a pretty dress. *What have I gotten myself into?* I wondered in growing terror.

Ben was waiting by the lift, and the smile he threw my way exposed every single white tooth in his skull.

"You look stunning, Mel!" he gushed, taking my hand and kissing it. I tried not to grimace. For once I was actually glad that Joel was there with me. I needed the buffer he could provide between Ben and me.

"Okay, did I miss the memo about the colour scheme tonight?" Ben asked jokingly, pointing to Joel's cream shirt and gold tie. Ben himself was wearing a navy suit with a blue striped shirt and darker blue tie – he looked so conservative next to Joel.

I laughed nervously. Joel turned to me with a question in his eyes, but Ben didn't seem to notice the edge of hysteria in my giggle. He wrapped a gold pashmina around my shoulders.

"It gets very cool in the air conditioning where we're going," he explained, taking me by the elbow and leading me into the lift. Joel followed, lips twitching like he was holding in a laugh.

I don't know what part of the rest of the night was the most surreal for me. It could have been the virtual submarine ride from the foyer of the restaurant to the actual dining area.

It could have been the enormous circular aquarium in the centre of the room, around which all the tables were aligned. Brightly coloured tropical fish darted around a forest of water plants, the lighting of the restaurant shimmered, all combining with the giant fish tank to make me feel a bit like Ariel in *The Little Mermaid*.

Or it could have been the way that Ben insisted that I taste the wine, and that I take the first bite of each of the five courses that were brought out to the table. That each time he spoke to me he touched my hand gently, caressing it with his fingers.

Only Joel smirking across the table at me stopped me from

completely flipping out, even as his enjoyment of my discomfort fuelled my frustration.

Ben clasped my hand in his across the enormous back seat of his chauffeur driven car as we returned to the apartment. Joel spun around from the front and winked at me. I sneered back. I wished I could just pull my hand out from under Ben's, but that seemed ungrateful. It wasn't just the dress … I'd gotten a glimpse of the bill that he'd paid in its entirety, without even blinking. Splashing that sort of money around without a second thought on a single meal horrified me.

Joel disappeared inside his room as soon as we got back. I wished he wouldn't leave me alone with Ben, but that was childish. I had to face the mess that I'd made for myself.

Ben took my hand and led me out onto the pool terrace, seating me in one of the chairs nestled around a table. He disappeared into the house and reappeared with two glasses of sparkling wine, a strawberry in each. He passed one to me and settled into the other chair, smiling over at me.

He clinked his glass to mine and took a sip. I glugged down more than I should have in one gulp, catching the strawberry in my mouth and chewing it viciously.

"Now you don't have a game to prepare for, I'd like to spend some quality time with you tonight." He leaned across to kiss me on the cheek. I flinched involuntarily away from him, and he stiffened, moving back.

I bit the bullet. "Ben, listen. I like you – you're lovely," I tried to smile at him, "but I just don't think it's right for me to … give myself to you again, when there's really no future for us."

Ben watched me for a moment, all seriousness now, inhaling deeply through flared nostrils. "There could be a future for us," he offered.

"How?" I asked. "Ben, you live in Dubai, I live in Sydney. And when I'm not there, I'm all over the place. I don't think you really want to give up your business here to move back to Australia to try something with me." God, I hoped he didn't suddenly decide that was exactly what he wanted to do.

He was silent, pondering, and I felt the nerves settle a little as I realised that if he was prepared to give it up, he would have said it by now.

"I appreciate that you're not the type of girl to lead a man on, Mel. Thank you for your honesty." His voice was chilly, but his face was calm. He stood up.

"I'll say goodnight now then." He leaned in and kissed me on the cheek, before walking stiffly back into the house. I'd upset him, but I'd done the right thing. And I'd done it without having to resort to the *you were shit in bed* get out of jail card.

I scuttled back to my room, the relief making my knees weak. My hands shook as I reached for the zipper at the back of the dress. I couldn't get a hold on it.

I left my room and knocked next door. Joel answered in his suit pants and the white singlet he must have been wearing under his shirt. His biceps rippled as he stretched. My mouth went dry.

"So, do I have to start calling you Aunty Stink now?" he asked.

I shuddered. "There's something else to add to the ever-growing list of *why bonking Ben was a bad idea*." I turned around. "Can you please unzip this for me? I can't get it."

Joel chuckled, but I felt his fingers on the zipper, and the panels fell away from my back. He stroked down my spine, making me shiver.

"You really do look gorgeous in this dress," he murmured, his breath hot against my shoulder. I froze. He was so close. I couldn't turn – his mouth was too near.

"I … this is …" I began, but rational thought fled as his hot lips branded the nape of my neck. A gasp burst from my throat. His mouth was still pressed against my skin, his hands sweeping down my sides, beneath the fabric of the dress, fingertips digging into my hips, pulling me back towards him.

I stiffened, not daring to breathe.

"You're very tense, Mel. I could give you a back rub." Joel's hands swept back up my spine.

I stepped away from him quickly. "Thanks, Joel, but I know how your back rubs finish." I hated that my voice was husky.

He laughed under his breath. "Not looking for that sort of happy ending tonight, Stink?"

I bit the inside of my cheek until I tasted blood, before turning back to him. "From you? Absolutely not!" My voice trembled with what might have been a lie. I didn't know anything anymore.

Joel shrugged. "Don't forget to pack tonight, Stink. Our flight's an early one tomorrow."

He closed the door.

As far as I was concerned it couldn't be early enough.

CHAPTER TWELVE
Broken

I moved back to my place the day after we got back from Dubai. I just couldn't spend another night in the same house as Joel. My nerves were frazzled from everything that had happened in Dubai, with Ben … and with Joel. And I still had to see him every day for training.

The nightmares, which had temporarily subsided while overseas, had crashed back into my brain at the worst possible time – midway over the Indian Ocean, on a packed flight.

Blood.

Gaping mouth.

Bulging eyes.

I'd jolted awake, gasping for breath. I'd tried to leap up, to run from the images, but my seat belt held me firmly in place.

"Mel, shh, it's okay." Joel's hand was on my shoulder, pressing me gently back into my seat. He'd handed me some bottled water, taking it back to unscrew the cap when he'd realised my hands were shaking too much to manage.

Except it wasn't okay. In no world was it okay to keep reliving that morning over and over.

I shook myself, hoping that being back in my familiar apartment would be the catalyst that would stop the dreams from recurring. I busied myself making a coffee as Connor refamiliarised himself with the place.

I needed to keep busy. I needed groceries, I had laundry to do, I had friends I needed to catch up with. Focusing on a checklist like this helped me not to dwell on nightmares of Steve …

Or on the spot on the back of my neck where I was sure I could still feel Joel's hot mouth.

What the fuck had he been thinking?

Nope, I told myself. *No dwelling. It happened, it was weird and it's not happening again.*

I unpacked my suitcase and chucked a load in the washing machine. One task ticked off.

Groceries. Thankfully my pantry was always stocked with staples, but I needed fresh produce. I needed milk that wasn't long-life.

I needed to burn some nervous energy.

Grabbing an empty backpack, I lifted my pushbike down from the hook near the door, dragged it down the stairs and hopped on. I pedalled the few kilometres to the local organic markets in Double Bay.

I'd never learned how to drive. No licence, no car, no interest in changing that situation. Anywhere I needed to go I could get to easily via Uber, or in this case, a ten-minute bike ride. Joel used to tease me about it, until I suggested that he teach me in his BMW. That shut him up like lightning. No one was allowed behind the wheel of his baby except for him.

I was halfway back to my place, backpack full of grass-fed beef, hormone-free chicken, fresh-caught seafood, and pesticide-free fruit and vegetables when a car honked beside me, the window buzzing down. I kept riding.

"I think those bike shorts are my new favourite!"

"There's a reason I'm not looking at you," I retorted, refusing to give him the satisfaction of glancing his way. "Now, drive on, you're holding up traffic."

"Oh, come on, Stink! Don't be like that. I was looking for you.

Can I meet you back at your place? I have something important to talk to you about."

I groaned. "Joel, please, can I just have *one* day of peace?"

"Either you let me come back to your house, or I'll keep driving like this and talk to you about it now."

I could hear the frustrated beeps of cars queueing behind him.

"Fine!" I grunted. "I'll see you back at my place!"

"Don't take too long, Stink!" Joel called as he roared his BMW off down the road. I found myself pedalling harder, sure there would be some smart-arse comment about how long it took me to ride back to my house waiting for me at the other end.

I wasn't disappointed.

"Lucky it's a sunny day, Stinky – I've been getting a nice tan here." Joel grinned, leaning against his car in the visitor space. I climbed off my bike, biting the inside of my cheek so he wouldn't see me wince from the stitch in my side.

"What was so important that it couldn't wait until tomorrow, Joel?" I opened the door and struggled with my bike on the stairs. Joel squeezed past me, hefting the bike over one shoulder and carrying it up. I followed, wanting to be miffed that he assumed I wasn't capable, but really just relieved because I'd just ridden like an utter maniac, so there was very little juice left in the tank.

"I got an interesting call today," he began as he hung my bike up on the rack. I moved into the kitchen and started unpacking the groceries. I tried to pretend I wasn't interested in what he had to say, but my curiosity got the better of me.

"Okay, who called?" I asked.

"The features editor for Woody Magazine," he replied casually. I turned to him, eyebrow raised, waiting for him to explain.

"He was wondering if he could entice you to be the cover girl for the May issue."

I groaned. "I *hate* that magazine, Joel. It's soft-core porn for kids whose parents have their Internet locked down so they can't access the good stuff."

Joel put on his best cajoling face. "Look, Mel, I know it's not really your cup of tea, but just hear me out –"

"What? You actually *want* me to do it?" I screeched. He grabbed me by the arms and held me still.

"Mel, think about this rationally. One, you're not getting offers from sponsors – sorry, but it's true. The money would be welcome. Two, it would thrust you into the limelight, and might attract sponsors that are a bit left of field and outside the tennis sphere. And three, if you go out there and do an interview showing how little the video thing worried you, people are going to forget about it a whole lot faster."

"But it *did* worry me. It *does* worry me," I argued pitifully.

Joel sighed. "Of course it does. You'd have to be a sociopath for it not to. Maybe think of this as a chance to refocus the conversation; shine a light on the fact that it's okay for women to enjoy sex, to be adventurous in bed, but it's not okay for men to take advantage of that. You can turn it around to a discussion about consent, and the fact that Pete Levine didn't get your consent to film what you did together."

I felt the fight go out of me. Joel was talking too much sense, yet again. I'd been so caught up in the mortification of the whole debacle that I hadn't even thought about the unfairness of Pete Levine walking away unscathed after taking advantage of me. Joel sensed the change in the tension in my body and released me.

"When would I have to do it?" I asked, turning back to my groceries.

"Not until we get back from the States. So, can I call him back and tell him you'll do it?"

"Yes," I sighed without looking at him.

"Great! Stink, you're a good sport."

"Why did they call *you* anyway?" I asked.

"Well, actually they DM'd me on Instagram after they saw my posts from Dubai."

I stiffened. I'd forgotten in all the drama in Dubai that Brad had mentioned keeping updated on what I was doing through Joel's social media.

"But you only posted on-court action shots, didn't you? Not that exciting considering every sports media outlet would have been posting similar."

Joel cleared his throat. "Well … I don't think it was the content so much as the fact that they knew I was with you, so they figured I might be able to put you in touch with them. You've seen all my posts, right?"

I shook my head. "I'm still on my social media hiatus. The Internet doesn't need more of Mel Black."

Joel snorted. "I'd hazard a guess that 'the Internet' would beg to differ with you on that."

I closed the fridge and turned to face him, finding him sitting in a chair at my table, looking for all the world like he lived here. I sunk into a chair as well. I reached behind me into the fridge and pulled out a couple of bottles of Platinum Blonde, my favourite beer. I passed one over to him.

"Have you heard anything more from the police?" I asked quietly, changing the subject. Joel shook his head, taking a swig from the beer.

"Nope. I called them this morning but there are still no leads whatsoever. Mel … these nightmares you keep having …"

I choked on a mouthful of beer. "Nope! We are not discussing this!" I spluttered.

"I just want to know how often they're happening. Do you need to talk to someone about them?"

I downed the rest of my beer, leaning over and reaching into the fridge for another.

"I've talked to *you* about them – don't make me regret that," I warned.

Joel shook his head, sipping slowly from his own beer. "I just wonder whether maybe you should talk to a professional. You're an athlete, Stink. You need quality sleep or your performance will suffer."

I rolled my eyes. "Oh, this is my concerned trainer talking, is it?"

Joel sighed. "Don't be like that, okay? I'm worried about you. I don't want … fuck, I wish I was there before you!" He rubbed at his forehead.

I leaned forwards, finger hooked around the neck of my beer. "Joel, don't try to pretend that you're coping with this any better than I am. You being there first, it wouldn't change what we saw."

"I could have stopped *you* from coming in. I could have saved *you* having to see." Joel's voice was agonised.

My heart lurched. "Jesus, Joel! Don't you dare feel guilty about this! I wish *you* hadn't had to see it either! Fuck, I wish *neither* of us had to see! I wish he wasn't …"

My throat locked up. I pushed back from the table and turned to lean against the bench, gripping the edges with white knuckles.

His chair scraped and the warmth of his body was like the sun on my back. His hands were on my arms, holding me steady.

"Please, Stinky. Just … promise me … if things get too overwhelming for you that you'll at least be honest with me about it, even if you don't want to talk to anyone else."

I inhaled until the lump in my throat was small enough to speak around. "I promise."

I wasn't sure I could keep that promise. He was clearly carrying enough guilt about the whole thing. I didn't need to be adding to it with my own issues. But it was easier to lie to him than to argue.

"Another round?" I asked, sliding my empty glass back towards the bartender. Amanda shook her head, indicating her still mostly full cocktail.

Brad watched me thoughtfully. "I'll have a Coke this time," he replied. "Got a shift at the hospital tomorrow, I can't be nursing a hangover."

I sighed. "You're a pair of buzzkills!" I grumbled, but I ordered two Cokes. I should probably pace myself too. Joel didn't see hangovers as an excuse to skip training.

"Hey, babe!"

I turned to see Thomas wrapping his arms around Amanda, leaning down to kiss her cheek. She flushed pink, tilting her head so their lips met. It quickly turned from innocent to almost pornographic, as he spun her on the bar stool and stepped between her knees, gripping her hips.

"Are they always like this?" I asked Brad.

He snorted, sipping at his Coke. "This is PG. Keep watching …"

"Do I have to?" I whined. Something inside my chest squeezed seeing how sweet the two of them were. Amanda's hands were clutching at Thomas's back now, sliding under his t-shirt.

"I miss making out," I sighed.

Brad coughed. "Well, maybe you should be looking for guys who want to make out with you, instead of ones who want to secretly film you deep-throating them."

I turned to Brad in shock. "Christ! That was harsh!"

He shrugged. "Sometimes the truth *is* harsh, Smellie."

"Speaking of harsh …" Amanda interrupted. I turned, noticing her bee stung lips and flushed chest, and the bright spots of colour on Thomas's cheeks. And then I followed Amanda's eyes.

Susie Keens.

Susie Keens, my ex's *fiancée*, wearing the tiniest body-hugging white dress, heels that could stab right through someone's torso and come out the other side, and a tacky white veil with a matching satin sash with the words 'Bride-to-be' emblazoned on it in hot pink.

She was surrounded by a bunch of girls who looked like clones of her: fake blonde hair, fake claw-like nails, fake tans, trout pouts – also fake. They were giggling and simpering over her, as they all downed glasses of champagne.

I felt like someone had shoved Susie's stiletto through *my* chest. I hadn't realised when that photographer had goaded me with talk about Grant marrying Susie that it was happening basically immediately.

"I'm not drunk enough for this fuckery," I muttered, turning back and ordering a Long Island Iced Tea. Brad sighed, but said nothing.

"Come on, Mel. Just one more flight, and we'll get you into bed," Brad crooned.

"Oh, come on! You guys are so lame, I was just getting started!"

Was it just me, or were the stairs all different heights? That was weird, I didn't remember them being that way before.

"Um, Mel, you were kicked out of the bar. And there is no way you would've been let in anywhere else."

"Who're you again?" I asked, flopping my head, trying to focus on the other person who was half carrying me up the stairs to my apartment.

"I'm Thomas, remember? Amanda's boyfriend? You asked me to give you make-out lessons?"

I chortled. "Well, it looked like you and Mandy-Moo had it down to a …" I swallowed bile.

"Quick, guys, she's going to vomit any second," Amanda's anxious voice rang out behind me.

"Nah, I'm good! I just need to sit down." I tried to pull away from Brad and Thomas, but they gripped me harder.

"Your door is right there, Mel. Just a few more steps and you can sit down on your comfortable lounge."

"Uh-huh," I grunted, as a key snicked in a lock and the door opened.

"Home, sweet home!" I crowed, taking two steps and collapsing face first onto the lounge.

I turned my head to the side, watching through hazy eyes as they talked about me like I wasn't even there.

Thomas: "Does she get this messy a lot?"

Brad: "Hardly ever. Although this is the second time I've seen her like it this year. She was like this the night that Steve …"

Thomas: "What set her off tonight?"

Amanda: "She was serious with Grant Johnson – you know, the NRL player? They were together basically all through high school."

Thomas: "And what's that got to do with tonight?"

Brad: "He cheated on her with that woman who was out on her hen's night. Susie Keens. It was going on for years – every time Mel travelled to compete."

Thomas: "Why didn't anyone tell her?"

Amanda: "We all thought she knew. Mel's … she's never been one to wear her heart on her sleeve. It was so obvious, none of us imagined that she didn't …"

"That I didn't realise that he was fucking her every time I was away long enough for him to get away with it?" I interrupted. I snorted as the three of them jumped like they'd forgotten I was there. Suddenly I felt stone cold sober.

"For the record, I didn't know. Grant was … he was very good at hiding things from me. I … I honestly thought he loved me. I never thought we'd be forever, but I thought it would be my career taking off that would end it. Not that he'd been pounding Bogan Barbie basically since I popped his cherry."

"Is it really that bad a thing, that he's marrying her then, if you never expected to end up there with him?" Brad asked gently.

I chuckled humourlessly. "It's not even that. I couldn't give two shits about him marrying Susie. It's just …" My throat got tight, and my eyes blurred.

"He's the first guy I ever trusted … you know? The first one I ever let in. Towards the end, things were shit, and I knew a breakup was coming, but when he turned up to meet me at the airport and she was with him … I have never felt so … betrayed!"

I was sobbing in earnest now.

Amanda sat beside me, her hand stroking soothingly up and down my back. "You had every right to feel that way, Mel," she reassured me. "What Grant did – that day, and every time he cheated on you – it was so shitty. He's a shitty person who never deserved your love."

"I feel like after the way that felt … anything more than just casual stuff … it's not something I can do. Grant fucking broke me."

I'd never said it out loud before. Never even really recognised it, but the truth of it hit me like a freight train. Pete … Ben … there had been no likelihood for anything long-term with either of them. Had that been what had made it possible for me to sleep with both of them?

"Well, that's absolutely untrue!" Brad murmured. "You'll find someone who is worthy of your trust, Mel. And when you do, that dickhead will be so far from your mind, you'll forget he even existed."

I swallowed, nausea rolling suddenly through me. "I'm going to be sick," I gasped, lurching off the lounge and rushing towards the bathroom. I barely made it to the toilet before my meagre dinner, and many cocktails, came hurling back up.

Amanda was behind me, gentle hands holding back my hair. When the last of the dry heaving finally subsided, she stood up and flicked on the shower, helping me to undress and climb under the warm spray.

"Thanks, Mandy-Moo," I whispered.

She smiled, placed a fresh towel within reach and walked to the bathroom door. "I'll be waiting on the other side, if you need me."

I had such good friends. I probably didn't deserve them.

I woke up with a mouth that tasted like Connor's litter tray, and a banger of a headache. Hello hangover.

Staggering into the kitchen, I poured a big glass of water, collapsing into a chair and sipping it slowly. Bit by bit, the previous night came back to me.

Susie … *way* too many cocktails … Brad and Thomas carrying me home … spilling my guts about Grant Fucking Johnson.

"Ugh!" I groaned, and my head throbbed as someone knocked on the door. I staggered over to answer it.

"Stink! Did you hear what happened to your ex?" Joel exclaimed as I opened the door. I took a step back and he moved into the apartment, stopping dead when he actually caught sight of me.

"Fuck, Mel, you look like shit!"

I rolled my eyes, then wished I hadn't, clutching at my head. "I might've had a few too many cocktails last night," I admitted, shuffling back to the kitchen and popping a couple of paracetamol.

Joel snickered. "Yeah, I got a message from Brad saying not to expect you for training this morning. Thought I'd better come and check that you hadn't asphyxiated on your own puke."

"Thanks for the visual," I grunted, sitting back down at the kitchen table. Joel sat opposite me. His mouth was turned up in amusement, but his eyes weren't smiling.

"What happened to my ex?" I asked, picking up my water glass and tipping it, only to find it empty. Joel stood, taking it out of my hand and turning to the tap to fill it for me.

"Turn on Wolf Sports – you'll hear all about it."

I hobbled to the lounge and flicked the TV on.

"Breaking news from New South Wales this morning. Eastern Sydney Cockerels player Grant Johnson is in hospital in a serious but stable condition after being stabbed in a bar room brawl in Bondi in the early hours of the morning. Johnson, who was celebrating his buck's night, was rushed to Saint Bernard's Hospital to be treated for a stab wound to the shoulder.

"Police are calling for any witnesses who have not yet come forward to contact Sydney Metropolitan Police on …"

I turned away from the TV in shock.

"Yeah, that was how I looked when I heard too," Joel said as he collapsed down beside me, passing the water to me.

I burst into tears.

"Hey, Stinky, what's wrong?" Joel asked, taking the glass away before slinging an arm around my shoulders. I shook and his arm tightened, pulling me against his chest.

"I don't know!" I sobbed against his shirt. "Last night I … I kind of had a breakdown about Grant. We saw Susie on her hen's night and it was a bit … triggering."

Joel's warm breath stirred my hair as he sighed, his hand smoothing the tangled waves away from my face.

"It's just … weird," I continued, "that last night I was … I told them – Brad and Amanda – how he broke me, and now, someone's tried to break *him*."

Joel's muscles tensed. "This is not your fault, you know that, don't you, Stink?"

I shook my head. "Of course it's not, but …"

"No buts! He got in a drunken fight with some louts, this is what happens to arseholes like him who think they're tougher than they are. Nothing to do with you at all. Don't you waste any of your energy on that dickhead. You are not broken – he is."

I hiccuped, the sobs dissipating as quickly as they had begun. I pushed away from Joel's chest, unable to meet his eyes.

"Sorry I cried all over you," I mumbled. Joel looked down, as if just noticing that his shirt was completely drenched.

"My shirt is always available to soak up your tears, Mel," he murmured, before jumping up and heading to the kitchen.

"I'll make you some toast," he said, before I had a chance to process what he'd just told me.

CHAPTER THIRTEEN
Tension ...

"Let's just call it what it is, Joel – a lucky fluke," I said as he unlocked the door to our villa. Joel snorted.

"What's with the negative attitude, Stink?" he asked. "You're in the final! You've gotten too far into this tournament for it just to be luck."

I shrugged. I'd been in a bad mood the whole time we'd been in Indian Wells. I *should* have been on top of the world – I was in my first ever final of a WTA Premier tournament. That was something to be ecstatic about. And I'd managed to beat out a few much higher ranked players on the way.

Well, I *was* happy about the place in the final. Happy and terrified. I'd never felt so much pressure to perform in my life. But that wasn't what was making me grumpy.

It was my dreams. Sometimes I woke up, drenched in sweat with that familiar gasping for breath sensation. Other times I managed to wake up before the dream turned into a nightmare. And that was just as bad – waking up gasping and drenched in a very different way, my body throbbing, clenching around nothing.

Every time it was the same. I was in my apartment, lying on my lounge, the weight of …him … on me. His tongue in my mouth, his knees pressing my thighs apart, hands on my breasts, sliding inside my bra …

Just as things started getting really exciting, I would roll to the side and I'd see what was lying on the floor.

Sightless eyes glaring accusingly at me.

Blood.

Gaping mouth …

As if my life wasn't complicated enough without my all too familiar nightmare taking on the added element of a hot sex dream about … him.

I knew that Joel had heard the noises that I was making in my sleep – the moans of pleasure, the sudden, hacking gasps for air. One night I had woken up and I swear he had been sitting on the edge of the bed, watching me. But I had been so out of it that I hadn't known whether that was just a hallucination or not. He hadn't said anything to me about it.

Living on basically no quality sleep, it was a minor miracle that I had made it to the final. But if anything, the dreams had helped me throw myself into my tennis in my waking hours. Anything to distract me from thinking about …

I was so used to the nightmare by now that the horror of it faded immediately as I woke. The sex dream though … I was constantly on a razor edge of arousal and I felt like there was nothing I could do about it.

Even surrounded by the virile masculinity of male tennis players, there was no way I would approach any of them. I could feel their smirks following me as I moved around the players' areas. I heard the not so quiet comments about things I'd done with Pete. I might be DTF, but I wasn't prepared to humiliate myself to get it from any of those arseholes.

Speaking of Pete, he was doing his best to avoid me.

I'd simply walked past him in the players' dining room just the day before, and as soon as he'd spotted me, he'd excused himself from the table where he was dining with a couple of other players and his coach, and had ducked very swiftly to the men's room. He'd still been in there when I left.

"So, Stink, I want you to be as relaxed as possible for your final," Joel said, snapping me back to the present. He eyed me up and down, my skin warming under his appraisal. "You definitely need to work off some tension."

"Yes, Joel," I muttered, trying to walk past him. He gripped my arm to stop me.

"You know what's great for relieving tension?"

I threw him a scornful look. "Let me guess, a throbbing cock inside me?"

"Sometimes it's like we share a brain, Stink." Joel's eyes went hooded and he grazed his knuckles across my lower stomach. I gritted my teeth.

Being near Joel was driving me nuts. I could still feel that spot on my neck where he'd kissed me in Dubai, as if he'd tattooed me there. Every time he touched me – even a congratulatory hug after a win – was setting me off. I was constantly over-sensitised. Brushing arms with a stranger in the supermarket would probably have me panting at this point.

I knew exactly what I needed. Joel was partially right. I needed an orgasm. Normally I had no problem getting myself off, but here, in a small apartment, with no lock on the bedroom door, and Joel who liked to walk in without knocking? That was a problem. Maybe I could take a nice 'peaceful' bath … behind the lockable bathroom door.

"Where are you going?" Joel asked as I ducked towards the hallway.

"Uh, just taking a bath!" I replied breezily.

Joel eyed me suspiciously. "You literally just had a shower back at the stadium," he reminded me. "You're not that dirty, Stink."

I shrugged, hating that my cheeks were flaming. Joel raised an eyebrow.

"Well, sorry if a quick rinse off with my trainer watching on isn't exactly peaceful. You just told me you wanted me to be as relaxed as possible for tomorrow," I snapped and Joel's lips quirked up at the corners. I was on fire. He one hundred percent knew what I was about to do.

"Fair enough. Go to town, Mel!" he said mildly, smirking. I escaped before he could make another dirty comment.

My hands shook as I ran the bath. Was I shaking with nerves, or … anticipation? I was a total deviant, because suspecting Joel knew what was happening in this room somehow made it more exciting.

Ew. But apparently not 'ew' enough to stop me.

I stepped into the water and sank down with a sigh, barely submerging before my hand slid down my belly and between my legs.

Jesus, I was so wet. Even in the water, I could feel how slippery I was. My finger glided over my clit, and I gasped to find it incredibly swollen and sensitive.

Yep, it had been far too long since I'd taken care of myself like this.

My fingers circled my clit, heat and aching flooding my lower body.

"Mmm," I moaned, taking a finger and sliding it inside myself. My slick pussy gripped my finger, and I thrust harder, adding a second.

I spread my knees wider, as wide as I could make them in the confines of the bathtub.

I arched my back, and the cool air hit my tight nipples. I gasped, reaching one hand up to pinch at a wet peak. The heel of my palm ground my clit even as I continued to finger myself.

My mind began replaying my erotic dreams, adding even more detail to the scene. I let my eyes slide closed, biting on my lip as I pictured … him … muscles rippling as he loomed over me. They were his fingers inside me, his palm rocking on my aching clit.

As I pinched at my nipple, in my mind his teeth were grazing across it. My insides were already coiling, tightening …

"*Ooh!*" I cried out as my orgasm crashed over me, my body pulsing and quaking with the intensity of it.

I lay, panting in the warm water, coming to terms with what had been the strongest climax I'd ever given myself. I didn't want to think too hard about the reason for that.

"Ungh!" a deep, pleasured voice groaned through the wall beside me. My heart stopped. That sound had come through the wall the bathroom shared with Joel's bedroom …

Holy shit! Was he in there going to town on himself?

Without my permission, my fingers started massaging my hyper-sensitive flesh once more until I was panting and rocking my hips to my fingers, and biting my lip as I came a second time …

Eventually I dragged myself from the water and towelled off, wincing at how tender my skin was. I checked my reflection in the mirror; hopefully I could pass the hectic flush on my chest off as a too-hot bath.

I wrapped the towel around me and unlocked the bathroom door, stepping out into the hallway to head back to my room to dress.

Joel's bedroom door opened at the same time, and he sauntered out, eyes bright, a satisfied smile fixed on his face.

"Can you believe how thin the walls are in this place?" he commented as he let his gaze rove over my towel clad body, my flushed chest.

"I'm feeling much more relaxed now, how about you?" he added, taking a step towards me. I stepped back, but the hallway was narrow, and I was up against the wall, the heat from his too-close body making me feel like he was touching me when he wasn't.

Damn him! I shouldn't let him get to me like this!

Taking a breath, I wracked my brain for a witty retort, but all my brain conjured up was the sound he'd made on the other side of the wall … and the sudden realisation that he would have been able to hear all the noises I made too.

The tension in my body was gone, but my brain was whirring.

"I'm taking a walk," I said, scuttling into my room to dress.

The resort we were staying at was a combination of traditional suites, which were contained in a ten-level tower, and villas, arranged around tropical gardens that wound around the pool and the tennis court and the little restaurants that dotted the grounds.

I realised as I caught a whiff of sizzling steak while walking past one of the restaurants in the dusk light, that I was starving.

Gee, could that possibly be due to the two mind-blowing orgasms you just gave yourself?

I took a deep breath and pushed those thoughts aside. I couldn't think about what had just happened in our villa or I'd go crazy.

I turned a corner, slamming straight into a bare chest. A broad, hairy bare chest. I looked up, into the shocked eyes of Pete Levine, obviously on his way back from the pool.

Fan-fucking-tastic!

"Hi, Mel! Uh, congratulations on your spot in the final! I bet that feels really good," he said nervously.

"It would … if people were more interested in my tennis, and less interested in my sex life – thanks to *you*!" I snarled.

Pete put his hands up, warding me off. "Mel, I can explain."

I took a deep breath, and really looked at him. I expected to feel the fire of rising rage. I expected my hands to itch to claw their way into him and tear him to shreds.

But I felt … nothing.

"You know what, Pete? I just can't be bothered. You're not worth my anger." I turned and walked away.

"Mel!" he called out. I almost didn't stop, but something in his tone made me turn to look back at him.

"I'm really sorry about Steve."

I nodded jerkily, heading back towards the villa.

"Hey, Stink!" Joel was in the kitchenette as I walked in, expertly flipping some beef and noodles in a wok. The smell of the stir fry made my mouth water.

"I'm starving!" I sauntered over and reached into the wok to snag a piece of beef, popping it into my mouth and tucking one leg under me as I sat.

"Sit straight, Mel." Joel chastised. I pulled my leg out from under me.

"You're looking significantly less tense since your bath," he said, sliding a cheeky sidelong look in my direction.

I flipped him the bird.

"Is that the magic finger you used earlier, when you were moaning in the bath like a porn star?" He gasped. *"Finger-bang Bathtub!"*

I rolled my eyes. "Title of my sex tape?" I asked. His lips curled upwards.

"It would be better than the first one; the soundtrack alone was enough to get me harder than steel."

"Oh, yeah? So what's your sex tape called then, Mr 'I fucked my fist listening to a chick coming on her fingers next door'?"

He turned the full force of those baby-blues on me. "Mel, you need to stop talking dirty to me, or I'm going to have to stop cooking your dinner and …"

"And what?" I asked, my voice suddenly throaty.

"And order you straight back into that bathtub for an encore."

I shook my head, surreptitiously squeezing my thighs together. "You're a sick man, Joel Herbert!"

He winked, a lopsided grin on his face. "Thanks!" It was like I was paying him the greatest compliment ever.

"Now, can we please never speak of it again?"

Joel saluted me. "It's our dirty little secret."

I rolled my eyes and changed the subject. "I just ran into Pete Levine out in the garden."

Joel looked sharply at me. "Do I need to help you hide the body?"

I laughed, shaking my head. "Not at all. It was so strange – I've been working myself up for when I'd have to confront him, but I stopped for a second and I thought, 'I just don't care enough about you to be angry at you'."

Joel watched me, an odd look in his eyes. "And you're okay?"

I nodded, confused. "Yeah, I'm fine, why?"

Joel shrugged and turned back to the wok. "No reason. Just checking."

We ate out on the little patio outside the villa, where there was a small table and chairs. The night was balmy. I really enjoyed the weather in California at this time of year.

"One day I might move to America," I said vaguely to Joel as I popped the last piece of beef into my mouth. The dinner he'd made was nothing short of awesome – I'd never give him the satisfaction of telling him, but he was an amazing cook.

Joel turned his sapphire gaze on me. "Why?"

I shrugged. "The weather's nice."

"The weather here is so much like Australia it's not funny," he argued. He had a point.

"It's far away from my mother."

Joel nodded. "Well, that's a good reason – for you at least. Me, I like being close to Mum."

I tucked my leg up underneath me – Joel didn't notice. "I like being near your mum too. I *love* your mum!"

Joel picked up his glass and stared down into it. "So, why'd you move back home then? You were welcome to stay with us for as long as you wanted."

I stared into the darkness, not wanting to delve into why living with him was difficult for me. Not even really knowing the answer myself.

"Well, Joel, we spend so much time together, with training, and travel and everything. Don't you like to have a break from me?"

I looked at him then, and he was staring at me, a strange smile frozen on his face.

"Stinky, you're my favourite person – to torment I mean. When you're not there, I get bored!" His eyes didn't look teasing.

I looked away. "Well, you'll just have to get your fix when we're together," I teased back, trying to lighten the weird mood. I stood up, needing to put some distance between us.

A spasm of pain went through my back. I gasped. Joel looked sharply at me, leaping to his feet.

"What's wrong Mel? Is it your ankle?" He crouched down and took my right foot in his hands, running his fingers lightly over it.

"No, not my ankle. My back just twinged a bit, that's all." I straightened up and gasped again.

Joel stood. "You were sitting on your leg, weren't you? Stink, you know you've been told not to do that!" Joel sounded exasperated. "Where's the pain?"

I pointed to my tailbone.

Joel sighed. "Go into your room and strip down to your panties," he commanded.

"Why?"

Joel was already heading back inside. "I'll come and rub it for you, just let me go get some massage oil."

I muttered crankily to myself as I shuffled into my room and undressed. I was still sitting on the edge of the bed rearranging my pillows when Joel walked into the room. I wrapped one arm around my boobs and shot him an angry look.

"Oh, come on, Stink. I distinctly recall you brazenly stripping your bikini off and sticking those beautiful breasts in my face less than a month ago."

I bit my lip to stop from retorting and lay face down on the bed, wearing nothing but a leopard print Lululemon g-string, half wishing that I'd had a chance to change into a proper pair of briefs. The other half of me was wondering what Joel was thinking of the skimpy thong.

"Joel, just promise me that this isn't just some stunt of yours to feel me up," I warned.

The lid on the massage oil popped, and I heard the slick sound of oil being warmed between his hands.

"Stink, I'm actually more concerned that you're match fit tomorrow. And believe it or not, you're in good hands; I have a diploma in remedial massage."

I was surprised enough not to comment. And then words failed me, because Joel's hands were working magic on my back.

He didn't get too deep into my muscles – obviously he didn't want me to be too tender tomorrow – but he did work out the kink in my lower back. When he was done with that, he moved more generally over my whole back, and even down the backs of my legs, my glutes, calves and thighs. I couldn't prevent the little sigh of happiness that left me as his palms swept across my shoulder blades.

When his hands moved off me, I groaned in disappointment.

Joel laughed under his breath. "Well, Stink, you know if you want me to keep going, I can, but it'll cost you." He chuckled again, but there was an edge to the sound. "I don't know if you're willing to pay the price." His voice was soft, mellow. It sounded like it did in my …

"Okay, this conversation is officially getting too weird," I said sharply, sitting up, forgetting that I was just about naked.

Joel stood up, and surprisingly his eyes didn't stray from my face to my breasts. "Are you sure you don't want me to keep going? I could do the front for you," he offered, waggling his eyebrows at me suggestively.

And just like that we were back in familiar waters, safe waters. I gave him a withering look.

"I'll take that as a no then. Have a shower and go to bed," he said.

"I hope I don't wake up sore in the morning," I said, standing and walking over to the door of the bathroom. I didn't bother to hide my almost nudity. He'd just rubbed down every inch of the back half of me, what was the point in hiding?

Joel smiled at me, softly, sweetly. I found myself staring at his full bottom lip. My insides fizzed.

"Have a little faith, Mel – you'll be fine tomorrow and you'll play your heart out."

I closed the bathroom door, showered very quickly, and when I opened it again to get into bed, Joel was gone.

Feeling a little put out for no good reason, I turned the light out and very promptly fell asleep.

"Mel, it's okay!"

I startled awake, sweating, my breath coming in gasps. I turned. Joel was sitting on the bed beside me, his hand on my arm.

"It was just a bad dream," he whispered soothingly to me.

For a moment I felt like I was still suspended in my dream. The ache between my legs intensified as his fingers stroked the length of my arm. I shook my head to try and rattle free the sudden desire to drag him into my bed, to seek comfort in the best way I could currently think of.

I sternly told myself that this was real life. And in real life I would *never* find myself wrapped around Joel Herbert, his hard body rocking against mine. But in my dream it felt pretty damn good, until I rolled over and saw Steve on the floor, and it all turned to shit.

I took a few deep breaths to calm myself down.

"Do you want to tell me about it?" he asked me.

I shook my head. "It's pretty much the same nightmare I've been having since …" He knew what I was talking about.

"Did it always start out with you moaning and rocking against your mattress?"

I grimaced into the dark. "No, that's a … recent development."

Thankfully Joel didn't press me for more information. "Are you okay now? Do you need me to stay?"

"No, I'm fine now, thanks, Joel," I murmured. The mattress moved as he stood up. In the darkness all I could make out were his white teeth as he smiled at me.

"Any time, Stink." He reached over, pushed a strand of hair out of my face and walked to the door, pausing for a split second before he walked out and closed it gently behind himself.

I shut my eyes and slept a dreamless sleep for the rest of the night.

CHAPTER FOURTEEN

Perspective

The plane jerked and I stiffened, clutching the arm rests. Joel glanced at me out of the corner of his eye, looking amused.

"With all the flying you do, Mel, I would have thought that you'd be desensitised to turbulence by now."

I glared at him coldly. The plane rattled around in the sky some more, and I gasped, ruining the effect. Joel laughed.

When we'd passed the rough weather, and the seat belt light flicked off, the man in front of me turned around and smiled. He was in his mid-fifties, I would have guessed, with a thick head of wiry salt and pepper hair that looked kind of like steel wool. His eyes were crinkled with laugh lines.

"You're Melanie Black, aren't you?" he asked me, flashing his teeth at me. He had an Aussie accent.

I smiled back at him. "Yeah, that's me."

"I was at Indian Wells, and I saw you in the final – that was too bad, you deserved to win."

I shrugged. "Well, thanks. Maybe next time."

He cleared his throat. "Would you be able to autograph something for me?" he asked timidly.

It would never cease to weird me out that there were random strangers out there who were in awe of me. I smiled at him and rummaged in my bag for a pen. Joel passed me one, and a piece of the airline paper that they give you in business class if you have the urge to leap a few decades back in time and write a letter to someone.

"Here you go, Stink."

I took the paper and pen from him with a quick smile.

"Who should I make it out to?" I asked the man.

"Can you make it out to Natalie, please?"

I looked at him questioningly.

"She's my daughter. She's twelve and she thinks you're amazing – she has pictures of you all over her bedroom. She wants to be a professional tennis player when she grows up, but she's not all that well at the moment … Leukaemia.

"We were supposed to be on holiday together; we had tickets to Indian Wells and Miami, because she was doing so well, but then she got sick again. She's back in hospital. I didn't want to go without her, but she wouldn't hear of me staying at home. She wanted me to go so I could tell her all about it when I got back." The man's eyes were watering. I found my own prickling as I put the pen to the paper.

Dear Natalie,

Be brave and keep fighting. Can't wait to see you competing at Wimbledon one day.

All the best,

Mel Black

I passed the paper back to the man, blinking the tears from my eyes. He read it and his own overflowed.

"Thank you so much, Mel. This will make her day."

Joel leaned forwards. "Would Natalie like it if Mel came and visited her in the hospital?"

The man's face lit up. "Oh, would you? That's something she would remember for the rest of her life!" His eyes clouded over – possibly wondering how long that would be.

"She'd love to, wouldn't you, Mel?" Joel said.

I nodded. "Of course I would!" I smiled at the man, who beamed back at me. Joel captured the man's attention then, exchanging details and asking him to get in touch when his daughter was well enough for a visit.

"So, Mel," Joel started, changing the subject. "Let's talk about your loss to Abigail Petersen. I want you to tell me what went wrong."

I rolled my eyes and sighed. "Well, not much that I could see. I mean, come on, Joel, I took it to a tie breaker! It was that close it's not funny!"

Joel grinned at me and squeezed my hand.

"That's exactly what I wanted to hear you say, Stink! You're far too hard on yourself sometimes. You played a great game. You can't win them all, you know."

I grunted. Of course, I still wished I *had* won them all. It would have been nice to be able to go home saying I'd won my first tournament since going pro.

"Stinky, you played *really* well. All you need to do is be ready to go out and do it all again in Miami."

I would almost be happy to bow out in the first round in Miami – I was feeling the burn out from competition in a way I never had before.

Steve. I kept thinking about him. And not just because of my nightmares, or the random times when images of that morning forced themselves into my brain. It was little things, like wanting to debrief with him about a tricky shot I'd aced, only to remember he wasn't there … he'd never be there again.

On top of that, after my long final at Indian Wells, I was feeling a twinge in my back again. I was too scared to tell Joel about it, because I knew he'd make a big deal out of it.

I nestled back against my seat and closed my eyes. California to Florida took about four hours, and I planned on trying to get a bit of nightmare-free sleep in there somewhere.

I woke with a jolt as the plane skidded to a halt on the runway. I turned to Joel, to find him looking at me with a strange expression on his face. I raised an eyebrow sleepily at him, and his mouth quirked into a smile.

"Wakey wakey," he chuckled. I grunted and clambered out of my seat.

Pain blossomed in my lower back. I bit my lip, but it didn't stop me crying out.

Joel was at my arm in an instant, gripping me tightly and supporting most of my weight. "Mel, is it your back? Where does it hurt?" he asked urgently.

I nodded. "Same place," I muttered.

The flight attendants were very good at their job – with the minimum of fuss I was off the plane and waiting under the watchful eye of a nurse in an infirmary inside the terminal. The door opened and Joel came in, carrying our suitcases.

I grimaced. "Can we leave now? I'm sure if I just go and rest for –"

"Yes, we can go – to the hospital! Mel you're obviously in a lot of pain. Why didn't you say anything?"

I shrugged, even that small movement hurting. "It just didn't seem like that big a deal."

Joel slammed his fist against the side of the bed I was lying on. I flinched.

"Not a big deal! Christ, Mel – this is your career you're toying with! Your health! There's no such thing as 'not a big deal'!"

I'd never seen Joel so angry.

"So, what are we going to do?" I asked in a shaky voice.

Joel scowled. "We're going to get you to a hospital, have an MRI to make sure there's no nerve damage, and then we're going to get you on the first flight home so that we can get you fixed."

"What about the Open?" I asked.

Joel looked down at me, and there was anger in his eyes, and something else. "Mel, be serious. You're not playing, no matter how minor this turns out to be. Your health is too important."

I didn't argue, but I felt a tear slip from my eye. He'd never really yelled at me before. Joel noticed it too, and he reached out a thumb, swiping the moisture off my cheek, before turning away.

The trip to the hospital in the back of the ambulance was a constant loop of Joel leaning over to ask if I was okay. In the end I snapped at him that I would tell him if anything changed, but to please stop bugging me. He didn't look happy, but he complied.

Thankfully the MRI showed no serious damage, although there was some not-minor inflammation around my sacroiliac joint, and they gave me the all-clear to travel with prescription pain relief. I didn't even try to argue with Joel at that point. I was withdrawing from the Miami Open on medical grounds. We were going home.

With me dosed up to the eyeballs, we got on the next flight back to Sydney. They settled me on the plane first, and before we even took off, I was fast asleep.

They must have given me the good drugs, because I couldn't remember the stopover at LAX, although Joel assured me that I seemed lucid, and I walked through the terminal from one flight to the next.

The first thing I remembered was waking up as the plane started to descend into Sydney. Joel was sitting at the end of my sleep pod, watching me. I wanted to ask him why he was freaking out, but I was too groggy. Yep, they gave me some *really* strong pain meds.

The plane landed, and Joel almost carried me out of the terminal, into a hire car and before it had even pulled away from the kerb he was on his mobile. I heard him mutter, "Yeah, we had one done in the states … no, but the SIJ is inflamed."

He hung up. "Julie says I need to get you to a physio as soon as possible," he said quietly. "And after that, you're taking it *very* easy."

I opened my mouth, but he held his hand up. "No, you're staying at my house. Stink, don't be stupid – you can hardly walk on your own, let alone look after yourself." How had he known I was about to ask if I could go home?

"So, Julie, huh?" I asked. Joel gave me a withering look.

"Who else should I call to discuss your injury? She's a physio who has worked on you multiple times in the past."

"Are you and her … are you together?" I pressed.

"Stink, why would we be together? She lives in Melbourne. I

kind of like to see the woman I'm dating on a regular basis." He grinned, but his eyes looked serious.

"The only girl you see on a regular basis lately is me," I muttered, shifting uncomfortably. It was just my back making me feel uncomfortable. It wasn't the way Joel was staring at me.

"Yeah, but Stinky you hardly count, do you?"

I felt a pang in my chest at his words. "Well, gee thanks, Joel, for making a girl feel special!"

Joel put his hand on my knee, his fingers gently tickling at the inside of my thigh. "I can make you feel special if you like, Stinky," he suggested, staring bedroom eyes at me.

I brushed his hand away. "Don't be gross!"

Joel laughed. "Hey, at least I stopped you thinking about your back for a minute," he said, and I sighed.

***

Sacroiliac Joint Dysfunction. If I heard those three words again in my life, I thought I would scream.

"I picked it when I saw the MRIs!" Joel had crowed a week ago when we'd gotten the official diagnosis from the physiotherapist.

"Hope you got good odds on that on Sportsbet," I'd muttered.

I'd been poked, prodded, zapped with electrodes and strapped with enough tape to keep a BDSM club in business for a month. I'd been ordered to rest for forty-eight hours and had spent the following week working on stretches and strengthening.

I was well and truly over it, and ready to get back into training. I had to be match fit in time for Madrid at the end of April.

Joel was stretching my hamstring. This was his favourite – me on my back, one leg straight in the air, him leaning his body against it. He looked down at me with such wicked delight that I flushed.

"How's that hammy, Stink? Nice and loose? Let me check." He placed his hand at the back of my knee, running it slowly towards my butt. There was no need for him to check as thoroughly as he was.

I dug my nails into my palms; I had to distract myself from the way his touch made me clench … everywhere.

"I think it's plenty loose, thanks Joel," I managed. He smirked and released me. I sat up, rotating my shoulders to loosen them.

"Now, Stinky, we've got a date with a sick little girl today."

"Oh? That Natalie kid?"

Joel nodded, holding his hand out to me. I looked at it for a second, then took it and he pulled me to my feet, caressing my fingers before letting me go. I flexed my fingers surreptitiously by my side and followed him upstairs.

Joel's BMW pulled up into the car park at Frankwright Children's Hospital, and he cut the engine. He reached into the back seat and grabbed one of my tennis racquets. I looked at him curiously.

"This is the one you used in the final at Indian Wells. I thought it might be nice if you gave it to Natalie."

I smiled at Joel. "Wow, that's actually a very sweet idea – I'm surprised!"

Joel winked. "I have my moments."

We found Natalie in the garden. There were a lot of kids there, many with bald heads, their eyes looking like they'd seen too much of the world for their age. Some of them were playing, but most of them were sitting quietly.

I felt my eyes misting up at the thought of the things these kids were missing out on because they were too sick. Like Natalie. By the time I was twelve I was already competing in junior tournaments around Australia. While I hated to think it, she was probably never going to have a chance to compete professionally. She'd lost that chance to cancer.

But it wasn't like I was about to say that to her. Who was I to bust the dream of a sick little girl?

God, why do you pick on children? Why do these tiny kids deserve a fate like this?

I recognised the man from the plane, sitting with a frail little girl in a wheelchair. She looked much younger then twelve. I swallowed my tears as we made our way towards her.

I was about five steps away when she turned and saw me, her little face lighting up with excitement.

"Daddy, it's Mel Black!" she cried, tugging on her father's sleeve.

I smiled down at her, willing the lump in my throat to go away. "Hello, Natalie!" I said, trying my best to sound cheery. "I hear you're a bit of a tennis fan!"

"Yeah!" the little girl exclaimed, staring at me in unmasked awe. If she were any older than she was, if she wasn't sick, I would have found that adulation a little unnerving, but on her it was just sweet.

"Well, I came to give you something, to help you get on your way to a professional tennis career." I held out the racquet to her. "This got me through to the final at Indian Wells, so I like to think it's kind of lucky."

Natalie took the racquet with reverence, unzipping the cover and pulling it out, inspecting all the little scuff marks on it like they were precious. I sneaked a glance at Joel, who had taken a step closer to me, his hand nestling into the small of my back.

"It wasn't luck that got you that far, though, was it Mel?" His hand started rubbing up and down my back in a very distracting way. I tried to ignore it, to focus on Natalie.

"Is he your boyfriend?" she asked bluntly.

I shook my head, feeling myself blush. "No! Joel's not my boyfriend, he's my coach."

Natalie leaned closer to me, gave me a look that asked me to lean closer too. I did.

"Is Pete Levine your boyfriend? Since you had sex with him and all."

I stood bolt upright, the heat in my cheeks exploding into a bonfire. Natalie's father looked mortified.

Joel saved the day. "Natalie, Mel and Pete Levine are two consenting adults, and what they chose to do together should have been private and special between them. But Pete Levine did something that broke Mel's trust, which was a very wrong thing for him to do."

Natalie nodded, accepting Joel's explanation. Her father gave him a look of respect. I gaped at him in shock. I had never expected him to be able to handle awkward situations with such eloquence. I realised with a jolt that I'd never really seen Joel as an adult before. Jokester, yes. Overprotective big brother type, definitely. Grown man …? It was like the world was tilting on its axis, showing me Joel from a different perspective.

I turned back to Natalie, determined to change the subject. "So, Natalie, when you're feeling a bit better, you get your dad to give me a call and I'll come and hit some balls with you." I offered.

Natalie's grin filled her whole tiny little face. "That'd be awesome!" she replied. I leaned down and gave her a hug.

About an hour later, after I'd posed for photos with Natalie and she'd shown me off to some of the other kids in the garden, and I'd answered about a bazillion questions about being a professional sportsperson, Joel ushered me back out of the garden, his hand returning to my back, stroking up and down.

"You hungry?" he asked as we reached the car. He opened the door for me, and it wasn't until I climbed in that he took his hand off my back. It felt almost odd that it wasn't there anymore. I nodded.

"Well, let's go get some lunch. I feel like celebrating." Joel started the car.

I looked at him with interest. "What exactly do you want to celebrate?"

He turned to me, his mouth twitching. "Today's the first time you've officially referred to me as your coach. So does that mean I've got the job?"

I felt my own lips twitching in response. "Joel, you knew you had the job."

His face broke into a toothy grin then. "Yeah, I know, Stink, but all the same, it's nice to hear you say it."

I rolled my eyes. "If I pay you a bonus, will you stop calling me 'Stinky'?"

He laughed then, loudly and joyously. I hadn't seen him so truly happy since before Steve's death.

"Not a chance, Stink."

I punched him playfully on the arm. Sure, he could be a dick a lot of the time, but if I didn't let him get too far under my skin, he was actually a lot of fun to hang around with.

He insisted on buying me lunch. I protested, until we pulled up outside a takeaway shop in Bondi. I didn't mind having lunch bought for me when it was under ten bucks. He winked at me and ordered fish and chips for two. Had I told him at some point that fish and chips were my absolute favourite greasy takeaway?

We carried it across the road to the beach, stopping by the car on the way so Joel could grab out a picnic blanket. We plonked ourselves down on the sand and I tucked straight into the fish – peeling off the batter and eating the scalding fish inside, then wrapping chips in the batter. Joel watched me, an enthralled expression on his face.

"What?" I demanded, scoffing down a batter-clad chip.

Joel snorted. "I've never seen anyone throw back deep-fried food with such … gusto." He sounded impressed. I popped another batter-clad chip into my mouth, grinning at him.

"You know as well as I do that it's all about balance. You'll just have to help me work it off this afternoon."

Joel looked away, clearing his throat. I leaned over and peered into his face.

"Joel Herbert, is that … a *blush*?" I teased, eyeing his face closely. "It *is*! I never thought I'd live to see the day when I could make *you* blush!" I giggled.

Joel turned to me with a leer and pushed me onto the blanket. I sat up and retaliated, pushing *him* down with a laugh.

He righted himself, brushing sand off his arms. "You really want to play this game, Stink?" he asked, as if he was giving me a chance to back down. I shoved him down again with a cheeky snicker.

I wasn't laughing long. He had me pinned on the blanket before I could even blink to register what was happening to me, his body pressed down against mine, lips curling as he gazed down at me.

"Get off me, Joel!" I pushed at his chest.

He chuckled, not budging. "Not until you surrender," he growled. I looked up at him. His sapphire eyes were sparkling.

Suddenly I was all too conscious of his firm body on mine, and of certain parts of his body that were pressing against me in a more than friendly way. I wriggled. He let out a tiny grunt, his hips rocking against me. Heat exploded between my legs.

"Okay, I surrender," I breathed, my chest tight, heart pounding. Joel didn't move an inch.

"Say it like you mean it, Stinky," he whispered. I felt the warmth of his breath on my cheek. He was staring straight into my eyes. Had I never noticed before how pouty his bottom lip was? I tried to speak, but I couldn't find my voice.

Joel's phone rang, rescuing me from a situation that had spiralled completely out of my control. He released me with a huff and sat up, reaching into his pocket and pulling it out.

I could hear the buzz of his voice as he spoke, but the actual words floated over me. I sat up and put my head between my knees. I didn't like the way my breaths were coming shorter and sharper. I didn't like the way my legs felt like they wouldn't be able to support me if I tried to stand.

I *definitely* didn't like the way my heart was beating raggedly in my chest, or the way I ached … everywhere.

"You okay, Stink?" Joel asked, nudging me on the shoulder. I looked up and glared at him. He didn't seem at all affected by having just rocked his semi-hard dick against me.

"What did I do?" he asked.

"You know exactly what you did, Joel!" I accused, the heat of my embarrassment fuelling my anger.

Joel laughed. "Oh, I know. It was fun, wasn't it?"

Yeah, for *him* it might have just been fun, but for me … I wasn't willing to think about that in too much detail. I shook my head.

"Why?" he continued, his voice softer as he moved back towards me, "Was it working?"

I stood up very fast, brushing the sand off my butt. My head swam and I staggered, trying to right myself. He was up beside me in a flash, his hands on my arms, holding me steady.

"Don't, Joel!" I warned crankily. He took his hands off me and held them up in a gesture of surrender. I stomped back towards the car.

"Hey, Mel, wait!" he called after me. He was beside me well before I reached the car. Damn him and his long legs.

"Don't you want to hear who that was on the phone?"

I grunted. Of course, *now* I was curious, but I didn't want to give him the satisfaction of asking.

"Well, I probably should just tell you anyway, seeing as it's about you."

"Who was it, Joel?" I asked, trying to keep my voice disinterested.

"Oh, just your new sponsor, that's all," Joel replied in a voice every bit as disinterested as mine. I stopped with a gasp, turning to him and grabbing him by both arms.

"What?! Who?" I demanded, shaking him. He laughed, but he looked anxious. That worried me.

"Well, you know how I said before that it might be good to look outside the tennis sphere for sponsors?" I nodded, wondering where this was going.

"Well, earlier in the week I was approached by Dudz who are interested in using you as the face of their new range. It would be a twelve-month brand ambassadorship deal, with options to extend for another year at the end. They just called to say that they're all ready to sign."

I felt the puff go out of me. I'd been expecting something really cringe, like tampons, or dildos or something. I'd been all geared up to shout at him and refuse.

"Oh, Dudz. That's pretty cool actually. Why didn't you tell me about it earlier this week?" I asked, mildly curious.

Joel looked sheepish. "Well, I wasn't sure what your reaction was going to be, so I decided to wait until it was certain to bring it up – I figured I'd find a way to talk you around to it."

I raised my eyebrows at him. "You figured you'd be able to talk me round, huh?" I asked, a warning in my voice. Joel smiled down at me, moving closer and putting an arm around my back, pulling me against him.

"Yes, well, I can be pretty persuasive when I want to be," he murmured. I gulped. This was *not* happening to me. I pushed him away before my resolve wavered.

"Okay, here's the deal. You stop trying to seduce me and I'll do the sponsorship with Dudz," I bargained in my most matter-of-fact tone. Joel took a step back and assessed me.

"You drive a hard bargain, Stink. Okay, I'll do my best. But it's just so much fun to see the look on your face!"

I rolled my eyes at him and hopped into the car. "So, what do I have to do for this sponsorship?" I asked. Joel turned the key and the engine roared into life.

"They want to do a photo shoot for online, magazine and billboard advertising, and a TV commercial. And there'll be some in-store appearances when the range comes out."

I shrugged, nodding. I could handle that. I mean, if I could writhe around in lingerie for Woody Magazine, I could have my photo taken in cotton underwear.

We lapsed into silence on the drive back to Joel's house. Silence was bad – my brain went into overdrive. Why was I suddenly having all these … feelings … for Joel?

It had to have been the dreams. If I hadn't had those stupid sex dreams about him, I wouldn't be feeling all hot and bothered when he got too close.

"Joel," I began quietly.

"Hmm?" He didn't take his eyes off the road.

"What would have happened before, on the beach, if your phone hadn't rung?" I asked in a tiny voice. Joel's breaths were suddenly noisier than usual. He pulled into his garage, cut the engine, and turned to me. I couldn't meet his eyes.

"Stink, don't you just wish you knew?" he teased, before getting out of the car. "Come on, we've got a greasy lunch to work off."

I got out of the car, feeling more unsatisfied than I had before I'd asked.

CHAPTER FIFTEEN
Panties & Amazons

"I really don't know if I'm ever going to be able to forgive you for this, Joel," I muttered as I walked towards him, wearing a satin robe over pink lacy lingerie. My dark hair fell in sexy, glossy waves down my back, and I was plastered with more makeup than I'd worn in my lifetime.

A couple of days ago I'd sat down with a female journalist for the interview portion of my Woody feature. I could barely remember how I'd responded to her questions. I just hoped that I'd made the one point that mattered to me – that adventurous sex was great, when everyone involved was fully aware of, and consented to, what was taking place.

The interview was a cakewalk compared to what I was about to do.

"You'll forgive me, Stink," he said, eyes sparkling. "You can't stay mad at me, it's impossible!"

I frowned. "Why do you have to be here, anyway?"

"I can go if you want me to," he offered, turning back towards the house.

I panicked. "No!"

His smile was a thousand watts bright.

"Joel, you got me into this, you have to stay and make sure they don't make me do something really ridiculous."

"Okay, Stinky, I'm not going anywhere." He collapsed into a chair, resting one ankle on the other knee.

"We're ready," the photographer said. I looked around Joel's tennis court, the location we'd agreed on for the shoot.

I slipped out of the robe, tossing it at Joel, and did my best to strut out onto the court in the enormous heels they'd dressed me in. The lingerie was *very* pale pink and *very* see through. I was glad I'd taken Joel's cheeky but no doubt well-meaning advice and had a Brazilian a few days before – nothing worse than pubes peeping through lace underpants.

A tennis racquet is the most unwieldy prop for a sexy photo shoot. I handled it awkwardly as I followed the instructions the photographer called out, but he insisted I was doing just great.

I threw a glance in Joel's direction. He was leaning forward in the chair, his elbows resting on his knees, his mouth slightly open, eyes roving my skin … hungrily.

"Wipe the drool away, Joel!" I called out with a syrupy smile. He leaned back, folding his arms across his chest and sending a sly grin my way as I changed positions for another pose, suddenly feeling much less awkward, and so much sexier, as I watched him watching me.

"Okay, we're done!" the photographer said, satisfied. I held my hand out to Joel for the robe. He pulled it back out of my reach.

"Just let me admire the view for a little longer," he murmured, eyes grazing my breasts, barely contained in the demi-cup bra. I snatched it from him, wrapping myself up self-consciously.

"You know," Joel began as he followed me into the house, "I can enjoy the view just as much in the robe as out of it."

I whirled around then, brow furrowed. "What the hell are you talking about?"

He approached me, stopping about a foot away. "The way this gapes … just here," he murmured, reaching out to touch the robe just below my collarbone, "it taunts me with the tiniest hint of what's beneath."

He traced the fabric down to where it rested against the curve of my breast. I watched his fingers leave a trail of goosebumps on my skin.

"You're panting, Stinky."

I gasped in a mouthful of air and stepped backwards into the bathroom, flinging the door shut in his face. I stripped out of the robe, glancing at my suddenly flushed chest, at the way my nipples were jutting obscenely through the lace bra.

Nope – we're not going there again, I told myself.

"Oh, come on, Mel. I'm a red-blooded male, and those panties …"

I opened the door and stuck my head out. "Can you *please* not use that word!"

"What word?" he asked, holding the door so I couldn't slam it in his face again.

"Panties!" I choked out. "Damn I hate that word!"

He let go of the door, and I shut it again as he guffawed. His laughter retreated as he showed the photographer out.

I finished pulling my clothes back on and stepped out of the bathroom, colliding directly with Joel's chest. He pushed me back inside, against the wall, pressing a finger to my lips to signal that I should be quiet.

I wrenched his hand away.

"What's going on?" I hissed.

He watched me, his eyes dark, worried. "Mel, just stay down here and be *quiet*, for God's sake."

"Why?" I asked.

"Ben."

I gulped, making a gesture as if I was zipping my lips shut. Joel smiled gratefully and slipped back out of the bathroom. I crept to the door and cocked my ear up the stairs. What the hell was Ben doing back in Australia so soon?

Joel opened the front door.

"Ben, what a surprise!" Joel said, his sincerity so believable. Clearly he was a great liar.

"Where is she?" Ben demanded, his voice unrecognisable … sinister.

"She's not here," Joel replied.

"Joel, don't be stupid, you can't hide her from me forever!"

"I'm not hiding *anyone* from you. She's not here."

"Did you think you could keep it a secret from me? Did you think I wouldn't find out? I have a right to speak to her."

"Well, actually, you don't. She doesn't have to see you if she doesn't want to … and there's no secret here." I sent a silent prayer of thanks to God for Joel sticking up for me.

"Oh really? I'm pretty sure that your mother doesn't know about it. How about I tell her?"

"No! Do you really want to upset her like that?" Joel asked.

I was suddenly confused. What was he trying to keep from his mother, to do with me?

"You've been keeping a close eye on her since Steve died, haven't you? What's your interest anyway?"

Were they still talking about me?

"I'm just continuing what Dad had always intended." I smiled at that.

"Well, I'm going to be moving back here now, so you're not going to be able to keep me away from her forever."

That was a threat if ever I'd heard one. This was a side to Ben I was very sure I didn't want to see again.

"Goodbye, Ben," Joel muttered and I heard the front door close again. There was silence, and then footsteps on the stairs. I waited for Joel at the bottom.

"What was *that* all about?" I asked shakily.

"Well, it seems like Ben's moving back to Australia," Joel replied.

I was less than delighted at the prospect, even as I realised that Joel hadn't really answered my question.

"He was talking about me, right?" I asked quietly.

Joel paused, then nodded. "Uh, yeah, he was talking about you. You're going to have to set things straight with him sooner or later."

I swallowed. "Yeah, I know."

"Can you see a trend happening here, Joel?" I asked through the change room door as I pulled on the cotton underpants and matching crop-bra. At least this shoot was happening inside, in front of a white screen, and not in full view of Sydney Harbour.

Joel chuckled. "Yeah, and it's a trend I'm really liking!"

"Pervert," I muttered under my breath. He heard and laughed harder.

I reluctantly unlocked the change room door and stepped out.

Joel eyed me appraisingly, chewing on his bottom lip. "Well, I have to say, I think I like this outfit more than the one from your last photo shoot."

I looked up at him disbelievingly, and then down at the bright turquoise cotton undies and matching bra. Sure, the underpants were quite cheeky – they let a lot of my butt hang out – but it was modest compared to the racy lacy lingerie from the Woody shoot.

He saw the look on my face and grinned. "It's cute in a kind of schoolgirl way," he explained.

I gave him a withering look. "You really are a perve, aren't you?"

He responded by pinching the exposed part of my bum and my stupid body, which clearly hadn't gotten the memo about Joel being a perve, sent a hot throb between my legs at his stupid touch.

"Uh, we have a problem," a tiny, leather-clad woman with black hair and loads of eyeliner said timidly to me. I looked to Joel.

"What's up?" he asked, using the voice he saved for women who weren't me. I scrunched up my nose in distaste – at least, that's what I told myself I was feeling. I hated the little pang in my chest.

"Well, you know that Dudz always launch a women's *and* a men's range?"

Joel nodded, waiting for her to get to the point.

"We had booked a male model to appear in the photos with Mel, to showcase the men's range. But we've just had a call and it turns out that his agency double booked him, and he's gone to the other shoot." She looked chagrined. "We might have to reschedule, if that's okay?"

Joel shrugged. "No need to reschedule – I'll do it if you want."

I gaped at him.

The Goth looking woman eyed him appraisingly. "Let me go and talk to my boss." She trotted off.

"Joel, what do you think you're doing?" I grated from between my teeth.

He grinned. "I'm saving us from having to come back and do this another day." The twinkle in his eyes contradicted his reasonable tone.

I folded my arms across my chest and narrowed my eyes. Well, it wasn't like he couldn't be a model – he had the right body, the right face. The right everything. Damn him!

The little Goth came cantering back. "She's happy for you to do it." She handed over a bundle of men's underwear.

Joel looked over at the Dudz rep: a power-suit clad Amazon with long, straight blonde hair and a pair of rimless glasses, which made her look hot in a dominatrix sort of way. I dragged my eyes away from her as she pulled the glasses down her nose and gave Joel a very suggestive stare over the top of them.

Nope – not going to react, I told myself as that weird pang in my chest throbbed again.

Joel traipsed into the change room that I had just vacated and changed into the men's underwear. I stood outside and tapped my foot impatiently. Or nervously. I wasn't sure what they wanted from this shoot, but posing in underwear with Joel suddenly seemed terrifying. Or exciting. Ugh.

Heels clip-clopped our way, and I turned my head to see Amazon strutting towards me.

"Now, Mel," she began, getting straight down to business. "You know that Dudz is a fun, flirty range of casual underwear." Her face was cold and businesslike.

I nodded, wide eyed. Up close she was even more perfect than from a distance. Did she even *have* pores?

"So, what we need from you and Joel today is fun and flirty. We've decided to go with the tennis angle for the campaign, so we'll start you out posing with racquets, but interacting with each other in a teasing way. Understand?"

I nodded again, but I felt a thrill of nerves tingle through me. Flirting with Joel. This was not good.

The change room door opened, Joel stepping out in a pair of lime green trunks, his ripped chest and shoulders glowing with his golden tan. I bit down hard on the inside of my cheek. He looked so hot! This was *really* not good. I was on a razor-edge of giving in to the hormones raging through me and dry humping his leg.

It's Joel, it's JOEL! I repeated to myself. Somehow it wasn't working as well as it usually did.

"Well, hello stranger," Amazon cooed at Joel. He smiled that heart-melting smile and leaned in to kiss her on the cheek.

"Georgie, great to see you. You look lovely as always." He let his eyes rove over her suit-clad body, as if he was mentally undressing her. Amazon actually *blushed*.

Apparently, Joel could make even the coldest woman feel hot under the collar. I scowled.

Amazon turned back to me. "Okay, let's get this over and done with." Clearly she was hoping to get it finished so she could have lunch with Joel. Or maybe have Joel for lunch.

"What's with the long face?" Joel muttered as Goth handed us a racquet each.

I refused to look at him. "How do you know her?" I asked. He knew exactly who I was talking about.

"I met Georgie at Uni. We got our Bachelor of Business together."

Yeah, I bet that's not all that they 'got' together, either.

"I didn't know you had a degree," I hissed.

Joel smirked at me. "Well, Stink, there are *lots* of things you don't know about me."

Amazon clapped her hands, and I snapped to attention.

"Remember, fun and flirty – *you* shouldn't have a problem with this, Joel." She puckered her lips at him. I almost puked.

"You know it!" he replied with a wink. I took a deep breath and tried to channel fun and flirty. All I got was 'raging hormone monster wanting to devour Amazon woman'.

"You know, I'm thinking about what almost happened the other day on the beach, Stink," Joel whispered in my ear. "Give it a go – but try not to get too excited and leave a wet spot on your cute new panties, okay?"

I wanted to be mad at him, but I just couldn't. I grinned, and suddenly I *was* in a flirty mood. I'd flirt my arse off if I had to.

I turned and smacked him playfully on the butt with the racquet. He smiled cheekily at me and retaliated with the same. The camera clicked frantically, but I wasn't paying attention to it, or to Amazon.

I was just having fun with Joel. Probably too much fun – I could feel my heart hammering against my rib cage as we teased one another, my blood pulsing wildly through my veins, all of it apparently heading south in a rush.

"I want to get some without the racquets," the photographer suggested. I turned and watched as Amazon shook her head.

"I think we've got enough now!" she said sourly.

But then Joel caught me around the waist and pulled me against him. I arched my body towards his, and he reached for my racquet, throwing it and his to the side, his other hand gripping my thigh just below my butt. I bit my lip and allowed my eyes to flick to his for a second, and then away. I couldn't handle the heat in his gaze. I was absolutely leaving a wet patch in my underwear.

His knee pushed my thighs apart, until it was wedged between my legs, his bulging quad pressing right against my pussy.

I could barely breathe.

"I said flirty, not *foreplay!*" Amazon's grouchy snarl snapped me back to reality.

Joel held on for a moment longer than was necessary, leaning down to press his mouth to my ear.

"Good job, Stink, you're very convincing," he murmured. I felt a little shiver go through me as his breath tickled my ear. He let me go, and I tried my best to stay upright, to not let him see my legs shaking.

Amazon clip-clopped her way over to us.

"Very … engaging," she said, giving me a dirty glance before turning her pearly white smile to Joel. I felt a thrill of satisfaction to see that he was clutching his hands in front of his dick. Maybe he wasn't quite as unaffected as he made out?

"You busy this afternoon?" she asked him. "We should catch up over lunch."

Joel smiled even as he shook his head. "I've got to get this girl home for some training," he explained, nudging me with his elbow. "How about dinner?"

I scowled at the way he called me 'this girl', like I was a bratty little child he was babysitting, and not the woman he'd just been grinding up against in front of a camera.

Amazon beamed at him. "Sounds lovely. Shall we meet at George's at eight?"

Joel nodded, and I stomped off to the change room to get dressed. I was pulling my shirt on when Joel zinged the curtain open and walked straight in.

"What are you doing?" I demanded. "I could have been naked in here!"

"That would have been fun," he growled, before turning around and pulling his clothes down off the hook on the wall. I couldn't help but stare at his back – every muscle stood out under his tanned skin.

"How long?" I asked on an angry whim.

"How long what?" His voice was muffled as he pulled his t-shirt on.

"How long did it take you to lose the boner you were sporting after you rubbed your leg on my pussy?"

A laugh barked out of Joel's mouth. "Honestly?"

I snorted. "Are you capable of that?"

"I haven't lost it yet."

Fuck. This was backfiring hugely for me. I was throbbing in every place that was capable of throbbing.

"Ever had sex in a change room before, Stinky?" he asked.

"Are you offering?" I retorted, then bit my lip. I really needed to filter, especially when it came to Joel.

"Well … no."

Disappointment rocked through me.

"I was just wondering what sort of sordid locations you might have had sex in."

"Joel, if you knew some of the places I've had sex, you wouldn't look at me the same again," I blurted. So much for filtering!

He gave me a sharp look, stepping into his shorts. I grabbed my bag and stormed out to the lift, jabbing at the button.

Joel caught up with me just as the elevator dinged, the doors rattling open. I stepped inside and poked the ground floor button.

"Elevator?" he asked, eyes lit like a Christmas tree.

"Uh yes, we're in an elevator, Joel," I replied, using a voice I would use with a very stupid person.

Joel rolled his eyes at me.

"Have you ever *fucked* in an elevator?"

"Um, no. Have you?" I wasn't sure I wanted to know the answer.

Joel chuckled. "We weren't talking about me. You told me I wouldn't look at you the same if I knew where you'd had sex. I'm just trying to test your theory out."

The lift opened at the ground floor and I escaped. Joel kept pace frustratingly easily.

"So, tell me. Where's the naughtiest place you've done the nasty?" he asked, nudging me with his elbow. I pressed my lips together. This was not a good way for me to avoid having sexy thoughts about Joel, but he wouldn't let up until I told him something.

"Okay, you tell me first and then I'll tell you," I bargained.

Joel took a deep breath. "Uh, let me think. Probably in the mosh pit for Princes of Lion two years ago."

"What? As in, in a crowd of sweaty, high teenagers?"

"Yep, it was exactly as bad as you're picturing. It's almost impossible to keep a hard-on when you've got spaced-out teens elbowing you in the back."

I screwed up my face. "Ew, Joel! That is the single most disgusting thing I have ever heard!" For a split second I wished it had been me.

"Your turn now, Stink." Joel sounded ecstatic.

I thought about it. I might only have had three sexual partners, but Grant and I had five years to get pretty adventurous.

"Okay. On the fifty-metre line at Sydney Football Stadium." It didn't sound very adventurous at all compared to Joel's crowded mosh pit. I peered up at him from under my lashes and he was watching me, eyebrows raised.

"How did you get … oh, of course, with *Grant*." Joel muttered, annoyance colouring his tone. Well, that was interesting.

"Yeah, and the sprinklers came on just as I was …" I looked down again.

"Coming?" Joel asked, a smirk in his voice.

"Mm-hmm," I replied awkwardly. "I guess you win. Yours was the kinkiest."

"Yeah, but you're the homemade porn sensation," he responded with a laugh. I cringed.

"Thanks for the reminder, Joel," I muttered. "I just love it that you've seen me like that."

"Oh, me too, Stink." He replied thickly. Something in his voice made me glance curiously at him, but he was looking straight ahead, his face unreadable.

We reached the car. I waited until Joel had started the engine before I asked my next question.

"Are you going to spend the night with Amazon woman?"

Joel looked at me out of the corner of his eye. "You mean Georgie? Why? You're not … *jealous*, are you Stinky?"

I was. And I hated it.

I didn't reply, and for once Joel didn't push me. We made the journey back to his house in silence. I changed into my tennis gear, ready for whatever training Joel had in store for me.

He seemed preoccupied when I went out onto the tennis court. He'd set up the drills he wanted me to do and I started immediately, pushing myself harder than usual, hoping that I could sweat out the swooping sensation that plagued my stomach when I looked at him.

Drills complete, Joel packed everything away, returning with racquets and balls.

"You look tense, Stink. Take it out on the ball."

He served it to me, and I smashed it back at him with as much force as I could muster. It hit him on the shoulder. I saw him wince.

That afternoon I found a way to make myself feel better that Joel would be out with Amazon tonight, while I sat at home and tried *not* to think about what they were doing …

Fuck.

Joel would have a lot of bruises. Maybe he'd be too sore to screw the Amazon. I grinned at that thought and lobbed another ball at him.

He called it quits when I managed to hit him on the upper thigh – too close to his favourite body part for comfort, I guessed.

"You're annoyed at me," he said, a tone of wonder in his voice. "You're *really* annoyed at me this time, not just play annoyed."

I refused to meet his eyes. "So what if I am?" I asked.

"You *are* jealous!" he crowed.

I ignored him to start my cool down, paying particular attention to the stretches the physio had given me for my back. Joel didn't like being ignored. He knelt in front of me, touching two fingers under my chin, pulling it up until our eyes met.

"Stink, I won't go out with her, if that's what's upsetting you." He sounded surprisingly genuine, which freaked me out more. I shook my head, breaking Joel's hold on me.

"No, don't spoil your night on *my* account. I mean, you must be about to explode – you haven't spent the night with a girl for how many days now? Is it into the weeks yet?" I teased, but my voice was strained.

Joel pulled his phone out. "I'm calling Georgie and telling her that I can't make it."

I started to protest, but he leaned over me, clapping a hand over my mouth. I was trapped. I squeezed my eyes tight shut and screamed in my head as he spoke into the phone; I so didn't want to hear his conversation.

He took his hand off my mouth, and I sat up. "What did you do *that* for?" I demanded. "I said it was fine!"

He stared at me and I fell silent.

"You'd better be nice to me tonight, Stink. I have some very good memories with Georgie I could be reliving this evening."

I groaned. "Call her back and tell her you can make it after all," I begged. "I don't know if I have enough energy in me to be nice to you."

Joel cracked a massive smile then. "It's okay, Stinky. It's worth it to know that you're jealous."

I bit my lip to keep from screaming incoherently in my frustration. I *was* jealous. But it wasn't because I wanted Joel. I didn't. I *definitely* didn't.

I just wasn't sure exactly what the reason was.

CHAPTER SIXTEEN

Push & Pull

"You deserve a bit of sightseeing," Joel shouted over the cacophonous buzz of the moped. I clung to his back as he weaved through the narrow laneways of the city. "Semi-final appearances at Madrid and Rome; you're on fire!"

Since my semi-final loss at Internazionali D'Italia, we'd visited the Colosseum, thrown coins in the Trevi Fountain, and eaten a lunch of crusty bread, cold meat and cheese on the Spanish Steps.

Joel had one more surprise in store for our last full day in Rome before we headed to Paris for the French Open.

"I'll explain when we get there, keep your panties on," he'd said when I'd asked for more detail.

I dug my nails tighter into his stomach, the memory of his teasing sending a wave of ... something through me. His muscles contracted under my fingers.

We pulled up on a random bit of pavement – Joel seemed to be quite at home with the Italian method of parking – and he crossed the road, threading between the traffic like a pro, heading towards the stone arch of a stucco building.

"This is the *Basilica di Santa Maria*," he told me in a hushed tone, leading me through the ancient church, through several stone archways and onto a colonnade, hemmed in on one side by the church wall and on the other by barred archways. Tourists were lined up to get up close to a big round stone face with a gaping mouth at the end.

I raised an eyebrow at Joel, who spread his arms wide, grinning.

"Here we are – *La Bocca della Verita*; the Mouth of Truth." Joel explained, passing coins to an attendant as the line progressed us closer. "Legend says that you put your hand in there, and if you've ever lied about anything, it'll bite your hand off."

I gaped at him in horror.

He laughed. "You game?"

I shivered all over. The claim sounded pretty far fetched, but I was a superstitious Catholic after all. I wracked my brain trying to catalogue all my past lies. There had been some doozies.

We reached the front of the queue.

"You go first," I said, pushing him towards it. He looked dubiously at the black gaping mouth for a long time. His hand stretched out towards it. He paused.

"Joel, don't!" I cried. He turned to me, expression grim. What lies had he told to make him feel *that* sick about it?

"Don't do it – I want you to keep both your hands!"

He chuckled but stepped back hastily. "Okay, do you want to do it, or not?"

I shook my head emphatically. The people lined up behind us chortled at our stupidity; we'd just watched over a dozen people pose with their hands in the stupid mouth, with no adverse effects. I dragged Joel to the side, and we left quickly.

Joel was subdued all afternoon. We ate pasta at a little café near the Roman Forum, and he was virtually silent. We returned the moped to the hire place, and walked back towards our hotel, over the Ponte Sant'Angelo. Still nothing.

I was going crazy – Joel was never like this.

My curiosity overwhelmed me as we returned to the apartment. Joel headed towards his room, but I grabbed him by the arm. He looked at me questioningly.

"So, what's your big lie?" I asked.

He refused to meet my eyes. "What do you mean?"

I snorted, keeping a hold of his arm. "I mean, you freaked the fuck out at that stone mouth. And you've been weird all afternoon. What's going on?"

"I don't want to talk about it," Joel said dismissively, pulling his arm out of my grip and turning away.

"Why not?" I demanded.

"It was stupid, I got caught up in the moment. That's all."

He reached his bedroom. I followed, forcing my way into the room even as he tried to close the door on me.

"I don't believe that for a second, Joel."

He barked out an angry laugh. "I don't owe you my secrets, Mel."

I took a step back, shocked. "What?"

"You aren't entitled to know every little thing about me! You don't get to push, and push, and keep pushing until I ..." He dropped his forehead into his hand, thumb and finger massaging his temples.

Irrational fury raged inside me. "Oh, well, while we're on the subject of 'pushing'," I snarled, "*you* don't get to push *me* either!"

"What are you talking about?" he asked wearily, dropping his hand to his side. He looked ... tired.

"I'm ... I mean ..." I stammered, then cleared my throat. "I mean, you keep doing ... things to me, and ..." I looked away, embarrassment scorching across my scalp.

"What things?" His voice was hoarse. "You mean, this sort of thing?"

He took a step closer to me. I took a step back, but his hand snaked around and pressed me to him. My nose was against his chest. I inhaled – woodsy aftershave and warm skin. My legs turned to jelly, his hand on my back the only thing holding me up.

I tilted my face up. His gaze seared me, his lips slightly parted. A little crease furrowed his dark brows, but his eyes were cobalt fire.

One palm held me still, the other slid up the side of my neck, tangling into my hair.

"Do you feel 'pushed' right now, Mel?" he whispered.

I bit my lip. I *wanted* to feel pushed. I wanted him to push me against the wall. I wanted his tongue pushing into my mouth. I wanted that muscular thigh of his pushing between my knees, forcing my legs apart. I wanted him to push my t-shirt up, knead my breasts with those long fingers. I wanted …

"Don't," I pleaded. "Please don't."

Joel's Adam's Apple bobbed as he swallowed. His lips pressed together, thinning. He untangled his hand from my hair and the pressure of his hand on my back disappeared.

"I'm sorry, Mel."

I couldn't respond. I turned and fled, grabbing my bag and running. Out of the room. Out of the hotel.

I wasn't sure it would ever be far enough to subdue these feelings. He pushed me but I was pulled to him.

I can't let this happen.

I couldn't sleep. When I'd returned to our apartment, it had been empty. Hours later, Joel still hadn't returned.

Something big was going on with him, but he wouldn't talk to me. Something was going on with us, but I couldn't think about that right now.

I wanted to text him. Just to be sure that he was okay. But I stopped myself. Fear sat like a stone in the pit of my stomach. I wasn't sure I wanted to know exactly what he was doing tonight. But I thought I might have had a good idea.

I got my answer at about two AM. The apartment door clicked open, then closed. Muffled, slurred words – Joel. Relief turned me boneless. But then, his words were met by a giggle. A high-pitched giggle that was way too feminine to be Joel.

The knot in my stomach swelled, until it was pushing up into my rib cage, squeezing the air out of my lungs.

I crawled deeper under my blankets, pressing my pillow around my ears as the bedroom door next to mine snicked closed, but it didn't shut out his low chuckle, and that grating, squeaky giggle on the other side of the wall.

I had no right to feel the way I did. I had no claim on Joel, and I didn't want one either. Yes, I felt things with him, but that was an itch I was never, ever going to scratch. It would be disastrous.

But I also didn't want him to be in the room beside mine, murmuring and moaning and making some other girl cry out, while I had to listen. I didn't want that at all.

***

"Bit too much to drink last night?" I asked Joel coldly as the plane reached cruising height and he unbuckled his seat belt.

"Something like that," he muttered, cracking open the complimentary peanuts and tipping half the packet into his mouth.

"Any hole in a storm," I commented, grabbing the in-flight magazine out of the holder and leafing through it as if I could read Italian.

"Any … what?"

I glanced at him out of the corner of my eye. His body was turned towards mine, his eyes slightly bloodshot, which somehow intensified the blue of his irises.

"I mean, you were clearly hard-up last night. You almost tried to jump *me*, and when I rebuffed you, you disappeared for hours, and then brought some random hole-with-a-heartbeat back to our room and had loud, drunken sex at three in the morning."

Joel made a weird, strangled sound. Was he choking on a peanut? I looked at him, worried, before realising with rising frustration that he was laughing.

"What the fuck is funny about this, Joel?" I demanded. He guffawed harder, reaching for the bottled water.

"Any hole in a storm – that's going in the phrasebook!"

I found my own lips curling at the corners as I realised my mistake. His laugh had always had an infectious quality to it.

"I meant, any port in a storm. Or maybe any hole's a goal – I don't know."

"Any hole in a storm is my new favourite saying!" Joel shook with laughter for a long moment, then took a deep breath, had a sip of water, and was suddenly completely sober.

"Mel, I'm sorry about what happened last night. I shouldn't have brought someone back to the room. It was really inconsiderate of me. I should have thought about how much it would upset you."

"Upset me?" I asked, looking back at the magazine so he wouldn't see the consternation on my face. "It kept me awake, that's about all it did. How drunk were you, anyway?"

He sighed. "Drunk enough that I can't even remember what her face looked like."

"She couldn't have been that memorable then, could she?" I asked cuttingly.

"She doesn't even rate as the most memorable woman I touched in the last twenty-four hours."

Why did that make my chest jolt?

"How many women did you touch yesterday, exactly?" I managed to ask over the sudden tightness in my lungs.

"Just one other."

I could not respond to that. Instead, I stared out the window, white, fairy floss clouds below, blinding sun all around.

When I had myself under some semblance of control again, I turned back to him, all business now.

"Okay, Joel. I'll forgive you. But if we're going to do this – work together I mean – we need some ground rules. First, no bringing other people back to the room."

Joel nodded.

"Second, no going out for hours on end without telling the other person where you're going, or when you'll be back. We're here to work, not to play." He nodded again, a little amusement creeping onto his face.

"Third –" but I didn't get to a third, because the plane shuddered, and I lost my train of thought. I closed my eyes. It got worse. I could feel the sweat on my palms as I clawed the armrests.

And then his hand was on my face, stroking. I couldn't open my eyes, so I just let him touch me until the shaking (both the plane's and mine) stopped. I opened my eyes. Joel was leaning close, his thumb on my cheek.

"It's okay, Mel. It's going to be okay," he whispered. I felt my body relax slightly. The seat belt light went off with a ding. Joel undid his belt, moving closer and wrapping his arms around me until I was cocooned in them. I didn't protest. I was so exhausted from the turbulence that I had no strength to argue with him.

I felt his lips brush my forehead once. I just let it happen.

When I felt calm enough, I spoke. "Hey, Joel," I began.

"Yeah?" he replied quietly.

"You know how I said once that if you'd been my big brother, I would have killed you by the time I was twelve?"

"I remember."

"Well, I'm glad you're not … my brother that is. Because if you were, I *would* have killed you, and then you wouldn't be here to act all big brotherly now when I need you."

He laughed into my hair. "I'm glad I'm not your brother too, Stinky."

I didn't know how to interpret that comment, so I decided not to try.

CHAPTER SEVENTEEN

In The City Of Romance

Paris. The city where people supposedly fall in love. You'd think that some of that atmosphere might have rubbed off on me.

You'd be wrong. I was about as far from feeling romantic as it was possible to be.

Playing on clay is in my opinion the most exhausting tennis you can play. You have to work twice as hard to get the same result as you would on pretty much any other surface. And I had spent the last ninety minutes working my arse off. Sweat dripped from me as I returned hopefully the last ball to Gordana Slavanisovich.

It *was* the last ball – a drop shot after a rally where I'd kept her out deep. She skidded for it on the slippery clay court and missed. I won the third set and the match.

The game ended to applause, and I wiped my forehead on my sweatband as I walked into the net to shake her hand.

"Vun day, Melanie Black, I vill beat you," Gordana muttered to me as we clasped each other's arms over the net. I smiled a little nervously at her – with her eastern European accent, it was hard to tell whether it was a joke or a threat. But she returned my smile pleasantly enough, so I guessed she meant it in a friendly way.

Joel was practically bursting with excitement when I arrived in the change room, where an ice bath was waiting for me. I stripped down to my underwear and sunk into it, gasping a little at the temperature.

"Great job, Mel! You were awesome out there!" He was grinning from ear to ear.

I rolled my eyes. "Jesus, Joel, you'd think I'd just won Wimbledon or something!"

He laughed at me. "Stink, if you think this is enthusiastic, wait till you *do* win Wimbledon!"

I smiled, starting to relax as the iciness took over.

"Okay, I doubt I'll ever win Wimbledon, but thank you for your support. It's just thrilling!" I couldn't help the teasing tone that slipped into my voice.

He sat on the bench beside the ice bath. "You know what's *really* thrilling?" he asked, his voice deep, "The thought of how hard your nipples would be right about now."

I crossed my arms over my boobs under the water. My nipples were as hard as rocks, and throbbing just from his words, his gaze.

"You are disgusting, Joel!" I snapped, but relief coursed through me. Things had been a bit off between us since our fight in Rome. Somehow, his teasing innuendo comforted me, reassuring me that everything could go back to normal.

"I think I've figured out why you've never had a long-term girlfriend," I continued, keeping my tone cheeky. "It's because you only know how to talk dirty and don't have a clue how to romance a girl."

Joel grinned widely. "That sounds like a challenge!"

I groaned and hopped out of the bath, gritting my teeth and stripping off my wet underwear, running the shower to a steamy temperature. Joel watched me from his seat. I glared at him.

"You know, Joel, it's kind of annoying that you've seen me naked loads of times, and I've *never* seen you naked. It's a bit of a double standard, don't you think?"

Joel stood up and stripped off his shirt, one eyebrow raised and a smirk curving his lips. "Should we rectify this glaring double standard?" He started to undo the drawstring on his shorts.

I froze at the sight of his broad, shirtless chest, my core

clenching at the thought of him under the hot water beside me, naked. I came to my senses just in time.

"No! Don't be gross!"

Joel huffed out a little laugh under his breath, and tied his shorts back up, pulling his shirt back on over his head.

"Is it alright if I take off for a bit, Stink? Are you right to find your way back to the hotel?" he asked, leaning against the wall and continuing to stare at me disconcertingly as I towelled dry. My head jerked towards him.

"Why? You want to go find some French hussy to bang?" I asked sharply. Joel's smile widened.

"Let me check the weather first. I can only go looking for a hole if there's a storm predicted."

"Ha-ha!" I said sarcastically. His smile faded.

"That's never going to happen again, Mel. I promise."

Earnest Joel was too much for me to take. I busied myself looking around for my bag. Joel leaned over and pulled my clean underwear out of it, passing it to me. The thought of him touching my stuff in such a familiar way sent another jolt through me. Nope, I didn't need to think about Joel touching my underwear.

I dressed hurriedly, shouldering one bag. Joel grabbed the other one and we walked out together. My hair was wet from my shower, sticking to the back of my shirt. I moved my head a couple of times to try and dislodge it, but I wasn't having any luck.

Joel reached out and slipped his hand under my hair, just at the nape of my neck. He freed it, running his fingers through it a couple of times. I tried to give him a grateful smile, my heart hammering at a million miles an hour, my skin rising into goosebumps where he'd touched me.

It's Joel! You know, the big brother you never had. Except big brothers didn't touch their sisters the way he touched me. Big brothers didn't joke about getting naked in the shower with their sisters.

Fuck.

We packed the stuff into a hire car and I climbed into the back seat. Joel leaned in and gave the driver the hotel address, speaking in infuriatingly perfect French.

"I'll see you back at the hotel in a couple of hours, okay?" he asked. I nodded, but before I could ask what he was doing, he closed the door and the car pulled away.

He was up to something, I could tell. I just didn't know what it might be. I *shouldn't* want to know so badly.

It was actually a relief to have some Joel-free time that afternoon. I didn't realise how much effort it was taking to keep my distance, until he wasn't there anymore, and I didn't have to keep up the pretence.

Back at the hotel I did some stretches for my back, ate lunch from room service, and ran a brush through my now dry hair. I was just about to do some channel surfing when the door clicked open and Joel walked in, a large paper bag in his hands and a look of intense satisfaction on his face.

"What's for dinner?" I asked, stretching out on the sofa. Joel put the bag down on the little bench in the kitchenette.

"It's a surprise. Now go get dressed."

I looked down at my yoga pants and t-shirt in confusion. "I *am* dressed."

"Just put on some jeans and shoes, okay?"

I shrugged and stood up, heading for my own room. I dragged on a pair of jeans. I changed my t-shirt for a low-cut long-sleeved top – the nights in Paris at this time of year were quite cool. I chucked on a pair of sneakers and finger-combed my hair.

"Do I look presentable?" I asked as I met Joel back in the living room. His eyes roved over me, pausing for slightly too long on my cleavage. I squirmed under his gaze.

"Maybe take a scarf – it could be cool out tonight," he suggested, lifting the paper bag off the bench. I retrieved my scarf and Joel held the door open for me.

"Where are we going?" I asked, a little disgruntled. "I don't like surprises."

Joel smiled smugly at me. "I thought we could dine alfresco tonight."

As we climbed into an Uber, I peeked suspiciously at him out of the corner of my eye. He noticed, grinning at me.

"Just go with the flow for once, Mel! Believe it or not, I'm actually not trying to annoy you tonight."

It was a short trip, and when we got out Joel gripped me gently by the elbow and steered me.

The night was cool and a little crisp, but the air was still and the sky was clear. We couldn't see the stars; a small country could have been powered for a year with the amount of electricity Paris used to light all its fancy landmarks.

Joel led me onto a wide bridge stretching over the River Seine. Lamp posts dotted little patches of brighter light along either side, and there were benches at intervals all the way down the centre. At the far end was an absolutely stunning building with a large dome, directly at the end of the bridge.

"*Le Pont Des Arts*," he explained, gesturing to the bridge. He reached into the paper bag and pulled out a picnic blanket. I gaped in stunned silence as he led me further onto the bridge.

There were people everywhere, sitting on the bench seats or leaning against the railing taking in the view. Some people were sitting on the ground, eating or chatting and laughing with each other.

Joel spread the blanket out to one side of the bridge and sat down, his back against the railing. He patted the space beside him, and reluctantly I sat. He started unpacking things from the bag: olives and cheeses and cold meats and bread and fruit. I gawked at him in astonishment.

"What are you doing?" I asked.

"I'm making you dinner," he replied with a smirk. "Same as I do every night when we're travelling."

I leaned back against the railing and watched. Finally he pulled out a bottle of red wine and two plastic wine cups. He poured a small one for me and a slightly bigger one for himself.

"That's all the wine you're allowed tonight, seeing as you have a quarter to prepare for, so you'd better make it last," he warned in a teasing tone. He clinked his cup against mine and took a sip. I stared down at the wine, at the array of beautiful food, and then back at him.

"This feels a little too much like a date for my liking," I muttered, sure that he could hear the thunder of my heartbeat. I looked away from him, straight at a couple who were kissing each other like there was no tomorrow, their hands wandering to places that it just wasn't appropriate for them to wander in public. Definitely the wrong place to look – it made me wonder what it would be like to be doing that with Joel.

"Don't get too excited, Stink. It's just dinner." Joel was already filling a plate with food. He passed it to me and then made one for himself.

I ate in silence. Joel was up to something. Even when I wasn't looking at him, I could feel the warmth of his eyes on me.

It wasn't until I finished my wine and felt the alcohol singing gently in my blood, that I decided it didn't really matter what he was up to, and that I should just enjoy a nice evening out with him.

"What's that building over there?" I asked, pointing towards the domed structure I'd noticed earlier.

"That's *l'Institut de Francais*," he replied. "It's a museum – it used to be a learning academy."

"And that's …" He pointed to the other side of the bridge we were on, where another equally spectacular building was nestled behind some trees, "*Musée du Louvre*."

I gasped, more at the husky purr of Joel's perfect French pronunciation than at all the incredible things that would be inside that building.

"You want to do the most touristy thing possible in Paris?" he asked, clearing the empty containers back into the paper bag. I couldn't help the grin that spread on my face.

"Really? It's open at night?" I didn't try to hide the excitement in my voice, and Joel beamed at me.

"Yep, it's open until late. The views at night are incredible."

I leapt to my feet. "What are we doing then, let's go!"

Joel's laughter bubbled over as he stood up, folding up the blanket we'd been sitting on and draping it over his shoulder. He put a hand on my arm and swung me so that I was facing the water of the river. He pointed towards the tourist attraction we were heading off to see. I couldn't believe I hadn't noticed it when we arrived.

"Watch," he whispered. I kept my eyes locked on the Eiffel Tower, which suddenly twinkled with what looked like millions of fairy lights. I couldn't tear my gaze away from it, but at the same time I was all too aware of Joel's arm pressed up against mine as we both leaned on the railing.

The show went on for a little while, and then the twinkling stopped, and the Tower went back to glowing in the Paris night.

I turned to Joel, who seemed to be trying not to laugh – his lips kept twitching further and further up at the corners.

"What's so funny?" I asked, my voice dreamy. Joel's smile widened.

"Just watching you is entertainment enough for me tonight." He started walking back towards the street and I followed. I wanted to know what he meant, but I couldn't find the courage to ask.

"When did you learn to speak French?" I asked instead.

"I spent a year here on an exchange program in high school," he replied carelessly, tossing the paper bag into a rubbish bin as we passed it.

"Really? What did your dad think about that?" I asked.

"He didn't mind so much. I stayed with a tennis family, so I played a lot. He didn't care where I was, as long as I was keeping up with my training. Mum was the one who pushed me to do it; she could tell that I needed some time away from Dad. We were constantly arguing back then."

"How old were you?" I asked.

"Sixteen."

"What else did you do, apart from play tennis?'" I asked.

Joel chuckled. "Oh, I had a lot of sex," he murmured. "French girls are *very* adventurous."

I rolled my eyes. "Of course you were having a lot of sex!" I snapped. "That seems to be all you ever do!"

Joel turned his blazing eyes to me as he hailed down a taxi to take us to the Eiffel Tower.

"You know, Mel, since I started spending every day with you,

I've been having a lot less than usual. The … Rome was the first in … months."

My heart skipped a beat.

"Oh, sorry, am I taking up too much of your valuable fucking time?" I asked in a sarcastic whisper.

Joel snickered. "No, Stink. I've just re-prioritised my life a little bit, that's all. Don't get me wrong, sex is still up there, but at the moment helping you with your career is more important to me."

The closer we got to the tower, the more my excitement grew. I forgot about the conversation with Joel and sat staring intently out the window as the tower loomed closer and closer.

Joel asked the taxi to stop a little way out, where there was still a great view along the broad avenue towards the tower, shining like a beacon in the night.

"It's so beautiful," I whispered. Joel took my hand. I was so shocked that I didn't try to brush him off. His fingers linked through mine, warm and strong. I realised I didn't particularly want to let go.

As we arrived at the base of the tower, the line for the elevator was relatively short. We took our place behind a couple who had their hands in each other's back pockets. I recognised them as the couple I'd been trying not to look at back on the bridge – the ones who hadn't been able to keep their hands off each other. As I watched they turned to each other again and kissed, their tongues slipping into each other's mouths.

I peeked up at Joel, finding him smirking down at me. I let my gaze slide away from him as if I had just been glancing around.

"What're you thinking about, Mel?" Joel asked, his breath tickling my ear. I jumped and turned to face him.

"Nothing really. Just enjoying being here," I lied, gazing up towards the top of the tower.

"Don't tell me you're actually enjoying hanging out with me, Stink," Joel said in a mock scandalised tone.

I pursed my lips while I thought of an appropriate come back. "Well, it could be worse, I guess."

Joel chortled. "Admit it, you're loving every second you spend with me."

I huffed. "Maybe you should admit that it's really *you* who's enjoying being with *me*."

Joel leaned closer. "Can't we both … maybe … just admit that we like hanging out with each other?"

I'm sure that I would have come up with some incredibly witty retort, but at that moment we reached the front of the line for the elevator, and I was saved from having to reply as we stepped inside. We shared the ride with a few other people, including the canoodling couple.

I scowled at Joel as the elevator inched its way towards the top of Paris's most famous landmark. He grinned back and reached out to pinch my chin gently.

"I've told you before how cute you look when you're cross, haven't I, Stink?"

I really couldn't stay mad at him, even though he drove me nuts. I bit my lip to try and stop the smile, but it broke free anyway.

"You look cute when you're smiling too," he murmured, his fingers straying towards my cheekbone. I stopped breathing for just a second – long enough that the parts of me that I didn't want responding to Joel started aching with desire.

The elevator doors clinked open, and I realised that I hadn't even been paying attention to the views – I'd been so focussed on Joel. But it turned out that we were only on the first observation level, and we had to change elevators to get up to the very top.

Joel led me over to the other elevator, the canoodling couple following us.

I stared out at the twinkling lights of Paris below as the lift took us higher and higher, but my head kept wanting to turn to where I could feel Joel watching me.

When the doors clinked open at the top, I rushed out. My heart was hammering, I hoped from the excitement of being at the top of the Eiffel Tower, and not because of Joel.

"Oh, my *God*! It's *sooo* beautiful!" the canoodling girl exclaimed in a strong British accent. They headed straight to the edge, staring out over the city. I moved to the edge also, gazing down at the glow of Paris, spread far below. Joel stood beside me, his arm just brushing mine.

"Not as beautiful as you are," the canoodling guy replied to his girlfriend. I smiled. What a clichéd line.

"Oh my God, oh my *God!*" the girl shrieked. I turned, wondering what she had seen that was so exciting.

Canoodling guy was kneeling in front of his girlfriend, holding out an absolutely *ginormous* diamond ring, while she fanned her face and looked like she was about to pass out.

"Jess, will you marry me?" the guy asked. Jess's knees wobbled and she held out a shaking left hand, her ring finger extended.

"Oh my God, yes!" she squealed and he slipped the ring on her finger. And then he was on his feet and they were canoodling harder than ever.

"Oh," I sighed, turning back to the barrier and the city far below me.

"Would you class that as a pretty romantic gesture then, Stink?" Joel whispered beside me. There was something odd in his tone.

I turned to him with an incredulous expression. "Yes, wouldn't you?"

He smiled at me, his teeth glinting pearly white in the night. "It's up there." His voice took on a different tone. He sounded almost … nervous.

"Mel, there's something I've been meaning to ask you for a while now." He stared at me intently. I wanted to look away, but I found that I couldn't.

"What, Joel?" I breathed.

"Well, we've been spending a lot of time together lately, and, well, I thought that maybe, you and I … this isn't coming out the way I'd hoped." Joel sounded flustered – he *never* sounded flustered. I couldn't breathe.

"Okay, I'm just going to come straight out and ask you." His hand went into his jacket pocket and he started fishing around. My own hand went to my heart, which felt like it was about to take flight out of my chest. Joel had something hidden in his hand. He started to lower himself down onto one knee.

"Joel, what are you doing?" I asked breathlessly. He couldn't be … no he definitely wasn't.

Except he was.

"Melanie Black, will you …" he paused for effect. I clapped my fingers over my mouth.

He reached his clasped hand up towards mine and turned it, so his fingers were facing upwards. His hand started to open.

"… share this Caramello Koala with me?" he finished, his palm flat, revealing a single wrapped piece of my favourite chocolate in the world. I let out the breath I'd been holding in a giant gust. Joel's laughter burst from him. I slapped his shoulder.

"Get up and stop making a fool out of both of us!" I hissed. He got to his feet, still chuckling. I stomped away.

When you're on the observation deck of the Eiffel Tower, there's really nowhere to go except back down again. I wasn't ready to do that – we'd paid enough money to be here, I wasn't cutting my experience short.

So, Joel caught up with me quite quickly.

"Oh, come on, Stinky, it was a bit funny, admit it."

I leaned against the railing and shook my head emphatically.

"Seriously, Mel, you didn't *actually* think that I was proposing, did you?" Joel didn't sound so teasing now.

I managed to turn and glare at him. "Of course I didn't! I had *no* idea what you were doing." I turned away, back towards the city below. A breeze gusted through and I shivered. Joel put an arm around me.

"I told you it would get cool tonight." He picked up my hand and turned it over, putting the Caramello Koala into it.

"You don't have to share it if you don't want to, Stink."

I looked down at the chocolate. "Good, I won't!"

I unwrapped it, taking a bite from the feet first. In my head I replayed the look on Joel's face as he'd gotten down to present me with the little chocolatey piece of heaven that I was devouring now. I felt my lips starting to twitch. It *was* actually quite funny, now that I'd gotten over the shock of it. I didn't want it to be funny, but it was. I wanted to be mad at Joel, but being mad at him was such hard work lately. It never used to be.

All I had left of the chocolate was the head, and I was all too aware of Joel's arm still around me, his hand rubbing my arm, keeping me warm. I looked at the last little bit of deliciousness and I sighed, holding it out to him.

"Okay, I'll share."

"Really? The head's your favourite part!" he replied, humbled. I took his hand and opened his palm the way he had done to me and popped the bit of chocolate into it.

"Yes, really. But how did you know the head is my favourite?" I asked, not daring to look into his eyes. He put the piece in his mouth.

"I've watched you eat enough of them to have worked it out, Stink."

I did turn to him then. He wasn't chewing – he was letting it melt in his mouth, just like I would have. He gazed at me, a fierce light glinting in his eyes. His body moved closer, his leg resting up against mine. I leaned closer. He leaned closer.

His Adam's Apple bobbed as he swallowed the last of the chocolate. I could smell the sweetness of caramel on his breath. His lips were so full, if I just moved a fraction closer, I could have tasted them.

He moved first and there it was. The tiniest brush of his mouth against mine.

No, Mel!

I turned my head very quickly to the side, shivering, although I was feeling very warm right at that moment. I put my hand up and pulled my hair over my shoulders, as if it could protect me from the fierce need inside me.

"It's getting late and cold. I don't want to wake up cramped in the morning," I muttered. I knew my cheeks were bright pink. For once Joel didn't comment and I was grateful for that. I was completely incapable of coherent conversation.

"Okay, Stink, let's get you to bed." He used the business-like tone of my coach, but in my head all I could picture was *him* getting into my bed too.

And that was something I couldn't *ever* let happen.

CHAPTER EIGHTEEN

Drop Dead

We had three weeks until Wimbledon. We'd flown home, even though staying in Europe would probably have made more sense, because Joel still felt bad about leaving Sandra alone. I totally got it. I wanted to be home too, even if just for a fortnight.

The first morning back in my apartment, I got up late, eating a couple of slices of toast and sipping at my latte while staring out my kitchen window. It was raining. I texted Joel and asked if I could have a day off training. He replied immediately.

> Joel: Of course, Stink, just try not to miss me
> too much x

I rolled my eyes as I grabbed my umbrella and raced out to the letterbox. That would be my exercise for the day.

The letterbox was stuffed with the usual bills and a large, padded envelope, damp at the edges, from Allied Australian Publications. My mouth twisted in confusion as I took the stairs two at a time back to my apartment.

Discarding the bills, I ripped into the parcel, pulling out three copies of Woody.

In the picture they'd chosen to use for the cover I was kneeling on the court, gripping the handle of the racquet in an overtly phallic way. There was a handwritten note from the journalist who had interviewed me attached to the cover with a paperclip.

Mel, I hope I've done your story justice – and that our readers don't miss the point entirely (spoiler alert, they might …), Kayla

I slid the note away, to see the headline they'd used for the cover story. *'I LOVE HOT SEX!'*

Oh, for fuck's sake. I rubbed my forehead. This was totally not the message I'd been trying to get across. But of course, sex was always the focus. And then I read the smaller print under the headline.

'As long as you get my consent first.' Mel Black talks tennis, relationships, and the infamous sex tape. Page 27.

I flicked through until I reached the feature. Another shot of me lying down, arching my back, filled one page. But there was a full article beside it. I glanced at the quote that had been highlighted in bold.

"I love exploring my sexuality, there's nothing better than trying new things in bed. But me consenting to get adventurous with a partner isn't blanket permission for them to act out their own fantasies without my knowledge."

I laughed giddily as I devoured the article in its entirety. Kayla had indeed done the best she could. If it got through to just one horny teenage boy the importance of communication and consent, then I'd feel like the shit with Pete had all been worth it … somehow.

By late morning I was stir crazy. I almost called Joel to ask him to pick me up and train me. But then I mentally slapped myself

Instead, I called an Uber, and spent four hours and untold sums of money at the local Eastmeadow Shopping Centre.

Thoroughly retail-therapied out, I walked in the door of my apartment and plonked my purchases down on the kitchen table. Something fluttered to the floor.

Melanie, the creamy paper read. I unfolded the note.

Mel,

I don't know if Joel told you, but I'm back in Australia – to stay. I dropped by to visit you, but you weren't home. I would really like to see you soon, if you're not busy. I'm staying

at my investment apartment in Kirribilli: 901/27 North South Road, until I get a chance to go house hunting. It would be lovely to see you. Drop by tonight if you get a chance.

Love, Ben

I looked away from the paper. I wasn't sure that I wanted to see him, after the conversation I'd overheard him having with Joel. He'd sounded frighteningly possessive. I thought I'd made it pretty clear that I wasn't interested.

I sank down into a chair at my kitchen table and thought back over the conversation I'd had with Ben in Dubai. I'd told him I wasn't interested, hadn't I?

No, I hadn't. I'd told him that there was no point in starting something up when he lived in Dubai and I was in Australia. Damn it! I'd thought I was letting him down easy. How was I supposed to know that he'd take it way too literally and move back here?

God, what should I do?

No answer.

I put my head in my hands. I couldn't come up with a solution on my own. I couldn't ask Joel, for a thousand different reasons.

And then another thought hit me. How the fuck had the note made its way to my kitchen table? If he'd dropped by while I was out, the most he could have done was slip it under my door. I shivered, suddenly feeling cold and very alone in my usually cozy apartment.

Someone had been in here while I was out. Amanda had known that I'd gotten home last night; I'd texted her so she wouldn't wake me early in the morning on her way home from work, thinking she needed to give Connor his morning feed.

There was one other option.

I stood up, took a deep breath, picked up the phone and dialled.

"Hello?" my mother's prim and proper voice answered.

"Hi, Mum," I began. I opened my mouth to speak again, but she didn't let me.

"Melanie! I can't believe you would do this to me! I feel like I can't show my face in church ever again!"

"Are you talking about Woody Magazine, Mum?" I asked.

"I'm talking about *everything*! What's gotten into you? I've heard stories about this … video … and now you're in your unmentionables on the cover of a sleazy men's magazine! And Maureen Turner told me that when she was dropping her daughter to work the other day, she saw a giant poster of you at Chatswood Eastmeadow, wearing underwear and spanking some boy with a tennis racquet!

"I didn't get you into tennis so that you could make an exhibition of yourself in this way! Your behaviour is getting completely out of hand. Have you been to confession yet? Because I'm getting very tired of always telling Father Shannon that you're just busy and you'll pop by to see him soon."

She stopped to take a breath and I jumped in.

"Okay, Mum, you listen to me!" I said. "What I do with my body is nobody's business but mine. If I decide that I want to pose *naked*, I'll do it. So you can just go tell Maureen Turner that she can stick it! And the 'boy' who's posing with me, that's *Joel*, Mum – remember? The son of the man who made me the player I am today. Mum, you've known him and his family for almost *six* years now!

"I don't play tennis because I want to make an exhibition of myself. I play because I love it and because I'm good at it. You haven't even spoken to me since before Indian Wells – did you know I made it to the final? Did you know that I'm now ranked in the top twenty female players in the world? I'm achieving my dream here, Mum!

"No I haven't seen Father Shannon yet and I don't plan on visiting him anytime soon. So you'd better stop making him promises that you can't keep.

"I don't want you snooping around my house when I'm not here. Either stay out, or I'll change the locks. I'm sick of you butting into my life!"

I hung up before she had a chance to speak again. She'd probably read the letter from Ben instead of just leaving it on the table. That would have been her style.

I collapsed onto the lounge, all energy sapped from me. It had always been this way with Mum – fiery screaming matches that left me drained immediately after.

I sent a group text to Brad and Amanda:

> Mel: SOS guys – need relationship advice stat!

Amanda replied within ten seconds.

> Mandy Moo: Be there in thirty. OK if Thomas comes too?

> Mel: Yep!

I grabbed a packet of rice crackers and cracked open a cold bottle of white wine and poured myself a glass.

By the time I heard the knock on the door, I was a little tipsy. Amanda and Thomas were outside, Amanda holding wine.

"Sounded like this might be needed," she explained. I toasted her with my half empty glass and grabbed two more from the cupboard.

"Oh, none for me," Amanda said. "I've got a shift at the hospital at nine-thirty. I can stay until then, but I can't drink."

"Thomas?" I turned hopefully to him. He nodded, accepting a glass from me. I threw him a grateful smile.

Another knock at the door. Brad grinned at me from the other side, holding up a bag of Chinese takeaway. I grabbed bowls and chopsticks, and we all moved to the kitchen table.

"So, what's the big dilemma?" Amanda asked, popping a dim sum into her mouth.

I scooped up a piece of honey chicken and chewed while I thought about where to start.

"Okay, so you remember that day that you came round to Joel's place, before I went to Dubai?" The three of them nodded, waiting for me to elaborate.

"Well, you remember Ben, Joel's uncle?" They nodded again.

"Oooh, the hot one!" Amanda said. Thomas threw her a mock hurt look and she grabbed his hand.

"Hot for Mel, not for me! You know I'm super turned on by your whole non-threatening nerd vibe!"

Thomas barked out a laugh. "Yep, I don't feel completely emasculated right now!" But he turned and pressed a kiss to her temple, and she snuggled in closer.

Jesus, I wanted what they had so damn bad.

"Yeah, that's Ben. Well, turns out he has a … bit of a thing for me. We stayed at his place in Dubai while we were there, and some … stuff happened between us."

Amanda was virtually bouncing out of her seat; she loved my spicy drama. Thomas watched with polite interest, I guess not really knowing what to expect next.

Brad … his face was frozen the way I imagine someone looks when they're trying not to be completely disgusted.

"Okay, so he seemed like a sweet, nice kind of guy. But, in the bedroom … oh my God, it was awful. Like, the worst sex you could possibly imagine; he was just completely clueless. But I didn't realise until after that he was into me for more than just … you know. Well, he did say a couple of weird things, but I didn't … well, I assumed it was just casual, or I would never have …

"Anyway, I told him that I thought there wasn't any point in starting something, seeing as he lives on the other side of the planet. He seemed a bit upset, but he took it pretty well."

I stopped to take a mouthful of wine and stuffed some fried rice into my mouth.

"So, what's the problem then?" Amanda asked, confused. Brad looked at me with an expression of horror on his face.

"Well, uh, it seems that he's decided that he likes me enough that he's moved back here."

Amanda gasped. Brad shook his head. Thomas looked from Amanda to Brad to me.

"Is your life always full of so much drama, Mel?" he asked.

I laughed nervously. "It didn't used to be," I replied. "This must just be my year for it."

I went on to tell them about the note, and about the conversation I'd heard him have with Joel before we'd left for Rome.

"So, I guess I'm even keener now to make sure he doesn't continue having the wrong impression about us."

Brad eyed me, brows drawn. "Mel, you should have told him the truth before. He's come back here for you, because you gave him the wrong impression! You should have made it clearer that it wasn't going anywhere. Hell, maybe you shouldn't have jumped into bed with yet another rando."

"I know that, Brad!" I snapped. "But I can't go back and change the past, can I?"

"Can I add something here?" Thomas asked. I shrugged, hoping he wasn't going to ream me out like Brad.

"I kind of think what you're saying is a bit unfair, Brad. This Ben dude, he didn't speak to Mel even once to talk to her about his plans to move back … did he, Mel?"

I shook my head, liking this guy more and more.

"I don't think it's fair to lay all the blame on Mel. Yeah, she should have probably made it clearer to him to begin with," he flicked an apologetic glance at me, "but he still had no reason to believe that moving here was any guarantee that Mel would be with him."

"Thank you, Thomas!" I cried, throwing a hard look at Brad, who refused to meet my eyes.

"So … do I confront him tonight, and tell him the truth, or avoid him and hope he gets the message?"

"Mel, you have to go and tell him tonight," Amanda said. "Thomas is right, Ben acted on a crazy assumption. But you don't need this hanging over your head. Get it over and done with and move on."

She stood. "And I really have to go to work now."

I stood too and she kissed me on the cheek. "Good luck, Smellie. Let me know how it goes."

Amanda held out a hand to Thomas, and I walked them both to the front door.

"Hey, thanks Thomas, for being in my corner tonight," I said. He smiled briefly at me and ushered Amanda out.

Leaving me alone with a stony-faced Brad.

"So … should I book an Uber to Ben's house?" I asked, plonking down on the lounge and pulling out my phone. Brad sighed and scraped back from the kitchen table, joining me on the lounge.

"I'm sorry, Mel. I was a bit of an arsehole just now, wasn't I?" He reached an arm across the back of the lounge, and I leaned against his side.

"I probably deserved it. I mean, in hindsight, you're right, I should never have slept with him in the first place. But you know me – jump first, check the depth later."

"You never deserve for men to treat you like you owe them something for sleeping with them, though. And I kind of feel like that's a bit what's happened here."

I shrugged. Possibly.

"I'll drive you to Ben's and I'll wait in the car to bring you home."

"Well, no time like the present to go and get this unpleasantness out of the way," I said, falsely bright. My heart was thrumming with nerves.

We made our way through the city, the wipers on Brad's car a rhythmic squeak.

"You know, Mel. I've been thinking about what you said that night … about Grant. I've been thinking about it a lot." Brad murmured.

"Oh?" I managed. I felt too strung out about having to confront Ben to have a D&M with Brad right now.

"I was thinking … you said you feel like casual is all you can do, because you don't want to put your trust in someone again, after what he did to you."

"Yeah."

"Do you trust me?" he asked suddenly. That got my attention. I turned and gaped at him. He continued to concentrate on the rain slicked road.

"What?"

"Do you trust me, Mel?" he repeated.

"Of course I do! You're one of very few people I do trust! You're always honest with me, even if I might not like what you have to say. And I know you've always got my best interests at heart."

Brad inhaled deeply. "Okay."

"Okay? Care to elaborate?"

"Not yet I don't," he replied under his breath. "Just … get through this drama with Ben, and we can talk more before you head to Wimbledon."

"Okay," I muttered, confused, but feeling an odd sensation like I didn't want to push Brad for an explanation.

Even in the rain the restaurants in the main street of Kirribilli were doing a bustling trade as we passed them. Ben's apartment building wasn't much past the main strip.

I wiped my damp hands on my jeans, remembering the way he'd spoken to Joel that day, demanding to see me, like he owned me or something. And now I had to let him know that there was no future for us, and I had no clue what his reaction was going to be.

I should have called Joel.

Brad pulled up outside and turned to me. He gave me an intense look.

"I'll wait for you here, okay? If anything happens, give me a call, and I'll break down the door if I have to."

I felt a surge of love for Brad – he was so dependable. I reached over and hugged him.

Brad gave me a small smile as I got out of the car and trotted through the rain to the door. I pressed the buzzer with number 901 on it and waited.

"Mel?" Ben's voice wafted through, warm and friendly. Not at all like the cruel tone he'd used with Joel.

"Um, yes, it's me," I replied, unable to keep the shaking from my voice.

Get a grip, Melanie! I told myself. *Get it done, and it's over.*

"Come on up."

The door buzzed and I let myself into the foyer, where there was a very old elevator. I pressed the button dubiously and it made its creaking way down the shaft. I was contemplating taking the stairs up, when the doors opened in front of me.

I stepped in, and after what felt like an interminable amount of time in the groaning lift, I was on the ninth floor.

Ben was waiting for me outside the doors. He leaned close and kissed me on the cheek. I stiffened, and he took a step back, but he didn't seem to think much of it, ushering me with a smile towards his apartment.

It certainly wasn't anything like the ultra-modern pad in Dubai. This one was all thick creamy carpet and big soft furniture. I could see straight through to a balcony with a view over the harbour, the Opera House sails gleaming centre-stage.

"It's a beautiful view, isn't it?" he asked, coming to stand behind me, a hand resting on the small of my back. "I was planning to sell and buy a house in the suburbs instead – with a yard for the kids. But that view just gets me every time."

He looked down at me with a cheeky grin. It looked so much like Joel's that I caught my breath.

I stepped away from him, out of reach of his hands. His talk of houses in the suburbs and kids, it was frightening. What had he pictured in his head about the two of us?

"Ben, I'm really sorry," I began, taking another step back and wringing my hands. "It's just that I'm not … into you, the same way that you seem to be into me," I finished lamely. Ben moved forwards until he was standing mere inches away from me.

"You seemed to be pretty into me in Dubai," he murmured in my ear. I took another step away.

"That's not really true you know. I mean, I told you that it wasn't going to work out."

Ben stared at me, blue eyes dark. "No, you said that you couldn't see a future for us when I lived on the other side of the world."

I took a shaky breath. "I'm sorry, but I was really just trying to let you down easy." The way Ben's eyes narrowed sent my heart buzzing nervously in my chest. He stepped closer.

"So, what you're telling me is that I left my business, my *home*, and came back here for *nothing*?" His voice was low and dangerous. "I did all this for *you*, because you *lied* to me!"

I stepped away again, backing closer and closer to the balcony.

"That's not fair, Ben! I slept with you *once*, and then told you I couldn't see a future. It doesn't matter what reason I gave; it was not an invitation to move across the world with no notice, no discussion, no anything! You should have called before you made such a huge decision, you should have talked to me."

Ben advanced on me and I backed hastily away, stumbling on the runner for the sliding door that separated the living area from the balcony. Ben grabbed me by the arms, as if to steady me, but his fingers dug painfully into the soft flesh in the crooks of my elbows. I gasped, but he didn't seem to notice that he was hurting me, his eyes blazing angrily into mine.

"I shouldn't *have* to talk to you about it! You stayed in my home, you *fucked* me for Christ's sake! You accepted my gifts, you were more than happy to let me buy you dinner. You gave me every impression that this would be a long-term thing, if I was back here in Sydney."

I felt my own anger heating inside me. "You buying me things and taking me out does not mean you own me! And I didn't keep the stupid dress – it's probably still hanging in the wardrobe.

"And … *fucked* you? I don't know about you, but I don't feel like I've been *fucked* unless there's some level of pleasure in it for me!"

"You didn't feel fucked because you can't feel pleasure unless you're acting like a filthy whore!" Ben roared.

I froze, any retort caught on the choking lump in my throat.

"Stop making excuses!" Ben warned, "Don't expect me to just let you go now that I've sacrificed so much for you!" He shook me until I could feel my teeth clacking together in my skull.

Adrenaline rushed through me and my voice returned. I screamed. It was enough to stop him shaking me.

"That's *exactly* what I expect you to do, you freak! It's not my fault you're *insane*!"

He gaped at me, but his fingers still grasped me, his nails digging into my skin.

I kneed him in the groin. The choking grunt that he made as he released me to clutch at his balls was supremely satisfying.

"Drop dead, you psycho!" I screamed, turning and running as fast as I could back towards the door.

"Don't think you can come crawling back after this, you ungrateful little slut!" he growled.

"Don't worry, I won't!" I slammed the door behind me with as much force as I could muster.

There was no way I was waiting for the lift – I was too full of adrenaline to stand still. I dashed for the stairwell and took them two at a time, leaping around the turns. I burst out the door and flung myself into Brad's car.

"What the hell happened?" Brad asked, his eyes roving over me as I collapsed back against the seat, gasping for breath. I had no energy to tell him the story.

"Just take me home, please," I begged breathlessly. Brad started the car and roared back onto the street.

CHAPTER NINETEEN

Free Falling

By the time we got back to the Eastern Suburbs from the North Shore, the adrenaline had worn off and I was trembling so hard my teeth chattered.

"Are you going to tell me what happened now?" Brad asked me as he took the key out of my quaking hands and let us into the apartment. I made my way to the lounge and fell onto it.

"Mel, what are these marks on your arms?" Brad demanded. I felt him touching me, his fingers cool on the sore parts of my forearm. I couldn't answer. My voice had gone into hiding.

"Did he hurt you anywhere else?" Brad asked, his voice quiet. I shook my head, eyes still closed.

I had that feeling I sometimes got when I was really drunk, and I lay down, like I was falling from a great height, even though I knew I was lying in my bed. Like I was free falling.

I opened my eyes to stop the sensation, and my vision was filled with Brad's concerned face peering down at me, his grey eyes grave. My own eyes filled up with tears. And once they started, I couldn't stop them – they flowed harder and faster, until my body shook with sobs.

Brad held me close, and I clung to him, the sobs slowly subsiding until I was just weeping pitifully. Brad leaned back to look at me.

"Do you want to talk about it?" he asked. I shook my head, wiping the tears away.

"Just don't let go of me, okay?" I whispered. Brad held me tighter.

"He didn't deserve you anyway, Mel. If he treated you badly, he doesn't deserve you."

"I wish I'd never met him!" I groaned against Brad's shoulder. "I wish he'd leave and never come back!"

Brad pulled me upright, so he could wrap his arms around me properly.

"I wish I could make him go away for you, Mel."

I looked up at him then. He reached towards my face and brushed a stray tear off my cheek. He seemed on the verge of saying something to me – his mouth opened and closed once or twice, like he couldn't decide whether to say it or not.

Instead, he leaned in and brushed his lips timidly against mine. I didn't fight it. I let it happen. It was soft, sweet. Comforting.

He broke away from me.

"Mel, you know what I said earlier, about trust?" I nodded.

"Well ... I want to earn your trust. I want ... there's so much that I want, but ... not now. Not while you're hurting about Ben. I don't want you to do anything unless you want to."

I leaned over and put my head on his shoulder. He stroked my hair gently.

"I feel safe when you're here," I whispered to him.

"I'm glad I can make you feel that way, Smellie."

A thumping on the door interrupted us. My heart started hammering in my chest and I looked at Brad in fear.

"Should I go and see who it is?" he asked. I hesitated, then nodded. If it was Ben, he wouldn't leave of his own accord, and he would probably break the door down. Brad got up and made his way to the door.

Please, God, let it not be Ben. Let it be anyone but Ben!

It wasn't Ben. It was Joel. He stormed into the lounge room, pushing past Brad and coming to crouch beside me. His eyes strayed to the bruises purpling on my arms.

"What happened?" he growled dangerously. I didn't want to talk about it, but his tone didn't leave room for defiance. I relayed as briefly as I could the events of the evening.

"Did he hurt you anywhere else?" I shook my head. Not physically anyway. Joel exhaled a deep breath. Brad hovered in the background.

"How did you know, Joel?" I asked, sitting up to get away from his agonised eyes.

"Ben called me, had a massive spray to me about you. He sounded like he was ready to kill you. I got straight in the car and came here to make sure you were okay." He turned to Brad. "I should have known that you'd have someone here already," he added darkly.

I scowled at him. "Hey, Brad was the one who took me over there. I had to do *something* – he seemed to think I was going to shack up with him and start having his babies!"

Joel stood up and glowered down at me. "Why didn't you call *me*?"

I glared back at him. "I don't have to ask your permission for *everything*, Joel!"

He turned away from me, his hands on his head, and started pacing the living room.

"This is my fault. This is my fault," he repeated.

"Um, I think I'll get going now," Brad said awkwardly.

"No, you don't have to leave," I replied, still glaring at Joel, who continued to pace, head in his hands. What was his deal?

"Actually, I think I do. See you soon, Mel?"

I tried to smile at him, but my face felt tight and uncomfortable. "Yeah, soon Brad."

He let himself out quietly and I turned to Joel once more.

"What's all your fault?" I demanded. He stopped pacing and dropped into the chair opposite me, his hands still on his head.

"I should have told you. I had plenty of chances, but I didn't tell you."

"Tell me what, Joel? Stop talking in riddles and just give it to me straight."

"Tell you about Ben. About what he's really like. When he thinks he can get something he wants, he turns on the charm, but as soon as you take it away from him, he completely loses the plot. I was worried that he might … after what happened in Dubai. But I didn't think he'd really go off the rails, otherwise I would have stepped in."

He unfolded himself from the chair and came over to sit beside me. He sat so his body was facing mine, turning the full force of his eyes on me.

"I'm sorry, Mel. I should have warned you, should have protected you, but I didn't think it would go this far."

"It's not your fault. It's not like you forced me to sleep with him," I said, my eyes dropping to the bruises on my arms. Joel's hand snaked into my vision, touching the marks gently. I flinched and he stood and stalked into the bathroom, returning with a tube of ointment, unscrewing the lid with his teeth. He squeezed some out and started spreading it gently on my skin.

"This should help the cuts and the bruising clear up faster," he murmured. I sat still while he massaged the ointment in.

"So," Joel began, a hint of teasing in his tone. "Brad finally kissed you, did he?"

"What?" I blurted, dumbstruck. And then it hit me – he had kissed me. I'd been half spaced out from shock at the time. But it had happened.

"Stinky, he was going to kiss you sooner or later. He's been wanting to for years." He looked at me from under thick, full lashes.

Wanting. Brad had mentioned something about that, too.

"Do you think he … does he …?"

Joel chuckled, but there was an edge to it. "Mel, he wants everything you're prepared to give him. If you haven't realised this before, then realise it now, because you're going to have to decide."

"Decide what?"

"Friend or lover – once you take that leap, there's no going back."

Those words, coming from Joel, squeezed at my heart.

"I can't think about this right now," I said, leaning my head back against the lounge. "I'm in no state to be thinking about anyone like that."

I sighed, looking down at the bruises blossoming on my arms. "I'm not an ungrateful slut, am I?" I whispered.

Joel sucked a breath in through his teeth. "He called you that?" he asked in a low voice. I nodded, feeling the tears welling up again.

"I'm also a filthy whore, apparently."

Joel pulled me against him, tucking me into his side. I put my head on his chest.

"Of course you're not! Ben, however, is a bad loser who lashes out when he doesn't get exactly what he wants. He's been like that ever since we were kids."

I wiped my tears on his shirt. I'd told Brad that being held by him felt safe. But being held by Joel … I couldn't find words.

"Do you want me to stay here tonight? Or you could come to my place, if you don't want to be alone," he offered.

As soon as the words left his mouth, I knew that being alone was *exactly* what I needed. I looked up at him and he met my eyes with nothing more than concern showing in his own.

"No, I'll be fine," I mumbled.

"Are you sure? I'm happy to stay if you want me to."

I shook my head. "Sorry, Joel, but it's … hard to look at you right now. You look so much like Ben."

Hurt flickered across Joel's face and he stood up very quickly. "Well, I'll leave you to it then," he said stiffly. "Just … call me in the morning, okay? First thing? I need to know that you're alright."

I nodded. "I'll call tomorrow. I promise."

Joel let himself out quietly. I sat staring at nothing for a long time. Connor came circling round my ankles and I picked him up, cuddling him close to me and lying back on the lounge. His purring was very comforting.

"See, Connie? I don't need men in my life – I've got you!" I whispered, kissing him on the head. He yowled in disapproval and jumped down. I snorted. Just like a typical male – they want to be all over you until you do something that makes them uncomfortable, and then all of a sudden they want nothing more than to escape you.

Well, that wasn't necessarily true. Ben had wanted to force me to be with him, even after I told him that there was nothing between us.

And I'd done loads of stuff that Brad would have every right to feel uncomfortable about, but he … he wanted, he'd said. There was so much that he wanted. He'd kissed me! I had been so overwhelmed with everything that had just happened with Ben that I hadn't really processed the fact that it had happened. We were going to have to have a conversation about it at some point. Joel was right, I was going to have to choose: friends or more than friends, with the potential to ruin everything.

And what about Joel?

Yes, what about Joel? The little voice asked snarkily in the back of my head. I couldn't think about him.

I fell asleep trying *not* to think about him.

I dreamed that I was on the balcony at Ben's house. He came up behind me, wrapping his arms around my waist. I didn't feel uncomfortable or scared in the dream at all — I felt happy and content to have him holding me this way.

I turned around to kiss him and found myself face to face with Joel. He was scowling down at me, his eyes dark with fury.

"Filthy whore! Ungrateful slut!" he roared at me, putting his hands around my throat and squeezing. I clawed desperately and in vain at his hands, leaning away from him. I felt the cold of the balcony railing pressing into my back, and suddenly I was falling headfirst towards frothing water below.

I woke up with a jolt on the lounge, upsetting Connor, who'd been lying across my throat. No wonder I'd dreamed that I had been choking. I got up and made my groggy way to the bedroom, where I fell into bed and into a blessedly dreamless sleep.

The phone woke me as the sun was peeking through my blinds, fighting valiantly against the heavy, dark clouds that were still rumbling around. I rubbed my bleary eyes and reached for my phone.

"Hello?" I grated, still mostly asleep.

"Stink? Did I wake you?" Joel's voice shook.

I yawned. "Yes."

"Don't turn on the TV, don't look at your phone, whatever you do. I'm almost at your place." He hung up.

I unlocked the front door so Joel could get in when he arrived, then I stumbled my way into the bathroom, and ran the shower. The hot water revitalised me a little bit, and by the time I'd washed my hair I was feeling mostly awake. I wrapped a towel around me and stepped out of the bathroom.

Joel was sitting in the living room, staring into space. He was white as a ghost and his lips were a tight, thin line. Something was very wrong. I had been planning on getting dressed, but I found my feet taking me out to the lounge room, where I sat in one of my chairs.

"What is it, Joel?" I asked. He looked at me and his eyes seemed lifeless.

"Ben's dead."

CHAPTER TWENTY

What If ...

My jaw fell open. I sat staring at him for what could have been seconds, or hours.

"What?" I whispered when I found my voice again. "How?"

"They think he fell. Or jumped. Off the balcony."

We lapsed into stunned silence. Eventually, I got up and went to the bedroom. I pulled on my clothes, barely feeling the fabric on my skin.

I returned to the living room, but instead of taking my seat in the chair, I sat down on the lounge next to Joel. He was still staring at the wall. The shock of this, so soon after his dad …

"Joel, I … I'm so sorry," I whispered. Joel didn't budge.

"Last night I dreamed that I was being choked by you, on Ben's balcony. And then I fell."

Joel jolted, turning to me. "*I* was choking you?" he repeated, his voice shaky. I nodded.

"I wouldn't ever," he whispered. I found myself wriggling closer, wrapping my arms around his middle, resting my head against his chest.

"I know you wouldn't."

God, I know that yesterday I wished Ben would leave and never come back, but I didn't mean THIS. You know I didn't mean this, don't you? I would never wish that someone was dead!

I felt cold, although the apartment was quite warm. I huddled closer to Joel and let him put his arms around me.

***

It was three days before the police showed up at Joel's door, but it wasn't him they were looking for. It was me.

The rain was still hanging around, spotting the court in dribs and drabs as I ran through my drills. Sandra appeared and Joel turned away to speak with her. I continued with the drill, turning all my focus onto the movement of my body – it helped me cope.

That was until I saw the others who had come down with Sandra. I'd hoped never to have to deal with them again.

Joel walked back over to where I had frozen. "They just want to ask you a few questions."

I gritted my teeth. Joel put a hand on my arm.

"Stink, I'll come sit with you if you want," he offered.

I shook my head and pulled my arm away from him. "It's okay, I can handle this."

I walked stiffly over to Taylor and Coughlin, nodding politely at the man, not really acknowledging his partner.

"Mel, we've got some questions for you about Ben Herbert." Coughlin sounded almost apologetic. I walked past them, taking a seat on the edge of the big lounge in the rumpus room. They followed and sat across from me. I glanced outside; Joel was watching me from the tennis court.

"Okay, can we get this over and done with quickly, so I can get back to work?" I asked primly. Taylor glared at me.

"Miss Black, when was the last time you saw Ben Herbert alive?" she asked, leaning forwards like a hunting hound on the scent.

"Why? I thought he fell?" I asked. "Is there something I don't know about this?"

Coughlin cleared his throat. "Mel, the autopsy –"

"Shut up, Coughlin!" hissed Taylor, "Melanie, answer the question! When did you last see him alive?" Taylor grated. I focussed on the reason they were here and took a deep breath.

"About eight o'clock the night he died," I replied. They would make more of that than was necessary. Well, Taylor would; she definitely had it in for me.

"And where was this?" Taylor continued.

"At his apartment."

"What did you two talk about?"

I sighed shakily. I didn't want to rehash this. "We argued about his reasons for coming back to Australia, and I told him that I didn't want to see him anymore."

Taylor looked triumphantly towards Coughlin, who was pinching the bridge of his nose.

"How would you describe your relationship with Ben Herbert, Melanie?"

"Brief," I snorted. Coughlin smiled and looked outside so that Taylor wouldn't see it.

"He pursued me for a while after Steve's death, and then while I was competing in Dubai, but I shut him down. Apparently not forcefully enough – he thought that if he moved back here there was a chance for us."

"Did you have a sexual relationship with him?"

I nodded. "We slept together once in Dubai."

"Was there any physical violence during your argument?"

I held my arms out, so they could see the bruises that were changing from purple to yellowish green. Coughlin leaned forward to look, a disapproving set to his mouth. Taylor gave the bruises a cursory glance.

"And what about you, Melanie? Did you defend yourself in any way?"

I grunted. "I kneed him in the balls. That was enough to make him let go of me so that I could leave."

"And what time did you leave?"

"About fifteen minutes after I arrived. And before you ask, I went straight back to my apartment and I stayed there for the rest of the night."

"Can anyone confirm that for us?" Taylor asked, a nasty tone to her voice.

"My friend, Brad Jacobs – he drove me to Ben's and he waited for me downstairs. He can tell you that he brought me home. And Joel," I looked outside. Joel was pretending to be busy moving the drill equipment, but I could tell he was straining his ears to hear every word that was being said.

"Joel came over not long after I got home."

"Can anyone vouch that you stayed at home the whole night?"

I got cross then. "No, they can't. I live alone, Detective Taylor. I don't have a flat mate, and I'm not in the habit of inviting people to stay over. I guess you could ask my cat – but he probably wouldn't want to talk to you, he's got better taste!"

Taylor scowled at me. Coughlin hid a grin behind his big hand. I flicked my eyes towards Joel, who was chuckling out on the tennis court. I felt better knowing that he and Coughlin were on my side when it came to Detective Taylor.

"Miss Black, we're not talking about me, we're talking about you! So, you're saying that you went straight home and stayed there for the night. You didn't leave the house? You didn't go back to Ben Herbert's house – alone – and strangle him before pushing him off his balcony?"

My breath caught. "He was *strangled*?" I gasped.

Coughlin interrupted Taylor's interrogation. "Yes, Mel. The autopsy showed that he was strangled with a piece of cord before he was pushed."

My fingers flew to my throat. I found that I was having trouble breathing. A warm hand landed on my shoulder. I hadn't realised that Joel had come inside and was sitting on the back of the lounge. I felt better almost immediately knowing he was there.

"Listen, Detectives, she hasn't done anything wrong," Joel said. "If you don't believe that she didn't leave her apartment again that night, then maybe you should question the bus drivers that were on that route, and the taxi and Uber drivers who picked people up in Vaucluse that night. Mel doesn't have a car, so if she left the house again, someone would have driven her there."

"And what about you, Mr Herbert? Where did you go after you left Miss Black's apartment that night?"

Joel shrugged. "I came home and went to bed. My mother can vouch for me."

Coughlin turned to Taylor. "If you want to look into the taxis and the buses, we can get into that straight away." He stood up. Taylor stood up briskly beside him, smoothing down her tailored pants and adjusting her jacket.

"Thanks for your time, Mel," Coughlin said pleasantly, giving me a smile. I couldn't return it – I was still too shocked.

Sandra came down the steps then, offering to show the detectives out. Taylor looked like she wanted to interrogate me some more, but Coughlin gave her a glance and she followed him back up the stairs. It seemed that he did have some control over her after all.

I heard the door shut upstairs and Sandra came back down. I was frozen on the lounge, touching my throat, remembering the panic of being choked in my dream. Sandra went to the fridge behind the bar and pulled out a bottle of juice. She poured three glasses and brought them back over to the lounge, putting one into my hand and passing one to Joel, before sitting beside me and taking a sip of her own.

Joel reached around and gently pried my hand from my neck. He squeezed it once, but he didn't let it go like I expected him to. Instead, he sat it down on his leg, which was resting on the back of the lounge, and put his hand over it.

"Sandra, I'm so sorry about this," I whispered, my throat raw and raspy. "This isn't something you … so soon after Steve."

Sandra patted me on the knee. "Don't you work yourself up about it, Mel. How on earth is this in any way your fault? You just make sure you look after yourself through all of this."

Sandra finished her juice and stood up. "Well, I'd better let you two get back to business," she said with a smile, heading back up the steps. I looked down at my juice, still untouched in my hand. Joel plucked it from me, walking back over to the fridge and putting it inside.

"You can drink that later when we're done with your training."

He smiled gently, beckoning out towards the court with his head. I followed.

He'd cleared up the equipment from the drills, and he handed me my racquet.

"Let's have a game, hey, Stink?" he asked me, taking his place on the baseline. He bounced a ball in front of him, getting ready to serve.

"Hey, Joel!" I called, before he served. He caught the ball and looked at me.

"Thanks. For the support, I mean. I don't really tell you often enough how much I appreciate it."

He grinned at me. "Hey, it's my job, Mel. I'm just doing my job."

He served to me then, before I could argue. It wasn't just that. He did more than he needed to, job-wise. I took a breath and set my mind to the game.

For the second time in less than six months I found myself back at Saint Gertrude's for a funeral. This time there was less of a circus outside, but there was still a decent pack of journalists; it was the funeral of a murdered man, a rich murdered man.

'The Herbert Murders' the media was calling it. I cringed at the name. Journalists conveniently forgot that these people had families who were grieving.

Deep down though, I wondered. *Was* there a connection between the two murders? It would be too much of a coincidence for there not to be – two brothers don't just both get murdered randomly, do they?

Ben's friend from Dubai had flown in for the funeral and he gave the eulogy. I paid little attention to his words. He was tall, slim, and Middle Eastern. He spoke perfect English with a rich accent. His skin was olive and flawless. He was dressed smartly in a charcoal suit, grey shirt and tie.

His smooth voice flowed over me and I listened without really hearing what he was saying. I glanced up at Joel. His teeth were slightly bared, his jaw clenched so tightly I was worried that it might shatter. He looked absolutely furious.

I very quickly tuned in to the eulogy.

"… he was generous with everyone he knew. Ben wasn't the type of person to hoard his wealth. He shared it with friends and loved ones, with no expectations in return. He was never interested in flaunting his fortune …"

I reached out and took Joel's hand, resting it on my thigh and placing my own hand on top of it. His head jerked and he turned to me. His face began to relax, although his lips were still pursed. The right corner of his mouth tweaked up, and he put his other hand on top of mine, leaning closer to me. I rested my head against his shoulder, listening to his breath hiss in and out. I felt the stiffness in his body ease.

The eulogy ended and the priest started speaking again. I wasn't listening to that either, but for a different reason. Joel's thumb was moving back and forwards very gently on my thigh. I sneaked a glance up at Joel's face, but he was watching the service. Was he trying to get a reaction out of me? If he was … no, he couldn't possibly be that bold, to do it in the middle of a funeral.

There was another option: that touching me in such a familiar way was becoming second nature to him … and I kept letting him.

Should I stop him? Or should I just let it happen? Before I could work out the answer, the priest announced a hymn and as we stood, Joel's hand slipped from my leg. I breathed a sigh of relief. I couldn't deal with how his touch made me feel right now.

On the way home from the funeral, Joel's phone bleeped with a notification.

"Can you check that for me?" Joel asked, navigating through the traffic from Bondi back to Rose Bay.

"Really? What if it's one of your fuck buddies?" I asked , picking his phone up from the centre console.

"It won't be," he assured me in a low voice.

I looked down at the screen. "It's a Tweet, from that guy, tennisfanboi, the one who leaked the …” Joel grabbed the phone, typing in his passcode and handing the phone back to me.

“What does it say?”

I skimmed the Tweet. “Holy fuck!”

Joel dragged the steering wheel to the side, pulling up to the kerb. “What is it?” he demanded, snatching the phone from me.

Police leak: the bar brawl was a red herring! Grant Johnson's stabbing back in February happened INSIDE his apartment, ya'll! Police treating as attempted murder … more to come …

“Where the fuck is this guy getting his info?” Joel exclaimed, putting his phone down and gripping the steering wheel with white knuckles. “He must have access to police files.”

But something else was niggling at the back of my mind. Something about this information turned my stomach.

“Joel …” I whispered, turning to him, my face suddenly cold.

“Stink, what's wrong?” he asked, voice thick with concern.

“What if … what if it's all because of … me?”

CHAPTER TWENTY-ONE
Nothing Good

"So, the cops have Tweeted a confirmation that Grant was stabbed inside his apartment," Joel said, looking up from his phone as I finished my warm-up stretches to one side of the court.

It was two days since Ben's funeral – since tennisfanboi's Tweet about Grant that still had my stomach tied up in knots. And only a week until we flew out for Wimbledon. I was training extra hours at the moment to make sure I was ready. This morning I was doing drills and weights, then taking a swim. After lunch I would play a game with Joel, and he would push me to my limits.

"You seem very interested in this information, for someone who told me the other day that I was completely overreacting when I thought that maybe this thing with Grant was related to Ben and to … to your dad."

"We've been over this, Mel. The world doesn't revolve around you," he reminded me with a little smile. They were the same words he had used in the car the first time I'd brought this worry up with him, after he got over the initial shock of my sudden suspicion.

But his words had done nothing to alleviate my concern. What if they – Steve and Ben – had died because of me, somehow? What if Grant had been almost killed because of me?

"Okay, but just hear me out," I said, walking over to where he had my drills set out. "The night that Steve … well, you know that he and I weren't on good terms." I swallowed around the knot in my throat.

"Stink, we went through this the other day. And the night Grant got stabbed, you had a breakdown in a bar because you saw his fiancée out on her hen's night – big deal."

"But Ben and I had a *huge* fight, and then …" I swallowed again, willing the prickling out of my eyes. I swiped a stray tear away. I didn't need all of this stress, with the biggest tournament of the year a week away.

Joel stepped closer, taking my shoulders in his big, warm hands, piercing me with those blue eyes. "Mel, how would anyone know that you had issues with all of them, and then somehow act on it almost immediately? It's not related, It's just a very weird coincidence."

Everything he said made sense, but still I couldn't shake the feeling that it *was* all linked to me.

"Brad knew – he was there every single time," I muttered.

Joel snorted. "You think *Lover Boy* did all of this? He couldn't hurt a fly!"

He was right. Brad was studying to be a paediatrician for crying out loud! He wasn't going around murdering men in cold blood because they hurt my feelings.

I started my drills, trying to wipe my head clean of all the things that were still battering against the insides of my skull.

It helped … a bit. But I was still preoccupied as we finished up on drills and moved into the gym for weights training.

Joel watched me guardedly. "You're dwelling, Stink."

I eyed him crossly. "Of course I am! I love a good dwell, don't you?"

Joel snickered, but his eyes were serious. "Mel, there are things that you don't know – things about Dad and Ben – that could be related to what happened."

"Like what?" I asked, intrigued.

Joel shook his head. "Believe me, you're better off not knowing."

"Do the police know about it?" I pestered.

Joel paused for a long while, then nodded very slightly. "I've told them the important parts," he muttered.

"Is it bad?" I asked. He didn't respond, staring away at nothing in particular. I sighed and that seemed to snap him out of it. He smiled brightly at me, falsely.

"Got any plans tonight, Stink?" he asked, changing the subject.

"Yes, actually, I'm having dinner with Brad, and Amanda and Thomas."

"A double date with Lover Boy! That should be a pleasant evening for you," Joel said. He turned to add some plates to the squat rack, but I caught the slight downward twist of his mouth.

I pursed my lips. Brad had called it a date too. I hadn't forgotten that he'd kissed me, or that he had told me he wanted more. Was that what tonight was? Us trying for more?

"Maybe," I muttered.

"It's a pity, though. I was going to see if you wanted to come and see Princes of Lion with me – they're playing in town tonight and I have two tickets."

I stopped in my tracks and gaped at him. Princes of Lion tickets were almost impossible to come by, and every time they'd been playing in Australia, I'd been overseas at a tournament.

It was tempting … very tempting.

But as soon as I thought about Princes of Lion now, all I could see was a girl with her skirt riding up, legs wrapped around Joel. I shuddered at the thought.

"Thanks for thinking of me, Joel, but I just have this visual of you fucking in the mosh pit now, and that's all I can see when I hear any of their songs."

Joel moved closer, a cheeky grin on his face and a glint in his eyes.

"Well, Stink, if you come with me, I could give you something else to think about when you're listening to them."

I couldn't exhale – he was standing so close that I could feel the heat from his body radiating out towards me. It was like a magnet, drawing me closer.

"I can't cancel on my friends," I said hurriedly, turning away to the squat rack.

Joel shrugged. "No worries. I'm sure I can find someone else who wants to go with me. I just wanted to give you first option."

I couldn't help myself. "If only you knew who it was last time – I'm sure she'd just *love* and encore performance!"

Joel chuckled. "Don't be jealous, Stink. You have a chance to be 'moshing' with me at Princes of Lion, and you'd rather have dinner with Lover Boy."

I stopped and whirled towards him.

"Let's just get one thing straight here, mate! I'm not the type of girl who fucks random guys in the mosh pit at a concert. I've got a bit more class than that. And if that's what you were hoping would happen between us tonight, then you would have been *very* disappointed!"

Joel put his hands up in surrender. "I'm hardly a 'random guy'."

I glared at him icily, working through my weights in silence, Joel hovering to spot me as usual. He seemed to sense that I wasn't in the mood to talk to him.

Our lap swimming continued in much the same fashion. As I showered, Joel made us some lunch. It had become our training routine.

"Hey, Stinky," Joel began as we finished up our lunch, trailing his finger along the edge of the table. I waited for him to continue.

"Sorry, Mel. You know I wouldn't ever try to make a move on you like that."

"It's okay," I replied awkwardly when I found my voice. Why did it cut me that he wouldn't have even *tried*? I mean, I would absolutely have told him where to go … wouldn't I?

"So, *are* you and Brad dating now?" he asked.

"No. Well, not really," I replied. He looked up at me then and his eyes were enquiring.

"Not really?" he persisted.

I shrugged. "I just … he's always so … I don't know how to explain it, but lately … can you tell I'm really confused about the whole thing?"

Joel smiled, a genuine, beautiful, white toothed smile. My knees trembled under the table.

"It's a big decision. You go down that path, you can't ever go back to the friendship you had. But if you really like him, you should go for it. He's a decent guy. You could definitely do worse."

I rolled my eyes at him. "Well, thanks for your permission, coach!"

He hissed out a laugh and put his elbows on the table, leaning towards me. "You know you don't need my permission, Mel," he murmured, his face suddenly serious. I found myself leaning towards him, until our noses almost touched.

"I never thought I did," I replied in a whisper. Oh God, his eyes! I forced my gaze to drop, only to stare at his lips, getting closer and closer to mine, so full and pink. As I stared, his mouth curved up in a smirk.

"You know, Stink, you can deny it all you like, but it's only a matter of time before you give in and beg me."

"Beg you for what?" I breathed against his mouth.

"For this …" His lips touched the corner of my mouth.

I leapt out of my chair so fast that it fell backwards.

"No! I'm never going to let that happen, Joel Herbert. I promise you. Never!"

I raced off the deck and up the stairs to the front door, heart battering against my chest. I couldn't be in the same house as him another second.

His footsteps approached. As I turned the handle on the front door, he was behind me, his hand on it so I couldn't open it. I turned and he was leaning over me, his palms pressed against the door on either side of my face.

"It's not happening," I muttered unconvincingly.

"What's not happening?" he whispered against the side of my face.

I let out a shuddering breath and my hands took on a life of their own, reaching up to rest against his hips. He moved until his leg was pressing between mine.

Another shaky breath and my fingers burrowed under the

bottom of his t-shirt. His skin rippled under my touch and he brought his hands down to cup my face, tilting my head back until I was gazing into the depths of his eyes. Until his mouth was very, very close to mine.

"Joel, I can't do this," I pleaded with him, turning my head away.

"Can't do what?" he asked.

"I can't do this with you." The words were barely more than a breath; that was all the strength I could give to them.

"We're not doing anything, Mel," he replied, even as his hips pressed against mine. Had I pulled him closer?

I tore my hands off his body. "I'm not. I can't."

He released me and I opened the door and escaped. My legs were jelly beneath me. Before I was even to the gate he was behind me again, his hand on my arm, holding me back.

"Let me drive you home." He sounded so reasonable that I felt the fight go out of me. I trudged back to his car.

It was a silent trip to my house. Maybe Joel realised that he'd overstepped a boundary today. A boundary that I was clearly incapable of keeping defined.

As I got out of the car, he spoke.

"Don't worry about our game this afternoon. Just have fun tonight. I'll see you at training tomorrow. Let's make it ten instead of eight, okay? Gives us both a bit of a sleep in."

I nodded, not having any words to say to him. He drove away before I had closed the main door of the apartment building behind me. I stood just inside the door trying to catch my breath.

"Have you been away from home more this year, or is it just me?" Brad asked.

I took a sip of my wine and leaned back against the aqua coloured leather lounge. "No, it's pretty much been the same," I replied, staring out over the waves.

Brad and I had arrived early, so just the two of us could have a drink before Amanda and Thomas joined us.

Brad leaned back next to me. "It just feels like you've been away more, that's all," he sighed and took another mouthful of his beer. "You and Joel seem to be spending a lot of time together lately."

I fiddled with the stem of my wine glass, ordering my stupid heart to stop fluttering. "He's my coach, of course I'm going to spend a lot of time with him; I *work* with him. That's all it is."

I heard the lie in my voice. I hoped that Brad didn't. I couldn't talk to him about what had almost happened in Rome … and again in Paris … and again today. Brad, one of the few people I could usually tell anything and everything, was not someone I could confide in about Joel.

"So, you've been getting into a lot of finals lately," Brad commented.

I sighed in relief that he'd decided to drop the whole Joel subject. "Yeah, I know. It'd just be good if I could actually *win* one. I was *so* close in Paris – Abigail Petersen's not a fan of the clay. I thought I had her, but I got a bit too overconfident."

I paused to take a breath. "You know what? We always talk about me, what's going on in your life?" I smiled winningly at him. It would be so good not to talk tennis … or Joel for a little while.

Brad grinned at me. "Just the usual. Uni, clinical placement at Frankwright paediatric oncology … missing you."

I swallowed nervously, choosing to ignore his last statement. "Oncology, wow, really? Wouldn't that be kind of … I don't know … depressing?" I thought about little Natalie, and the courtyard full of bald kids with not enough meat on their bones.

Brad shrugged. "Only if you let it be – I prefer to think about the positives. I could help make a difference to kids who might not have much of a chance otherwise."

"Hey, do you know a girl called Natalie up there?" I asked.

Brad smiled. "Oh, yeah, she's a cutie, that one. A real battler. She's got a very rare form of leukaemia, and it's quite aggressive, but she never complains or gets upset about all the treatments she needs. Isn't she the one that you went to visit that day?"

I nodded.

"Well, she's definitely a massive fan of yours – she has your autograph framed beside her bed, and pictures of you in a little folder."

"How's she doing?" I asked.

"She's not one of my patients … and I can't really disclose … but she's midway through another chemo round."

Another one. My eyes prickled at the thought of that brave little girl idolising someone like me. I didn't deserve her devotion. There were people out there in the world who were far more deserving than me – people who were making a difference to society. People like Brad.

"I think what you're doing is noble." I patted him on the knee. He put his hand on top of mine, capturing it and holding it on his thigh. He grinned, his slightly crooked teeth gleaming.

"I really do miss you, Mel, when you're gone," he murmured.

I smiled uncomfortably. "I miss you too, Brad." I just wasn't sure I meant it in *exactly* the same way he did.

"Well, fancy seeing you two here!" a voice from above my head spoke. I knew instantly who it was. I tried to take my hand off Brad's leg, but he tightened his grip on it. I didn't want to embarrass us both by wrenching it away, so I let him have his way.

"Joel, how are you? Who's your friend?" Brad asked, his fingers caressing the back of my hand.

Joel smiled brightly down at both of us. Beside him, Julie looked as awkward as I felt. Joel had his arm around her. She wouldn't meet my eyes. What was she doing here?

"Julie, this is Brad, a *friend* of Mel's." I could feel Joel's eyes on me as he said it. "I thought tonight was supposed to be a double date, Stinky?"

"Oh, it is," I assured him, narrowing my eyes at his smirking face. "Amanda and Thomas are meeting us a bit later."

"Well, since you've snagged a table for four, mind if we sit with you guys until your friends get here? It's crazy busy tonight." Joel didn't wait for either of us to respond, plonking himself down beside me, putting an arm up on the back of the lounge behind me. Brad gripped my hand harder.

I leaned out past Joel and turned to Julie. I would try and be polite, even though her presence was sending pangs of some strong emotion through me.

"So, Julie, what are you doing in Sydney?" I asked pointedly.

"Oh, I've moved here," Julie said, tossing her long red curls over her shoulder. "Didn't Joel tell you? I've been up here for a few months now."

I leaned back and caught Joel's eye. "No, he *didn't* tell me that."

Joel shrugged sheepishly. I distinctly remembered him telling me that he wasn't with Julie, because she was in Melbourne. I tried to convey through my eyes that I was not happy about being lied to.

"Julie's coming to Princes of Lion with me tonight," he announced.

Brad's eyes widened. "How did you snag tickets for that? I heard it was sold out within minutes."

"Oh, I was on the VIP pre-sale. I never miss a Princes of Lion concert … do I, Mel?"

I threw him my dirtiest look and he grinned. Why couldn't I shake his cocky exterior, just once? I finished off my wine and stood.

"Brad, let's head back to my place, where we can have a bit of privacy." I looked pointedly at Joel then – let him think what he wanted about that.

"But … what about Amanda and Thomas?" Brad asked, confused. I kept my eyes on Joel, who smiled serenely at me, his arm around Julie, who was looking from him to me, her eyebrows furrowed.

"It's really only you I wanted to spend time with tonight," I snarled. Brad stood hurriedly, chewing on his lip.

"Enjoy, kids," Joel said. I scowled at him and turned jerkily to leave. Brad followed hastily, a little flustered.

"You too," I replied icily, wrapping my arm around Brad's waist and dragging him through the crowd.

"Mel!" Amanda called out. I stifled a groan. I just wanted to get out of there. I could still feel Joel's eyes on us.

"Hey guys," I mumbled as Amanda and Thomas weaved their way through the crowd towards us.

"Do we have a table? I thought you booked?" Amanda asked.

"We did. Mel wants to go home though," Brad explained, his voice tight.

"I have a headache," I lied, although there was a tightness at the base of my skull that could easily turn into one.

"Oh, that's a shame. Are you sure you couldn't just stay for even half an hour? I have some paracetamol here somewhere." Amanda rummaged through her purse.

Thomas stilled her hand. "If Mel's feeling unwell, we really should let her go home, babe. She's got a huge tournament coming up, she needs to look after her health."

I smiled gratefully at him, and he gave me a little nod.

"You guys could always go and hang out with Joel and his date," I suggested, failing utterly to keep bitterness from my tone. Brad's arm around my shoulders tightened.

Amanda grabbed me into an awkward one-armed hug, and Thomas patted me on the shoulder as they headed towards the bar.

Back in Brad's car, he turned to me, a serious look on his face. "You were kind of rude to Amanda and Thomas."

I shrugged, sinking further into the seat.

"I also don't appreciate being used as a pawn in your little game with Joel."

I glared at him. "Uh, *excuse* me, but I'm not the one playing games here! What was the go with you making sure he saw my hand on your leg?"

Brad shook his head. "Well, what's the go with you making up excuses for us to leave? And then winding yourself around me to walk out?"

"I, well, I uh … I hate walking in heels."

Brad smiled humourlessly. "Listen, I'll take you home, but I'm not coming in tonight. Whatever is going on between you and Joel, I hope you get over it soon."

The fury bubbled over. "*Nothing* is going on between Joel and me!" I shrieked.

Brad started the engine, lips pursed. "So, you can tell me without a word of a lie that seeing him there tonight with that redhead didn't make you feel anything?"

"Nothing," I lied. Brad snorted disbelievingly.

I sat in stony silence for the short trip back from Bondi to Vaucluse. Brad pulled up out the front of my apartment building and cut the engine.

"Listen, Mel, I don't want to fight with you."

"Goodnight, Brad," I said tersely.

I moved to open the door, but he grabbed my arm, turning me back towards him, pulling me close, covering my lips with his. I gasped in shock, his tongue slipping through the gap, stroking gently against mine.

Suddenly, all the frustrated, confused, swirly feelings in my stomach overtook me and I gripped his neck, my tongue caressing his. A sound from deep in Brad's throat vibrated through our joined mouths.

Nope. This is a bad idea.

I broke away. Brad and I stared at each other in shock.

I turned and practically leapt out of the car. Even once I'd made it safely into my apartment, I could see his car idling outside through my bedroom window for long moments before he finally drove away.

I kicked off my shoes and stalked into the kitchen in search of more alcohol.

———

My phone rang after I'd downed three more glasses of wine. I fumbled for it.

"Why are you calling me, Joel? To gloat about how much fun you're having at Princes of Lion?" I slurred.

There was a pause. It was too quiet. It couldn't be later than ten-thirty – the concert would still be in full swing, but I couldn't hear any noise on the other end of the phone.

"Joel? Are you there?" I asked.

He cleared his throat. "Yeah, I'm here. And no, I'm not at the concert."

"Why not? Where's *Julie?*"

"It doesn't matter. Listen, I just had a call from Natalie's dad."

"Oh, okay."

The silence stretched. I tried to focus through the fog of wine.

"What happened, Joel?"

"Natalie lost her fight. The funeral's tomorrow. Her dad thought you might have wanted to be there."

The tipsiness leeched straight out of me.

"Of course I want to go." My shoulders slumped and I rubbed at my forehead. "That's just awful. Poor little Natalie."

Joel cleared his throat again. It sounded like he was trying not to cry. "Yeah, it's fucking horrible. Funeral's at ten. You want me to pick you up?"

"Please. I'll see you then."

"Are you … are you alone?" he asked and the agony in his tone was lightning through my chest.

"I'm home … alone."

"Will you be okay?"

My vision blurred. "I … I think so. I'll see you tomorrow, Joel."

I hung up the phone before he could hear me start to sob. Because if that happened, he'd want to come over. And if he came over nothing good would come of it.

CHAPTER TWENTY-TWO

This One Chance

"I feel like all I ever do lately is attend funerals for people who should still be alive," I muttered thickly to Joel as I pulled on a black coat over my grey pants and cream jumper. The day had dawned crisp and cold. I slipped my feet into a pair of tan ankle boots and sat down on the edge of the bed.

"Trust me, Stink, you're not alone there," Joel replied from the doorway. I looked up at him. He was wearing dark grey pants and a black shirt with a cream-coloured suit jacket over the top, and tan shoes. I grimaced – we were colour coordinated. Well, it wasn't my fault; I'd gotten up and ironed this outfit before he'd arrived. How was I supposed to know that he was going to wear those colours?

The BMW's air conditioner blasted warm air over me, flipping my hair around my shoulders. The inside of Joel's car was so warm that I struggled out of my coat.

Joel watched me. "Hey, Stink, I'm sorry for interrupting your date with Lov … Brad last night." He actually sounded like he meant it.

I sighed. "It's okay, Joel. I don't think … I think he wants things that I'm not … that just aren't going to happen. I feel like I might have screwed it all up last night, actually."

He took his eyes off the road to stare at me. "How?" he asked sharply.

I shrugged and looked down at my lap. "Well, we sort of kissed again."

"You *sort of* kissed?" Joel asked sharply.

"He said some things on the drive home that … riled me up. I was ready to leave the car mad at him, but then he kissed me. And …"

"And what?"

"And I kissed him back … for probably longer than I should have. I stopped as soon as … Brad and I shouldn't be anything but friends. But I kind of think that the kiss might have given him the wrong impression."

"Because a kiss from Melanie Black is life changing." Joel murmured.

I glanced at him out of the corner of my eye, wondering if he was making fun of me. His face was unreadable. I blushed, deciding it was probably better not to know.

We lapsed into silence for the rest of the trip, and it wasn't until we pulled into a parking space near the Botanic Gardens that he spoke again.

"Well, Stinky, I have to admit I feel sorry for the guy." He turned to look at me.

I raised an eyebrow at him. "Why?" I demanded.

Joel sighed. "Because he's been wanting to kiss you for years, and you finally gave him a taste of it. He's going to want more, Stinky."

I thought about Brad's words the night he took me to Ben's: *"I want … there's so much that I want …"*

"Oh God," I muttered. "I'm a horrible person. I only kissed him back because …" I came to a choking stop. I'd been absolutely on the verge of blurting out, *"To make myself forget the way my chest ached when I saw you with Julie."*

Joel sighed beside me. "You're not a horrible person, Mel. You just do things sometimes without thinking about the consequences until it's too late."

I couldn't argue with that.

"But hey, at least I didn't sleep with him, right?" I tried to joke.

"Thank God for small mercies," Joel muttered.

We walked side by side towards the Oriental Garden where the funeral was being held. Joel's warm, male scent blew across me in the breeze, and I shivered.

"Cold, Stink?" Joel asked me quietly. I shook my head stubbornly, but the wind gusted harder and I trembled for real. Joel chuckled and slung an arm around my shoulders. He was *very* warm. Against my better judgement I nestled in closer to his body.

"You don't have to act so tough all the time, you know. I know that you're really a big baby under all the bravado," he said wryly. I tried to wriggle out from under his arm, but he held me firmly against him.

I grunted unhappily. "Well, you don't have to act like a dickhead all the time. I know that there's more to you than that. At least, I think there's more … actually I have no idea."

Joel snickered quietly. "I have to keep you guessing, Stink."

I snorted. "Why? Do you like it that I'm always confused when I'm around you?"

He turned and scooped a hand under my chin until I was staring into his face. "You're so cute when you're confused, Stinky."

I rolled my eyes. "According to you, I'm cute no matter what sort of bad mood I'm in."

He shrugged. "So, I'm in trouble for telling you that you're cute now am I?"

I didn't have a reply for that. He pulled me closer against him. I tried to ignore how much I liked being that close to him.

"You like this, don't you Mel?" It was as if he'd read my thoughts.

I feigned ignorance. "I have no idea what you're talking about, Joel."

He chuckled. "I think you do. I think you like being in my arms way more than you'll ever admit."

I laughed sarcastically, if a little nervously. "Well, you'll never know, since I'm never going to admit it, will you?"

He stopped walking and I was dragged to a halt. He turned me until my whole body was facing him.

"I wonder if I could make you admit it," he breathed, his arms circling my waist, pulling me against him. I clamped my fingers down on his arms, but I couldn't figure out if I wanted to push him away or drag him closer.

I sucked in a breath. "Joel, this is totally inappropriate. We're here to attend a child's funeral! Get off!" My voice was panicked. I was cranky with him; that was all. It had nothing to do with the fact that it had taken every ounce of my self-control not to close the gap between us myself.

He leaned away, a self-satisfied smile on his face. Then he sneaked in and brushed those full lips briefly against my cheek.

"You're right, Stink. I'll make you admit it some other time."

We crested a hill, and there was the funeral spread out on the other side. There were hundreds upon hundreds of people there. School kids in their uniforms stood out the most for me. Well, almost. It was the little pack of kids with beanies covering their bald heads, looking pale and drawn to one side, under the watchful eye of their parents and medical staff that really caught my eye. I wondered morbidly which one of them would be next.

There weren't really any seats, except for some for the family down at the front, circled around the distressingly tiny, bright pink coffin. People were either sitting on the grassy verge or standing. We stood towards the back. Joel relinquished his hold on my shoulders, only to wind his fingers through mine. I let him.

I needed to talk myself *out* of this stupid attraction to the smug, crass, sleazy, funny, stunningly gorgeous, strangely deep, intensely frustrating, confusing, contradictory man who was currently holding my hand.

I didn't need to be attracted to him. I *really* didn't need it. I just had to convince myself that I didn't *want* it either.

The secular celebrant began the service with some words about Natalie. I'd never been to an Atheist funeral before. I found the notion that this was our one life at once strangely cathartic and terribly depressing. If this was Natalie's only chance to live, if there was no eternal life, then what sort of cruel world did we live in?

"Natalie knew that there was a good chance her life wouldn't be a long one, but she never let that thought get her down. She enjoyed the things within her grasp to the fullest. Her love of reading and writing, and of course, tennis," the celebrant said, and I bit my lip against the sudden tremor that thrummed through me.

I'd never get to play that game of tennis with Natalie. I'd never get to see the joy on her face that would have brought.

It made me wonder what things *I* hadn't done on this earth that I should do, just in case the Atheists were right, and we only got this one chance at finding joy in what we had *now*.

One thing forcefully sprang into my head, and I glanced up from under my lashes at the object of my sudden thought. He must have felt my gaze because he met my eyes. The wind whooshed through again, blowing my hair all around me.

Before I could scoop it out of my face, Joel's hand swooped in and with gentle fingers he brushed it off my cheek and tucked it away behind my ear. His thumb lingered on my cheekbone just a tad longer than was really necessary. His eyes were cautious as they met mine, and he tucked his bottom lip between his teeth, like that would hold in something that was clamouring to get out of him.

I turned away, focusing as best I could on the rest of the cere-mony. When the celebrant finished and the crowds started to shift away, I turned to Joel and indicated with a jab of my head that I wanted to go see Natalie's dad, Frederick.

There were a lot of people around him, but when he saw me, he pushed his way through the mourners towards us. His eyes were red-rimmed, but he was composed.

"Thank you so much for coming, Mel. It was one of the last things that Natalie asked me, before she went."

I pushed aside my shock. "I'm truly sorry. Natalie was a beau-tiful little girl, and I wish I could have gotten to know her better." My eyes prickled, but I really didn't want to cry. What right did I have to cry, when her own father was here, dry eyed?

"She talked about you a lot towards the end. The one thing she was really cranky about was that she never got to play that game with you."

I swallowed the lump in my throat. "She knew? That she was

…" I felt horrible asking, but it just seemed surreal to me, that a child could know that she was dying and accept that fact.

Frederick nodded. "She was the one who told me I had to let her go. She was trying to hold on to watch you play at Wimbledon, but it wasn't meant to be. She kept saying that she had a good feeling about Wimbledon for you."

He looked back towards the coffin briefly, then turned back to us. "I hope you don't mind – all she wanted in the coffin with her was the racquet you gave her. She said that at least then she'd feel like she got to play with you."

I lost it then, totally and completely. The prickling became a burning, and the tears were flooding down my face like a torrent. I let Joel pull me close to him.

"Mel's really honoured that Natalie thought so highly of her. We've got a good feeling about Wimbledon too, and I'm sure that Mel will do everything she can to do Natalie proud," Joel replied. I felt him reach out and shake Frederick's hand – I couldn't really see it through the blur of tears.

"Mel and I have made a donation to the hospital," Joel added. "We hope it makes a difference."

"I'm sure it will," Frederick said. "Thank you so much!"

As Joel drew me away from the crowd, I let the tears take over completely. He pulled me against his chest and I sobbed onto his black shirt. The air was so icy, my tears made the fabric cold almost immediately.

Joel's hands moved up and down against my back rhythmically, until I was semi-calm. I didn't move my face from his chest though. It felt too nice, too comforting to be enveloped in his arms.

"I'm sorry I cried on your shirt again," I mumbled. I felt Joel's chest shake with … what? Tears? Laughter?

"I told you my shirts are always at your service for all tear-soaking purposes."

"Mel," a familiar voice said behind me. I hid against Joel's chest, wiping at my streaming eyes.

"Hi, Brad," Joel greeted him warily.

I turned and gave him a watery smile. "Hi," I replied bashfully. I felt kind of weird seeing him so soon after what had happened last night. He held his arms out as if he expected Joel to pass me over to him.

Joel started to release me with a little sigh of resignation. Something snapped in my brain. I clung to his waist and he pulled me back against him.

Brad dropped his arms, and the look on his face made guilt roar in my chest. I shouldn't have kissed him back last night. This new, strange awkwardness I felt in his presence was the consequence. I hoped that it would wear off. I hoped that by the time I got back from Wimbledon, things would be back to normal, the kiss in the car forgotten. I doubted it would be that easy somehow.

"I just wanted to tell you how sorry I am, Mel," Brad said formally. I reached out and touched his arm briefly.

"Thanks, Brad."

"You had a special connection with her," he added.

I smiled at him again, a little warmer now. I felt Joel's hand move from my shoulder to my waist. I ignored the tingling his touch sent through me. Or tried to ignore it anyway. Unsuccessfully.

"I was about to take Mel out for lunch. Do you want to come?" Joel asked.

Brad glanced at me, eyes wary, then shook his head. "No, thanks. I've got classes this afternoon anyway." He turned to me. "Mel, I'll see you when you get back from England?"

I nodded.

"Well, good luck."

Brad leaned in and kissed me on the cheek, then stepped back and, giving me a wistful look, he turned and walked away.

"That was ... awkward," Joel said as we headed towards the Opera House. I turned and looked at him, expecting a smug expression. But all I saw were serious, pouty lips, and eyes that cut through me like blue diamonds.

Stupid me, I wanted him to kiss me, so badly. When I looked at him, I could understand the things that Brad had said to me ... *'there's so much that I want'* ...

"Well, if it's going to be that awkward after thirty seconds of tongue kissing, I'm *really* glad I didn't take him to bed."

Joel chuckled then. "After what the world knows about Melanie Black's bedroom antics, I think Brad Jacobs wouldn't have been able to walk straight for a week!"

I scowled. "You know, I am capable of sex that isn't … pornographic." I grated the word out. "In fact, I quite like sweet, vanilla sex, when it's with the right person."

I just hadn't found that person yet.

Joel sighed. "Of course you are, Stinky. So, what am I buying us for lunch?" He moved his arm back up around my shoulders. Was it wrong that I was disappointed that he wasn't caressing my hip anymore? Yes, it was.

"I don't mind, Joel. If you're paying, then whatever you decide will be fine."

We ended up getting dumplings from Opera Kitchen and sitting on the steps of the Opera House to eat them. The sun was finally burning away the chill in the air, and I took my coat off and sat in my cardigan, enjoying its warmth on me.

Joel finished his lunch and leaned back against the steps, propping himself up on one elbow and facing me.

"Have you heard anything more from the police?" I asked tentatively. Joel shook his head.

"I'm starting to wonder whether they'll ever solve them," I said.

"Wouldn't be the first time murders went unsolved."

I turned to face him. "Aren't you desperate for justice? I mean, it was your dad and your uncle, Joel."

He shrugged.

"Finding who did it isn't going to bring either of them back, is it? I don't know if anything would make me feel better about it. I'm certainly not counting on anything making me feel better anyway."

Thoughtlessly I reached out and grabbed his hand. His long fingers clasped around mine.

"How are your nightmares?" Joel asked. "They didn't seem to worry you on our last trip overseas."

I shrugged. "They come and go. There were a few nights after

Ben when it was bad again, but it's almost like I'm so used to them now that it doesn't shock me the way it used to. I don't know. I've just learned to live with them."

Joel threw me a dubious look, but when I didn't elaborate, he sighed.

"How are you feeling about Wimbledon, Stinky?" he asked. The sudden change of topic caught me slightly off guard, and I paused for a moment to figure out my answer.

"I feel okay. I feel probably about the same as I do going into any tournament. I think my fitness is much better, thanks to you." I looked down at him, and he grinned back, winking.

"Well, at least I'm doing *something* right," he said.

"What is that supposed to mean?" I asked him, intrigued. His eyes slid away from mine.

"Nothing, forget I said that," he muttered, but there was absolutely something he wasn't telling me. I leaned back against the steps until my face was parallel with his.

"I know you don't 'owe me your secrets'," I began, using a fake deep voice to quote his words back to him, "but … I'm here and I can handle the hard stuff, if you want to talk to me."

He met my eyes, his own dark and … hungry. He stared at me in silence for a long time.

"You have the most beautiful eyes, Mel, like melted chocolate," he whispered, catching me off guard and making me forget what I'd said in the first place. I blushed and looked away, afraid that if I held his gaze, I wouldn't be able to hold myself back from him. I sat up swiftly.

Joel sat up beside me. "Come on, training time."

I nodded without looking at him and he stood, pulling me up by our still joined hands.

I couldn't voice it, but I'd just realised that whenever I asked him something that he didn't feel comfortable answering, he turned to seduction to distract me. I wondered why that was, but I knew that if I asked he'd just do it again, and I wasn't sure that my resolve could handle it *another* time today.

Besides, I had the biggest tournament of the year just around the corner. I forcefully pushed all the little intriguing questions about Joel out of my head.

I had to focus on Wimbledon. I wasn't just playing for myself anymore. I was playing for Natalie. For Natalie who couldn't realise her dreams because of circumstances out of her control. And for Steve, who's dream it had been to see me succeed, and that had been taken away from him too.

Like I needed any more pressure to perform.

CHAPTER TWENTY-THREE
Adjectives

I wiped the sweat from my face. The weather in London was uncharacteristically muggy. I set my jaw and walked back onto the court for set two of round one. Against Yu Yang.

The little Chinese girl looked like she hadn't even broken a sweat in the first set, the one she'd won in a tie breaker. Well at least it had gotten to a tie breaker. I had to win this next set. I couldn't face the shame of bowing out in round one, when everyone had such high hopes for me.

Please God, I begged silently, pitifully. *Please let me get past round one, for Natalie's sake.*

I took my place at the baseline to serve.

God must have listened to me.

All the doubts that were lurking inside me vanished, to be replaced by steely determination. I eyed Yu Yang calculatingly as I served. She was good. She was freakishly good. But I was going to beat her.

The further into the game I got the surer I became. The second set was mine six four. I'd found my form. The third set was even more decisive – six two. As the crowd applauded and I shook Yu Yang's hand over the net, I waited for happiness to settle over me. Or relief. Or anything, really.

Nope … just low-level anxiety, bubbling away in the pit of my stomach like a simmering pot, just waiting for someone to turn up the heat and watch it explode.

I was subdued as I completed my press conference and my recovery. I was morose as I inhaled my chicken and rice. I was downright miserable in the car on the way back to the serviced apartments we were staying in.

Joel watched me surreptitiously as I climbed out of the car. He knew something was up, but I wasn't sure I wanted to talk to him about it. I wasn't sure that he'd understand.

I did some yoga to try and clear my mind, but I still felt mopey. I watched some British TV to try and distract myself, but that didn't work either. It didn't help that I could feel Joel watching me the whole time, and that made me think about the things I was trying to *stop* myself thinking about.

Joel served up steak and salad for dinner and I plonked myself down at the dining table, picking at it grumpily. Joel sighed.

"You're fretting, Stink," he said. I shrugged and Joel leaned closer. "What's up? You should be fired up – you had a decisive win and you've got a day off tomorrow."

I moved a cherry tomato around on my plate. "It's nothing," I muttered.

Joel was having none of that. "Just get it off your chest, Mel!" he commanded.

My head snapped up to look at him and I just blurted it out. "I have never felt so much pressure to win in my life! Natalie told her dad she had a good feeling about me. Everyone has been saying things like 'when you win at Wimbledon' and … your dad … he would have …"

"He would have known that no matter what happens, Mel, you're doing your best, playing your best."

"No, it doesn't feel like that's enough anymore," I blubbered, my tears overflowing. I wiped angrily at my streaming eyes.

Joel had gotten quite comfortable with my extreme emotions – I'd certainly given him a lot of practise with them these last few months. He leaned towards me over the table and pulled my hands into his. They we so big they made mine look tiny and delicate.

"Okay, lets deal with this, once and for all. You don't owe anyone anything when it comes to your tennis. If you start feeling like your performance is all for others it's never going to end well for you, even if you do win here at Wimbledon, because there will always be the next one, and the next one, and the stakes will start to feel too high.

"Do this for you, Mel. Sure, you can feel inspired by Natalie and by Dad. But at the end of the day, this is for you. Okay?"

I nodded.

"Anything else that you want to get out, while you're already crying?"

"Brad probably hates me because we kissed and then I freaked out!" I wailed.

Joel huffed. "Stinky, Brad doesn't hate you. He could never hate you. He loves you."

I shook my head, tears plopping into my salad. "He doesn't love me. No one can fall in love just like that." I lifted one hand from Joel's, snapping my fingers to emphasise my point.

Joel chuckled. "Stink, people *can* fall in love just like that. People can fall in love from the first time they clap their eyes on someone. And it's not like this has happened overnight anyway. He's been your friend for years. You think you're incapable of making a guy fall in love with you? You probably do it all the time and you don't even realise it."

I didn't like the things that Joel was saying. They made me feel warm and fluttery, and at the same time as if my heart and lungs were suddenly too big to be contained in my chest.

"But I don't love him – not like that, anyway."

"Well, if he loves you, he'll understand. He'll realise that he can accept it and take whatever piece of you that you're willing to give. Or if not … well, that's on him, not on you."

Joel's eyes became more serious. "You've got a very important tournament to play. You need your wits about you for this. As your coach, I can't have you moping about something like this. I need your focus to be on your game. And … as your friend … Stink, I hate seeing you so miserable."

He reached into his pocket and he pulled out his mobile phone, sitting it on the table in front of me. I looked at it, but made no move to pick it up.

"Give Brad a call, Stinky. Tell him you're sorry, make it better between the two of you. And then we'll go out and do something fun this evening, and tomorrow you can train, and relax, and get ready to smash Slavonisovich on Wednesday."

He was smiling so beautifully at me that I couldn't help but feel my own lips pulling up at the corners.

I took a deep breath. "Okay, Joel. But I'll use my own phone."

I stood up and walked into my bedroom. I didn't want Joel to hear this conversation. I sat on the edge of the bed and dialled. It rang and it rang. I was about to hang up when Brad answered.

"Hey, Mel," he panted. "Sorry, I was working out. What's up?"

I swallowed the lump in my throat – he *was* acting a little brusquely towards me. Normally he was so happy to hear from me when I was overseas. I tried not to let regret overwhelm me and focussed instead on making it better.

"Working out? Why, got a hot date tonight?" I joked, then winced straight away. That was probably not the best thing to say, considering the last 'date' he'd been on.

Brad grunted. "Nope. I had a bad experience recently, so I'm steering clear of women for a while."

Ouch!

God, please let me find the right words to make things okay between us again.

"Brad, I'm so sorry about that night. I shouldn't have … we shouldn't have … what I'm trying to say is that … I shouldn't have kissed you back. It … I gave you the wrong impression that night."

Gee, thanks God, that was just sooo articulate!

The breath hissed through Brad's teeth. I gulped. He wasn't going to let me off easily, that much was for sure.

"I don't wish you hadn't kissed me back," he muttered darkly.

"Well, I'm sorry anyway. You're one of my best friends, Brad, and you'll always have a place in my heart. But … I don't think I'm ready for what you want."

There was a silence on the other end of the phone. I felt the hope just oozing out of me. Then he spoke, and his voice wasn't cold or angry anymore.

"Do you think you'll ever be ready for that?" he asked tentatively. I pinched the bridge of my nose.

"I don't think … this isn't a conversation for over the phone, in different time zones."

Brad sighed. "You're probably right. Dinner when you get back?"

I sighed in relief, and I'm sure he could hear it in my voice when I replied, "Dinner would be great, Brad. But before I go I need to know … we're still friends, right?"

Another silence. Then, "Of course we are, Smellie. Friends always and forever. No matter what."

"I'm so lucky to have you, Brad," I whispered. "See you soon."

"Good luck, Mel," he murmured and hung up.

I lay back on the bed and breathed out all the air in my lungs – it felt like the first time in over a week that I'd been able to do that.

There was a knock on the door, but before I said anything, Joel waltzed in. I looked up at him from the bed, a little crossly, but I couldn't be truly annoyed now that I'd cleared the air with Brad.

"You were listening," I accused, but it came out teasing, not really angry.

Joel grinned unapologetically. "Of course I was, Stink. I have to make sure that my star pupil is in winning form." He winked at me.

I sneered cheekily at him. "Uh, I'm your *only* pupil, and I don't think that's the right word really."

He chuckled and shrugged. "Well, what are you then?" he asked me, lying down on his stomach on the bed beside me and propping his head up in his hands.

"Um, well I guess you'd call me … I don't know, Joel – you're the educated one, you tell me what I am!"

His eyes danced merrily. "I can think of a lot of words that describe you, Stinky. I'm just not sure you'll want to hear them."

I rolled onto my side and propped myself up on one elbow. "Try me," I offered. Joel watched me carefully. I raised one eyebrow at him and waited. He smirked back.

"Okay. Let's see. You're naive, feisty, sometimes very silly … entertaining, impulsive … this could take a while, you know, there are tonnes of adjectives out there."

I tapped my fingers on the bedspread and grinned antagonistically at him. "Come on, you can do better than that."

Joel looked away – not his usual style – and traced the pattern on the bedspread with a fingertip. Then he turned back to me and his eyes were blazing.

"Well, you're very fit … and I don't just mean that in the athletic way …" I felt my breath hitch up a notch. Joel grinned at me – he knew he was getting a reaction now.

"In fact, I'd go as far as to say that you're beautiful … especially when you're naked." He winked at me and I felt the blush spread on my face.

He jumped off the bed. "And you're about to be very excited."

I went from breathing too fast to not being able to breathe at all. What kind of excited did he mean?

"Get up and get dressed – we've got plans tonight."

I looked at him curiously as I clambered off the bed and opened my suitcase, pulling out a pair of jeans. I was getting used to Joel springing 'surprises' on me like this.

"Do I need to dress them up or down?"

"Stinky, you'd look stunning if you wore a sack – whatever you want to wear is fine."

With that he left the room, closing the door behind him with a final lopsided grin in my direction. I waited until my heart returned to its normal rhythm and then I dragged on a pair of skinny jeans and a baby blue cami top with a plunging neckline. I slipped on a pair of flats and dabbed a bit of lip gloss on.

I opened the door and stepped out. Joel was waiting in the living room, lounging on the sofa in a pair of jeans and a baby blue shirt. I rolled my eyes.

"Do you spy on me and match your outfit to mine or something?" I asked incredulously.

Joel laughed, eyes dancing. "I was about to ask you the same thing. Do you want me to change?" he asked, standing up and starting to take his shirt off. I gulped at the sight of his abs, and I took the two steps across the room to him, pulling his shirt from his hands before I got way too carried away by his body.

"No, I'll change," I insisted hastily, tugging his shirt into its correct position. I might have smoothed it over that washboard stomach just a moment longer than was strictly necessary, and I couldn't help the tiny little sigh that escaped my lips.

Joel looked down, past my face, to my breasts – I was braless in this top. He groaned softly. "No, don't change, they look awesome," he murmured, his hand grazing up my belly.

I pushed him away, flushing. "Well, let's go then, since we've established that neither of us is changing!" I snapped at him, stomping towards the door. He snorted and followed me.

"Are we getting a cab?" I asked while we waited for the elevator. Joel shook his head, smirking. I was instantly suspicious.

"Where are we going?" I demanded.

"Curious – there's another adjective for you," Joel joked. "We're going to a concert, seeing as I missed out on Princes of Lion in Sydney."

I looked sharply at him.

"They're not playing here, though."

Joel laughed. "Did I say it was them?"

I folded my arms across my chest. "Who then?" I asked.

"Impatient. Another one."

I huffed and looked away as the elevator came to a halt at the ground floor.

The night air was balmy. I was warm in jeans, but not uncomfortably so. Joel looked smug beside me as we walked through the bustling streets of Soho. It wasn't exactly convenient to the tennis, but it was definitely more interesting.

"I had some awesome nights out here when I was nineteen," Joel said. I looked up at him and he grinned down at me.

"You came here when you were nineteen?" I asked.

Joel nodded. "Yeah, during the semester break from uni. I came with a couple of mates and we stayed for a month. It was insane – the amount of beer I drank … I can't even remember how many girls I picked up."

"Okay, stop right there – too much information, buddy!" I snapped, holding up a hand.

"Jealous, Stink?" he asked cheekily. I clapped my upraised hand over his mouth before he could continue. His eyes twinkled merrily, his grin widening under my hand.

"I'm *not* jealous of you, or the countless skanks you've boned!"

Joel reached up, and with very little effort he pulled my hand away from his mouth, keeping hold of my wrist and pulling me against him.

"You sure?" he asked teasingly, releasing my wrist and trailing a hand down my arm and down my side until it rested on my hip.

"Yes, I'm sure Joel," I breathed, totally unconvincingly. He leaned down until his mouth was level with my ear.

"I think you're in denial, Melanie Black."

I managed to pull away then, folding my arms protectively across my chest. "I think *you're* wishing I was one of them, Joel Herbert," I accused.

Joel winked at me. "Well, it would be unforgettable, that's for sure." He raised one eyebrow at me suggestively. I huffed.

"Okay, Mel, I promise that I'll be a gentleman for the rest of the evening," Joel assured me chastely.

I rolled my eyes. "I'll believe *that* when I see it," I grunted. Joel picked up my hand and passed it through the crook of his elbow. I watched him surreptitiously as we walked. He was wearing such a pious expression on his face that I almost laughed, but I stopped myself just in time. I was too interested in seeing how long he could keep it up for.

We arrived at a blacked-out glass door with a bouncer standing outside it. Joel produced two tickets from his pocket and the bouncer opened the door and let us in. There was a set of steps leading down.

"This isn't a sex club is it Joel?" I asked nervously. Joel the Gentleman gave me a horrified look. I tried not to grin.

"I would never take a lady to any such establishment!" he gasped. I did grin then and he winked at me, before returning to his chivalrous persona, taking my hand and assisting me down the steps.

It was dimly lit at the bottom of the stairs, but there were a lot of people on the dance floor, surrounding an empty stage.

Joel led me towards the bar and ordered two bottles of water. He unscrewed the lid on one and passed it to me. I thanked him with a mock curtsey. Two could play at this game. I took a sip from my water.

The crowd started whistling and I turned my attention to the stage. I dropped the bottle of water. Joel managed to grab it mid-air, taking the lid from my hand and securing it. I gaped at him and he smiled indulgently at me.

"I thought you'd enjoy this," he leaned close to my ear so I could hear him over the music. I held him down at my level and turned my lips to his ear.

"I don't *believe* this!" I exclaimed, bouncing up and down with excitement. "How did you know he was going to be playing *here*?"

Jace McKenzie was notorious for doing sneaky little gigs in small independent venues. Even hardcore fans didn't often know about them until it was too late.

Joel tapped the side of his nose and didn't say anything more. He moved through the crowd until we were much closer to the stage. I bounced along in time to the beat behind him, and when he stopped, he positioned me directly in front of him.

I was sure I hadn't said anything to Joel before about my love affair with Jace McKenzie; with his unique, soulful Brit-alt-pop sound.

I was hoarse from screaming about six songs in, when Jace slowed the tempo down, and the opening chords of the song that had first made me fall in love with him began.

Joel turned me towards him and put his arms around me, pulled me close against him. I was so euphoric that I didn't try to resist. I put my arms around his waist and swayed with him in time to the music.

Joel leaned down and his lips were against my ear, and when the lyrics started, he sang the words along with Jace. He had a husky singing voice that sent my nerves tingling. I closed my eyes and let the song flow over me, feeling Joel's warm body against mine.

The song lifted towards its climax and I took a deep breath. Joel stopped singing and I opened my eyes. His face was so close to mine that I could feel my lips tingling from his breath on them. I realised that my hands weren't on his waist anymore – they were under his shirt, my fingers splayed against his skin. One of his hands was under my hair, curled around my neck. His eyes were closed.

The song ended and the audience screamed for more. I tore myself away from Joel and turned, cheering and clapping and acting as if what had just happened, hadn't.

I made sure that I kept some distance between us after that. I didn't let him turn me towards him again. If he put his hand on my waist to keep me close to him in the crowd, I pulled away slightly.

When Jace left the stage for the last time, and the audience started moving towards the door, I looked down at my watch. It was almost one.

"Did you have a good time?" Joel asked quietly as we climbed the stairs and headed back out onto the street.

I refused to look at him. "Yes! It was … I have no words. Thank you so much, Joel. How did you know I like Jace McKenzie?"

Joel snorted. "I'm not sure if 'like' is a strong enough word, Stinky. And I've heard you singing in the shower enough times to have worked out your obsession with him."

I flushed, my eyes downcast. "Did *you* have a good time?" I asked. I didn't like him thinking about me in the shower. I didn't like thinking about him thinking about me in the shower. It made me throb in places I was trying not to feel when I was with him.

Joel sighed. "I had a fucking great time, Mel," he replied fervently. I looked at him then. His eyes were blazing.

"A gentleman wouldn't use a word like that in the presence of a lady," I chided him teasingly.

He bit his lip and bowed his head. "I apologise, Miss Black, for my language," he responded formally. "And now I'd better get you home to bed, before I turn back into a pumpkin."

I giggled despite myself. I didn't want to find him charming, but it was almost impossible not to.

"Okay, you can drop the act now, Joel. I'm not sure I like you as much when you're not being a rogue."

He glanced sidelong at me and before I knew what was happening, I found myself up against the wall of the nearest building. People continued to walk past us as if nothing was happening. As if I hadn't suddenly found myself pinned between solid brick and six foot four of pure muscle and sex.

He leaned down and pressed his lips to my neck, just at my hairline, behind my ear, even as he pushed one knee between my thighs. Goosebumps erupted all over me and I trembled. I didn't have the strength to fight him off. I wasn't sure I wanted to.

My breath was coming in little panting gasps as Joel's lips lingered on my skin, the warmth of his leg meeting the heat of my pussy through my jeans, creating pressure on the seam of denim that was rubbing right where I needed it most. His breath was warm on the nape of my neck as his lips moved against my skin, up towards my jaw, my earlobe. I longed to rock myself against that strong leg, to turn my head, capture his full bottom lip between my teeth.

But instead, I stood frozen. The wanting feeling was far too big.

After a moment he pulled away, silently offering his arm to me, his lips moist and quirked up into a funny little half-smile. I somewhat shakily linked my arm with his and let him lead me away.

"My sincerest apologies for the brief roguish lapse, Miss Black," he said. I grinned, relieved that he was joking it away. Relieved that I hadn't given in like I'd wanted to. Like I still secretly wanted to, somewhere down in the pit of my stomach where there was a seed of disappointment that he had stopped when he did.

Not a good idea to think about that.

The elevator seemed to take forever to get us up to our room. It felt too small, too crowded, though it was only the two of us inside.

Joel unlocked the door and held it open for me. I walked inside and went straight to my bedroom door. When I turned back, expecting him to be across the room at his bedroom door, I was startled to find him right behind me.

"A gentleman always walks a lady to her door," he explained with a smile.

I opened the door and took a step back. "Thank you, Mr Herbert, for the lovely evening. And I'm willing to forgive the little indiscretion on the journey home. I'll put it down to the overwhelming excitement of the concert."

I took another step back, preparing to make my escape, but Joel grabbed my wrist and pulled me close again. He leaned down and kissed me on the cheek. It would have been a very polite kiss except he lingered there too long, and his lips parted slightly and moved towards my ear.

"A gentleman always kisses a lady goodnight," he whispered.

"Well, goodnight, Joel," I murmured. My voice trembled.

"Goodnight, Mel. Oh, I just thought of another adjective."

"What?" I whispered.

"Horny," he replied with a grin, and turned and walked away before I could argue. Not that he wasn't completely right, damn him.

It wasn't until much later when I was in bed trying to sleep that I realised that 'pupil' wasn't even an adjective – it was a noun. And Joel couldn't find one noun to describe what I was to him.

Well, that was depressing.

CHAPTER TWENTY-FOUR

Wimbledon

I shoved all thought of Joel from my mind as I warmed up for my round two match against Gordana Slavonisovich. I really hoped that today wouldn't be the day that she would finally beat me. I didn't think it would. Physically I was in my best shape ever, thanks to Joel and his positive reinforcement and the diet and training schedule he had me on.

Whoops, I wasn't supposed to be thinking about Joel, was I?

But it was impossible not to – he was always *there*. He was playing a very important role in my life. I had to acknowledge that.

He'd been a little weird after the night of the concert – it seemed that every time he knew he got too close to breaking down that final little barrier that I held between us, he backed off. It only confused me more. Was what I felt something real? Was he just playing with me? I didn't want to find out.

I desperately wanted to find out.

I shook my head to clear the thoughts; they had nothing to do with this game against Gordana. I had to concentrate on my sport.

Joel handed me my racquet as I finished re-lacing one of my shoes. He watched me closely. "Something's different about you today, Stink. Normally you're a little agitated just before a game, but today you seem very quiet and focussed. Not that it's a bad thing, by any means. It's just interesting."

I shrugged, not meeting his eyes. "I don't know, Joel. I guess I've just realised that it's not worth it to worry," I lied. Joel grinned at me, and I could feel the tension bubbling to the surface at the sight of his smile. I ruthlessly stifled all of those feelings and walked out onto the court – cool, calm and collected.

I won in straight sets: six one, six two. I shook Gordana's hand and she shook her head. We all have a hoodoo player – a player that we always lose to, no matter what, so I guessed that I might just happen to be Gordana's.

Now I had another day off before round three. Another day of trying to keep my distance from Joel – a task that was rapidly becoming next to impossible.

"You want to go out and do something tonight?" Joel asked me once we were back in the apartment. I dumped my bags inside the door and went straight to the lounge, flicking on the TV and finding the most mindless thing on: some reality show about a bunch of girls vying for the affections of an obscure European Prince. I shook my head vaguely, not taking my eyes off the TV. Not wanting to look at him.

"But you go out if you want, Joel. Don't feel like you need to entertain me."

Joel plonked himself on the lounge beside me, close enough that his shoulder touched mine. I stiffened, shifting to put some space between us.

"Do I smell bad?" he asked, turning the full force of his baby blues on me. I pursed my lips, shaking my head again.

"Relax then. I won't bite." He patted the space I'd just vacated at his side. If I didn't move back, he'd only shuffle over towards me, so I complied. My arm tingled with heat where his skin met mine, and I felt far too warm and achy in places that weren't supposed to be reacting to Joel.

I focussed entirely on the TV then, on two contestants who were having a slanging match about who the Prince kissed first.

Joel snorted. "I can't understand why anyone wants to go on these shows," he said with a shake of his head. I turned to look at him out of the corner of my eye. "I mean," he continued, "do they actually think this Prince is going to fall in love with either of them?"

I shrugged. "People have fallen in love in stranger ways," I muttered.

Joel turned towards me. "Were you in love with Grant?" he asked me suddenly. I wasn't expecting the question. I bit my lip and tried to focus on his words and not his big, warm body pressed against my side.

"I thought I was back then," I replied thoughtfully. "But, looking at it now, I don't think it was real love. How does anyone know at that age whether they're in love or not? He made me feel special. So when everything went down with him and Susie … I thought I was heartbroken. But now, I think what I was feeling was humiliation."

"So, not Grant. Have you ever been in love then?" he persisted. Again, I paused, all too aware of his arm on the back of the sofa behind my head.

I shrugged. "Who else have I had a chance to fall in love with?" I asked. "Why are you so interested anyway? Have *you* ever been in love?"

Joel eyed me cheekily. "I've been far too busy having great sex to fall in love."

I grimaced. "Don't tell me you've never had feelings for *any* of the women you've been with," I grunted in disbelief.

Joel sobered up. "I didn't say that. I've got a lot of affection and respect for most of the women I've slept with. But no, I haven't been in love with any of them."

"Not Princes of Lion Girl?" I asked slyly. Joel's mouth tweaked up at one corner and he shook his head.

"What about Julie?" I forced myself to ask.

Joel sighed. "No, I'm not in love with Julie, Stink. We're just friends."

"Ah, the good old fuck-buddy," I grouched. Joel shook with silent laughter.

"So, if you've never been in love with anyone you've slept with," I said thoughtfully, "what about women you *haven't* slept with – there has to be a few of us scattered around."

Joel loomed over me, his bulging arms caging me in. "Any time you want, Mel, I'll change you over to the other list."

I rolled my eyes, worried that if I opened my mouth, I would just tell him to go right ahead and have his way with me. Have every possible way with me. I took a couple of deep breaths until I was calm again.

"Sure, Joel, but beware, my kink is kissing and running."

Joel chuckled but didn't move away from me. His hand came down off the back of the sofa and touched my hair.

"Stink, if I kissed you, there is no way you would want to run."

I really should be running now. I shoved roughly at his torso while I still had a shred of resolve left. He barely budged.

"Get off me you sleaze!" I whined. Joel laughed again and flopped back beside me. We sat in silence for a few moments – Joel apparently absorbed in the never-ending bitch fight on the prince show. Me sulking, wondering how much longer I was going to be able to hold off against him.

"I've been in love before," Joel murmured out of the blue.

I turned and gaped at him. "Really?" I asked incredulously.

His eyes met mine. "Yep."

"What happened?" I asked quietly, leaning closer to him.

"She's made it pretty clear what she thinks of me."

"Who is it?" I gasped. "Are you *still* in love with her? What does it feel like?" I leaned against his side, our eyes locked into each other's. His face was inscrutable.

"It feels like a constant ache, here." He placed a hand over the centre of his chest. I found myself mirroring the movement. My heart thrummed against my palm.

Then Joel broke into a smile and slung an arm around me. "But it doesn't matter, Mel. Who needs love anyway when I've got you around to annoy?"

I sighed, but I didn't pull away. I let him hold me against him. I should move away from him, put that all important distance between us. But the stupid, reckless, infatuated part of my brain wouldn't let me. I remained under his arm on the lounge, pretending to watch TV when really I was imagining us naked, his lips … his hands … his tongue … exploring me everywhere.

Jesus, Mel, get a grip! You can't have that with Joel. Sex will ruin what you two have right now. You can't do that. Ever.

Round three versus Katinka Norieva. I was cold and detached on court. There was no room for nerves – all the emotions roiling inside me when I was alone with Joel had sapped all the strength for any other feelings out of me.

This was a good thing, I decided, when I won the second set and consequently the match. I couldn't remember the last time I'd won two back-to-back matches in straight sets.

Joel rubbed my back as I walked into the change room. "Congratulations, Stinky. Two days off now until your next match. Anything you want to do?"

You, I thought, then blushed. Joel looked at me curiously.

"I think I should train extra hard over the weekend. I want to keep up this straight sets winning streak if possible." I kept my voice light, afraid that he'd hear something in my tone that would twig him to what was really going on inside my head.

Joel shrugged. "If that's what you want, I'll support you. I told you I had a good feeling about this one."

I rolled my eyes. "Whatever, Joel. I get into finals all the time, but this is *Wimbledon*. I'm not going to win."

He nudged me with his shoulder. "Not with that sort of attitude you won't. Stink, I know you hate watching yourself play, but I think we'll watch the footage of that game between now and your next match. You were incredible. I need you to realise that."

I decided to humour him.

Round four versus Abigail Petersen. I went into it with a whole new outlook. No longer cold and distant.

I'd spent the previous night lying on the lounge while he sat on the floor, his head next to mine, providing me with a running commentary of my game against Norieva. And I had been able to forget that his lips were within kissing distance of mine. Now, I had something else to focus on.

I was going to win Wimbledon. Watching the game back had made me see something clearly for the first time – I was playing the best tennis of my life, and if I was ever going to win, it was going to be now.

We'd spent the hour after that going over Petersen's game – her strengths, her weaknesses. We'd strategised. I'd never been more prepared going into a game.

It paid off. Another straight sets win – six one, six one. Joel winked at me as he walked into the change room, bumping my fist with his own. I grinned, feeling relieved that the tension between us seemed to have dissipated … for now at least.

Quarter-finals here I come.

Saturn Phillips. The world number one player. She was six feet of pure muscle and she terrified me. Never mind the fact that I'd never played her before, but her sheer power … it was overwhelming. And she didn't just grunt when she hit the ball. She screamed, which was pretty off-putting.

"Don't get worked up about it, Stink. Just keep your cool, like you have been for the last four rounds, and you'll be fine. You're on *fire* – the media is touting you the player to watch. You've got this in the bag. Saturn's getting old – you're younger, faster and fitter."

I gave Joel a weak smile and let him pat me on the cheek, my head spinning that I was about to face down the world number one player in the quarter-final of the biggest tournament of the year.

I won the first set. Saturn won the second and she was burning up the court. I felt my grip on the match slipping as she won the third game of the final set. I hadn't won a game in this set yet and judging by the strength with which she was sending the ball my way, I wasn't sure I would.

I lined up on the baseline and allowed myself a brief glance up into the stands at Joel before I served. He grinned at me. I chuckled under my breath, feeling my fear vanish. I served.

Saturn didn't score any more points after that. I won the third set and the match.

Semi-final versus Joanne Mercer. I'd only played her once and she'd beaten me.

Again, Joel spent my day off going over her past few matches and together we dissected her game.

"You know, Joel," I began as we both stretched and got ready to go to bed, "you're a great coach. I don't know what I'd do without you."

He grinned and tweaked me on the cheek.

"Thanks, Stinky. I was thinking earlier that I can't remember enjoying myself as much as when I'm helping you win games."

I smirked. "Oh my God, I'm better than sex!" I teased, relieved that we were back in that comfortable place where we *could* tease each other.

"You're better than sex …" he murmured in agreement as he walked towards his room. Everything south of my navel contracted violently.

He looked back over his shoulder from the doorway of his room. "Sleep well, Stink. You've got an American to beat tomorrow."

The morning air was hot and heavy as I walked onto the court. Joanne Mercer smiled at me from the other side of the net. I'd always liked her – she was friendly to everyone and she was a good winner. I wondered if today was my chance to find out if she was a good loser as well.

She smashed me in the first set, six games to two. I took a break, towelled the sweat off and went back out for another try.

The second set went my way, six four. Joanne maintained her cheery facade even as we went into the deciding set. I wondered if that was a tactic to try and throw me off guard. I breathed deep and positioned myself to receive the ball.

I went into a whole other dimension when I won that final set. I looked up at Joel, who was beaming hugely at me.

"Only one more match between me and that trophy, Sensei," I teased as we prepared to head back to the hotel. Joel put his hand on the small of my back and ushered me out. We wouldn't know who I was up against until the other semi-final was played that evening. But since it was narrowed down to two players, Joel decided we'd start discussing both of them.

"Di Gunn is older, she's trying to make a comeback after having a year off to have a baby," Joel explained. I nodded impatiently – this was information I already knew.

"That she's gotten to the semi-final means that she's very focussed on proving herself. But she *is* older and she's only been back a couple of tournaments. It's her home crowd, though, so there'll be a lot of support for her."

"What about Heather Roach?" I asked. I didn't know much about the young Canadian. I hadn't played her before. I hadn't seen her play before.

It seemed that Joel didn't know much about Heather Roach either.

So of course, she was the one that I was facing in the final.

Okay, Mel, you've got her number now. She's got a niggle in her ankle. She seems to be favouring her left leg. Whatever it is she's definitely not enjoying it when you send her across court. Work her as hard as you can, keep her running back and forth.

I'd noticed Heather limping very slightly when she had to run for the ball. I self-consciously moved my own right ankle around in circles. It was feeling fine, but there was nothing to say that Heather Roach wasn't over there right now reminding herself about my weak ankle too.

I took a swig of water and searched the stand for Joel. He met my gaze with an intensity that sent tingles thrumming through me. I was running on nothing more than nervous energy anyway – that's what happens when you're in a tie breaker inside a tie breaker. What I mean is, we'd each won a set and now on the third we were locked at six games each.

So, there was very little fuel left in the tank. The only thing keeping me going was the knowledge that if I won, I'd won at Wimbledon. I'd never even imagined I'd get to the final, let alone have a shot at *winning* it.

I thought about Steve and Natalie, and I prayed silently that the Atheists were wrong, and that they were both watching me from Heaven. I looked up at the watery British sun, sending a silent promise to both of them. *This one's for you.*

The bell went off and I walked back onto the court silently. Heather Roach nodded at me across the court.

I served and all thoughts of everything else disappeared – Joel, Steve, Natalie – everything except winning.

Serve, return, forehand, backhand, volley, run, run, run, backhand. That was the extent of what was going on inside my brain. I didn't even have room to keep score.

I scored a point and the crowd erupted. I looked at the umpire, who was calling the game – I'd won.

I'd won.

I'd *WON!*

I dropped my racquet right then and there, hands pressed over my heart. Heather Roach was standing at the net waiting for me to come and shake her hand. I practically floated towards her.

"Congratulations, Mel!" Heather greeted me in her mellow Canadian accent. "You deserve this. I'm a big fan of yours."

"Thanks, Heather!" I said with feeling. It wasn't often that a competitor was so nice after you beat them.

And then I looked up and saw Joel. I'd just won my first ever

Grand Slam event, at Wimbledon no less, and without him I couldn't have done it.

I raced across the court, skidded to a halt briefly to shake the umpire's hand, and then I climbed the barrier into the shocked and delighted crowd. I navigated my way up the stands, people clapping and cheering as they moved aside. I ascended towards the coach's box, Joel watching me, eyes burning. I flung my arms around his neck and clung to him. I could feel his laughter where our bodies were touching (which was a lot of places), and his lips pressed against the side of my neck. He didn't even seem to care that I was oozing sweat and I probably stunk. My top had ridden up a bit at the back and Joel's hands sneaked up under it, his fingertips caressing my spine.

"You did it, Mel! You really did it – I told you that you could do it!"

"You did tell me, Joel." I couldn't fail to notice that his hands were still under my top. I felt dizzy from the win and from his proximity to me.

I was about to throw caution to the wind, to open my mouth and just blurt out the words that had been on the tip of my tongue for weeks now, but just as I took a breath to say *"kiss me"* to Joel, he turned me back towards the court. His eyes weren't on me anymore.

"Go, Mel, this is your moment!"

I turned and raced back onto the court, to where I was being beckoned by the match officials to the podium that had been hastily erected.

I stood in a daze, not paying attention to anything happening around me – not the words that the match official said into the mic, not Heather Roach receiving her runners-up award, not Princess Kate waiting to present the trophy to me.

I just watched Joel. I watched the way his facial muscles moved as he grinned down at me from his place in the stands. I let my eyes rove over his impressive body as he clapped.

It was probably a good thing that the presentation had started when it did – who knows what would have happened if Joel and I hadn't been interrupted then.

And then Princess Kate was shaking my hand and passing the trophy over to me. I held it above my head and the crowd cheered. I grinned stupidly, my eyes prickling when I thought about all the people I'd done this for. Steve and Natalie. Brad and Amanda, who'd always been there for me. Even Mum, who had gotten me into tennis in the first place.

And Joel. Of course, Joel.

When it was over, when I'd blurted some unknown words into the microphone for the crowd, when I'd done a lap of the court and shaken the hands of the people who were hanging over the edge, when I'd mindlessly answered press conference questions, finally I was able to leave the spotlight.

"Do I have to do my recovery today?" I whined at Joel when I found him waiting in the change room for me. "I don't think I can sit still long enough."

Joel laughed and took the trophy from my hands. "Ice bath and take a shower and then we'll get out of here. I can always give you a rub down when we get back to the apartment."

I was on such a high I didn't even bother reacting to his innuendo. I iced myself and showered in record time, slipped into clean underwear and a dress, and we avoided the worst of the rabble outside the players' entrance to get into a taxi.

"Well Mel, we're going to have to make an appearance at the WTA party tonight now – you'll be the star attraction."

I grimaced. I didn't like tennis parties. But I could see his point.

The taxi dropped us out the front of the building and we clambered out, weighed down with all my tennis gear. Joel carried most of it. I followed him in a daze.

The staff in the reception area crowded around to congratulate me. I accepted their praise with grace, all the time backing towards the elevator.

I sighed out a deep breath when the doors closed and we were finally alone.

"I can't believe it, Joel, it just feels so surreal," I said, leaning against the side of the lift.

He beamed at me. "Better get used to it fast, Stink. Everyone's going to want you — you're a piece of history now."

I grunted at him. "That makes me feel old — a piece of history."

"Oh, you're so old, almost twenty-three!" he teased.

I wrinkled my nose at him. "Well, sorry that I'm not ancient like you. Twenty-eight this year. Do I need to start reminding you to book in for your prostate exam?"

Joel snorted and I giggled.

"Stink, get the key out of my pocket — my hands are full."

"Could you be any less subtle about making me fumble around in your pants?" I said, but reached into his shorts pocket for the key, blushing as my hand brushed against his crotch. I dragged the key out and swiftly turned to unlock the door, biting my lip hard because words wanted to spill out — words that I just couldn't say.

Joel dumped our gear just inside the door. I walked in, sucking in a deep breath. He came up behind me, hands spanning my hips, fingers caressing.

"Mel, I'm so proud of you," he whispered in my ear. I turned around to face him, trying to figure out what was safe to say. There were too many things I wanted to say.

Joel didn't give me a chance to say anything.

His lips crashed into mine and my resolve crumbled.

CHAPTER TWENTY-FIVE

Getting In Too Deep

I felt that kiss everywhere. I gasped and he used that moment to slip his tongue past my lips.

Oh God, the taste of him was like crack! As his tongue tangled with mine, the ache between my legs intensified to the point where I had to break the kiss to pant.

My body curved towards his, pressing against him, his hands slid from my hips to grip my butt. And I could *definitely* feel his dick straining against his shorts urgently where his hips met mine.

He leaned back in to kiss me again, but I turned my head to the side.

"Joel, this isn't … I don't think we should …"

"Liar," he murmured into my ear, his teeth grazing my earlobe. An involuntary moan rolled up through my throat.

His hand slid up under my dress and pushed my underwear aside, his finger slipping inside my slick folds. My pussy clenched emptily as he stroked me.

"Yep, definitely lying," he whispered. He was right, damn him! Was I about to make the biggest mistake of my life?

Stuff it! I thought, dragging his head down, pressing my mouth against his. He responded with a groan, his tongue slipping back into my mouth and sending electric pulses shuddering through me.

"Didn't I always tell you that one day you'd realise you wanted me?" Joel asked cheekily as he broke our kiss to trail his lips along my jaw.

"Don't spoil the moment, Joel. Just fuck me."

He responded by lifting me up off the ground and carrying me into his bedroom.

He sat me on the edge of the bed with surprising gentleness and slipped my dress off over my head. Kneeling on the floor in front of me, he nudged my legs apart and wedged himself between my thighs. He reached around with one hand and unhooked my bra with practised ease, pressing his searing lips to my shoulder as he pulled it off. He leaned back and just … stared at me.

My pussy throbbed as his gaze roved over my breasts, my stomach, my thighs, as I sat on his bed wearing nothing but a pair of Dudz. I bit my lip, a moan slipping between my teeth.

"So fucking beautiful," he murmured, his hands sliding over my shoulders, my collarbone, and down the valley between my breasts until his hand rested on my navel. He pushed me gently until I fell back against the mattress and he loomed over me.

I swallowed heavily and reached for his waist, tugging his polo shirt up and over his head, exposing his impressive body, those cut abs. My palms met his skin, my fingertips trailing down the hard planes of his chest and across that washboard stomach, feeling the skin ripple under my touch.

Why hadn't I just given into this a long time ago?

Damn it, Joel had been right! He'd known all along that I was fighting a losing battle against my own desire for him. He'd known it even before I did.

Joel's hungry gaze devoured me. He pressed the significant length of his body against me, and I gasped as I felt the pressure of his cock on my thigh. My pussy clenched again, wetness soaking my underwear. His mouth found mine, tongue teasing mine, teeth nipping at my bottom lip.

His fingers found my nipples. He caressed them with his thumb, then gave them a pinch, earning a squeak of pleasure from me. He broke away from my mouth, kissing down my chest, towards one cupped breast. His fingers were replaced by his mouth, his tongue laving, flicking, his teeth grazing to a point where pleasure became almost painful.

He slid a hand down my belly, tugging at the waistband of my underwear. I lifted my hips obligingly and he pulled them down my legs and off. His own shorts and trunks followed, and I gasped as I looked down and caught a glimpse of his thick length as it bobbed against his stomach.

"You like what you see, Mel." It wasn't even a question; he knew he was a near perfect specimen of manhood. I responded by reaching down and grasping him, stroking that stunning cock. It jerked in my hand and I panted, giving him a squeeze. I grinned as he choked out a moan, thrusting into my hand.

"This isn't how I …" he began, then stopped. I wondered what he'd meant to say, but before I had a chance to ask, his lips, his tongue, were teasing my mouth again.

His hand cupped my pussy, his fingers dipping into my dripping entrance, then out again, circling my wetness over my aching clit. I gasped and let my legs fall wider.

Joel ground the heel of his palm against my clit, his fingers thrusting into me. One, then two, stirring me.

"You feel so fucking good," he growled. I rolled my hips and dug my nails into his back, clutching him closer to me, licking into his mouth.

The tingling started in my toes, an ache spreading out from deep within me.

"I'm so close!" I broke away from his mouth to gasp. He responded by curling his fingers inside me to stroke the hypersensitive, ridged spot as his thumb flicked my clit.

Once.

Twice.

Three times.

I exploded, crying out as my pussy contracted around his fingers, every muscle in my body spasming with the strength of the orgasm. Joel's forehead met mine as his fingers continued to thrust gently inside me, slowly bringing me down.

"Mel," he whispered, and there was some strong emotion in his voice that I couldn't decipher.

"Yes, Joel?" I responded, reaching down between us and wrapping a hand around his dick once more, guiding him towards me.

He leaned closer, kissing me on the tip of my nose in a surprisingly tender way, and then he was in me. Filling me. Stretching me.

Part of me.

I wrapped my legs tight around his hips and clutched him to me, rocking back and forth in sync with his thrusts.

"You have no idea how long I've been waiting for this," he murmured against my cheek as he pushed even deeper inside of me, his cock rubbing against my already over-sensitised g-spot, his pelvis grinding against my clit. I felt my body tightening again, that delicious ache building deep within.

I had no space in my brain to stop and think about his words. He reached down and grabbed a handful of my butt, angling me back slightly so his cock rubbed harder against that sensitive spot inside me.

"Oh God, Joel!" I sobbed out, clawing my nails into his back. He leaned back and caught my eyes as my orgasm exploded. I couldn't look away. I drowned in the ocean of his eyes as I clenched around him, moaning incoherently.

"Was that good?" he asked a moment later, still rocking back and forth inside of me, his hands tangled into my hair as my pussy continued to flutter around his cock in little aftershocks.

I nodded, not trusting my voice at that moment.

"Because *that* was fucking amazing for me," he continued, and for a second I wondered how it could have been so amazing when he was still hard and throbbing inside me, still very obviously not finished. But then he leaned back so he was kneeling and lifted me until I was straddling him, sending all thought fleeing my brain. His fingers kneaded my butt as I gripped fistfuls of his silky hair. His lips found mine and he feasted on my mouth, as he continued to rock me back and forth on him. I moved in sync with him, riding his gorgeous cock, digging my nails into the nape of his neck.

He clutched me tighter to him, burying his head in my shoulder and stifling his own groan as he pulsed inside me, flooding me with heat.

We sat like that for a few moments, just getting our breath back, and then he lowered me back down on the bed and pulled out of me, lying beside me and cuddling me. I nestled into the crook of his arm, like that spot had been made for me.

"Wow!" I breathed. Joel was silent. I turned my head to see whether he'd fallen asleep, but he was watching me through heavy-lidded eyes.

I blushed. I'd just completely lost control of myself, with Joel to boot – the one guy I had always said I wouldn't touch – couldn't touch. Shouldn't touch.

But looking at him now, I couldn't regret it. What we'd just done was so different from any sex I'd ever had – in the best possible way. It scared me how much I wanted it again already. And not just the orgasms, but the feel of him so close to me. Part of me.

"Mel," Joel whispered. I rolled towards him and pressed my lips gently to his. This was getting into dangerous territory now. This post-sex snuggling was crossing another line. One that I didn't think either of us wanted to cross.

"I'd better go shower – we've got a party to get to," I dead-panned, trying to save some face.

I got off the bed and walked to my bedroom without looking back at him.

I don't know how I managed to shower and do my hair when every fibre in my being was screaming to me to just go back into his room and climb back into bed with him. But I did.

I opened the wardrobe and pulled out the one special dress I'd brought with me; after the dinner debacle in Dubai I always came prepared. As I stepped into it, I imagined his expression when he saw me in it, before immediately peeling it off me. And then I had to stop for a second to get my breath back again.

The deep teal green body-hugging sheath dress clung to my thighs, pressing them together and heightening those deliciously achy post-sex sensations. I spent a good few minutes staring at my reflection in the mirror, trying to get my heart under control. It was just the sex that was making it flutter like this. Just the amazing sex.

Despite my best efforts to remain composed, the second I saw the look on Joel's face when I walked out of the bedroom, I knew that my expression would be all too readable to him.

"Wow, you look … incredible," Joel said, his eyes roving over my body before meeting mine. I couldn't hold his gaze; I felt suddenly shy. I looked down at the sexy green dress I was wearing, with a very rare pair of heels.

"We'd better get going or we'll be late," I muttered.

Joel took a deep breath. I sneaked a glance up at him from under my lashes. He was wearing a pale grey pinstripe suit with a teal green shirt underneath, open at the collar. Why was it that we always seemed to unintentionally match when we went out? Normally I would have made some smart-arse comment about it, but the words just dried up in my throat. In some stupid way I kind of liked it that we were colour coordinated.

I walked to the door and stopped to wait for him. He approached, then paused, facing me. He was just too close, it was intoxicating. Why was I unable to resist feeling aroused when I was near him? If anything, having sex with him had made those feelings more intense.

He made no move to open the door. Neither did I.

Seconds inched by.

Eventually I took a deep breath and turned the handle. I walked out, feeling his eyes on me the whole way down the hallway.

Then we were in the limo that the WTA had sent for their 'guest of honour'. It was the longest ride of my life. It felt like there was a live wire running between Joel and me. His hand was resting on the seat between us, as was mine, less than an inch separating them. I was gritting my teeth, resisting the almost irresistible urge to weave my fingers through his and hold on tight.

Don't be so stupid, Mel, I told myself firmly. *It was just sex. It's out of your system now and soon enough these feelings will go away. There's nothing else going on here. Just sex.*

Joel helped me out of the limo at the other end. Wherever his hand touched my skin felt hot to the point of burning. I was immediately hustled away by media for photos with Heather, and unfortunately, Pete and his opponent, Donatello Herrera.

Joel was left behind, and he watched me with a faraway smile as I was carried away by the tide of journalists.

———

"You look like you've been enjoying yourself this afternoon," Pete commented quietly as we posed for the cameras. I gritted my teeth through the fake smile I was forcing. Donatello was on my other side, smiling vaguely at the camera.

"You have no right to comment on how I look, Pete Levine!" I hissed, then proceeded to ignore him until the photographers released us.

I caught Joel eyeing me from the bar. He noticed me looking and winked, toasting me with the beer in his hand. I wanted to go and drink with him, but I wasn't sure I could handle being that close to him right now.

"Hey, Mel, wanna dance?" Clayton Banks asked behind me. I turned and grinned at him.

"Sure, why not? We haven't caught up in ages!" I commented as Clayton led me onto the dance floor. "Congrats on making it to the semis."

Clayton beamed at me. "Come on, Mel, don't congratulate *me* – you're the Wimbledon champ here! When we get back home, they'll probably have forgotten my name!"

I giggled. "I don't think so, Clay. You have a penis, remember? You're instantly more interesting to sports journalists."

Clay barked out a laugh at that. "Don't forget I'm the only openly gay Australian tennis player with a penis."

I sneaked a look out of the corner of my eye. Joel was standing at the bar, watching me over the top of his beer. I dragged my eyes away from him, turning back to Clayton with a smile. He'd seen where my eyes had taken me and he smirked knowingly.

"Mixing business with pleasure, Mel?" he murmured.

I shrugged, feigning nonchalance, but my blush gave me away. "No idea what you're talking about, Clay."

He snickered at me. "No judgement. I've known Joel Herbert for a long time – his family and mine go way back – he's a really decent guy. Smart. Hot as fuck." I caught Clayton watching Joel in a more than friendly way.

I smacked playfully at his arm. "He's *straight*, Clayton Banks!" I hissed.

Clay grinned at me. "Hey, it's a free world, I'll look all I want thanks."

After my dance with Clayton, the evening passed in a blur for me. A blur of flashing cameras, cocktails, polite conversation with players and coaches and media, cocktails, tipsy small talk with some of the female players, more cocktails. And yet at no time through the whole night did I lose sight of where Joel was.

It was as if all my senses were suddenly tuned in to his frequency. If he talked to another woman, I felt it like the stab of a hot knife. If I happened to be talking to a guy when I caught him glancing back in my direction, I made sure to smile brightly and laugh, as if whoever I was talking to had just made the funniest joke. I think a lot of men that night decided that I was a little nuts. I sort of decided I was too.

I was sipping at my third Tequila Sunrise when his voice was in my ear.

"Okay, I've had a fun night playing games with you, Mel, but now I want to take you home." I heard the suggestion in his tone and my insides burst into flames. I tried desperately to keep my cool.

"Alright, Joel," I didn't like the way my heart skipped a beat when I said his name, although I was pretty sure it was just because I knew exactly what would happen when he 'took me home'.

There was a car waiting at the bottom of the steps, and Joel opened the door for me. I slid across to the far seat and he followed me in. The door closed, and the driver moved away from the kerb.

I wanted desperately to ask Joel what was going on here – why I suddenly felt like I couldn't be near him without going almost insane with the urge to hike my dress up and climb onto his lap. I'd thought that need might ease off now I'd slaked my thirst for him, but it was even more unbearable. I couldn't possibly admit that to him.

I didn't have a chance to work out what to say, because the second I turned to him his lips were on mine, his hands were on my waist and I was flying. It wasn't until his hand slipped along my thigh, up under my dress that I remembered we were still in the hire car, and the driver would be able to see everything. I broke away from Joel with an effort. He looked at me curiously.

"Just until we get back to the hotel," I whispered. He grinned at me, stroking my cheek, his thumb brushing across my lips. I opened my mouth and he slipped it inside. I sucked on it gently, his moan coiling me tighter. It was like the entire evening had been hours of protracted foreplay, and I was wound tight, ready to burst.

I wasn't sure I was going to be able to make it up in the lift. Joel was pressed up against me, his hands on my butt, his mouth at my throat, leaving me gasping for breath, desperate for him.

The lift came to a halt with a little dinging sound and the doors slid open. Joel didn't stop kissing my collarbone.

"Are we going to go inside, or do you want to do this here?" I asked breathlessly. Joel broke away and grinned down at me.

"Whatever you want, Mel. Here's pretty good, don't you think?"

I almost let him have his way. Only the worry that the lift might head back down and pick someone else up stopped me. I straightened up and tugged at his hand. He followed willingly enough. I could feel his lips on the back of my neck as I unlocked the door and stumbled inside.

The door closed and he pinned me up against the wall, kissing me hard and fast. I was defenceless. Not that I was trying to resist all that hard. Or at all.

He reached under my dress.

"Fuck, Mel!" he grated out, finding nothing but hot, wet flesh. I grinned against his mouth.

"VPL is a very real problem, Joel," I teased as I reached down and unbuckled his belt, unzipped his fly and pulled his penis out of his pants. He lifted me up against the wall and lowered me onto him. I bit my lip to prevent myself from screaming out right then.

He moved inside me, holding me against the wall, his hands supporting my butt and his forehead pressed against mine. The coil tightened even further as his hands squeezed my butt cheeks, his fingers slipping between them as he pounded me, muttering darkly between his thrusts.

"I can't believe," *thrust* "that you were just," *thrust* "walking around that party," *thrust* "with no," *thrust* "fucking," *thrust* "panties on." *Two quick, deep thrusts.*

I moaned into his shoulder as I came.

He set me back down again, holding me until I was back on earth enough to stand on my own, before stepping out of his pants and peeling me out of my dress. I dragged his jacket off him and unbuttoned his shirt. I giggled as I looked at him standing there with a massive boner, naked except for his socks and shoes, and I bent down to take them off him.

When I straightened up, he grabbed me to him and carried me into his bedroom.

Spread out naked on his bed, my hair splayed around my face and shoulders, with Joel watching me intently as he crawled up the bed towards me, was utter torture. Despite having just come on him, I ached for more.

Joel stopped just short of my mouth, his lips finding my jaw, his hands tangling in my hair. I reached towards him, but he grabbed my wrists in both hands and held them above my head.

"Uh-uh," he murmured. "No touching for you. It's my turn." My breath caught in my throat as he started feathering light kisses down my collarbone and between my breasts. My nipples hardened in anticipation, but he continued on past them, kissing down my stomach, pausing to dart his tongue into my belly button.

I arched towards him with a gasp, pressing my belly against his face. He moaned into my skin. I longed to grip my hands in his hair and guide his mouth exactly where I wanted it. I think he realised; he lifted his head, eyes burning.

"Don't move your hands or I'll have to start all over again," he warned, as his teeth found my hipbone, nipping and then gently soothing the spot with his tongue, kissing across my lower belly to nibble and tease my other hip. His fingers slid over my breasts, my nipples, flicking and twisting and strumming them until I was squirming, moaning and almost crying from the painful pleasure.

He was torturing me.

And then his hot mouth descended on my inner thigh, his hands leaving my aching breasts and pressing my knees wider. He gazed at my glistening pussy. It contracted so strongly he moaned.

"So fucking perfect," he hissed, before touching his tongue to my leg, just inside my knee and running it up my thigh.

Closer.

Closer.

And then he stopped. I watched in thwarted need as he repeated the process, licking up from my other knee. And up. And up. And skipping the part that was now weeping for his tongue. Over and over he continued this path.

"Joel!" I begged, rocking my hips. "Stop torturing me!"

His breathy laugh made my pussy squeeze once more.

"I'm not torturing you," he murmured, his hands sliding up my inner thighs as he stared intently at my pussy. "I'm learning you."

And then his nose nuzzled the top of my slit. I bucked under him, but his hands pressed my hips down into the mattress, holding me firmly in position.

A tiny flick of his tongue, just where I needed it, made me cry out so loudly I was sure that people in the hotel foyer would hear.

He flicked and teased, then swept his tongue away from my swollen, throbbing clit, until I was shaking with need. And then back again and away. Back and away.

The ache was building inside me with each flick, and receding when he stopped. Then when he returned the sensations were more violent than before. Fucking torture.

My breath was coming in short, staccato pants and my legs were shuddering with every swipe of his tongue.

And then he took one hand off my belly, and seconds later I felt the longed for thrust of fingers inside me.

I dissolved into a screaming, panting, shuddering mess. He wrung every cry from me, lapping at my quivering flesh and lazily thrusting his fingers as I came down from the high he'd just taken me to. Disobeying his orders, I reached down, trying to push his head away from my over-sensitised clit. He resisted, massaging every last shudder from me with his talented tongue.

"Joel!" I gasped.

He finally released me, kissing his way slowly, sensuously back up my body.

"That was … mind blowing!" he murmured with feeling, grinning like a cat that got the cream. Quite literally.

"You're telling me," I replied breathlessly, licking my lips and eyeing his throbbing dick. "But now, it's my turn."

***

I lost count of how many times we had sex that night. We would fuck until we were both satisfied, and then we'd nap for a little while, just to start all over again.

What had surprised me the most about the night was that after that first hot bang just inside the front door, he'd been incredibly tender with me. The gentle kisses he'd dropped on my lips, my shoulders, my breasts, my belly, and lower … The way he had stared at my face every time I climaxed, his expression devouring me. He'd whispered sweet little things in my ear in between, telling me how beautiful I was, how perfect it felt to be inside me.

I was pleasantly numb between my legs by the time he came in me for the last time, as the grey British sunlight was making its watery way in through the blinds. Joel didn't pull out straight away. He lay inside me, brushing a wayward strand of hair off my face. I closed my eyes for a moment – his gaze was too intense for me. It made me want to say things to him that I knew I just couldn't.

"I'm impressed, Melanie Black. That was quite a night."

I opened my eyes – he was still looking down at me. I grinned sheepishly at him. "Well, I do remember you offering to break me in once."

He leaned down and pressed his nose against mine. "And here I was, stupidly thinking I was just teasing."

"You only ever tease," I responded, not being able to hide the frustration from my tone.

"Would you like me to be serious with you?" he asked me, his voice smouldering.

"Maybe, sometimes," I managed shyly.

Joel smirked at me. "Okay, seriously, last night was pretty close to the best night of my life."

While that was incredibly flattering, it was making it even harder not to say those things that I didn't want to say … couldn't say to him.

"We'd better get moving – we're flying home this afternoon," I said instead.

With a sigh Joel moved off me. I felt suddenly self-conscious about being naked around him, but not because I didn't want him looking at me. He'd just spent the whole night exploring my body more thoroughly than anyone ever had before. But it was more than just physical nakedness; I felt like he'd exposed things inside me that I wasn't ready to be fully aware of.

I escaped to my bedroom and took a shower, got dressed and stuffed everything into my suitcase. When I couldn't find any other excuse to hide away in there, I steeled myself and joined him in the kitchen.

Joel was cooking a vegetable omelette. It smelt great. I felt almost timid as I poured myself a glass of juice. I fought an insane urge to kiss him as he smiled at me from the fry pan, to run my hands around his waist and rest my head against his back. What held me back was the fact that he didn't seem to be having any uncontrollable urges to touch me.

I couldn't handle the silence any longer.

"Okay, so what do we do now?" I asked in my most matter-of-fact tone. Joel served the breakfast out onto two plates and carried them to the table. I followed.

"Well?" I prompted. Joel sat down and picked up his cutlery, taking a bite.

I was starting to feel silly for asking when he replied, "We go home, and we start working towards the US tour."

I shook my head. "You know what I mean! This isn't going to … change things, is it?"

He looked thoughtful for a moment. "Mel, nothing has to change if you don't want it to."

I felt my brow furrow in confusion. "If I don't want it to," I repeated. Joel fixed his blue eyes on me.

"*Do* you want things to change?" he asked. I bit my lip, not sure how to answer that.

"Well, no … I suppose not," I replied. As soon as the words left my mouth, I wished they hadn't. I didn't want to decide now when I was so confused. And so tainted by the incredible night of sex we'd just shared.

But it was too late. Joel shrugged, his eyes flicking away from mine and off into the distance. "Great! No change then."

I leapt in headfirst. "But, Joel, *everything's* changed now! We can't just pretend that last night never happened! I don't *want* to pretend it never happened. What if I want to do it again?"

What if I want to do it every night for the rest of my life? No, I couldn't say that to him! *Bad, terrible idea, Mel!*

Joel smiled at me, that smile that he used when he wanted someone to melt for him. But it was too late for that with me – I was only beginning to feel the first inkling of just how too late it was.

"Stinky, if you ever want to do that again, you just let me know, and if I'm free, I'll be there."

I grunted. I really didn't like the way there was an *if* involved. But really, what had I expected?

I shrugged, feigning nonchalance. "Yeah, well, it was fun. I guess if I'm bored some time, I might take you up on that."

The smile slipped from Joel's face just a tad. Clearly that hadn't been what he wanted to hear. Well, it was give and take. If he wasn't prepared to give something more to me than just a fuck, then I wasn't prepared to give him my body.

Woah, wait a second! What *did* I want from Joel? My brain was too scrambled to answer that.

I remembered a time when he'd told me that all good relationships needed good sex, and I'd thought that if sex was all you had, then how could you possibly have a meaningful relationship?

But over the last few months I *had* built more with Joel than just a teasing relationship and one night of the greatest sex of my life. Hadn't I? There had been times when he'd been sweet, and protective, and kind, in between the teasing. He always had my back. He made me laugh.

But if he wasn't going to put his heart on the line, there was no way I was going to.

CHAPTER TWENTY-SIX

Misery

A hero's welcome greeted me at Sydney Airport. I wasn't feeling very heroic though. I felt gritty and tired, and I was sure that I had sleep crusted all over my eyelashes. But people didn't seem to care at all – they just wanted to wave flags and posters and cheer at me.

And of course, there were several TV cameras with journos waiting to accost me with questions.

Joel grinned and took my carry-on luggage out of my hands.

"Go bask in your glory, Mel," he muttered in my ear. I raised my eyebrows, but didn't look him in the eye as I moved into the fray to sign some autographs, pose for pictures that I'm sure I looked disgusting in, and generally just give people a piece of me that I didn't have to give.

When I managed to fight my way free of that debacle, I spotted Joel waiting for me near a café.

"I wish I'd been able to shower before I had to get through that crowd," I muttered grumpily. "I feel like a troll."

Joel gave me a sidelong glance. "Yeah, you're looking pretty troll-like, actually."

I couldn't tell whether he was joking or not. He'd been all strange since the Night of Amazing Sex. He fluctuated wildly between Jokey Joel and Serious Joel. I couldn't get used to his mood swings.

I wondered if this was what he was always like when he had sex with a girl he'd been pursuing for a while.

Something had occurred to me on the plane, as I lay awake trying to sort through the tangle of emotions I was feeling. I hadn't said anything to Joel about it yet, because of his weird mood. But I had to raise the issue sooner or later. Preferably sooner.

I spent the next ten minutes working up the courage to blurt it out. By that stage we were in the hire car.

I was just about to open my mouth and let the words come out however they would, when Joel tugged at my elbow and pointed out the window.

"Look, Stink, you're as big as a building!" he joked.

I leaned over him – he didn't try to touch me inappropriately, which disappointed me greatly (much to my embarrassment) – and looked in the direction of his finger.

There was the billboard; it was the first Dudz ad that I'd seen. I *was* as big as a building, but so was Joel. I was leaning against him, one of his hands was gripping the back of my thigh, just below my butt. My hand was braced on the wall beside his head, and in our other hands we were both holding tennis racquets loosely by our sides. Like tennis was forgotten because we'd found each other.

Fuck. It was the hottest Dudz ad I'd ever seen.

There was a caption underneath that read, *"On and off court, I play to win" (Mel Black, 22, professional tennis player)*. Then there was another line right at the bottom: *Dudz – for any game you like to play*

I leaned back. "I don't remember saying that," I grumbled.

Joel smirked. "You probably didn't – Georgie's job is to come up with marketing gold like that."

Oh, Georgie, I'd forgotten about her. Another one of Joel's conquests. Well, I'd just joined that list. My sudden, searing jealousy gave me the strength to ask the next question.

"So, should I go get tested?" I asked.

Joel looked at me curiously. "Tested for what?"

I took a deep breath. "STIs. I couldn't help but notice that we had unprotected sex the other night." Many times. "Birth control isn't an issue, but do I need to go and get tested?"

I felt sick asking the question, but I knew that as a responsible adult I had to. Well, while on the subject, if I was a responsible adult, I wouldn't have had unprotected sex with Joel. I probably shouldn't even have had sex with him at all. But my brain and my body weren't keeping close company these days.

Joel gave me a thoughtful look. Well, at least he wasn't mad at me for bringing it up. He took a few deep breaths before he answered me, and he refused to look at me, instead staring down at his hands like he'd suddenly discovered the face of Jesus etched into his palm.

"I've never had unprotected sex before, Mel. I should have been prepared, I'm sorry, but I wasn't planning on having any sex while we were in England. I've been tested before and it's always come back clear. I'm not saying that you shouldn't get tested, but I think that if you did it would be all clear."

Was it wrong that I believed him? Was I being naive? I didn't think he would lie to me about this.

"When was the last time you were tested?" I asked.

Joel continued to stare at his hands. "When we got back from Europe," he replied quietly.

I inhaled deeply through my nose. "Of course you did, after the little one-night stand in *our* hotel room in Rome!" I snapped. I had no right to be furious with him, but I was. I turned and looked out the window, pointing my whole body away from his.

"Yes, Mel, after that one-night stand. Don't you act all high and mighty about it – ten seconds on Google and I can remind you about *your* one-night stand."

I turned back to him and gave him a withering look. "That was *two* nights," I snapped.

Joel laughed sarcastically, leaning back against the seat. "Yeah, because that makes all the difference, doesn't it, Stink?"

I hated that he was right – I was in no position to be judging him over his indiscretions. And that just made me all the angrier with him.

"So, anyway, I was tested just after Rome and I haven't been with anyone else since then, so you should be okay."

I eyed him sharply. "You haven't had sex in the last two months?" I asked in disbelief. Joel shook his head, his eyes sliding away from mine once more.

"Not even Julie?" I persisted.

Joel hesitated, then shook his head. "Not even Julie."

The anger in me deflated somewhat, and I collapsed back against the seat.

"So, you're telling me that you went without sex for *two* months?" I repeated, still not quite able to believe it.

"In case you haven't noticed, I've been spending pretty much every waking moment with you. When have I had time to go out looking for sex?"

I clenched my jaw. "When have you *ever* had to go looking for sex? I thought that sex just fell into your lap."

Joel chuckled angrily. "It might seem that way to you, but the only time recently that sex has just 'fallen into my lap' was a couple of nights ago in a hotel in Soho."

The hire car pulled up outside my apartment building. The driver very politely waited for us to finish our argument.

I glared at him. "That didn't just fall into your lap, Joel! You'd been working towards that moment for *months*! Don't think I didn't realise it – you and your innuendo, and the way you would come so close to me that I thought I was going to go insane if I didn't just act on it. You knew *exactly* what you were doing. It's so frust –"

He didn't let me finish. He kissed me instead. I tried to fight it, God's honest truth I did, but within seconds I was clutching him to me desperately. He broke away from my lips for a second, his hands roving down to my hips, his lips curved up into a cheeky grin.

"You're so sexy when you get all angry, Stinky," he muttered, and his lips were on mine again.

"Ahem," the driver cleared his throat pointedly, and Joel and I jumped apart guiltily. "Will there be another stop after this one?"

Joel looked at me, his eyes burning. I shook my head.

"Just the one stop, thanks," I choked out. The driver got out and huffily dumped our bags on the sidewalk. I slid out of the car and Joel handed over some cash. The driver tore off down the street as soon as the door was closed.

It felt weird to have to do something as normal as carry our luggage upstairs, knowing that as soon as we got inside we were going to be all over each other. I tried not to think about it too much. I tried not to worry that it was a bad and stupid mistake to be doing this again. Hadn't I decided that I wouldn't let him touch me if he couldn't define what our relationship would be, now that we were having sex?

It seemed that my resolve wasn't as strong as I'd hoped, or non-existent more to the point, because as soon as we were inside the door Joel grabbed me, dragged my t-shirt off over my head and flung me onto the lounge, and I didn't make one noise or action of complaint. In fact, it was quite the opposite – I was actively encouraging him as he lay down on top of me and kissed me enthusiastically.

His hands roved expertly over my body – he knew every little curve of it by now, and exactly where to touch to get the best reaction from me. He was a lightning-fast learner and he'd had a whole night of practise.

His mouth was on one breast, his hand down the front of my yoga pants, his fingers circling my clit, thrusting inside me, circling again, in a way that was going to send me over the edge if he kept it up for much longer.

"You remember in California when I kept having those dreams?" I asked him breathlessly.

"Mmm hmm," was his muffled reply – he didn't take his mouth off my nipple. I gasped and the ache down low turned to a throbbing.

"Well, this is how they all started out."

He did pull away from my nipple then, and looked down at me with a smirk.

"Really?" he asked. He slid my yoga pants and underwear right off and dropped his own pants. I tugged his shirt off and dragged him back down on me.

"Yes, really," I moaned as he slid into me. "But they didn't end like this. I wish they *had*."

I felt a chuckle bubble out from Joel's lips, which were pressed against my collarbone. "I wish they had too; then maybe this would have happened sooner," he groaned against me as he lifted me up and moved into a sitting position with me straddling him. His teeth latched onto my nipple again, and I cried out as I moved on him. His hands caressed my butt and slid up and down my back.

I buried my head in his shoulder as I got close to the edge, but he pulled me back so he could see my face, cupping both my breasts and teasing my nipples with his fingers as I coiled tighter, and tighter, and overflowed into waves of ecstasy. I vaguely wondered as I cried out, what he found so fascinating about my orgasm face.

When I was done, Joel lifted me off him and put me down on the floor, climbing on top of me and feeding himself deep into me.

I wrapped my legs around his waist and pulled him closer, kissing him furiously, our tongues tangling, dancing as he fucked me slowly. He broke our kiss, pushing my hair out of my face and leaning back to look at me.

"Why is sex so different with you?" he asked in a low voice as he moved inside me gently.

I bit my lip. "Different better, I hope?"

He picked up the pace, and I swallowed heavily as I felt the ache inside start to hike up again.

"Better, *definitely* better," he groaned. "I can normally last for hours, but with you ... fuck, Mel!"

I clung to him as we both came together. He propped himself up on one arm and looked at me; his lips swollen from kissing and his eyes bright from coming. I smothered the urge to reach up and stroke his face – I was still totally unsure about what the protocol was for this particular kind of casual sex.

Joel smiled at me as he pulled out of me and sat up, propped against the lounge. I lay and watched him, feeling uncomfortable about how much I liked looking at him: naked, sex-mussed, with a five o'clock shadow from our long flight.

"I think I need a shower," I muttered, struggling to my feet – my legs wouldn't hold my weight properly. Joel was just too good at what he did. It wasn't fair. How could one man get so much talent in the sack? No wonder he slept around – it was almost like he owed it to womankind to show us all how great sex could really be.

I clenched my fists as I thought about that. I didn't want him to sleep with anyone else but me. But it was hardly my decision, was it? I couldn't just have him all to myself, not unless … no, I was not going there.

"Mind if I join you?" he murmured in my ear. I felt tingles all over me as his breath tickled my neck. I shrugged mutely. It seemed that I was unable to deny him anything he wanted.

Bad, bad situation to be getting into, Melanie Black.

I led the way into the bathroom, flicking on the light. I froze in the doorway. Joel bumped into me, not having expected me to stop so suddenly.

"What's up, Stink?" he asked, peering over my head into the room. I stared for a moment at the reflection of the two of us in the mirror, naked, and hated the way I liked it so much, then I focussed on the reason that I'd stopped.

"I'm not really sure, but something feels weird in here. I normally leave the shower curtain closed, but it's open. And I never fold my towel like that before I hang it up," I pointed to the towel rack, where my fluffy white bath towel was neatly draped. "I normally just chuck it over the rail."

Joel shrugged in the mirror, but his eyes were serious.

"Maybe you left it a bit neater knowing that you'd have Amanda coming in to feed Connor," he suggested. I shook my head – it was such a long time ago, or it felt that way, and so much had happened that I couldn't remember how I'd left it.

That reminded me that I hadn't seen Connor since I'd gotten home – that in itself was weird. Usually he was circling my ankles like lightning when I walked in the door, begging for attention and food. I pushed past Joel and walked into the bedroom, calling his name.

I heard a bemused meow from under the bed. I bent down and took a peek under – there he was, eyeing me grumpily. I guess he'd probably gotten annoyed that the first thing I did when I got home was have sex on the lounge. And the living room floor.

I grinned in relief. That was when I noticed the bedding. It was all put together differently. Just as neat and tidy as I would have left it, but not made up the way I liked it.

I added this to the mystery of the bathroom. Maybe I'd left it in a mess and Amanda had tidied up.

Or maybe my mother had been dropping by even after I told her not to. That might be more to the point. I'd have to change the locks. I growled and stomped back into the bathroom. The water was running and Joel was already in the shower.

I paused, uncomfortable again. Sex was one thing, but showering together just felt too intimate, too … couple-y. I knew that Joel wasn't interested in being a couple. But maybe he didn't read as much into the whole showering together thing as I did. Maybe he showered with all the girls he slept with.

I'd only ever showered with Grant, and that was only after we'd been sleeping together for a couple of years.

"Come on in, the water's warm," Joel joked as he stuck his head around the curtain, and I swallowed my nerves and stepped in.

He looked even better all dripping with water than he did dry, and I coughed as my breath caught in my throat. I reached for the soap and self-consciously started to lather myself up. I could feel Joel watching me, and I blushed and tried to pretend that it didn't totally weird me out.

I felt the words bubbling to the surface. "Okay, Joel, I have to know. What is this?" I asked quietly.

Joel smirked at me. "This is called a shower, Stinky. It's what people do when they want to get clean." He moved closer to me and grabbed a handful of my butt. "Or dirty," he muttered suggestively. I could feel his erection pressing against my hip bone. How could he be ready to go again already? I took a step away from him.

"Don't avoid the issue. What is going on here?" I gestured to him and then to me, back and forth with my hand.

Joel shrugged. "Well, we're … having sex. Stink, it's no big deal. People *can* just enjoy having sex with each other without there having to be something going on. Nothing else has to be different. I can still be your coach."

I looked down. Yes, we could just enjoy having sex and keep on going the same as usual. I could handle that, I thought. But there was one thing I knew I *couldn't* handle, and I had to bring it up, no matter how afraid of his answer I was.

"Will you be having sex with other girls too?" I asked in barely more than a whisper. There was a long, awful moment where I could hear nothing but the sound of the water splashing down.

"Well, I don't have any immediate plans to sleep with anyone else, Mel," Joel said. "And, I promise that if that changes, I'll be honest with you."

I sneaked a peek up into his eyes, and he was gazing down at me earnestly. I believed him. I wasn't sure if that was a total mistake, but I did believe him.

He reached out and pulled me against him. His chest was the perfect height for me to rest my forehead on, and I did, because I couldn't gaze into his eyes the way he seemed to be able to gaze into mine. But then I found myself staring down, past his washboard stomach and further to … oh my God. He really was raring to go again.

Should I, or shouldn't I? I couldn't decide. And then I realised that if I couldn't decide, it was probably best to say no. I closed my eyes so the sight of his huge erection wasn't able to affect my judgement.

"I think you should go home now, Joel," I muttered. "I have to unpack and I badly need sleep."

And I have a lot of issues to sort through, I added silently.

Joel switched the water off without a word and stepped out of the shower. He dripped his way over to the shelves where I kept my towels and pulled one out, drying himself matter of factly. I tentatively followed, pulling the towel that I was sure I hadn't folded like that from the rack.

Joel walked naked out to his suitcase by the front door and unzipped it. I followed him, my towel wrapped around me. I could definitely get used to him walking around my apartment naked.

Uh, what's gotten into you, Melanie Black??? What are you thinking? You can't have him. You don't want him, not in that way at least. Do you?

I wasn't sure about anything anymore. Which was why I was sending him on his way. The longer we spent in this weird little situation, the more likely it was that I would convince myself that this was real, that this was something more than sex. That I wanted something more with Joel Herbert.

Joel didn't seem to mind me standing watching him as he got dressed. In fact, he grinned at me as he dragged his underwear on. I tried not to be affected by the way his muscles moved under his skin. I failed.

When he was fully clothed and his suitcase was all zipped up, he opened the front door and winked at me.

"Thanks for a great time, Stink," he said with feeling as he dragged his suitcase out the door.

It felt like such an inadequate goodbye, but what had I really been expecting after all? *"Mel, I can't live without you"*? No. Or … maybe? No, definitely not.

I stood frozen in the doorway. I wondered whether he would kiss me goodbye, and then I decided that him kissing me would be a bad thing. It wouldn't be at all helpful when I was trying to sort out how I felt about this whole situation.

He stopped at the top of the stairs and half turned back to me, a look of indecision on his face. I held my breath.

"Hey, Stink, you can have a few days off if you want – you've earned it. Come round on Saturday and we'll start talking about America then."

With that he turned and walked down the stairs without another word, leaving me standing in my doorway wearing nothing but a towel and fighting off wave after wave of misery.

Stupid, stupid girl! I admonished myself. *You knew when you were getting into this that it was just a physical thing. Why are you suddenly upset that it's nothing more than that?*

I trudged back inside, ignored my full suitcase near the door and went straight into my room. Connor had emerged from under the bed and was glaring disgustedly at me from my pillow. I dropped my towel in the doorway and moved over to the bed, dragging the covers back and huddling down under them, lifting Connor under with me.

"I know, mate. Mummy's making some pretty dumb mistakes this year. I'm disgusted with me, too," I whispered to him. He turned his lamp-like gaze towards me and started purring.

He was just about the only male in my life that I knew exactly where I stood with.

CHAPTER TWENTY-SEVEN

I Won't Say It

The first four days after we arrived home were torture. Joel sent me one single text, with a date when he needed me back for training. And that was all I'd heard from him.

Every single moment of those four days had me on the verge of texting him, calling him, catching a fucking Uber and just showing up at his house. I tried to keep myself busy by going out every day, taking a run or a ride (in the opposite direction to Joel's house), walking on Bondi Beach, hitting the shops – anything to stop me from acting on these urges.

I discovered one down side to being a Wimbledon champion: my face was suddenly recognisable to so many people. Every time I went out in public I couldn't help but be aware of people whispering and pointing. I had to paste on a smile when people came up to me and wanted to chat, to congratulate me on my win, to ask for autographs and photos. I wanted to be able to enjoy it, but I was in a black mood.

Damn Joel Herbert! I should be on top of the world, but all I could think about was him.

Even once I was back at training, things were … different. I trained hard early in the mornings and sometimes of an evening as well. In the mornings I did drills and weights with Joel, but as soon as they were done, I escaped the awkwardness to do my own thing.

My own thing generally being moping around my house and annoying Connor who wasn't used to me being up in his grill all the time.

It was over a fortnight before everything settled down even a little bit. I went through the motions of attending media events, interviewing for newspaper and magazine articles, signing a new sponsorship deal with Martel, and putting myself out there the way people expected me to. But none of it gave me any pleasure. Nothing made me feel anything. And it was all because of Damn Joel Herbert, or DJH as I had started calling him.

When I did have a tennis related commitment Joel took me, but we were very careful not to speak about anything unrelated to tennis, our upcoming America trip, sponsorships, my training regime or my diet. It was all strictly professional.

I felt like screaming.

Something had to give. I had to do something to stop myself feeling this way.

God, I pleaded as I lay awake in bed for the third night in a row, *just let me get over this silly infatuation and get on with my life!*

I wasn't sure if he was listening to me anymore.

The next morning, I crawled out of bed after managing maybe four hours sleep, peering at myself in the mirror in the bathroom. The circles under my eyes were purple. I looked about forty, not almost twenty-three.

Almost twenty-three. Ugh. Almost twenty-three and what did I have to show for it?

Well, if I was being positive, I had a Wimbledon title. I had my own apartment which was paid off now courtesy of the winnings from Wimbledon. I had a regular income from Dudz, and now Martel, who were paying for all my playing gear now too. I had a cat who liked me most of the time.

I had friends … and just like that I was on the downward spiral again. I hadn't spoken to Brad once since I'd gotten back from London. Texts left unanswered, every call sent to voicemail. How the fuck was I supposed to face him knowing he had feelings for me, after what had happened with DJH overseas? I was afraid that Brad would take one look at me and figure out what was wrong. And he'd end up hating me because of it.

Of course, there was Amanda, but she was so busy with nursing shifts and Thomas … I tried to think of something else positive to pull me back out of the slump.

DJH was the only thing that came into my head. I tried to salvage something good from the whole mess. Well, he was an incredible coach.

He was gorgeous and an amazing lover … but I couldn't think about that because I wasn't sleeping with him ever again. He made me laugh. Well, he used to make me laugh. Now he was always Serious Joel.

I forced DJH from my mind and showered hurriedly, dressing in my training gear and getting on my bike to head over to his place.

He had the drills all set up for me when I arrived. I stripped out of the jumper and track pants I'd worn over my training gear. He looked at me strangely for just a second, then his eyes flickered away. He never looked at me when he spoke to me anymore.

"You're not getting enough sleep," he commented sternly, his eyes focussed about a foot above my head. I shrugged.

"I've got a lot on my mind."

He did meet my eyes then for a second, searchingly. He opened his mouth as if he wanted to say something, but then thought better of it, pressing his lips together. He turned and demonstrated the drill he wanted me to do. I complied in silence.

Why can't we just talk about it? Why can't we just have a massive fight about whatever it is that's making us act all weird, then have some hot make-up sex and get over it, go back to normal? the voice in my head screeched as I picked up a skipping rope. But that would be stupid. It was sex that had made things weird between us in the first place. Having more certainly wasn't going to help.

But it would be fantastic …

No Mel! No more sex with DJH for you!

Drills finished, Joel motioned in the direction of the weights equipment. I paused and shook my head. I couldn't handle the weirdness anymore. But I couldn't find the courage to speak up and ask him to explain what was going on.

"I'll do weights at the gym this afternoon," I mumbled. I expected him to argue, to tell me that I should do them now, while he was there to supervise. Instead, he just shrugged.

"If that suits you, Stink," he muttered. I took a deep breath and willed the tears back inside my skull. I wouldn't cry over him. I had no reason to cry over him. He'd made it perfectly clear to me that it was just about sex. But now it wasn't about anything, apparently.

I was scared. I wasn't able to resist him, but I had to because I couldn't bring myself to put it out there. I was worried that he'd reject me. I couldn't come back from that.

I left in a huff, the best way to mask the world of hurt I was feeling underneath. I powered home on my bike, as if riding faster would leave my worries behind. Of course, it never works that way. They were still waiting for me when I got home.

Another problem was also waiting for me at my front door, disguised as Amanda. I wasn't sure how I knew she was going to make my life more difficult – maybe it was the sheepish look on her face.

"Hey Mel, how are you?" she asked me too brightly.

"Fine," I replied warily, unlocking the door and climbing the stairs. She followed me.

"Want a cup of tea?" I asked automatically as I held my door open for her. She nodded as she walked inside and plonked herself down on the lounge. I went straight into the kitchen and put the kettle on.

"So, how have you been? Busy I bet. I've seen you on TV like a thousand times in the last week!" she said, speaking loudly over the bubbling of the kettle. I turned around and leaned against the bench, my arms folded.

"Amanda, you know I love you, but whatever ulterior motive you came here with, spit it out now," I snapped.

Amanda gazed at me wide eyed, looking much too innocent to be anything but guilty. Then she sighed and all the pretence slipped from her face.

"Okay, let's get the nasty bit out of the way, and then we can talk about other stuff."

I held my breath, having a sneaking suspicion about what she was here for. Or rather, on whose behalf she was here.

"I feel really silly coming over here to ask you this, Mel, really I do – it's not like we're in primary school anymore. So, I'm just going to say it. Brad's upset because you've been avoiding him. He said that he's tried to call you a few times and you haven't answered, and you haven't responded to any of his texts."

I screwed up my nose.

"So why didn't he come round himself to confront me?" I asked, even though I felt intensely relieved that he'd sent Amanda instead. I didn't think I was ready to deal with an emotional showdown at the moment.

Amanda grimaced. "Well, he's worried that you don't want to see him. He doesn't want you to feel crowded at all."

I felt so guilty. I should have just been honest with him from the start: that I wasn't in a place to acknowledge his feelings for me, because I was … what was I? I was pining after something I couldn't have. Was that why Joel had backed off all of a sudden? Because he could tell I was getting too into it, and he didn't want to encourage that?

Stop! No thinking about DJH, Mel!

"I'll call him today," I promised Amanda. "You're right, I've just been really busy with work – I was waiting for it all to calm down, but I should have at least told him that. I'll call him."

Amanda seemed to relax. "Okay, I'm glad that's over. Now, tell me all about England! I bet you partied hard the night after the win?"

Thank God the kettle boiled right at that moment, and I was able to turn away from her to pour the tea. There was no way I would have been able to mask the expression on my face, and she would have known something was up.

"Uh, yeah, Joel and I went out to the WTA after party. You know how much I hate to go to the social things, but I was sort of obligated."

I composed my face and turned back to Amanda. I passed a mug of tea to her, sitting on the chair opposite her and taking a sip of my own. It scalded my tongue.

"Did you do anything else fun?" she asked me over the top of her mug. I took a few deep breaths while I pushed away the memories of all the 'fun' things I'd done just before and just after that party.

"Actually, yes, Joel got us tickets to see Jace McKenzie," I answered, pleased at how airily I was able to say his name.

"Wow! That's awesome! You love him!" Amanda said. I felt the blush rising and there was nothing that I could do to stop it.

Amanda was looking at me funny. "What's going on, Mel?" she asked hesitantly. I looked away and took another sip of my tea.

"Nothing, why?" My voice sounded suss as I shook my head too hard.

"Oh, Mel, you're in love with Joel, aren't you?"

I choked on a mouthful of tea and almost spat it across the room. "No! *God* no! What made you think that?" My voice was on the edge of hysteria.

"Uh, apart from *that* reaction, every time you say his name your voice gets all sweet."

"I'm not *in love* with him," I insisted, sounding less certain about that than I would have liked.

Amanda shrugged. "Well, if you say so." She didn't sound convinced.

The need to confide in *someone* suddenly overwhelmed me, and the words started spewing out of me.

"I had sex with Joel while we were in England. And not just once – lots of times. And it was the *best* sex of my entire life. And then when we got home, we had sex again." I didn't tell her it was on the lounge she was sitting on, because she'd probably be horrified.

"And the reason that I haven't answered any calls from Brad is that I just don't know what to do. I feel things when I'm with Joel that confuse me. I *hate* being confused. And I don't want to drag Brad into this mess until I've worked it out."

I stopped blathering and looked at Amanda properly. She was gaping at me. I took a gulp of my tea and waited in intense embarrassment for her to say something.

"You … had sex with Joel?" she whispered. I nodded, looking down into my cup, where I could see some tea leaves floating about in the bottom. If a gypsy was here to read my fortune, I wondered what those leaves would say.

Amanda laughed. I looked up, wondering what was wrong with her. She was grinning at me like a fool.

"Well, it's about time! You have no idea how painful it's been for the last few years wondering when you two would finally admit that you are *totally* in love with each other!"

I plonked my teacup down on the coffee table and glared at her. "He's *not* in love with me. And I'm *not* in love with him. It was just sex. He's made that perfectly clear."

"But you want more." She didn't pose it as a question. I shrugged.

"I don't know *what* I want. I don't know *how* I feel. It's awful, Amanda. And I'm scared to talk to Brad because I just … can't handle his feelings for me right now. I'm too much of a mess."

Amanda sighed. "You're in love, Mel. Just admit it – you love Joel Herbert. You've been in love with him for years, but you've been in denial."

I continued to shake my head.

"You need to tell Joel. You need to be honest with him. Believe me, I think you'll be surprised by his response."

I gave her a withering look. "Amanda, I know Joel. I know what he's like. I know that he's not interested in love. Not with me anyway," I added, remembering that he'd told me he'd been in love but that the girl hadn't been interested.

"Just tell him."

I shook my head. "I'm not telling him something when I'm not even sure it's true! I'm not going to say, *'I love you'* to him when I don't even know if that's the way I feel!"

"You've never been in love before, have you, Mel?" Amanda asked, leaning back into the lounge.

"What's that got to do with it?" I snapped.

Amanda shrugged. "How do you know you're *not* in love, if you've never felt what it's like to be *in* love?"

I had no answer for that.

"Even if you don't tell him you love him," Amanda continued, "you need to at least tell him that you're interested in more than just sex with him. Take it slower and see how things go."

I groaned. "I can't fucking do that. I just can't. I won't."

Amanda stood. "Be honest, Mel. It's scary, but it's the only way you're going to get past the way you're feeling now."

She walked calmly to the door. I couldn't get up – I was paralysed with fear at the thought of doing what she suggested.

Amanda turned at the door. "Just be honest. And if you can't be honest with yourself, or with Joel, at least be honest with Brad. You owe him that much."

She closed the door quietly, the muted click as the latch clipped into place giving emphasis to her departing words.

No, I wasn't in love with Joel. Maybe I wanted to have sex with him exclusively, but I wasn't in love with him. Maybe I wanted *him* to have sex with *me* exclusively. But that wasn't love. Was it?

I just couldn't go for five minutes without DJH being in my brain. I stood and walked to the door, lifting my bike from where I had left it leaning against the wall.

I'd go to the gym, work out like a fiend, and hopefully forget about it all for an hour or so.

I love the feeling of a really hard workout; when I feel the burn in every muscle in my body and the endorphin high is intense.

I wished I felt like that today. But nope.

For starters I hated the way everyone looked at me out of the corner of their eye. They knew who I was and they just wanted to stare at me, but they knew it was rude, so they didn't. I would have preferred them gape openly at me than sneak surreptitious glances my way.

I was sweating a hell of a lot too, and that wasn't an attractive way for curious people to be seeing me. I imagined them going home to their friends and loved ones: *"Guess who I saw at the gym today, smelling like the north end of a south bound camel"* …

And yet for all of these bad things, working out at the gym was infinitely more preferable to being with DJH at the moment.

Yep. Definitely not able to go for more than a minute or two without thinking about him.

I finished my workout and went to take a shower. The hot water was soothing on my skin, washing away the slickness of workout sweat. I towelled briskly and dressed in clean clothes to head home, my hair wet and tangled around my shoulders.

The girls at the reception counter gave me a pair of giant grins and asked shyly if I would pose for a picture with them. I smiled mechanically and dropped my bags. One of the girls called a PT over to take the snap. He winked at me, reminding me of another PT who I was supposed to be keeping out of my head.

Like that was even possible. The trainer handed the camera back to the girls and turned to me.

"Hey, Melanie, can you tell Joel that Andrew said hello? He's coaching you now, isn't he?"

I nodded stiffly. "I'll tell him," I promised, leaning down to pick up my bags. A child was squatting beside them looking up at me curiously, his brown hair flopping around his blue eyes.

"Oh, hi there, mate," I said, trying to be nice because he was only a little kid, even though he was unzipping my bag as he stared at me totally unabashedly. "Are your parents around?"

"Shaun! Stop that now!" a familiar voice rang out. I winced. I knew that voice and I wasn't in the mood to deal with its owner. The little boy stood up, a sheepish look on his face, and he trotted away. I unenthusiastically followed his steps with my eyes.

"Oh, hi Mel," Julie greeted me.

"What are you doing here?" I asked warily.

"I work here," she replied in a short tone. The child was standing at her feet, tugging on her shorts.

"In the crèche?" I asked in disbelief.

"No," she replied reluctantly. "I'm the physio here. Joel put in a word for me." She bent down and picked the child up, resting him on her hip in a very motherly way.

"Oh," I replied. I actually took a good look at the child then, and I felt my legs start to tremble under me.

"Is that your son?"

Julie looked tenderly down at the child in her arms. He looked about three to me.

"Yep, this is Shaun. Shaun, this is Mel." The boy looked at me with serious eyes. Serious eyes that were horrifyingly familiar to me. I clutched at the counter as my legs threatened to give way.

"He looks just like his father," I muttered breathlessly. That's when the world went black.

CHAPTER TWENTY-EIGHT

Illegitimate

I came to in a wave of dizziness. I was on a massage table in a room with ambient lighting and indoor palms and ferns everywhere. Andrew the PT stood over me, looking concerned. I sat up and breathed deeply through a wave of nausea. As my vision began to clear I saw Julie hovering nervously.

"Are you okay, Mel?" she asked cautiously. I nodded, holding my forehead and refusing to look in her direction. I looked down at the floor, where the little boy was playing in the corner with some Lego bricks. That made me feel sick again.

"Andrew, can we have a moment?" I grated out. The trainer left hurriedly. I think he sensed that there was about to be one whopper of a showdown in the room.

Julie took a seat in a chair against the wall. I looked around – everywhere except at the child on the floor.

"This your office?" I asked, buying time while I figured out what I wanted to say. Julie nodded, looking around herself.

"It's nice," I commented.

"Mel, listen –" Julie started. I didn't let her finish. So much for trying to say this diplomatically. I was just going to blurt out the first thing that came into my head.

"No, you listen to *me*! I don't like being lied to and it seems that both you and DJ … Joel … have been doing exactly that! You have a child together … he's a fucking *father*!"

"Mel, just let me —"

"Let you what? I thought you two had never met before that day in the change room, but obviously I was wrong. I mean, I knew that you were sleeping with him, but I didn't know that it has been going on for," I turned to look at the child, "what, four years? You're a decade older than him! Oh my God, I can't believe I slept with him! I can't believe I actually thought that there might be …" I let that trail off. It was dangerous to go there, especially out loud.

Julie came and stood directly in front of me, staring me straight in the eyes. I pouted childishly at her.

"Have you said your piece, Mel?" Julie asked me in a stern-mum tone. I shrugged belligerently.

"Good," she continued. "Now before I say anything, I want you to promise not to use the F word, or any other swear word in the presence of my son. You clear on that?"

I nodded grudgingly. I knew better than to swear in front of children. But I had a good excuse: I'd just had a pretty massive shock.

"Okay. I can tell you're pretty mad right now and I totally understand that. But don't blame Joel."

I snorted. How could I *not* blame him? He should learn to keep his impressive penis in his pants. He'd told me he'd never had unprotected sex with anyone but me. Well, I was starting to realise how big a liar he was.

Julie gripped me by the shoulders.

"Seriously, Mel, *don't* blame Joel. This isn't his fault; I made him promise that he wouldn't tell anyone. But I suppose you would have found out sooner or later, so we may as well just come clean now."

"What's that supposed to mean? *'You would have found out sooner or later'*? I shouldn't have to find out like this! I shouldn't have to deal with this! He should have been honest with me before we … did you know that we slept together?"

"Yes, I knew. He told me."

I gaped. So, he talked about his sex life with the mother of his child? His sex life with *other* women? That just totally creeped me out.

"Mel, I made Joel promise not to tell anyone because it's not his secret to tell. It's mine."

I sneered at her. "It's his too! Does the kid call him Daddy?"

Something I said must have made Julie snap, because she glared at me, eyes ablaze. "*Shaun* has a name, and no, he doesn't call Joel 'Daddy'. Why would I teach him to call Joel that?"

I shrugged, returning her gaze with a glare of my own. "What, so you'd rather your son grew up not knowing who his father is?" I was disgusted, and I was pretty sure that DJH wouldn't want that either.

Julie looked away, towards the child still mashing his Lego blocks together.

"It wouldn't be right to let Shaun think of Joel as his dad." She turned back to me. "Mel, Joel's not Shaun's father."

Relief flooded me, so intense that I nearly passed out again. "Joel's not the father?" I repeated, stunned. Julie shook her head.

"No. Shaun's never going to know his father."

I breathed through the feeling of my heart beating vitally in my chest once more.

"What, don't you know who the father is?"

"I know exactly who the father is, but he's dead, so of course Shaun's not going to know him. Mel, Steve was Shaun's father."

My vision blurred. "Woah. Okay, just give me a minute to process this. Steve? As in Steve Herbert?"

Julie nodded.

I rubbed at my temples. "Does Joel know?" I whispered. Julie nodded again. I swallowed, trying to make my mouth feel less dry.

"Does *Sandra* know?"

Julie looked away. I had my answer right there.

"I can't believe that he cheated on her. I can't believe that *you* … Julie, why? You knew he was married!"

She turned back to me suddenly, tears in her eyes. "I *loved* him, Mel! I was in love with him. I know it was stupid and wrong, and don't think that I don't regret every day what I've done. But Mel, love isn't something that's rational. You can't pick and choose who you fall in love with. I made a stupid decision because of love."

I pursed my lips. Her words were too close for comfort for me, and I didn't want to let my mind follow that path.

"So, Steve knew that he had a child with you?" I asked.

Julie nodded. "He wouldn't meet Shaun or openly acknowledge he was the father, but he set up a trust which regularly deposited money into an account that I could access, so that he felt like he was contributing to raising Shaun. I don't know how he kept it from Sandra."

My eyebrows knitted together. "But now he's … gone. So how does the trust work now? Wouldn't those sorts of things have been frozen when Steve died?"

Julie shook her head. "Don't ask me the ins and outs of it, because I have no idea. All I know is that the trust is under Joel's control now. He's making sure that there continues to be money available for Shaun."

Holy fuck. The gravity of the situation really hit me then. Joel had an illegitimate half-brother and he was now responsible financially for that child. A child that Sandra didn't know her husband had fathered to Julie.

"How long has Joel known about this?" I asked quietly.

"Since the Australian Open. Since that night that we spent together."

I swallowed the bile that was rising in my throat. "So, you were banging the father, but you decided to upgrade to the son? You've been having sex with your son's *brother*?" I looked away, disgusted.

Julie looked askance at me. "I've never slept with Joel. What on earth gave you that idea?"

I pressed my lips together so she wouldn't see how shocked I was. Another lie he'd told me.

"I wanted Joel to meet his brother. I knew he was coming to Melbourne for the Open. Steve tried to make me promise not to tell him, but I was adamant – Joel should know he has a brother and Shaun deserves to know he has one too. Steve was … unhappy about it, to say the least."

I recalled the way Julie had snapped at Steve the day I sprained my ankle. At the time I'd just thought she was angry at him for being unreasonable about what I could safely do, but clearly there had been so much else going on that I'd had no idea about.

"Joel gave me the perfect opportunity, when he asked to take me out that night."

"So, you let Joel think you were DTF to get him on the hook, and then you dropped the brother bombshell on him? Why are you making him do this? Lie to his own mother, look after a child that isn't even *his*! Don't you feel a little guilty about all this?"

Julie's shoulders slumped. "Of course I do. I told him that I didn't expect anything from him, but he insisted on continuing his father's agreement. He helped me to move up here so that he could take a more active role in Shaun's life." She looked at me earnestly then. "Mel, he's a really decent guy. In fact, I'd go as far as to say he's one of the nicest, most genuine people I've ever met."

I met her eyes for a split second, before looking away.

"Yeah, well, if you like him so much, why aren't you together – he was more than happy to let me think that was the case."

"Well, aside from the fact that it would be wildly inappropriate, and I'm not attracted to him in that way … he's in love with someone else."

I looked up at her, desperate for more information, but Julie's face had closed down, and I knew that I wouldn't get anything more out of her on that side of things. I tried another line of questioning.

"How did Joel take it? When he found out I mean. I guess it would have been a shock. I mean, he had every intention of sleeping with you that night, and instead he finds out his dad got there first."

Julie had the grace to look ashamed. "I really don't think he ever planned to sleep with me. He certainly didn't try to make a move, and I didn't tell him about Shaun until after we'd had dinner and drinks and coffee. I didn't tell him until we got back to my place, and I couldn't avoid it any longer, because the evidence was right there."

She looked down at Shaun with a loving expression.

"Well, if he wasn't making any moves, what on earth did you talk about all evening?" I asked.

Julie turned back to me, with a wry expression on her face. "You, Mel. We talked about you."

I reeled. "Me? Why?"

Julie smiled at me. "Joel wanted to know how best to rehabilitate your ankle. What exercises to work on, how long it needed to be rested. He was very focussed on making sure you got better."

Well, that made sense. He had just been appointed my trainer at that point, so I guess he was just doing his job.

"So, when he found out, what happened?" I prompted, hoping that Julie's talkative mood would continue until all the questions swirling in my head had been answered.

The smile slipped from Julie's face. "He was furious. But not with me. With his father. He couldn't believe that his dad would do that to his mum. And he was angry that when Shaun was born Steve hadn't come clean about the whole thing. It was a lot for Joel to take in. I sat up for hours trying to explain everything to him. He took off at about three. I guess he needed some time to come to terms with it, because when he came back a few hours later he seemed much calmer."

I froze, my heart stuttering. "Wait a minute. You say he left? For a few hours early in the morning?" My stomach dropped.

"Yeah, he said he needed to clear his head and he'd come back in a little while. He was gone for about three hours." She looked up, noticed my expression. "No, Mel! Don't even *think* it – he didn't!"

"How do you know? He was … God knows where when it happened. He had the perfect motive. You lied to the police for him. Why?"

Julie's head dropped. "I offered to. I said it would make him look bad if the police knew that he couldn't back up his alibi. I knew that if they questioned him, if they suspected him, it would get out about Shaun, and I really didn't want that. So, I gave him an alibi."

My stomach was doing somersaults.

"But, Mel, I know he didn't do it. I know that he wouldn't have killed his own father!"

I thought I agreed with her, but everything was just all upside down all of a sudden, and I didn't know what to believe.

"What about Ben?" I muttered, more to myself than to Julie. But then I noticed the look on her face when I said his name.

"Julie, what about Ben?" I pressed.

"Ben?" she asked, but I could hear the fear in her tone. She knew more about this than I did, that was for sure.

"Yes. Don't pretend you don't know who I'm talking about – Joel's Uncle Ben … *Shaun's* Uncle Ben. Steve's brother. Seriously Julie, you'd better just tell me everything, or I'm going to jump to conclusions here."

Julie's shoulders slumped. "You're going to take this totally the wrong way, Mel, but I'll tell you. I don't know how, but Ben found out about the trust. He got suspicious about what it was for and why it was left solely to Joel to administer, when Joel already got a portion of the estate.

"So, Ben started asking questions. Joel managed to fob him off, and we thought it was all over when Ben went back overseas. But then I noticed this man following me, everywhere I went – to Shaun's daycare, to work, to the supermarket … everywhere."

The breath caught in my throat. "Ben found out. And he came back," I muttered.

With a sickening lurch in my stomach, I remembered the conversation I'd overheard between Joel and Ben the day I'd been hiding at the bottom of the stairs. Ben asking, *"Where is she?"* and *"Did you think you could keep it a secret from me?"* He hadn't been talking about me at all. He'd been talking about Julie and Shaun.

"When Ben found out he went berserk. Well, that's what Joel told me anyway. He was mad that Steve hadn't left him much in the will at all. He didn't think it was fair that a bastard child got more than he did." Julie's voice was hoarse. "He threatened Joel. He said that he'd tell Sandra everything if Joel didn't give him a portion of the trust."

I put my head down between my knees. "So, he was blackmailing Joel, and suddenly …" I looked at Julie. "He had a motive … both times. How have the police not …? How have they not found out that Ben paid a guy to follow you? And the trust? How have they not found out about that?"

Julie shrugged half-heartedly. "The trust is innocent enough, from what I understand. On the surface it's Joel's. What he chooses to do with the money in it is up to him. I have no idea about the private investigator. Maybe Ben covered his tracks really well. I don't know. But Mel, Joel didn't do it. I *know* he didn't do it!"

I dug my nails into my palms. I wanted so badly to believe her, but a part of me fought against being so naive.

"How can you be so sure? You only have his word about what he did that night when he left your house."

Julie looked at me earnestly. "But he was with his mum the night Ben …"

I shook my head. "He came round to my place that night for a while. How do we know he didn't make a detour via Ben's place on the way home? He might have been able to convince Sandra to lie for him too – to say he'd been home the whole time."

Julie slumped back into her chair. "Mel, you don't actually believe he could have done it, do you?"

I felt my body trembling all over. "I don't know what to believe. I don't know what to do."

Julie tensed. "You're not going to tell the police, are you?" she whispered.

"I don't know … I have to go." I took one last glance at Shaun. Joel's brother. That was weird. I slid off the massage table and walked to the door.

"Hey Julie, I'm sorry."

I walked out before she could ask me what I was sorry for. Lucky, because I didn't even know myself.

I pedalled as fast as my legs would take me, but nothing would slow the flurry of thoughts, suspicions, fears, that swarmed between my ears.

Should I go to the police, tell them what I suspected, and let them do their job?

I instantly discarded that option – rightly or wrongly I felt a stab of loyalty to Joel. I couldn't do that to him.

So, what *were* my options? Just pretend I didn't know anything about it, go on as normal, and eventually the police might uncover the truth? Or confront DJH, ask him outright whether he killed his dad and his uncle?

I could never pretend, I wasn't a good enough actress; Joel would know something was up. The second option terrified me: I was afraid of what I might learn, but also I'd have to actually have a direct conversation with DJH, which we hadn't managed in weeks.

I still couldn't muffle the ache inside my chest when I thought about him, but I had to do something. I had to decide.

I knew what I had to do. It was always the only option. Before I could chicken out of something else in my life, I turned my bike towards Rose Bay.

CHAPTER TWENTY-NINE

Confrontation

I climbed off my bike, and I was at the door ringing the bell without any idea of how I was going to do this.

DJH answered the door.

"Hey, Stink. I thought you were doing weights at the gym this afternoon?" His tone was subdued. I missed the flirty one, the tone that, now it was gone, seemed to have been so easy between us before we'd complicated things with sex. Well, I was about to make things even more complicated.

"You have a brother?" I hissed. Nothing like jumping straight into the deep end.

His mouth dropped open in shock and he threw a glance over his shoulder. "Keep your voice down," he muttered, dragging me inside, upstairs and along the hallway to his bedroom. He closed the door behind us and sunk down onto the edge of his bed. I momentarily forgot why I was there.

I'd never been inside Joel's room before. I was surprised at how neat it was. I don't know what I'd expected; naked girls on the walls, dirty socks in the corner and an unmade bed perhaps. It was nothing like that. The king-sized bed was made immaculately with a blue comforter spread out on top. The walls were decorated with black and white cityscape photography. A couple of personal photos graced the top of a chest of drawers, nestled in between a phone charger, a bottle of cologne, cufflinks, and Joel's wristwatch.

I found myself walking over to the photos to take a closer look. One was Joel with his mother and father. He looked about seventeen, younger than he'd been when I'd met him. He had been a gorgeous teenager, but that was only to be expected, really.

The other photo shocked me. My eyes were staring out of it. I was laughing, my hair wet around my shoulders. Joel's arm was slung around me, but he wasn't looking at the camera. He was looking down at me, a grin on his face. I couldn't remember the photo being taken, but judging by the bikini I was wearing, it had been at the pool party that Steve had thrown for me when I finished high school.

I reached out towards the photo, but before I touched it, I stopped myself. I turned back to Joel, who watched me warily.

"How did you find out?" he asked.

I crossed my hands over my chest, reminding myself that I was furious with him for lying to me. "I ran into Julie at the gym today. She had Shaun with her."

Joel paled. "Did she say anything to you?"

I nodded. "Of course she did! She had to. Joel, Shaun looks so much like you it's not funny! I thought he was *yours*! I totally freaked out and she had to tell me everything, so I'd stop thinking that you had a son!"

Joel looked up at me from his hands. "You thought he was mine and you freaked out?"

I glared at him. "Would you be freaked out if you found out that I had a kid you didn't know about?"

Joel paused, then nodded. "Okay, I get your point. So now you know."

I noticed the look of relief on his face. "Yes, now I know! And if you're so relieved that I know now, why didn't you tell me yourself? You have no idea how horrible it was for me to find out the way I did!"

Joel looked taken aback. "I promised Julie I wouldn't tell anyone! And now that you know, you have to promise not to tell anyone either. Stink, you think this has been bad for you – imagine how I feel, keeping this a secret from Mum! It's been the hardest thing I've ever done, but I've managed. Please don't say anything to her."

He looked beseechingly up at me and I felt my anger fading. "I won't tell her, Joel."

I saw his shoulders relax as he realised that I was telling the truth. I couldn't feel as reassured. I was too nervous about the next thing I needed to talk to him about.

"So … I guess you were pretty mad at your dad when you found out?" I asked tentatively.

Joel looked down at his hands. "That's an understatement! Cheating disgusts me. And … it hurts too, you know? Realising that the perfect family you thought you had wasn't enough for your own father. But I had to rise above my personal feelings, for Shaun. He needs me now that Dad's gone. I've got to be there for him and to support Julie."

I was so close to sitting down beside him and drawing him into my arms then. But I had to see this conversation through. I had to do what I'd come here to do, but I was scared; scared to ask, scared to hear his answer, and not just because if he answered yes it would mean he was a murderer. Scared because I wasn't sure that him saying yes would make any difference to how I felt.

"Joel, was it you?" I blurted, my eyes fixed firmly on his face. His brows furrowed in confusion. I couldn't blame him; I wasn't exactly making myself clear. I forced the words from my mouth, before I lost my nerve.

"Did you … kill … your dad? Julie told me that the night it happened you left her place for a couple of hours early in the morning. You were angry … you'd just found out he'd been having an affair. Did you want to … to punish him?"

Joel stared at me with such an expression of horror on his face that I kept talking, stumbling over the words that came bubbling up next. The words that I had been trying not to say to him since Wimbledon.

"I need to know, Joel, because I think that … well … I might want … more … with you. But I need you to be honest with me. I need to know if you killed him … them, because if you did … well, I don't know what I'll do."

My words clammed up in my throat when I realised Joel was staring daggers at me. He sat, glaring at me, for the longest moment of my life.

"I thought you didn't want things to change?" Joel sounded furious, and his brows knitted together over his eyes. I stared at him wide-eyed. *That* was the most important thing he'd taken from everything I'd said?

"Well, maybe I … maybe when you asked me before, I was too confused about what I was feeling. You didn't give me much time to process it, you know."

Joel looked away, running a hand through his short hair. "Okay, so let me get this straight. You came around here to accuse me of murdering my father, and to tell me that you want to … what, start a relationship with me?" He turned his icy eyes on me then, and the world came crashing down around me.

"Um, well, yes … maybe? But … also Ben."

Joel glared at me. "What about Ben?" His voice held a warning, and involuntarily I took a step towards the door.

"Well, Julie told me about Ben threatening you, trying to black-mail you into giving him access to the money in the trust for Shaun. I just thought that you might have … you know … to protect Shaun?" My voice shook.

I'd never seen Joel look so angry. He stood up and towered over me. I took another step backwards but Joel caught me by the arm. He held on tight enough that I wouldn't be able to shake him off. I stared down at his hand on my arm, paralysed with fear.

Joel's other hand snaked up and tilted my chin until I couldn't help but look up at him. He flinched when he saw my expression. "You're afraid. You're actually afraid of me." I didn't like the hurt in his voice.

"Stink, do you actually believe that I could have killed my father and my uncle, no matter how selfish and … and greedy they both were?"

I didn't respond, but he could see the answer in my eyes. He sighed, but he didn't let go of me. Instead he stepped closer, until the fronts of his thighs pressed against the fronts of mine.

I couldn't think straight when he was that close to me. I was stranded somewhere between fear and desire. I had no idea which one would win out.

Joel didn't give me the opportunity to figure that out. He gripped me by the back of my neck, kissing me fiercely. I was stunned momentarily, but it didn't take long for my body to take over and reciprocate.

I could feel a lot of things in Joel's kiss. Frustration. Fear. Need.

My mouth mirrored his need. I needed to be closer to him. It was never going to be enough. An overwhelming emotion was brewing in the pit of my stomach, but I pushed it away. It was just too complicated to deal with right now.

I gave in and let him draw me down.

He hadn't answered all my questions. I started to realise that the answer didn't matter to me. That if he'd done it, I would never tell another living soul about it. I would do that, for him, I realised. Oh shit!

"Melanie Black!" Joel growled at me and my attention snapped back to him.

"Don't be afraid of me, please, Mel," he whispered, his hands stroking my face gently. He leaned down and kissed the hollow at the base of my throat. I moaned and arched myself towards him, my body responding automatically to his expert touch.

Everything felt raw ... intense ... altering. His hands undressed me, roved over my skin. His lips trailed down from my neck to my stomach and between my legs, his tongue making slow, sensuous love to my pussy, my clit, until I rocked to his mouth, crying out and knotting my fingers into his hair.

His body was a warm comforting weight as he crawled up, fitting himself against me, the expression on his face as he pushed into me like a homecoming.

Afterwards we lay naked on his bed, my legs still entwined with his and his arms encompassing me, holding me against his chest. It was then that I realised that my suspicions were stupid. This was

Joel. He was a lot of things, but he wasn't a killer. How had I ever even entertained that thought?

As if he could read my mind, Joel spoke very softly against my hair. "If I tell you now – and I promise you that I've never been more serious in my life, Mel – that I would never, *could* never, kill my father or anyone else for that matter, would you believe me?"

I gazed into his eyes and I answered him truthfully.

"I feel stupid for even letting myself think it in the first place. I'm just so confused about so much."

"Me too, Stink. Believe me. But let's try not to think about all those confusing things for now, okay?"

He turned me so my back fitted against his chest, my butt tucked against his cock. His hand stroked over the curve of my hip and around to my stomach. I could feel his heart beating steadily and strongly against my back. My own slowed, changing pace to match his.

Oh, God! I'm in love with him! And not just in a let's see where this goes sort of way, but in a want to spend the rest of my life with him way – a let's move in together and get married and never spend another night apart again sort of way.

I must have gasped aloud with the sudden revelation, because Joel shifted behind me, his fingers moving away from where they'd been stroking my belly. He turned me until he could look at me properly. "What's up?" he asked.

I looked up to face him, but I found the sentiments that had seemed so true in my head just a moment ago, were suddenly terrifying when I opened my mouth to voice them.

I tried; my mouth opening and closing over and over like a goldfish that had just jumped out of its tank. Joel grinned and my heart ached at how beautiful his smile was.

"Spit it out, Stinky, whatever it is."

I leapt off the bed, climbing back into my clothes with lightning speed.

"Where's the fire?" Joel asked, propping himself up against the bed head. I shook my head, clipping my bra back on with hands that trembled. I already had his door open while I still had my head stuck inside my shirt.

"I've got to go!" I choked out as I made my escape.

Heavy clouds were gathering as I pushed my bike down the drive. I turned to look at them, hoping I'd make it home before the rain started. I caught a glimpse of Joel standing in the doorway of the house, wearing only a pair of jeans and leaning against the door frame, watching me leave.

CHAPTER THIRTY
Revelations

Why? Why had I realised this *now*? Why couldn't I have just gone on in blissful ignorance of my real feelings for Joel? I couldn't even call him DJH anymore. I couldn't blame him for making me fall in love with him.

I could blame myself though. How could I have been so stupid? How could I have let myself fall in love with a guy who was a serial flirt, who collected women the way kids collected Pokémon cards?

If I let Joel know that I loved him, he'd run so fast I'd choke on his dust. How was I going to face him, knowing how I felt? How could I keep him from figuring it out and freaking out on me?

It was almost a surprise when I looked up and realised that I was at the front door of my apartment building. Had I been so deep in my own head the whole way home?

As I climbed off my bike my mobile rang. I pulled it out of my pocket.

It was Joel.

I didn't answer. If he wanted me, he would leave a message. If he *really* wanted me, he would call back. If he called three times, I'd answer the third. Yes, that would be okay. And I'd tell him that I'd forgotten I had some important appointment. I'd act all blasé about it and he wouldn't suspect a thing.

I scrambled up the stairs with my bike slung over one shoulder.

When I reached my landing, I juggled the bike while I sorted through my keys for the one to unlock my front door, reaching out to slip it into the lock.

I froze.

The door was slightly ajar. I put down my bike and left it leaning up against the wall. Through the crack in the door, I could see that the apartment was in darkness. My heart kicked up a notch.

Should I just leave, go to the police and get someone else to check it out for me? No, it was probably nothing – I'd probably forgotten to lock it. I'd been pretty distracted all day.

Still, I locked my key between the knuckles of one hand before I pushed the door open.

Blood.

Gaping mouth.

Bulging eyes.

The flashback hit me with such force I gasped. I pulled back the hand that had started to reach for the light switch – this felt way too familiar. I wasn't sure I wanted to see what was going on inside my apartment.

I was terrified. I wanted Joel with me so bad it hurt.

My mobile rang again, making me jump nearly out of my skin. Joel again. Call number two. I cancelled the call. I was stuck with one foot inside my apartment, one outside. Afraid to go in, afraid to run.

"You haven't returned my calls," a voice inside the apartment accused. In my fear and confusion, I didn't put two and two together. The only calls I could remember not returning were the two from Joel just now. But it couldn't be Joel's voice inside the apartment. I took a step inside and flicked on the light.

"Brad! What are you doing here? How did you get in?" I demanded, feeling so relieved my knees were weak. "Did I leave the door unlocked?"

Brad was sitting in the lounge chair beside the TV. Connor was curled up in his lap, purring loudly.

He shook his head. "You don't even remember, do you?" he

asked, a hint of hurt in his voice. I walked in and sunk down on the lounge, staring at him blankly.

"Remember what?" I asked.

Brad shook his head in disgust. "You gave me a key last year, remember? At the same time you gave one to Amanda, so that if she couldn't make it over to feed Connor, I could instead."

I collapsed back against the lounge – I *had* forgotten. "So, you've been letting yourself in to keep an eye on things when I've been overseas?" I asked.

Brad nodded. "Unlike *some* people, I keep my promises."

I flushed, finally remembering the calls that I hadn't returned. Had it only been earlier that day that I'd had a conversation with Amanda about it? It felt like weeks ago, so much had happened to me in the last few hours.

"Listen, Brad, I'm really sorry. It's been so hectic for me the last couple of weeks. It really has! I'm not kidding. I was going to call you this evening."

Brad's cold face shifted, softened, his grey eyes concerned. "Mel, I've been really worried about you. You have no idea how hard it's been for me to give you space, when all I want is to …" his voice trailed away.

I stared at him hard. "What do you want, Brad?" I prompted, although I had a feeling this was not a conversation I wanted to be having right now.

Brad stood up swiftly and moved onto the lounge beside me, his eyes earnest as they locked with mine. "I love you, Mel. I've loved you for as long as I can remember. All through high school, I had to watch you with that douche Grant Johnson, and wonder what you saw in him. The last year has been amazing, you were single, I felt like I could have more of you.

"But it's not enough for me anymore. I need you, Mel, I want all of you."

I gaped in shock. He stopped talking and looked at me expectantly. I supposed he was waiting for me to answer.

I had no idea what to say.

"I … I can't … Brad, I'm sorry, but I can't deal with this right now." I shook my head, looking down at my lap, afraid he'd read in my eyes the reason why I couldn't deal with it.

"Why not?" His voice was bitter. I should look him in the eyes, tell him the truth. But I couldn't.

"I just ... can't."

I heard the breath hiss through his teeth. "It's Joel, isn't it? Damn it!"

I sneaked a look up at him then, shocked at the fury in his voice. Shocked that he'd worked it out.

"No! It's not Joel! I'm just ... not in a place to be starting *anything* right now."

"Don't lie to me! I'm not blind, Mel! I've seen the way he looks at you. I've seen the way *you* look at *him*! He's not in love with you, Mel. He just wants you to think that you have feelings for him so that he can get you into his bed!"

I swallowed the hard lump that was forming in my throat. Somehow hearing my own deep-seated fear voiced out loud by someone else made it a thousand times more painful.

"I'm not in love with Joel," I muttered, but the words lacked conviction.

"Oh Christ, Mel, you *are* in love with him! How could you be so *stupid?*" Brad grated out, taking my hand from my lap and squeezing it. I snatched it away from him and stood up. Time to be honest.

"I don't know! I don't know why I feel like that about him! But I can't switch it off you know! Just like I can't magically make myself feel things for you that aren't there! Believe me, Brad, it's just not there for me. I'm sorry that it is for you, but it would be wrong of me to lead you on. That's why I haven't returned your calls ...

"I know I should have told you earlier, but I just ... couldn't find the right words. I'm probably using all the wrong ones now, but I can't lie anymore."

Brad stood up and folded his arms across his chest. "Have you slept with him?" he asked quietly, dangerously.

"What?"

"Have. You. Slept. With. Him?" he grated.

I took a step away. "Uh …" I stammered, "that's none of your business!"

Brad slammed the palm of his hand against his forehead, as if he were trying to knock loose some horrible image inside his mind.

"Of course you have!" He glared icily at me. "When? Before the night we kissed?"

I took another step away from him. "No, Brad!"

He looked down at the floor, snarling out his next words through clenched teeth. "You always make the wrong choices, Mel. *Always!*"

"What's that supposed to mean?" I demanded. Outside my kitchen window the sky lit up with lightning, followed by a rumble of thunder in the distance. Outside a storm was brewing. Inside my apartment, one was already in full swing.

"You choose the wrong men! You spent seven years with Grant Johnson, even though he was sleeping around behind your back for most of that time. Then you get yourself involved with Steve Herbert –"

"Leave Steve out of this, Brad!" I snapped.

"Steve Herbert treated you like a commodity. To him you were nothing more than a vehicle for him to keep his foot in the tennis door, because his own son had been such a disappointment to him. He treated you like dirt unless you were doing exactly what he wanted. Mel, I don't know how you couldn't see all this for yourself!"

I shook my head. "It wasn't like that at all – sure I complained to you about Steve a lot, but he was … he was like a father to me! He didn't just care about my career. He cared about *me*. Besides, I guess, unlike you, I try to see the good in people."

Brad glared at me. "Yeah, well that's worked out really well for you, hasn't it? I mean, look where that got you with Ben! Another massive mistake! You jumped into the deep end before you found out what he was really like – a psychopathic stalker!"

I looked down at the floor – Brad didn't know the half of how bad Ben had turned out to be.

"But you weren't satisfied until you humiliated yourself with *every* male in the Herbert family. You let Joel Herbert the serial slut work *his* magic on you, and now you're well and truly under his spell. He'll chew you up and spit you out just like he does every girl he sleeps with."

Tears burned behind my eyelids, but I didn't want to give Brad the satisfaction of seeing me cry.

My phone rang again. I let it ring out.

"Get out, Brad," I whispered, moving towards the door and opening it for him. "Please, just get out."

"Don't worry, Mel, I will. I'm going to end this now!"

He stormed out before I could gather my thoughts enough to ask what exactly he meant by that.

When the door closed behind him, I flopped down on the lounge, finally releasing the wracking sobs I'd been holding in for hours.

Brad had said a lot of angry shit and not all of it was true. But what he said about Joel … that hurt. In my head I'd known things with Joel could only ever be casual – that was my MO as much as it was his.

But my heart … it was dreaming about more.

Brad's feelings for me would no doubt disappear very quickly now; he clearly didn't have much respect for me and my decisions.

'I'm going to end this now'. Thinking about his parting words sent ice creeping up my spine.

Another sheet of lightning lit the sky as my phone beeped with a voicemail.

It was from Joel.

"Mel, listen, I don't know why you're not answering, but I hope you're okay and that you're not mad at me. I don't know what made you run out like that. I really need to talk to you. I think we need to sit down together and discuss this, before it gets out of hand. I'm not going anywhere – I'll be home all night, so if you can … look, please just give me a call and I'll come round, or you could come round here, or… well, whatever. Just call me, please."

I clutched at my aching chest. Joel wanted to end things with me because I was too involved. Brad wanted to end … what? His feelings for me? I couldn't work it out.

Connor pawed at my leg and yowled. I looked at my watch – almost eight. Today had been so long and yet so short. I wished it was over and that it hadn't even started at the same time.

"Okay Connie, I'll get your dinner," I mumbled, my throat thick from crying. I clambered off the lounge and slouched my way into the kitchen, reaching into the cupboard for the big plastic tub of cat biscuits.

Lightning split the sky outside, thunder following so fast and so loud that I flinched. Connor hissed and clawed me.

I gasped in pain, blood welling from my arm. The rain started to pound against my windowpane.

All the floating pieces suddenly clicked inside my skull.

I dropped the biscuits. The container split and they spilled, skittering to all corners of the kitchen. Connor jumped off the bench and started inhaling them off the floor.

I didn't stop him. I didn't stop to clean the mess.

I took a shuddering breath and ran to the door. I stopped just inside, then raced to the bedroom, struggling into a rain jacket before hurrying back out the door.

It was dark. It was pouring down with rain. It was freezing cold. But I had no choice. I manhandled my bike down the stairs, flicked the lights on, and rode out onto the street.

I hoped I wasn't already too late.

CHAPTER THIRTY-ONE

Betrayal

Joel was in serious danger.

And here I was, riding my pushbike through Sydney traffic in the torrential rain. Racing to save the man I loved from being murdered. By my best friend.

Pain sliced my chest thinking about what Brad had done … to Steve … and Grant … and Ben.

And I might be too late to save Joel. I might be too late to tell him that I loved him.

The tyres of my bike splashed along the rain-drenched streets. I ignored red lights, sweeping around corners like a maniac with a death wish. Even then, it had never felt like such a long journey to Joel's house, but finally it loomed before me. I keyed the code into the gate and watched it slowly slide open. I dropped my bike just inside the gate and hurried towards the house.

The front door was ajar. My stomach sunk as I tiptoed my way towards the house, stopping just outside under the shelter of the porch, to allow myself a breath. Inside it was very dark, which was unusual – Sandra was all about ambient light of an evening.

Wrenching off my rain jacket, helmet and shoes, I slipped inside. My drenched clothes and skin dripping on the floors as I climbed the stairs to check the bedrooms first. All deserted.

I crept down the stairs. The living room was also in darkness. I paused to adjust to the gloom; although I could navigate this house with my eyes closed, I didn't want any nasty surprises sneaking up on me. I'd already had enough nasty surprises for one day.

I scanned the room: empty. I slipped silently through the master bedroom; also empty.

I couldn't let myself feel relieved. There was still a whole other level to this house.

I turned and tiptoed down, thanking God that this house was so well-built that the stairs didn't creak. There was no one on the lounge. The TV was off. The room was mostly shadow, the gym end was in utter darkness.

No one was home.

Then I heard a moan from the far end of the room. I raced towards the sound, not caring if I made noise now.

It was Sandra. She was tied to one of the machines. Her mouth was gagged with what looked like a CANTEEN bandana. I gagged; who would use an item from a kids' cancer charity to gag someone?

Someone who worked in a kids' cancer ward and probably had things like that just sitting in his car.

"Sandra!" I hissed, crouching down beside her. She looked up at me with fear in her eyes and I tried to swallow mine.

With shaking hands, I fumbled with the knot on the gag and managed to drag it free from her mouth. Sandra took a deep, shuddering breath. I leaned around behind her and tried to untie the rope that was holding her against the machine.

"Joel," she gasped croakily. My heart stopped beating for a second and I stopped trying to untie the rope. I leaned around until I could see her face.

"Where is he?" I asked frantically. I followed Sandra's horrified gaze until I was staring at a still form on the floor near the lounge, mostly obscured from view.

I leapt away from Sandra and staggered towards Joel's lifeless body, breath scissoring in and out of my lungs. My legs gave way and I collapsed to my knees beside him.

He was lying half on his side, facing the back of the lounge. I rested one trembling hand on his shoulder and rolled him over until he was on his back. His hair and face were matted with blood, and more oozed sluggishly from a split on his forehead, just on his hairline.

"Joel," I whispered in agony. I was too late. Tears burned my eyes, but they refused to fall.

Joel's chest rose and fell once, and I stopped breathing.

He wasn't dead.

"Joel!" I hissed, shaking his shoulder to try and wake him up. He groaned, opening his eyes a slit.

"Oh Joel!" I cried, not caring whether Brad was still in the house or not anymore.

"Mel?" Joel rasped. His hand went up to his forehead and touched the bloody wound. "Ouch."

"You're bleeding," I explained. He leaned up onto one elbow and tried to hoist himself up. I slipped an arm under his and helped him prop himself up against the back of the lounge.

"Is he still here?" Joel asked.

I shook my head. "I don't know. I don't think so. Oh Joel, you have no idea how relieved I am that you're not …"

"Is Mum okay?" he interrupted. I nodded.

"I'm fine, sweetie, just glad you're okay," Sandra called from where she was still tied to the weights machine.

Joel sighed woozily and I held his face gently, taking a closer look at the wound. I thought he might be concussed.

"Mel," he began, but I put a finger to his lips, pulling my phone out of my pocket.

"Shush. I'll call the police and an ambulance." I swiped to unlock my phone and dialled triple zero. My hands shook so much I could barely punch the number in.

"Mel," Joel said again, more insistently. I looked up from my phone. He was squinting, trying to focus on a place somewhere above and behind me.

My brain screamed at me to not turn, to not look in the same direction, but my head started swivelling to the right, craning behind and up.

I didn't even get a glimpse of what was there before he pounced.

His hand snaked around my throat, gripping so tight that I couldn't expel the air caught in my lungs.

He dragged me to my feet and spun me around, still choking me, and holding me against him. Something cold and pointy pressed against my neck.

"Well, what a surprise – you see, Joel, you see what you've done to her?" The voice was rumbly and rough, and something about it was horrifyingly familiar, but in my panic, I couldn't place it.

One thing was certain: the voice did not belong to Brad.

"Leave her out of this," Joel growled, managing to sound menacing. He struggled to his feet, swaying, and I saw just how much blood was in his hair and on his face. And on the floor. My stomach churned.

The knife dug deeper into the skin on the side of my neck.

"Don't come any closer, or I swear I'll do it!"

I stared wide-eyed at Joel, his eyebrows knitted together as he glared at the man behind me. I blinked, lightheaded as I struggled for enough air.

"Let her go – you came here for me, not her."

"Oh, but don't you see? I *did* come here for her. Everything has been for her."

My attacker spun around, spinning me with him. I stumbled, felt the sting as the knife at my neck pressed deeper.

"Now I'm going to have to get rid of all three of you," he sighed.

Sandra stared at me with resignation in her eyes. *No!* There was no way I was ready to die!

"Why are you doing this?" I wheezed.

"Mel, you should be thanking me! I'm doing this for you! *Someone* has to protect you from the people who want to take advantage of you. From the mistakes you keep making."

"Mel's perfectly capable of looking after herself!" Joel grunted. My attacker swung us back around so that he could face Joel, who was holding onto the back of the lounge for support. He was deathly pale behind all the blood. How much had he lost? How much could a person lose before they were in serious danger?

"Is she?" my attacker growled back. "I'm not so sure about that. Well, it hardly matters anymore. It seems I can't stop others from using her, so she's better off dead."

Something warm trickled down the side of my neck – the knife had pierced me.

Joel's expression was horrified, furious … terrifying through all the blood. I really didn't want that to be my last image of Joel before I died. I squeezed my eyes tight shut and pictured him naked, arms wrapped around me, our legs entwined. Had it only been earlier that day that I'd been in bed with him?

"Joel, I …" I grated, gagging before I could say the next words – *"love you"* – as the hand around my throat tightened again.

"Mel," Joel moaned desperately. He couldn't save me. He could hardly even keep himself upright. I struggled for breath to force the words out. I had to tell him. I couldn't die and not tell him.

"Drop the weapon!" another voice growled behind us. The pressure of the blade on my neck eased slightly, and I sucked in a shuddering breath, even though I could still feel it biting into me.

"Let her go or I shoot!"

My attacker still had his hand around my throat, even if the knife wasn't pressed there anymore. I couldn't open my eyes. He squeezed it a little tighter and I gurgled pitifully.

The bang was so loud that I flinched, trying to bring my pinned hands up to cover my ears.

It was still reverberating when the attacker's hand loosened around my throat, and we both thumped to the floor.

It was still reverberating when pain blossomed in my shoulder. I opened my eyes and looked down at the blood very quickly soaking through my t-shirt.

It was still reverberating when the world went black.

CHAPTER THIRTY-TWO

Floating

There were flashes of awareness.

A blurry outline of a police officer leaning over me.

The high-pitched whirring of the siren in the ambulance.

A room with bright lights that smelt of antiseptic.

People peering down at me. Mum. Father Shannon. Sandra. Brad.

I had no strength to show them that I knew they were there. I had nothing more to give.

I let the darkness hold me under for a little longer. I wasn't ready to face the real world just yet.

CHAPTER THIRTY-THREE

Recovery

I knew I could open my eyes, that I was conscious. I just wasn't sure that I wanted to face what was waiting for me.

Don't be such a baby, Melanie Black! I chastised myself. I forced my eyelids open.

Brad was slumped in a chair beside the hospital bed, looking haggard. He must have sensed my gaze, because he looked up from his lap, his grey eyes exhausted. When he saw me looking his eyes widened, and he was at my side in an instant.

He hadn't shaved or brushed his hair in days. I started to reach my left hand up to touch his stubble, but pain sliced through me. I gasped, and Brad reached under the covers to wind his fingers through mine.

"You were shot, Mel," Brad explained in a voice that sounded dead. "The police shot … the intruder, but he was close enough that the bullet passed through him and ended up in your shoulder."

I looked down to where the pain was. My shoulder was wrapped in thick padding. I tried to swallow the lump in my throat, but it wouldn't go away.

"Mel, I'm so sorry!" Brad's voice was agonised. "I keep wondering if I hadn't fought with you, then you wouldn't have ended up going over there, and then you wouldn't be stuck in this hospital bed." His thumb stroked the back of my hand.

I fought to speak around the lump and the dryness in my mouth. "Joel?" I rasped.

Brad sighed through his nose, but he nodded. "He had a concussion from the blow to his head, but he's recovered pretty well from that."

"Well, don't be sorry, Brad. If I hadn't thought that … well, if you hadn't argued with me, Joel and Sandra might be dead now."

Brad looked away from my eyes, staring towards the machines I was hooked up to. "But you would be safe. *You* wouldn't be lying here with a hole in your shoulder."

"But if Joel … if he'd died, I … I love Joel." The words sighed from my body, like it was a relief for them to finally be out there.

Brad watched me, mouth tight. "Even if he doesn't love you back?" he asked.

I nodded. "Even if he doesn't love me back." I let that thought sink in, and the lump in my throat throbbed.

Brad sighed, his grey eyes meeting my brown ones. "I know, Mel. And I'm sorry. Well, I guess now we both know what it feels like to love someone who doesn't reciprocate."

I leaned my head against his arm. "I love you too, Brad. You're my best friend. That's never going to change, no matter how many men come and go in my life."

He snorted. "Yeah, I'll be the one you know you can always rely on."

I turned my head and pressed my lips to his arm.

The door opened and Amanda rushed in, stopping dead when she saw me.

"You're awake," she said. She looked from me to Brad, and back again, and suddenly she was sobbing, her face quickly getting red and splotchy with tears.

"Oh Mel!" she blubbered, collapsing on the bed, lying down beside me and grabbing my other hand. "I'm so sorry. I don't … I can't believe I …"

I looked at her in confusion. "What are you sorry for?" I asked.

She looked up at Brad and my stomach dropped. "Someone better explain what's going on," I muttered.

"It's all my fault! I should have known that he seemed too good to be true."

I narrowed my eyes at her. "What do you mean? Who are you talking about?"

Amanda refused to look at me. "Thomas … it was Thomas."

Fuck.

The voice that had been horrifyingly familiar, that I couldn't place, suddenly all meshed in my skull.

"No!" I gasped. "Why? How?"

Amanda shrugged, tears plopping onto the blanket. "I don't know. No one knows. He's still in intensive care. They're not sure when, or if, he'll wake up."

"Steve?"

Amanda nodded mutely.

"And Ben?"

Another nod.

"And … Grant?"

Brad intervened. "Amanda, we don't know any of that for sure. We might never know. He might die before they can question him."

Amanda shook her head. "I just know it was him! He asked me a heap of questions about you – even before we were dating, that night we met down in Melbourne. I thought he was impressed that I knew a famous person. He was … he was only with me because it meant he could get closer to you …"

A cold shiver ran down my spine.

Brad slipped his hand out of mine and walked around the bed, pulling Amanda up gently, moving her until she sat in the chair he'd vacated. She shrunk into it, shaking, clinging to him.

"Those detectives spent three hours with her," he explained. I shuddered. I'd had enough experience with police interrogation to know what she'd been through.

A nurse bustled into the room at that point. She glared disapprovingly at Brad and Amanda.

"Alright, I think Melanie has had enough excitement to last her a little while," she said, coming to the bedside and checking the IV line connected to my right arm. My good arm. My tennis arm.

"Time for you to shoo!"

With a look of apology, Brad gathered Amanda under his arm and drew her, weeping, from the room.

I ate a little after the nurse checked me over and then I slept again. I'd never felt so exhausted in my life.

I woke to the door opening. Groggily I peered over.

Mum took a shuddering breath and came right up to the bed, wrapping her arms around me gently. The way she had when I was little and I'd woken up from a nightmare.

"Mel, oh my beautiful girl," she whispered against the side of my face. "I'm so sorry."

I cleared my throat. "Water," I rasped and she sat up, pouring me some from the jug at my bedside. I drank to give me time to process her being here.

"What are you sorry for?" I asked.

"I'm sorry that I treated you like a disappointment. You never were. When your father died, I … my faith became so much more important to me. And I'm afraid that … I think I let my beliefs tarnish the way I saw you. And then I … I almost lost you too!"

"Mum … I …" I began, but had no idea what I wanted to say.

"I know our relationship is … strained, but sweetie, I'm so proud of you. You've grown up to be a strong, capable young woman and you've done that without any help from me."

She smoothed hair off my forehead and gazed down at me, with eyes that were just like my own.

There was a knock on the door. We both looked over, to see my two favourite detectives letting themselves into the room.

"We need a few moments of your time, Miss Black," Taylor said, looking from me to Mum and back.

I sighed. "I'd better get this over and done with," I muttered to Mum, who leaned down and kissed my forehead before vacating the room.

I took a deep breath, enduring Taylor's questions and Coughlin's concerned looks, for over an hour. I relived every minute of that dreadful day.

I was exhausted by the time the conversation was over and my shoulder was throbbing with pain. A nurse came in and checked on the machines strapped to my arm and injected something into my IV. I started to feel sleepy almost immediately.

"We're not going to get much more out of her now," Taylor grunted to Coughlin. I watched them through half-closed lids.

There was another knock at the door and a uniformed police officer poked her head in.

"He's awake, Detective Taylor."

That was all it took to clear the room of police, and I was able to close my eyes and let sleep claim me.

I woke up drenched in sweat and gasping for breath, my shoulder screaming in pain.

The nightmare had been so real. *I could smell his cologne as he held my throat. I could feel his sweat dripping on me as he struggled me onto the floor. The agony of the knife was so real as it sunk into my chest. I looked up in shock into Thomas's smiling face.*

It took three days for me to recover enough to be discharged. Three days of pain meds, and sleep, and sporadic visitors. Brad, Mum, Sandra.

Amanda avoided me.

So did Joel.

Brad came to collect me and while we waited for my discharge papers, he told me that Detective Taylor had managed to extract a full confession from Thomas. The murders of Steve and Ben. The attempted murder of Grant. The attack on Sandra, Joel and me, with intent to kill.

"We knew Thomas was at the Australian Open. He heard you and Steve fighting, the morning before Steve was ... and something just snapped. He was already targeting Amanda, even before ... Steve ... because he knew she was close to you."

"Well, that worked out perfectly for him, then, didn't it? He found out about Ben and Grant, because he was there with us all, when I was pouring my heart out about them. But I still don't understand. Why?" I asked in frustration. Brad turned my hand over in his and traced the lines on my palm with his fingers. It felt nice.

"Who knows what goes on in the head of a psychopath, Mel? He went to insane levels of effort to get close to you, without you realising." Brad tilted his head to one side, watching me. I faltered under his gaze and looked down at my arm, at the little Bandaid where the IV had been removed. He looked at me the way I was sure I looked at Joel.

"We might learn more when the trial gets underway."

Brad was right. There wasn't any point in me worrying over it. I'd find out the whole story sooner or later. All I cared about really was that they'd caught him before it had been too late for Joel.

Joel.

The door opened and a nurse came in with papers to sign. I sat up straighter on the bed and reached for the pen. My left arm still hung virtually useless by my side. I was going to need a lot of physio to get back into competition shape.

I added that to the rapidly expanding list of things I needed to speak to Joel about. Along with telling him that I loved him, and yelling at him for not coming to visit me. And asking him if he felt anything for me at all. And getting ready for heartbreak when he let me down.

"I just don't know what to do, Brad," I blurted once we were safely in the car and driving through the evening peak hour traffic. "I really need my best friend right now. And I know that you probably don't want to hear about it, but you're the only person I've told about … Joel … and I just need to talk about it."

Brad flexed his fingers on the steering wheel, and he wore a little smirk that didn't reach his eyes.

"Spit it out, Mel."

"So … you don't think there's a future for me and Joel, do you?" I asked timidly.

"Smellie, I don't know. It's not really any of my business, is it? What do *you* think?"

I sighed. "I'm doubtful."

Brad's knuckles were white on the steering wheel. "But you can't change the way you feel about him."

I shook my head.

"Well, I can't change the way I feel about you."

I fixed my gaze out the passenger window. I couldn't look at him while he said these things.

"But Smell, I love you enough that I just want to be a part of your life – whatever part you want me to fill. I'm not going anywhere. Maybe you love Joel enough to just want to be a part of his life too, even if it's not the part you were hoping for."

I wasn't sure that I could swallow my pride enough for that. Not telling him how I felt at all would be better than the humiliation of having it thrust in my face every day that it was unrequited.

"I'm so confused," I muttered.

Brad chuckled under his breath. "Join the club, Smellie. Life is just one discombobulating event after another."

I rolled my eyes, surprised that he had managed to make me smile. I nudged him with my good arm. "You know I hate it when you use those big words, Bradley."

We pulled into my driveway, and the smile I'd finally managed to find lurking inside me slipped from my face. It finally hit me. I'd come very close to being dead. Suddenly I really didn't want to go inside my apartment, to be properly alone for the first time since it had happened.

Brad must have seen the way my face changed. He stopped the car, but he didn't cut the engine.

"Are you okay?" he asked, concern seeping into his tone. I stared straight ahead, not wanting Brad to be able to meet my eyes, to see the sudden fear in them. I felt silly and paranoid for being terrified to go into my home, but I couldn't make the rational side of me overcome the emotional one.

"I can't do this …" I whispered.

"I can take you away if you want – we can go have dinner somewhere."

I took a deep, shaky breath. "No, Brad, it's okay, I've got to do it sooner or later."

"I'll carry your stuff up for you."

Inside my apartment almost everything was as I'd left it. Even a ravenously hungry Connor met me at the door.

"I'll feed him," Brad offered, heading to the kitchen, where I noticed the mess of Connor's food had been cleaned up.

"Did you or Amanda come and tidy for me?" I asked.

Brad shook his head. "It was your mum. I came over the morning after, and she was here, mopping your floors. She said she felt like she had to do something useful because she felt so helpless, seeing you unconscious in the hospital."

Tears welled, but I managed to blink them back. A big chat with Mum was long overdue. We hadn't talked frankly with each other in … I couldn't remember when. I could barely remember Dad, I'd been so young when he died. But I'd never even wondered how it had affected Mum over the years.

"You want me to make you a cuppa?" Brad asked.

I shook my head. "I think I just need to have tonight to settle back in. I'll call you in the morning, okay?"

Brad paused, then nodded, taking my bag through to the bedroom, then heading for the door. "You can call me any time, you know. Middle of the night, I don't care. If you need me, you call."

I walked over to him, hugging him as tight as I could with my good arm. "Thanks for everything, Brad. I love you, you know."

He sighed. "Yeah, I know."

CHAPTER THIRTY-FOUR

Facing The Truth

Nothing was better than a cup of tea made just the way you like it, especially after drinking the dirt water they call tea in hospital.

Connor was curled on my lap and I was ignoring the increasing throb in my left shoulder. I wasn't ready to take one of the pain pills they'd sent me home with, because I was sick and tired of sleeping.

My phone was on the lounge beside me. I'd ordered some Indian on Uber Eats and every time I picked it up to check the delivery status, I found myself straying to my text messages and staring blankly at the cursor as it flashed in the new message bar under Joel's last message.

Call me

It was sent the same time he left the voicemail.

I wanted to text him. I couldn't possibly text him.

A belting knock sounded on the door. My brow knitted – no way my food had arrived so quickly! Tipping Connor off my lap, I approached the door and opened it.

"Miss Black, we need to search your apartment," Detective Taylor said. I gaped at the team of gloved police waiting behind her.

"Why?" I demanded.

"We have uncovered some new evidence from Thomas Blackthorn's home, and we believe it may be linked to corresponding evidence here."

"Do I have a choice?" I asked. She shook her head.

"We're collecting evidence for a serial murder case, Miss Black. This is very important. You'll need to vacate until we have everything we need."

"And how long will that take?" I asked faintly. Connor bunted up against the back of my leg and I stooped to pick him up, hissed in pain, and gave up. Taylor actually looked mildly sympathetic.

"I'd suggest you find somewhere else to stay overnight, at least. You'll need to take your cat, too. It's essential that we do a full sweep of the entire apartment."

"Why?" I asked again. Taylor refused to reply, instead pushing past me and gesturing for her team to head inside.

———

Less than twenty minutes later I was sitting in the stairwell outside, with an overnight bag, eating rapidly cooling Indian food next to Connor, growling resentfully in the cat carrier. Police tape barred my apartment door, muffled murmurs coming from the forensics team inside.

I didn't know what to do next. I couldn't ask Brad to take us in – his granny flat was tiny, there was barely enough space for one person, let alone two and a grumpy cat.

I pulled up Mum's number, but paused over dialling. She and I needed to talk, but me showing up with Connor in tow and asking to sleep in my childhood bed … I couldn't swallow my pride enough for that.

And of course, the other option – Joel – was completely off the table.

"I can't call him, Connie, I just can't," I muttered. "He doesn't want to see me."

"Who doesn't want to see you, Stink?"

I almost tipped down the stairs, I leapt to my feet so fast. He stood in the stairwell, arms across his chest.

I gaped. "What are you doing here?" I asked.

Joel's lips twitched downwards. "I ... heard you'd been sent home today. I just wanted to check ... you know, that you have everything you need, and maybe talk rehab for your shoulder." He looked behind me to the police tape over my door. "What's happening in there?"

"Apparently there's some important evidence they need to gather. And then they have to do a full sweep of my apartment. No idea why – they won't tell me anything." I shrugged, then hissed at the pain in my shoulder. "So, I'm temporarily homeless."

Joel snorted. "You're ridiculous, Stinky. Let's get your shit and get down to my car. Mum will be delighted to have you."

And what about you? I thought grumpily as I grabbed my overnight bag in my good hand, while Joel juggled Connor and all his stuff. *How delighted will you be about this?*

The silence in the car on the way back to Joel's was awkward. Silence had never been awkward between us before London.

"How's your head?" I asked to break the tense quiet. I'd seen the stitches just below his hairline. I peeked at him out of the corner of my eye. His hair was shorter. It suited him.

Oh, Mel, who are you kidding? You'd love his hair no matter how he wore it!

Joel ran two fingers over the stitches self-consciously. "It's okay. How's your arm?" Joel asked, the way an old school acquaintance would ask you how you'd been when they bumped into you in the street. I gritted my teeth.

"It's been better, but you'd know that already if you'd ..." I trailed off. Joel's mouth twisted, but he didn't say anything. I pursed my lips and turned to face the road again.

God, why can't I just tell him the things I feel; get it over and done with? I silently asked. As usual no answer appeared magically out of thin air.

Joel took Connor straight into my usual guest room, leaving

immediately. I slammed the door behind him, gritting my teeth because the movement hurt so much.

I opened Connor's cage and he leapt out and scuttled under the bed, tail up like a bottlebrush.

There was a knock on the door.

"What do you want?" I snapped.

No answer. I groaned and got to my feet, reaching the door and wrenching it open. Connor's litter box was outside. Joel was nowhere to be seen.

I sighed and dragged it into the bathroom. I stripped my clothes off and ran the shower cold. I needed something to soothe the hot anger that was racing through my veins.

I strained in the mirror to see the hole where the bullet had entered me at the back of my shoulder. They'd stitched the hole shut, but they told me not to wear a dressing on it anymore – it needed to breathe. The black stitches stood out against the angry red wound. I was going to have one doozy of a scar there. I sighed. Nothing I could do about it.

I climbed into bed naked and with wet hair. I was so tired I felt like I would sleep for a century.

So of course, I couldn't sleep at all. Anger pulsed under my skin. I tossed and turned.

It was about three when I gave up. I pulled an oversized t-shirt out of my bag and dragged it over my head. It fell almost to my knees.

The house was silent, sleeping. Why could everything else seem peaceful, when I was full of turmoil? It didn't seem fair.

I filled a glass with water from the tap in the kitchen and guzzled it in one breath. I filled it again and padded quietly out towards the patio. The door slid open silently. I curled up on a love seat that overlooked the garden and pool below.

The moon was full and it lit the night better than any artificial light. I pulled the t-shirt over my knees. The neckline was so stretched that it slipped off my left shoulder. The cool air on my wound actually felt nice. I didn't pull it back up.

"I've never seen a bullet wound before."

I jumped, spilling the glass of water down the front of my t-shirt.

"What are you doing?" I hissed crankily. "You're supposed to be asleep!"

His mouth tweaked. "So are you."

He didn't move to sit beside me, for which I was grateful. I was suddenly hyper-aware that underneath this thin and now see-through shirt I was completely naked. He stood to one side and peered at my shoulder with detached interest, like I was a medical specimen.

I glared up at him and felt the rude retort die in my throat.

In the moonlight the gash on his forehead looked much more dramatic. Conscious of the direction of my gaze, his hand went up and touched the wound. His mouth quirked wryly and he shrugged.

"Chicks dig scars, don't they, Stink?" he asked me. I rolled my eyes, but the shudder in my breath gave away how even that throw-away comment cut me deep.

"You didn't even come to see if I was okay," I accused, dragging my eyes from him and staring out across the silvery, sleepy harbour.

"I wasn't sure you'd want to see me."

I pulled my knees up to my chest and wrapped my arms around them. "Could you not have just shown up anyway? If I didn't want you there, I would have let you know."

Joel chuckled humourlessly. "I'm sure you would have, Stinky." I hazarded a glance his way. He was watching me with wary eyes.

"What happened the other night? Before I got there, I mean." I leaned back against the seat and watched him expectantly. He sighed and looked down, scrubbing a hand across his jaw.

"Mum answered the door. I'd told her it was probably you. He held her at knife point and threatened to hurt her if I didn't do what he said. He forced us downstairs and tied Mum up. He said he hadn't wanted to get her involved, but … well, you heard the things he said when you got there."

"Why did he hit you?"

Joel shrugged. "I argued with him. He didn't like that. He didn't like that his reasons for doing it weren't really …" Joel's voice trailed off.

"Weren't really what? What reasons?!" I demanded, gesturing with my left arm. I felt the burn and I gasped, letting my arm drop to my side.

Joel took a step towards me and then stopped. "Stink, your shoulder's worse than you're making it out to be, isn't it?"

I could hear the concern in his voice and I looked away. "Don't try to change the subject, Joel. What did you argue with him about?"

Joel heaved out a sigh. "He accused me of hurting you. Of misleading you. I disagreed."

I couldn't look at him. I didn't want him to know that I thought Thomas might have been more right about that than Joel would like to admit.

"He said that you didn't know what was good for you, that you keep making bad decisions. That you need a man who'll treat you right, who'll look after you the way a woman deserves to be looked after."

I gagged at that. "What, did he think that would be *him*?" I asked incredulously.

"I don't know, he wasn't making much sense. All I know is that he definitely thinks that I'm not the right guy for you."

I turned and faced the pool again, gritting my teeth to stop the tears from falling.

"And you told him that you weren't hurting me and he hit you?" I clarified. Joel didn't answer right away. I wanted to look at him, but I didn't let myself. If I did, I wouldn't be able to hold the tears back.

"Something like that. It's all a bit blurry after that. I don't remember anything until you were there."

I felt his fingertips feather-light on my arm. I kept my chin high and my eyes focussed into the distance.

"Mel, if I *am* hurting you, I'm really sorry," Joel murmured. I took a few deep breaths.

"And I'm sorry that you got hurt because of me," I replied through my teeth. "So, I guess we're even then."

I heard his frustrated sigh. "This little cut? It's nothing. In a few weeks it'll be nothing more than a great story to tell."

I shrugged. "Well, I'm glad you'll be able to get over it that easily." I wasn't talking about the scar anymore.

Joel was quiet for a long moment. "Is there something you want to say to me, Mel?" he finally asked. I dropped my chin to my chest then, because the tears were spilling now and I really didn't want him to see me crying over him.

"There's no point, Joel," I replied bitterly.

"Why do you fight the way you feel about me?" He sounded amused.

My emotions overflowed. I leapt up from the love seat and turned to face him, not caring about the tear-tracks on my cheeks. I tried to focus on his face, not his body, clad only in boxer shorts.

"Why do I fight it? What, does it annoy you when a woman doesn't swoon at the sight of you? Does it make you feel less of a man if you can't make a woman's heart melt? I can't afford to make myself that vulnerable around you, Joel! It's not fair that you can steal my heart! I don't want you to have it!" I snapped my mouth shut.

Oh God, had I just, in a weird, roundabout way, told Joel I loved him?

Joel was smirking now. That just made me even angrier, and I screwed up my face to try and keep the tears from getting worse, wiping hurriedly at the fresh ones that were rolling down my cheeks.

"I stole your heart?" he asked, his mouth hitching up even further into that cheeky grin that I would have said annoyed the living daylights out of me, if I wasn't totally in love with it. With the man it belonged to.

"You know you did – you've been trying to for months now! I hope you're happy – it's yours! You'll probably just break it anyway. I'm so *angry* at myself for letting this happen!"

I stopped and stared at him. He was *laughing* at me! I couldn't believe it. I felt my face burning red hot and I snapped.

I lunged at him, pummelling at his torso with all the strength I could muster in my right arm. I lashed out again and again, my fist making contact with his ribs, his stomach.

Joel just stood there and took it like I was tickling him with a feather duster. He watched me with that ridiculous grin on his face.

I slowed down my attack and then stopped altogether, dropping my face into my good hand. I didn't want him to look at me. Could I have made any more of a mess of this?

"I didn't steal your heart." Joel spoke with such quiet assurance that I almost looked up into his face, but at the last minute remembered how blotchy and red I would be. I kept my face hidden in my hand.

"Yes, you did!" I snapped childishly, my words muffled because my fingers were over my mouth.

"I didn't steal it, Stinky. I traded it. Yours for mine."

I froze. I couldn't look up at him. I hadn't heard right. I was going insane. I was starting to hear voices.

Cool hands pried my fingers away from my cheeks and tilted my chin until my face was pointing directly at his. I didn't look up into his eyes. Instead, I pouted stubbornly.

"That's a pretty fair trade, don't you think, Mel?" Joel asked in that softly spoken tone that always made me weak at the knees.

"Don't lie to me, Joel. It's not funny, you know," I grunted, looking everywhere but at him. He sighed and manoeuvred his face until I couldn't help but look at him. I closed my eyes.

"Mel, look at me please," he commanded. I pursed my lips but opened my eyes. He was so close that I couldn't think straight. I swallowed the saliva that rushed into my mouth.

"Why is it that you always have to argue with me? Here I am, trying to tell you that I'm in love with you, and you still want to disagree!"

"I – I …" I stammered, not knowing what to say.

Joel snickered. "What can I do to prove it?"

I dragged my face out of his hands with an effort and stomped over to the glass balustrade.

"You're in love with me?" I asked, whirling around to face him.

He stopped in his tracks and watched me with a half smug, half pleading expression. "Would I say it if I wasn't?"

I opened and closed my mouth, trying to work out a cutting, clever retort to that. But I had no words.

"Trying to catch a fly, Stinky?" Joel chuckled. I snapped my mouth shut, hearing my teeth click together.

"You want to prove it? Stop calling me Stinky!" I snapped, putting my good hand on my hip and eyeing him grumpily. He laughed out loud and closed the distance between us in two graceful strides.

"Melanie Elizabeth Black, I love you," he murmured. "I've loved you for longer than you can possibly imagine." He wasn't even touching me, but his gaze felt more intimate than if I was standing naked in front of him. "Now, are you going to swallow your pride and respond?"

"Joel," I groaned. I couldn't bring myself to say the words, even when he'd had the courage to say them to me.

"Just say it, Stink, so I can kiss you already," he whispered. I heard my breath hiss as I gasped. I ignored the fact that he'd just used the nickname he'd promised not to.

I knew I had to say it. I knew it was time to tell the truth. But I was stubborn, I couldn't quite swallow all of my pride.

"I don't know why I have to say it out loud – you already know it anyway," I grumbled. "But yes, I'm in love with you." I sighed, reaching up to brush my fingertips down his cheek. He deserved better than that.

"I love you, Joel Herbert." I whispered.

His mouth met mine, but he could hardly kiss me he was smiling so much. And that made me smile too. Soon we were both grinning like fools, and we'd given up on kissing for the moment.

"You *love* me," I sighed in wonder and pressed my cheek to his, loving the way I could *feel* his smile. He turned his head until his lips were at my ear.

"*You* love *me*," he replied. His mouth traced down from my earlobe, along my jaw to my chin, and then he found my mouth again.

He wasn't smiling anymore. He was kissing me in that way that I should have realised was about more than just seduction. He'd always kissed me like someone who loved me, I'd just been too blind to recognise it. I wrapped my right arm around his neck and pulled him closer.

His hands slid down my back and slipped under the bottom of my t-shirt. He broke away and gasped as his hands met my naked butt.

"I wasn't going to do this tonight," he moaned against my hair, even as I felt the physical evidence that it was *definitely* what he wanted to do, jabbing me in the hipbone.

I dug my nails into the back of his neck. "Why the Hell not?" I asked huskily.

"Because I didn't want you to think that I only said I love you so you'd sleep with me again."

I giggled breathlessly. "I'm going to regret saying this, when your ego gets so big it needs its own postcode, but you wouldn't have needed to say it to get me in bed with you. You were right – I can't resist you."

"Now she tells me!" he joked, his hands moving off my butt and caressing up and down my back. I clung to him, pressing my lips to his collarbone.

"Mel, I love you, and if you said to me that you wanted to sleep alone tonight, I'd respect that. The last few weeks have been … a lot." He leaned back and waited for me to answer. I bit my lip as if I was thinking about it.

"Well," I replied after a pregnant pause, "actually …" I grinned when I noticed that he was holding his breath. "I think I might just spend the night in your room, if that's okay."

He didn't need any more encouragement. He scooped me up into his arms, like I weighed nothing, careful of my shoulder, and carried me inside. I laughed, and it was the most carefree sound I'd made in as long as I could remember.

CHAPTER THIRTY-FIVE

Healing

I could finally lift my arm above my head without feeling like it was about to fall off. The relief seeped through me, making my knees feel like jelly.

"You're coming along in leaps and bounds, Mel. I told you that you'd be fine, as long as you did the work."

Julie smiled at me as she helped me stretch out my shoulders. I'd be sore in the morning, but it meant that my shoulder was getting better. It meant that soon I would be able to compete again. The thought made me impatient.

I'd already missed all of the US tournaments. Tokyo was just around the corner. I really wanted to try my luck, but I was sure that Julie would tell me not to push it. An instruction that Joel would no doubt agree with wholeheartedly.

Thinking about Joel made me smile ridiculously. It had been six weeks since I got out of hospital. Six weeks since he'd told me he loved me.

Julie saw me grinning like a fool and smirked. "You can't stop thinking about him, can you?" she asked. I batted at her with my left hand, pleased that I could actually use it again.

"I can't help it," I sighed.

Julie chuckled. "I know what you mean. I used to be like that when I thought about ..." Her voice trailed off. I knew she had been about to say Steve. But for more reasons than one she felt it wasn't appropriate to speak about him.

"How do *you* feel, Julie, now that Thomas has been found guilty?" I asked, gazing out over Sydney Harbour. Joel's gym and tennis court were perfect for Julie to help me rehab. The best part was that it was private.

In some sense, my injured shoulder was a blessing – it had kept me out of the public eye for the weeks following the shooting. The weeks where the speculation in the media was going berserk.

"I feel … at peace, I guess. I don't think that has much to do with that boy pleading guilty or anything. I think it's more to do with Sandra."

We'd all been shocked to discover that Sandra had taken the revelation about Julie and her illegitimate child in her stride with no surprise whatsoever.

"I should have known that Steve would have told her. He loved her. He really did – more than anything else. More than me." I heard Julie's voice break, and I put a tentative arm around her shoulders.

I actually really liked Julie, now that there was no need for me to be ten different shades of green thinking about her and Joel together.

"I'll never regret it though. How could I when I got Shaun out of it?"

I smiled. "He's a cool little kid, I'll give you that much. And he's going to be a stunner when he's older."

Julie sniffed and rolled her eyes. "Yeah, like you're not biased! He's definitely going to take after his brother."

"My ears are burning!" Joel announced behind us and we both jumped.

"How do you do that?" I asked, feigning annoyance.

Julie smiled and slipped out from under my arm. "I'd better go and see what my wayward son is up to – probably terrorising Sandra." Julie made her escape.

I looked up at my man. His eyes sparkled, bluer than the harbour. He moved closer and slipped his arms around my waist.

"How'd you go today?" he asked.

I grinned. "Great! I'm definitely getting better. I think I'll be able to get back into competition soon."

Joel's eyes narrowed. "How about you just take it easy, Stinky? There's no rush."

I pouted and Joel smirked.

"I want to go to Tokyo," I muttered without any real conviction. I was pretty sure what his answer would be. I was right.

Joel shook his head. "Okay, here's the deal. You skip Tokyo, keep working hard, and we'll aim to have you ready for San Diego."

I rolled my eyes. "Is that a directive from my coach, or my boyfriend?" I couldn't help the little smile that lit up my face as I said the word 'boyfriend'.

Joel noticed it and grinned. "From both."

I sighed, but I nodded. I could see that what he was saying made sense. There was no point in rushing back into it and ending up injuring myself further.

Joel drew me off the court and into the rumpus room. I broke free of him and went towards the stairs, but he caught my hand and pulled me back. I looked at him curiously.

"The sentencing hearing was this morning," he reminded me.

I nodded, the smile slipping from my face. We'd been told that we could attend if we wanted. I couldn't think of anything worse, and Joel and Sandra had agreed with me. I didn't want to be in the same room as that psychopath ever again. Not after what we'd learned during the hearing.

Thomas Blackthorn, who'd seemed like such a lovely, doting boyfriend to Amanda, had 'kindly' offered to feed Connor of an evening while I was away, so Amanda wouldn't have to rush before her shifts at the hospital. And while he was there, he'd installed hidden webcams, covering every corner of my apartment. The police had found footage on Thomas's computer of me in the shower, sleeping, changing … and one video of Joel and me on my lounge, and on my living room floor. That was how Joel had managed to get into his crosshairs.

Thomas had also been responsible for leaking the Pete Levine video – the anonymous tennisfanboi Twitter account that had always posted about me belonged to Thomas.

"I just checked," Joel muttered, "life in prison."

A huge sighed gusted out of me and I collapsed onto the lounge.

"Well," I managed after I took a few deep breaths. "That's … good." It seemed totally inadequate, to say it was good that the person who had ended two people's lives was stuck in prison for the rest of his. But what else was I supposed to say?

Joel inhaled deeply and let the air hiss slowly out of his lungs. "It's over."

He pushed me down on the lounge, covering my body with his, kissing me with wild abandon. If there hadn't been a preschooler upstairs playing in the living room with his trucks I would have let nature take its course.

I broke away from him. "I'm glad you feel relieved, but maybe we should find a more appropriate venue for this," I murmured. He sat up, pulling me against his side. I snuggled as close as I could.

"You're right, Stink. You should probably go take a shower, anyway." He leaned over and distractedly kissed the bullet scar on my back. It was healing very well; shiny pink skin having replaced raw redness. Joel always kissed me there.

I got off the lounge and trotted up the stairs. Julie and Sandra were sitting on the rug in the living room while Shaun zoomed cars under the coffee table. The two women got on surprisingly well. It was pretty clear that Sandra liked having a child in the house.

Inside Joel's room I stripped off my exercise clothes and stepped into the monster shower in his en suite. The warm water felt great on my skin, and I closed my eyes and put my face into the spray, before grabbing some shampoo and lathering it through my hair.

How he moved so quietly I'd never know.

"Is this a more appropriate venue?"

His words were my only warning that Joel had joined me in the shower. I managed not to jump – I was getting used to him sneaking up on me.

"I suppose this will do," I replied coyly, turning towards him and tilting my head back under the spray to rinse the shampoo from my hair. I opened my eyes to see Joel staring hungrily at my breasts, thrust in his direction, shampoo bubbles slowly sliding over them. I smirked up at him as I ran my fingers down my chest and across my rapidly puckering nipples.

"I'm a lucky man," Joel murmured, reaching out to cup and fondle my breasts, and I glanced down to see his dick hard against his belly, sending a shock wave of aching heat between my legs. I looked back up into his eyes as I slowly went to my knees in front of him.

A choking gasp erupted from him as I took that throbbing length into my mouth, laving my tongue around the head before sucking it deep into my throat.

"Fuck, Mel, you're going to be the death of me," he cursed, but I watched him brace himself against the wall, his hips thrusting slightly. I reached around and gripped his muscular butt, letting him know it was okay for him to fuck my mouth.

"Ungh!" he groaned as I felt him hit the back of my throat. I moaned around his beautiful cock, sucking harder.

"Do you want me to come in your mouth?" he rasped.

With a pop, I let his cock go. "Well, you have a choice to make," I began, taking his cock in my hand and caressing it. His eyes were locked on my hand on him. "Either I can keep going and finish you off with my mouth ..."

"Or?" He demanded between gritted teeth.

I grinned, standing up. "Or you can bend me over and get us both off."

"Bend over," he demanded darkly, and with a shiver of raw anticipation, I complied.

Quite some time later, I was dried and dressing in the clothes that Joel had picked out for me – I'd moved most of my wardrobe over from my apartment. My apartment was being leased out; after learning about what Thomas had done in there, I had decided I'd rather be a temporary house guest of Sandra than live there again.

Joel watched me from the bed, dressed in jeans and a button up shirt in a colour that matched mine. He thought it was cute when we were coordinated, since we'd always unintentionally dressed that way before we were together.

I eyed him suspiciously. "Why are we getting so dressed up?" I asked. "Do we have plans tonight?

Joel shrugged. "Nope." He sounded suspiciously innocent. I glared at him and made for the door. He grabbed my wrist and dragged me down on top of him on the bed.

"What's the hurry?" he asked as he trailed his fingers up and down my sides. "Isn't it nice just to be alone?"

I struggled. "Your mother already thinks I'm a sex addict without us fuelling that suspicion any further."

Joel chuckled. "No, she thinks *I'm* the sex addict, not you. And she's wrong, anyway."

I snorted. "Yeah right, pull the other one, pal!"

Joel turned the full force of his blue eyes on me and I stopped talking.

"I'm not a sex addict. I'm a Melanie Black addict." He grinned at me, then leaned down and nuzzled at my neck.

I giggled and squirmed under him. "Well, they don't have AA meetings for that."

Joel wrapped himself around me. "Thank God for that. I *never* want to beat this addiction!"

The doorbell rang. I leaned away from Joel, but he made no attempt to get up.

"Aren't you going to answer the door?" I asked. He sat up, shaking his head.

"I think it's probably for you," he murmured. I wrinkled my nose at him, but left the room, heading down the stairs and opening the front door.

"Hi, Mel."

I looked out at Brad and Amanda, opening my mouth, but then shutting it when I realised I didn't know what to say. I hadn't seen either of them in six weeks. I'd actively avoided them for six weeks.

"Hey Brad … Amanda," I said shyly as I moved aside to let

them in. Brad looked at me for a long moment as if he was looking at a stranger, but then his eyes softened, and the stiffness went out of his shoulders as he walked inside.

Amanda followed, and I couldn't help but notice that she wouldn't look at me, and her hands were shaking.

"Uh, do you want to …" I began, but I wasn't sure how to go on.

"Go sit out on the patio, Mel," Joel's voice echoed from above. I looked up, finding him leaning over the loft railing, smiling tenderly down at me. "I'll make some drinks and bring them out in a little while."

Seated, and thankful for the distraction of the harbour glowing in the late afternoon light, I tapped my fingers on the table.

"How have you been?" I asked, chancing a glance at Brad.

He shrugged. "Good. For a while there I wasn't sure if you cared anymore."

I hung my head, ashamed. "It's not like that, Brad. I wasn't sure if you'd want to speak to me now that Joel and I …" I couldn't finish that sentence. I didn't need to.

"He loves you," Brad murmured.

I smiled despite the little tug of sadness I felt for Brad. "I know."

"Smellie, you're happy. That makes me happy."

I turned to him then. "Sorry I've been avoiding you," I said. Brad smiled, then nudged me with his shoulder, jerking his head towards Amanda. She sat slumped with her head bowed, hands in her lap.

"Mandy-Moo," I said. She flinched but didn't look up.

"Nothing that happened was your fault, you know that, don't you?" I asked, turning my chair and reaching out to untangle her hands from her lap, winding my fingers through hers.

"Yes … no … I don't know. I just feel so guilty." She sniffed and I realised that she was crying. I moved my chair even closer, wrapping an arm around her shoulders as she shook.

"He had us all completely fooled," Brad added, sounding like he had been saying this to her for weeks. Another flash of guilt burned through me. I should have been the one to tell her. My radio silence would have seemed like an accusation to her.

"Brad's right. I can't remember how many times I thought, *'oh, this Thomas guy, he's perfect for Amanda, and he seems so steady and sensible and so infatuated with her'*."

"I'm seeing a psychologist about it all," she confessed, as if there was something wrong with that.

I squeezed her shoulders. "Well, you're more sensible than me. I've just been distracting myself from the unresolved trauma by throwing myself at Joel!"

Amanda giggled wetly. Brad shook his head, looking mildly ill.

Mental note – don't mention sexy-times with Joel in front of your best friend who is in love with you.

"Have you all kissed and made up?" Joel asked, and I looked up to see him walking out with a tray of cocktails. I smiled gratefully. Alcohol would definitely help.

"Thanks, mate," Brad said as he accepted one of the drinks. He even gave Joel a small smile as he took a sip. Progress!

After a Sandra Herbert home-cooked meal and multiple drinks, things were decidedly less frosty between all of us. Amanda was actually laughing at something Joel said, and the haunted look in her eyes wasn't quite as obvious.

"He is obsessed with you," Brad murmured in my ear. I turned to him questioningly. Joel and I had barely touched each other all night.

Brad half-smiled. "The way he looks at you … I feel like we're all about to go up in flames."

My heart thrummed and I glanced at Joel. He was looking at me, and suddenly I did feel like I was about to spontaneously combust.

"You know what, Mel?" Brad muttered next to my ear, as Joel and I continued to stare at each other. "You didn't make a mistake this time." Brad stood up. "And our Uber is approaching, Amanda. Time for us to go."

I stood too, heading over to Amanda and grabbing her hand. We walked to the front door like that.

"Want to get brunch tomorrow?" I asked as I opened the door for her.

She nodded with a small smile. "Yeah, that would be great, Mel."

I kissed her cheek, before turning to Brad and wrapping my arms around his waist. He squeezed me briefly, before holding me away from him. "Don't be a stranger again, okay?"

I nodded. "Okay, I promise."

Joel and I watched as their Uber turned out of the driveway. Once it was gone, I spun, flinging myself into his arms.

"What's gotten into you?" he growled in my ear. I smiled and planted a kiss on his collarbone.

"I'm just happy, that's all," I replied, snuggling closer to him. 'Thanks for making me talk to them."

"Stink, they're your best friends. It was agony knowing that I … that maybe you weren't talking to them because of me."

I rubbed my nose against the hollow in his throat. "You are perfect, Joel Herbert."

He chuckled, his lips in my hair. The evening air was cool, but Joel was warm, and it felt so nice to be in his arms.

"Hey," I said, leaning back so I could see into his eyes.

He grinned down at me. "Yes?"

"Something's been bugging me."

"What's that, Stinky?" Joel asked. I didn't even flinch when he called me Stinky anymore. I actually kind of liked it. To be honest though – I'd kind of liked it all along.

"What *were* you doing for those few hours when you left Julie's house the night you found out about Shaun?" I asked.

Joel's grin slipped, but only slightly. "Well, I was wandering around the streets of Melbourne, worrying about your ankle, worrying that if I *seemed* like I was worrying about it too much, you'd realise that it was about more than just your career … that it was about how much I fucking loved you."

I looked up at him in disbelief. "But … you'd literally just found out that you have a half-brother! Didn't you have better things to be thinking about than me and my stupid ankle?"

Joel lifted a hand to my face and rubbed his thumb across my cheekbone. "Mel, it's been a very long time since I've gone even a minute without thinking about you."

I held up a hand. "Hang on! You were in love with me back in *January*? This wasn't just a recent development?"

Joel chuckled at me. "Melanie Black, I've been in love with you since you were eighteen."

I gaped at him. He laughed. "Dad saw how I felt about you straight away, and he forbade me from making a move. And you were still with Grant … So I settled for teasing you instead – like a stupid kid in the schoolyard who pulls a girls hair when he likes her. You have no idea how relieved I was when you split up with him.

"But then I started to worry that I had ruined any chance I might have had with you *because* I'd spent all those years teasing you."

I frowned. "I honestly never had a clue that you felt that way about me. I mean, I've known for a while that you wanted my body, but I figured that was just because you're a sex fiend."

Joel snickered under his breath and reached down to squeeze my butt. I felt the pulse deep inside me that I hoped I would always feel when he touched me like that.

"Mel, I did always want your body. But I wanted *everything* else that came with it as well."

"You hid your true feelings very easily," I grouched.

"It might have seemed that way to you, but every time you left a room I was in it was all I could do to keep myself from running after you and grabbing hold and never letting go. It's been even harder since Dad died because I knew that his disapproval wasn't stopping me anymore."

I looked up into his stunningly blue eyes. "Well, why didn't you make a move earlier?"

He smiled beautifully at me. "I told you – I thought that I'd spent so many years teasing you that you actually believed I was an idiot who only thought with his dick and lived just to make your life Hell. I was terrified to reveal how I felt in case you laughed at me."

If my heart wasn't already liquid for him, the vulnerability in his voice would have melted it.

"To be fair I did think that for a while. But then you started to show me that there was more to you than the sex-crazed Adonis. You had me very confused there for a while. Don't get me wrong though, the sex-crazed Adonis is a lot of fun too." I reached my hands up and put them on his chest, feeling the beat of his heart through his shirt.

He laughed breathlessly. "I know you like that part of me, Mel. That part of me likes you too, so much."

I rocked myself against him, feeling the part we were talking about bulging against my hip.

He took a shaky breath. "Don't start something unless you're prepared to finish it, Melanie Black. I don't have the sort of self-control around you that I should have."

I grinned, liking the fact that I could make him feel the way *he'd* been making me feel all year.

"You had plenty of self-control over the last five years," I reminded him, moulding myself even closer to his body.

He trailed his fingers up and down my arms. "Yes, and now that it's no longer necessary, it's just disappeared altogether."

"Shut up and kiss me," I whispered, tilting my head up towards his. He smiled a stunning smile – not the one that I'd seen him use on other women. A special one that was just for me.

He pressed his warm lips to mine.

"Joel's making a baby with Mel!" Shaun's little voice cackled from the doorway. I broke away from Joel with a giggle, and he pressed his forehead against mine, moving one hand up to stroke my face.

"Sorry!" Julie hissed behind him, and I looked up to see her scooping a pyjama clad Shaun into her arms.

"Who told you that's how babies get made, Shaun?" Joel asked.

"Kim at school. And she said that before people make babies like that, they have to get married first."

"Damned Catholic preschool," Joel muttered jokingly in my ear. I grinned.

"Joel's got to marry Mel now!" Shaun crowed, squirming in his mother's arms.

"Sure Shaun, we'll get married. You can be my best man!"

I gaped at Joel, not sure if he was joking or not.

He laughed at the look of shock on my face. "One step at a time, Mel. Maybe we should move in together first."

I chewed on my lip for a moment. "Well, we pretty much live together now," I replied.

Joel grinned. "Yeah, well … I have an investment property in Bondi. I've had it for years, but my tenant has just given their notice and I thought that maybe we could move in there. Just you, me and Connor. Mum's asked Julie if she'd like to make their stay here with her more permanent." Julie's lease had expired around the time I got out of hospital, and with the rental market the way it was, Sandra had offered for them to stay for a while. It worked great for my rehab, and Sandra seemed to love having both Shaun and Julie around, even knowing the truth about Shaun.

I felt the slow smile spreading on my face, but I was trying not to get too ahead of myself. "But Joel, we've only been together six weeks. Don't you think we should … wait a bit? I mean this is a massive commitment for a man who was a terminal bachelor until six weeks ago."

"Well, if you want to count it like that, we've been 'together' since Wimbledon. And we've been unofficially dating since the French Open really."

I eyed him sharply and he smirked. "Just because you're clueless and don't see what's happening in front of your nose, doesn't mean it's not real. And besides, I've been waiting for you for five years – I think that's long enough, don't you?"

A smile burst onto my face in full force. "Just think, Joel – we'll be able to 'make babies' in every room. The lounge room, the kitchen bench, the washing mach–"

My words were cut short by Joel's urgent mouth on mine, by his excited groan.

Thank you, God, I thought as Joel's tongue slipped into my mouth. *I asked you for a man who would love me for me, who would care about me, and all along you must have been pulling your hair out wondering why I hadn't just taken what was waiting in front of my face.*

Joel's hand reached around my waist, pulling me tighter against him and distracting me from my silent prayer. I only really had one thing left to say to the Man upstairs, so I thought it quickly before Joel could distract me any further.

God, you definitely got it right this time! Thanks.
AMEN.

Acknowledgments

My husband and children have put up with a lot in the last few months as I got my baby ready for the world. Thank you for your patience and understanding, and knowing that when I was screaming and ranting, it was never about you, it was always about the damn book!

Lani Belle, I wouldn't even be here if it wasn't for you! You're the best cheerleader a writer could wish for, thanks for responding to all my random late night ramblings, beta reading like an absolute pro, and loving my characters as much as I do! Book besties for the win!

Elena, you might have freaked me out with some of your feedback, but once I came to terms with it, I ended up with a much better story.

Leisha Vas, you brought my cover vision to life, and you've been so patient with all the changes we had to go through on the way.

Amanda Girvan, your proof reading was spectacular, we will absolutely be working together again in the future!

About the Author

Layla has been writing stories ever since she could pick up a pencil and shape words. The most memorable works of her tween and teen years included a rap version of 'Little Red Riding Hood' and an embarrassingly pornographic high school camp/murder mystery (which was possibly a sign of things to come).

Layla lives on an acreage in regional NSW with her husband, two rambunctious children, five mostly feral cats, and two wilful Corgi puppies named Kingston and Empress (you can meet them in her novel Hating Dr Fox). Oh, and some angry Plovers that swoop her every spring without fail.

When she's not writing, or reading, she's bellowing Taylor Swift at the top of her lungs.

Join Layla's Facebook Reader's Group, Layla's Pining Woodies, for early access to WIP's, character art, and the unhinged life of Layla.

www.laylapine.com

facebook.com/laylapine.author

instagram.com/laylapine_author

tiktok.com/@laylapine_author

Also by Layla Pine

Aussie Cravings (Contemporary Romance)

Strokes at Midnight—an insta-lust, one night stand, opposites attract, right person wrong time sports romance (with a splash of surprise pregnancy WITH A TWIST)

Hating Dr Fox—a city to small town, second chance, hate to lovers, reality TV show romance (with a splash of explosive secrets from their past)

Singing My Tune—a taboo, forbidden, teacher student, musical theatre college romance (with a splash of emotional damage)

Renegade Strangers (Paranormal Romance)

Greenrock (book 1)

A human girl … A mysterious stranger … A forbidden attraction … A deadly craving …

Taiga (book 2)

A female dying for revenge … A male who hates what he is becoming … locked within the confines of a shady government facility, their blood calls to one another …

Standalone Titles

My Soul For A Donut (Coming 2025)

He owns her soul … but she's stealing his heart … What happens when you get a bit drunk and accidentally sell your soul to the son of Satan … for a gluten free donut?

Jemma Bliss is about to find out …

www.ingramcontent.com/pod-product-compliance
Lightning Source LLC
Chambersburg PA
CBHW040342130726
47911CB00033B/541